THE ARMY
OF THE
REPUBLIC

THE ARMY
OF THE
REPUBLIC

STUART ARCHER COHEN

ST. MARTIN'S PRESS   NEW YORK

This is a work of fiction. All of the characters, organizations, and events portrayed in this novel are either products of the author's imagination or are used fictitiously.

THE ARMY OF THE REPUBLIC. Copyright © 2008 by Stuart Archer Cohen. All rights reserved. Printed in the United States of America. For information, address St. Martin's Press, 175 Fifth Avenue, New York, N.Y. 10010.

www.stmartins.com

Library of Congress Cataloging-in-Publication Data

Cohen, Stuart, 1958–
    The Army of the Republic / Stuart Archer Cohen.—1st ed.
        p. cm.
    ISBN-13: 978-0-312-38377-0
    ISBN-10: 0-312-38377-0
    1. Terrorists—Fiction. 2. Terrorism—United States—Fiction. 3. Water rights—United States—Fiction. 4. Domestic fiction. I. Title.
    PS3553.O4337A89 2008
    813'.54—dc22

                                                                      2008019522

First Edition: September 2008

10 9 8 7 6 5 4 3 2 1

For Donald, and his dreams

ACKNOWLEDGMENTS

Much of this book is constructed out of the goodwill of strangers who invested their stories in a venture over which they have no control. I deeply thank the following people for their contributions and hope they see some part of their wisdom reflected in it:

In Buenos Aires:
Fernando Vaca Narvaja, Ricardo Rajendorfer, Marcelo Larraquy, Luis Vicat

Sixties and seventies activists:
Peter Bohmer, Stew Albert, Pat Sturgis, Mike James, Mary Sturgis

Present-day activists:
Erica Kay, Brenna Wolfe, Geov Parrish, Leslie Howes, Lexie Woodward, Martin Fleck, Tim Simons, and Deane T. Rimerman

Gary Perlstein, who helped me look at things from the other side

David Cantor, William Fletcher, Don Stollworthy, Andrew Kidde, and

Markus Hoffman helped in diverse ways. In Juneau, I thank Paul Grant, generous dispenser of hypothetical legal advice, Lauren Brooks, Margo Waring, Kevin Maier, Thomas and Amy Fletcher, and the long-suffering employees of Invisible World.

At St. Martin's: George Witte, who saw something others didn't.

A thanks also to those who prefer not to be named, doing their duty as they see fit in their own eyes.

With special gratitude to my Seattle friends, who, after all these years, still meet me at the airport. They gave me the support, advice, and connections that made this book what it is:
David Perk
Mikala Woodward
Warner Lew

My agent, Joe Regal, who stood by me for seven skinny years. Joe Regal shows up!

In a category by herself:

Suzanne (my queen)

It is rather for us to be here dedicated to the great task remaining before us—that from these honored dead we take increased devotion to that cause for which they gave the last full measure of devotion . . . that this nation, under God, shall have a new birth of freedom—and that government of the people, by the people, for the people, shall not perish from the earth.

**—Abraham Lincoln, at the dedication
of the Gettysburg cemetery**

A benevolent man extends his love from those he loves to those he does not love. A ruthless man extends his ruthlessness from those he does not love to those he loves.

—Mencius

Part I

THE ARMY OF THE REPUBLIC

1

*T*elevision is the closest thing we've got to God in America, an all-present eye that creates the world, ceaselessly and seamlessly, twenty-four hours a day. A comic book bible made of light; they build their phony universe with pictures, pictures, picures!

"Business figure John Polling was shot to death today outside a Seattle apartment building. . . ."

A visual of an ambulance in the black drizzly cavern of television night, a cordon of hard-eyed cops, a dead body under a sheet.

"Yes!" Tonk shoots his fist into the air, does a few quick struts across the living room. "Check it out, America! The big man goes *down!*"

It's kind of awesome to see the divine stamp of Big Media imprinted on our sketchy little lives. Lilly, Sarah, and Kahasi say nothing, sit uneasily with their tea and toast. People are frightened by large moving objects, and an assassination is a very large object, moving very fast.

But not fast enough to scare Tonk. Handsome football hero Tonk spins away from the screen and cups his hand to his ear. "Hear that popping, everyone? That's the sound of champagne corks hitting the ceiling in every state of the Union!"

"Shut up, Tonk!" Sarah says, "I'm trying to watch this!"

"Tonk . . ." I trail off. I'm in a quiet mood, tarnished by the long night and that last image of Polling's girlfriend screaming her lungs out as she looked down at his body. I'm having trouble making this all lie flat. "We did something horrible to someone who deserved it. It's nothing to celebrate."

Polling had been visiting Seattle "on business," says the news gal, and we all snort at that one. She follows it up with a couple of euphemisms about his career. "Financier," she says, "Controversial modernizer of public—"

"Try *swindler*," Sarah spits at her. *"Criminal! Murderer!"*

Not exactly a room full of sympathy for John Polling. Polling was a man who'd gotten everything he wanted. He'd feasted on the war and let the People pick up the tab, bought out public assets at a fraction of their value. He had deals with everybody worth owning and a small enterprise of lawyers and PR flacks who cut the water in front of him like the bow of an icebreaker. He was a master con man. He beat every rap. He was bulletproof.

Metaphorically, at least. When his goons clubbed an organizer to death in a Boston parking garage eight months ago, the clock started ticking on John Polling.

Ms. Blah Blah goes on: "The assassination was claimed by a previously unknown group calling itself the Army of the Republic."

"That's right!" Tonk cries. "Corporates, meet the Army of the Republic."

On the screen, Polling's body is being carried to the ambulance yet again in a flash of blue strobe lights. At the bottom of the screen, the crawler's giving the latest entertainment news: PARAMOUNT SIGNS PITT FOR REMAKE OF *HIGH NOON*!

Tonk looks at his watch. "Eight-oh-one, Lando. Where's the hack?"

"Chill, Tonk," I say. "Your watch is fast."

We watch another fifteen seconds, and then Tonk erupts again: "Hack on!"

The crawler at the bottom of the screen has changed now. The show biz news had given way to a communiqué hacked in by our IT group.

JOHN POLLING FOUND GUILTY OF CORRUPTION THEFT RACKETEERING AND MURDER. SENTENCE CARRIED OUT

BY THE ARMY OF THE REPUBLIC ON BEHALF OF THE
PEOPLE OF THE UNITED STATES OF AMERICA. FOR
DETAILS GO TO WWW.ARMYOFTHEREPUBLIC.ORG.RU.
STAND UP FOR YOUR COUNTRY!—✌ PEACE ☮☮☮☮☮☮☮
JOHN POLLING FOUND GUILTY OF—

"One thing they know now," I announce. "They're not dealing with
amateurs."

I think of Gonzalo in his electronic cave, watching our message
shimmy across Polling's fake obituary in blue-screen blue. Tens of
millions of our e-mails are ripping away to mailboxes all over the
country from servers in Russia, Brazil, Estonia. Our site will be frantic now, all the busy bees of the Internet clicking into the chronology
of Polling's whole stinking career, with every charge leveled against
him and which strings he pulled to beat it. This time, we'll be the ones
telling the story, not the Corporates. I hope McFarland is catching
this.

We're on the crawler a good three minutes before the network
techs break through our hack. The basketball scores start playing
under the footage of Polling's shocked widow ducking into a limousine. She's trying to hide her dazed expression, but the cameramen
crowd in and turn her reddened eyes into entertainment. I flash on
some imagined Thanksgiving dinner, a young John Polling holding a
little boy in pajamas, and then those useless second thoughts that
keep skating in and out of my head start coming back. They disappear when Polling returns, waving triumphantly at the cameras in
front of an American flag. Yeah, that's the man.

"Here comes the mockumentary."

They start in with more footage about Polling, showing him climbing the stairway of a private jet and standing in front of his corporate
logo. A few shots of construction machinery with army tanks nearby,
then the pipelines and highways that illustrate his privatization of the
Philadelphia water system and the Ohio Turnpike. A shot of him
shaking hands with the president. No word about the organizer his
security force had murdered, only the inevitable network cheap shot
from a think-tanker with spectacles and a pale, sappy complexion.
"Susan, we have unconfirmed reports that the terrorists shot Mr.
Polling in nonlethal areas like the knees and groin first to inflict

maximum suffering before they killed him. In essence, it looks like John Polling was tortured to—"

"That's a lie!" I shout. "Goddamn them, that's a lie!"

Everyone looks at me and I can see by their alarm that I shouldn't have gone off. I'm the guy who never goes off, but I haven't slept in two days and things feel distant one second and then suddenly raw and infuriating. Sarah stands up and puts her hand on my shoulder. "Let them sell their crap, Lando. Because you know what? They're running out of buyers."

I look at Sarah, with her long curly brown hair and her cashmere sweater. In another life she's a career girl, busting balls for the networks. In another life she's a model. But not this life. "Let's go, you guys. We need to set up for the meeting with the DNN people."

Tonk and Sarah drop me off at the Transit station and go on to the funnel. I catch my image in an empty window, surprised to see myself with short blond hair, a smooth white chin where my black beard used to be. That owlish face above the sports jacket. Too much waiting, too much adrenaline. I close my eyes and suck in the cool Seattle mist, try to expel John Polling in one long breath.

It doesn't last long. At the station the big screen's playing sanitized Greatest Hits from the life of America's most successful criminal. *"Innovator." "Water Entrepreneur." "Billionaire."* All running into the career-topping *"Gunned Down by Terrorists!"* The Blue Wave howls through the tunnel.

At the Pike St. stop little knots of people gather around the monitors with slack mouths and upturned faces, getting their dose of phony scripture from another think-tanker. I catch fragments of his speech as I pass each screen. "Don't know who this Army of the Republic—" "name of convenience—" "established terrorist groups—" "Jefferson Combine—" "the American people—" The reason God banned graven images: he knew people would confuse pictures with reality, and that men would use them to create a lying vision of the world. God sure called that one.

A couple of Whitehall boys manning the tollbooth, staring up with a smile at the Hammer on his morning TV rant. The Hammer looking good in his Harley T-shirt and tattoos—a Fascist for the youth crowd. "Army! Get real! This is three or four *bleeping* amateurs who pop out and sissy-punch somebody, then crawl back and hide under their mama's skirts."

I smile and keep moving. I guess he hasn't seen the hack.

This is the riskiest kind of meeting, between a surface group and us. They reached us through Lilly, who roomed with one of the DNN organizers at the UW. The two had kept up, and I told Lilly to drop a very discreet hint to her friend that she had some connections with people who knew people. Three days ago the DNN decided to click on the link.

Everybody is in place now. My sunglasses are on. Today I've gone Youthful Professional, which is less invisible than guy-in-a-sweatshirt but an easier sale to authority figures if there's anything to explain.

I take up my first position at a coffee shop across from the Borders bookstore, get a triple shot to travel and dump in a few packets of sugar. Within a few minutes the contact comes fluttering down the street in her red neck-scarf and her Nordstrom shopping bag. Past the store windows and their Halloween themes, paper jack-o'-lanterns grinning at her "gal out shopping" disguise. We're all in costume here. She turns into the Borders, and I wait for confirmation.

Our part goes perfectly. Sarah does a bump pass and disappears. Kahasi picks up the DNN person a minute later exiting the back entrance, as instructed in the note. She's heading for the newsstand at the Pike Place Market, where Tonk has stashed the directions in the back copy of *Model Railroader* magazine. The contact looks conspicuously inconspicuous as she pulls it out, takes a big obvious scan of the area, stuffs the directions into her pocket then disappears into the labyrinth of stairways and corridors of the market. A minute later she pops out the back and heads down the stairs to the water. The funnel. Kahasi watches from the pier as she walks five blocks north. "She's clean," he says.

She turns into a restaurant and Sarah is waiting for her in the bathroom, checks her pockets and her clothing. The text comes in over my phone. CLEAN.

I start the car and pull up in front of the restaurant as she walks out. I roll down the window. "Always nice to meet another model railroading fan. Need a ride?"

She's prettier than her picture, with black hair and dark eyes set above a slightly long chin. A handsome, resolute sort of face, but looking quietly freaked at the moment. "Yes, please."

I unlock the passenger door of the Toyota and she climbs in. I smile at her. "I'm Lando." We shake hands; then I reach down to the floor of the car and give her a big floppy hat and a black satin sleep mask. "Put on this hat and this mask, please, then lean back and pretend you're sleeping. No peeking."

We make a few turns and then approach the tollbooth at I-90. Privatized last year to cover the deficit. I flip a dollar into the basket. Click. *Get it while you can, fuckers.*

We cruise along without speaking and I find myself listening to the sound of the transmission revving upward to the next gear change, then starting at a lower pitch and revving up once more. A comforting machine noise that makes things normal. We're on a straight part of the highway and I can't help taking a moment to scope out her body, which, from the corduroy legs sticking out from beneath her red raincoat, is a rather pleasing one. Need more data. Her wavy black hair is falling across her shoulders, with one little strand dyed purple. Armenian? Italian? She reminds me a little of Lilly, but less flower child.

"So," I said, "you're Emily Cortright. You live at the Apex, downtown, Seattle's favorite communal apartment building. You graduated from the UW in Environmental Sciences then did a two-year stint at cooking school—*interesting*—then you abandoned the food service industry for law school at Lewis and Clark. You've been organizing at the DNN three years and two months. Which brings us to the one burning question that jumps out at me from your bio."

"And that is . . ."

"Do you do Thai?"

I see her mouth curl into a smile below the black circles of the sleep mask. "Everyone does Thai now," she says. "The new thing is Coastal Peruvian."

I like her voice. There's something very calm about it, sweet, almost old-fashioned. "Okay. Excellent. I'm glad I know that. If we ever need an event catered, you'll be my first phone call."

"Thanks. And you are . . ."

"I'm sorry, Emily, but at this point the 'getting to know you' part has to be kind of one-sided. Not that I don't trust you, but these days you never know when information is going to become a liability."

Her voice firms up. "Well, who do you represent?"

"And you need to know that because . . . ?"

"Because I was sent to make an offer and I have to know who I'm making it to."

I wonder for a second what McFarland would want me to answer. "I represent the Army of the Republic."

"Oh," she says softly. It's quiet for a minute.

I pull off in Bellevue and make my way toward Sarah's apartment. We've selected it carefully, a ground-floor one-bedroom right next to the underground parking garage that we can move things and people discreetly into and out of. I park right by the door and ask Emily to keep the mask on. We're through Sarah's door in less than ten steps. The apartment itself has been purged of anything remotely political. No Malcolm X posters, no heavy theory by troublemakers like Chomsky or Klein. A few canned photos of ballet slippers and nature scenes hang on the mostly empty walls, and the bookcase is heavy with mindless historical romances we picked up from the Salvation Army for a nickel each. It's an environment that you forget as soon as you turn your head. Her computer's loaded with a decoy memory card filled with Web sites about self-improvement and eating disorders. Not a trace there of the real Sarah, a survivor of the Earth Liberation Front who watched her eco-vandal *compañeros* get hard time as "terrorists" and decided to step it up a notch. The *orga* covers the rent, along with three other houses and apartments around Seattle. The rest of us have to keep our day jobs. Emily looks around as I close the door behind us. I catch her staring at me.

"You were expecting the guy with the flat-top, right? USMC tattooed on his biceps? Or the guy with hair down to his shoulders and pierced everything."

"You're just so . . ."

"Young Corporate?" I loosen my tie and take off my jacket. "I can only aspire." She laughs, a good sign.

She takes off her raincoat, and I have to admit that I can't help but enjoy that small moment of undressing. She's wearing a ribbed white turtleneck and her red silk neck-scarf, and she's covering up her chest and waist with some sort of Guatemalan vest. She's long-limbed and robust. I can hear Tonk saying *Mamacita!* in my head, and shutting him up brings me back to the cool calm Revolutionary mind-set that has to be. We're professionals here, right?

"Can I make you some tea? Root around in the fridge for something edible?"

"I'm okay, thanks."

I move to the kitchen and open up the cupboard. "Are you sure? We've got Bi Luo Chun green. The label says it's grown on a single island in the middle of a lake in China. Or here's Lipton. Very exclusive—it only comes from several huge warehouses in Oakland and New Jersey."

She acquiesces and sits down on the beat-up sofa as I putter away. I entertain a brief fantasy of blowing off this whole meeting and just riffing with her about how bizarre and ironic life is. Instead, I bring her a mug of tea and a biscotto, then half sit in front of her, resting my butt on Sarah's desk.

She looks down into the cup. I can see her fumbling for an opening. "You're really from the Army of the Republic?" she says, then there's that uncomfortable shifting of facial expressions. "Is it true your organization killed John Polling?"

I don't blame her for being squeamish. "You feel sorry for him, don't you?" I shrug. "So do I. He was a human being. Somebody's father, somebody's husband. But, let's do a brief postmortem of the man before we get too nostalgic. He made his first fortune fleecing taxpayers on the war, then used his political connections to develop supposedly protected wetlands in the Everglades. His next stage of self-actualization was to borrow money from the federal government to take over the public water supplies of most of the mid-Atlantic seaboard, resulting in increased rates and reduced water quality—"

"I worked on the DNN Water Project for a year. I'm totally familiar with that."

"Good. Then you probably know that racketeering charges were brought against him four years ago and he beat them on appeal to a court stacked with his cronies. And that last February he was linked to security agents that murdered Jeff Lansing, an antiprivatization organizer, but was never prosecuted because the Justice Department dropped the case."

"I know about Jeff Lansing."

She says it as if there's nothing more to add about him, and that annoys me a little. I say, very slowly, "Polling's thugs beat Jeff Lansing until his eyeballs exploded." She flinches a tiny bit. "You know why they did it?"

"Why?"

"Because they wanted to send a message to people like you."

She's quiet for a few seconds, then recovers. "So the Army of the Republic really did kill him?"

I take a deep breath. "The Army of the Republic judged John Polling and executed a sentence on behalf of the American people. But let's move on. You're the one who sent the Bat-Signal. What's up?"

She shifts positions so that she doesn't dissolve quite so much into the spongy couch. "We want you to declare a cease-fire."

I take in the idea and grin. "Is that all?"

She stumbles on into her pitch. "I don't mean just you, personally, I mean all of the militants. Democracy Northwest feels that Americans are decisively against this government and they're ready to stand up to it. They're sick of the corruption and the wars and they're sick of watching their whole country get parceled out to Big Business."

"Seen your Web site already, Emily."

"Sorry." She flashes a coy little smile at me. "I didn't realize that only one of us is licensed to diatribe here." That takes me by surprise. A pretty bold cut: I like her. She brushes a curl of black hair off her forehead and rolls right on. "But my point is, Americans are tired of this Administration and they're ready to act. If they ever had a majority, they've lost it."

"Yeah!" I rub my scalp, massaging out a little stab of caffeine headache at my temple. "You're right, Emily: They have lost their majority. The problem is, you don't need a majority to control this country. You need maybe thirty percent, because forty percent of the people won't act. They're equally happy with a dictator or a president as long as you don't take away their guns or cut off their last little trickle of gasoline. That leaves thirty percent who might actively oppose you, and you've got the entire security and media apparatus to attack them with. It's like that in every country in the world."

She tilts her head toward me. "That's a pretty unforgiving analysis."

"It's an accurate analysis." I put my cup down so I can make my point better. "I mean, I wish every cop that fired on a demonstration would suddenly say, 'Hey! These guys are right! I'm *not* going to shoot that kid in the face with a rubber bullet because he doesn't want to see the last redwood get axed! I'm *not* going to club that old man whose pension got ripped off!' I mean, I really wish I could believe that this whole country would rise up because of their democratic ideals and sweep these fuckers away. But I'm a student of history, Emily, and I'm a member of the Church of What's Happenin' Now. And in that Church, thirty percent call the shots. It's our thirty percent against their thirty percent."

Her eyebrows come together. "So you think you're going to fight a guerrilla war and defeat them militarily?"

"No! They've got the Pentagon, for Christ's sakes. Our strategy is, you go straight to the top. You take down the brain of the machine, the guys who are getting all the benefits. The open and notorious crooks like John Polling. You punish them for their crimes, you mess up their toys and their tools, and maybe that lazy, numbed-out forty percent in the middle starts to see the Boss-man isn't so untouchable after all, and they say, 'Hey, aren't these the guys that ripped off my pension and got my kid's leg blown off in the last oil war? Who put them in charge?' And I'll tell you: Nothing will bring down a government faster than when Uncle Joe and Aunt Sally and Jim Bob from the hardware store show up on Main Street with their Masonic rings and their beer guts hanging out and say, 'Get the *fuck* out of my government!'"

She answers slowly, picking her words carefully. "I have the same hopes you do, Lando, but I'm not sure your methods can achieve it."

I'm pacing back and forth now, sweating a little bit from the tea. "You don't think there's a hundred million people out there trading high fives at the water cooler because Polling got what he deserved? I mean, sure, a lot are probably saying, 'Oh, I don't approve of their methods!' But down in that Old Testament part of the brain, way down there where lightning bolts still reach out of the sky and strike down those who transgress, *people need justice!* We are that lightning."

She doesn't answer, and I feel a little silly standing up in front of her. I sit down on the floor, knees folded up and my back against the wall. Aside from everything else, she's still a woman around my age and we're all alone in this room and the intimacy comes flooding over me every once in a while.

"You say you're the lightning," she says after a bit, "but lightning doesn't form institutions and it doesn't put Uncle Joe in a mailgroup and tell him when, where, and why the demonstration is going to be. And without that, Uncle Joe doesn't hit the streets."

I nod from my crunched-up position, push back my newly short hair. I can see why she's the number three person at the DNN. "I grant you that point. What does that have to do with a cease-fire?"

Now she stands up, comes to rest on the arm of the couch, looking down on me. The harem girl disguise is gone; she's all lawyer. "The Government's using Terrorism to legitimize themselves. You know that. It's a package for them: Islamic fundamentalists and groups like yours. They lump you together in their propaganda and they present themselves as the only alternative to chaos."

"People don't believe that crap!"

"They don't have to believe it one hundred percent; they just have to believe it enough to stay on the sidelines. This struggle is a war of narratives, Lando, and you don't control the narrative. They do. They've got the reach and the repetition, and you're Brand X." I start to object but she rolls over me. "We need a wide movement based on a simple fundamental idea with high symbolic value, and that idea is *vote*. Not an Internet vote, or an electronic vote, but a real vote, with paper ballots, counted one at a time. That's something everybody in America can understand."

"That's a plausible argument."

She softens up a little. "And it would be extremely helpful if the militant groups like yourselves and the Jefferson Combine issued statements that they were going to put down their arms and work peacefully for change. I think that could have a profound effect on people. And it would take a card out of the Government's hand."

The headache's pulsing again and I push on it with my fingertips. "Okay. Sounds great. But what's your strategy when the Regime starts shucking and jiving?"

She leans forward, and her voice gets harder. "The government exists by the consent of its people. Right? We take back our consent. We stop cooperating in the thousand ways that the government and its backers need cooperation. We do general strikes. We boycott. We inform and organize. We go into the streets and shut cities down. We challenge them head-on with the full weight of the American people behind us and we don't quit until the Administration crumbles. In other words, we get Uncle Joe into the street."

"Just Seattle?"

She becomes less certain. "We're working with groups in Boston and New York, too. That part has just started coming together."

I don't say anything. The truth is I've kept our link to the DNN live for exactly this reason. No underground group can be effective without a much larger surface group to exploit its psychological gains. Revolutions are always essentially political, rather than military. That's what Mao and Ho understood, and what Chiang Kai-shek and General Westmoreland never did. India, Czechoslovakia, Serbia, Poland, East Germany, Russia. They all booted out their tyrants without firing a shot. I suspect that Emily Cortright is no stranger to history.

She clears her throat. I see the awkwardness come back into her face. "Lando, I'm sorry, but I have to ask you again: How many people do you really represent? I mean, I'd never even heard of the Army of the Republic until a few hours ago. But, I mean . . . is there someone else I should talk to? Is there any sort of central committee of militant groups?"

I stand up and fetch her empty tea mug from the table, throwing out an answer from the kitchen sink and winding it through the living room as I come back to face her. "Outside of the East Coast, the militant groups are pretty much autonomous. There is no central council or chain of command. This isn't like the Montoneros or the PLO. Nobody can snap their fingers and get you a cease-fire." She looks disappointed. "That being said, I can probably touch base directly or indirectly with most of the West Coast groups. Just realize that nobody's in charge of this movement. Everyone does what they see fit in their own eyes. Like in the Book of Judges. 'At that time there was no King in Israel, and each man did as he saw fit in his own eyes.'"

"The Book of Judges?"

"You know, after Joshua, before Samuel. The twelve tribes each doing their own thing in the Promised Land. That's where the Resistance is at now."

She looks at me quizzically, like she's trying to figure out exactly which flavor of fanatic I am. "Are you, uh . . . Do you read the Bible a lot?"

I play it off. "It puts me to sleep. And when you have insomnia, that's a very good thing." She nods but doesn't say anything. "And you're thinking I can't sleep because my conscience bothers me."

"No, actually I was thinking about a class on the Old Testament I took at the UW. What did you study in college?"

"Who said I went to college?" Her face stiffens, and I feel like a moron. "I'm sorry. Little factoids like what obscure topic I studied in college are the kind of thing that can make a profile snap into focus. Nothing personal. I'd like to tell you, actually. I wish we could just sit here for hours and talk about books and movies and where we grew up."

A deeper truth there than I like to admit, neatly put on display by the cluttered silence it brings over the room. I hand her the sleep mask. "I'll take you back now."

We get into the car and she leans her head against the seat so that her hair spills down over the blue upholstery of my late-model utterly un-rememberable Japanese sedan. I take a different route back, a longer one, avoiding the highway, not so much for security reasons as to spend a little more time getting to know her. That's part of my job, after all. It's noon now, and I imagine the news about Polling is mostly out, except for the mistress, which will be a great new plot twist for tomorrow. We discuss a few details of the DNN's timeline; I implore her again about proper security precautions. Then we do chat a bit about books, about her favorite artist, Marie Cassat, and mine, Caravaggio. As we reach downtown I tell her she can take off her sleep mask and that I'll drop her a few blocks from her apartment. We continue north toward Belltown and the conversation seems to run out, which disappoints me a little. She's silent for a time.

"So, does it bother you at all?"

It comes out of nowhere but I know what she means. "Canceling John Polling's account? I didn't say I was the one that did it."

"Your organization did it."

My throat feels heavy and I can hear a slight strain in my voice.

"We didn't kill John Polling," I say. "The People of the United States killed John Polling."

She starts to frame a reply but leaves it there. We get a few blocks from her house and I pull over to the curb. She opens the door a few inches then stops. "Well, it's nice meeting you," she says. Like the end of a first date.

"Yeah, you, too. I'll be in touch. Give me a couple of weeks." I feel almost like leaning over to give her a kiss. Instead we find ourselves looking at each other for a few seconds too long. "I'm riding the tiger here," I say, without really intending to.

"I know." She touches my shoulder. "Thank you, Lando."

I leave the car downtown for Tonk and head back through the Blue Wave. A new entertainment is flashing across the monitors above the platform. A mob is swarming toward a limousine. A zoom to the window and I'm startled to recognize the face: James Sands, water privatizer and corporate predator. Almost up there in Polling's league. I feel a buzzing in my chest that moves up to my throat as he gets out of the car to face them. He raises his hand. The crowd closes in. My train comes roaring into the station but I just stand there, watching. It's a picture I can't escape.

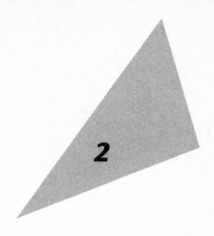

2

I was in the limo on the way back from Barrington when Walter called. It felt good to hear his easygoing voice after a particularly acrid meeting.

"Jim! You were wondering how much more they could hate you . . ."

"What's up?"

"About sixty nuts from Protect Our Water just showed up at headquarters. I recommend you go in the back way."

I felt my stomach start churning again. My creditors had just handed me my ass, and now the Flat Earth Society was weighing in. "Screw them. It's my building."

"I'm not on-site yet, Jim. I think you might be wiser to end-run 'em—"

"I'm not going to run from these people, Walter." He didn't say anything, so I went on. "Maybe this is a good opportunity for me to talk to them directly."

"You're starting to sound as crazy as they are."

"Okay. You're on record as warning me not to." I spoke to my driver over the seat. "Go to the front door, Henry."

We pulled up and Henry turned around. "You sure about this, Mr. Sands?"

I looked at them clustered on the sidewalk. Most were probably just confused and misinformed. Maybe in their shoes I would be angry, too. "Sometimes people just need to be listened to."

I opened my door and the crowd started to spread toward us. There were kids, but also a surprising amount of gray-haired people, and a few young children. They were holding placards that said WATER BELONGS TO THE PEOPLE and HANDS OFF OUR WATER! Amateur little signs, handmade with Magic Markers like the posters for a child's lemonade stand.

I got out of the car and raised my hand to get their attention. I half shouted "Hello! I'm James Sands," but before I could get any further a middle-aged woman came straight toward me, her face a mask of anger. "James Sands!" she barked. "You greedy pig! How much is enough for you?" Her face disappeared behind Henry's shoulder as he interposed himself between us. "Great business plan!" yelled an older man who looked like a retired accountant. "Your buddies bankrupt the country and you come in and buy us out cheap!"

"That's an oversimplification," I answered him, "but I understand where you're coming from. You think—"

My words were drowned out by a round of chanting that sprang up: "Our Water! Your Greed! Our Water! Your Greed!" His mouth started moving along with the others. They pressed closer as their slogan caught on and grew louder. There was a young woman with a bandanna covering her nose and angry blue eyes, a housewife whose baby watched me quizzically over her shoulder. An old man with age spots on his hollowed cheeks and thinning gray hair looked at me as if I was the final evil he had roused himself to confront. They were too densely packed for me to move forward; all of them were chanting or yelling catcalls. I'd been wrong; it didn't matter what I said. I was just a symbol. "Whitehall!" I yelled. It sounded frightened, so I cleared my throat and lowered my voice. "Whitehall!" A camera thrust in the air, a flash.

"Get your filthy hands off our water!" shouted one of them, a balding man with glasses who kept shifting his attention between me and the mob he was trying to inspire. "Our water! Your greed! Come on, everybody! Our water! Your greed!"

The blood seemed to surge to my brain, and I stuck my finger inches from my assailant's face. "Well, it's not your treatment plant and it's not your pipes! You want your water? Go drink out of Lake Erie!"

"Fuck you!" he shouted, and as he reached for my hand one of the Whitehall people came up behind him and guided him down to the ground. "Fuck you, brownshirt!" he shouted at the guard, and then I heard him bawl as Security made a quick movement. He was quiet after that.

Walter appeared in front of me. "Stay close to me," he said tersely, and he began pushing roughly through the crowd toward the front door, his eyes moving across the crowd.

Then, strangely, I felt a soft impact on the back of my head and heard a snapping sound. Liquid started running down my neck, and a sudden nausea clouded my stomach. In the next instant I felt something like a slap in the face, then saw something red go flopping at my feet. A yellow blur flickered past my eyes; a blue one flew over my shoulder. They seemed to come from every direction at once, bursting with wet little sighs across my back and my shoulders. Directly in front of me a young man had pulled a giant green water gun from beneath his coat. A stream of liquid came shooting out of it into my face, and I realized from the stinking saltiness that it was urine.

I felt the panic rising from my stomach. "Walter!" Walter grabbed me and pushed my head down as he bulled us through the crowd. As we went in the door, I glimpsed one of our people tackling the kid with the water gun. Somewhere behind me a baby started crying.

In my office I took off my piss-soaked tie and jacket and threw them onto the floor. I was shaking. A towel materialized, a fresh set of clothes, and I rushed into the bathroom to shower off the filth, yelling over the steam to my assistant, or whoever else might listen to me, "They've gone too far this time! Just too fucking far!" My hand was still trembling a little as I combed my hair and examined myself in the mirror, as if I might get a glimpse of what it was in that face that they so hated, something I hadn't noticed in the last fifty-eight years. I couldn't find it. On the contrary, I was often told that I resembled a certain heroic lawyer in a popular television show. He was a slightly younger, better-looking version of me, with hair that was coal black while mine was salt and pepper, and a graceful body instead of my bulky, Eastern European peasant build. But the same long face was there, the same dense black eyebrows. The irony was that he always played the earnest and upright prosecutor plodding relentlessly toward the People's justice in all those cases labeled *The People vs So and So*, while I was, to many, exactly that goddamned So and So.

Walter was standing there when I came out, unshakable and heroic. He'd gotten rid of his jacket, and I saw his black nylon shoulder holster hanging beside his ribs. Even though he stank of stale urine, he was as calm and focused as if he'd just come off a coffee break. "Thanks, Walter. I appreciate your help out there."

He looked me in the eye. "I'd do it again in a heartbeat, Jim." He went back to business. "I took your clothes to have them analyzed. We need to know if there was anything in those balloons besides water. When I find out who was supposed to screen that crowd, I'm going to have their ass."

"Punks!" I couldn't stop myself. "You should tell our guys to beat the shit out of that little asshole with the water gun!"

"You'd regret that one very quickly. Don't worry. He's looking at six years for his little stunt." I sat down at my desk and Walter started thinking out loud. "I was told that they showed up five minutes before you got there. Who was the joker with the video camera working for? And how'd they know just when we were coming? We need to interview the people in charge of your motor pool and scheduling. I want to take a look at Barrington's personnel, too. Those didn't have to be water balloons, you know. They could have been hand grenades. And there wouldn't have been a damned thing we could do about it."

I nodded, but my mind was somewhere else. Finally I said, "I used to be one of those people, you know."

Walter stopped dialing his phone and gave me a puzzled look. "What do you mean?"

"After college, in the eighties. Central America and all that." I gave a little laugh. "I remember being out there with a sign heckling Oliver North and John Poindexter. *'NO to the Shadow Government!'* I really hated them."

My friend considered that, then pressed out an arch little smile. "Looks a little different when you *are* the Shadow Government, doesn't it?" He laughed at my reaction. "Don't take me so seriously, Jim!"

He went back to his calls while I sat and stared at my desk, too unnerved to get to work. Some part of me still wanted to explain everything to the protesters, while another part just wanted to turn a fire hose on the bastards and wash them down the street. I logged on to my computer and glanced at the headlines. There it was, with a time stamp that showed it as being only ninety seconds old:

Water Exec Attacked by Mob

It had a picture of me grimacing as a balloon crushed against my head, an amorphous cloud of water arching into the air. The caption said "Direct Hit."

I stared at the image, at the cowering way I raised my shoulder to protect myself, and the expression of surprise and fear on my face. The guys over at Halliburton would certainly get a kick out of this.

Walter put away his phone. Someone had brought him a new white shirt to put on and he washed up in my bathroom and came out wearing one of my spare ties. "How'd things go with Barrington?"

"I've had better meetings, but it's nothing I can't handle." The friendly folks at Barrington Capital Fund had called me within hours of John Polling's assassination to demand a meeting. It hadn't been a cozy one. My Cascadia pipeline stretching from the Columbia River to the Southwest was the boldest private water project ever attempted, a jigsaw puzzle of rights-of-way and supply contracts that would cement Water Solutions as the largest private water provider in the world. We were heavily leveraged, though, and lawsuits in Seattle and Oregon had put us dangerously behind schedule. Now companies ten times our size were looking for an opening to pry Cascadia away from us, and Barrington was turning the screws, trying to make me put up my personal assets to secure any further financing from them. John Polling had been the white knight in that particular scenario, ready to ride in with his billions and bail us out. But John wasn't riding anywhere now.

"Well, Jim, this little water-balloon skirmish actually ties in with what I wanted to talk to you about today." He dragged a chair alongside my desk, went on in that rural twang of his that always sounded like the wise old football coach in the movies. "I want to show you some pictures."

He pulled the photos out of a manila envelope They had that off-kilter photojournalist feel and crisp little digital stamps indicating the date—hard facts put together by hard men. I put on my reading glasses and leaned forward.

The first shot showed a crowd of protesters outside our Evansville facility. There were probably fifty people of various ages holding signs saying PROTECT OUR WATER. Some were waving their fists or had their mouths frozen open in mid-slogan, making them look crazed with fury.

"That's Evansville," I said. "I've seen these."

He didn't answer, but went to the next group. "Portland," I said. Another band of protesters, many of them with their faces covered with black cloths or bandannas. Their signs identified them as the DNN, one of the protest groups that had cost us so much time and money. I could see our Security people standing like statues with their batons across their bodies. Behind them, our slogan, THE FUTURE OF WATER! He pulled out another group. "San Francisco," I said. And the next, "Phoenix."

The following picture showed a mass of rubble and broken glass, a gaping hole with an overturned desk and our big Water Solutions sign, now with some of the letters hanging upside down and others blown completely off the wall. "Seattle."

He pushed the next one in front of me: a body in a pool of blood. I couldn't help glancing away, but when I looked back I realized that it was John Polling. "Jesus!" I'd known Polling as a warm and generous man, a good listener, an art collector, a kind host. Now I knew him as a victim, flung out on the ground with his head blown open.

I pushed the crime-scene photo aside. "I take it you have a reason for showing me these."

"I do. Let's take another look at these, if you don't mind."

He went back to the first group, last April in Indiana, and pointed to it with a pen. "Look at this guy, with the black bandanna."

He looked somewhere in his twenties, with dark eyes and unruly black hair that had been tucked under a stocking cap. A punk kid with zero understanding of economics or how the world really worked.

Walter leafed forward to another photo, dated two months later. "This is San Francisco. Now, look." He indicated a man in a red bandanna and baseball cap. His hair was now light.

"He looks like . . ."

Now Walter pulled out a composite showing side-by-side enlargements of the man with the black hair and stocking cap and the other man two thousand miles and two months later with the blond hair and the baseball cap. "It's the same guy!"

"That's right. These aren't spontaneous citizen protests. These are targeted actions by a well-organized network of radicals. As was *this*." He went back to the photo of our bombed-out Seattle office. "And *this*." Forward to the photo of John Polling.

The bloody corpse angered me, but I stifled it. "They're interesting pictures, Walter, but where are you going with this?"

"We've been playing defense here, Jim. Water Solutions spent twelve million dollars protecting its assets last year, and we've got four arrests to show for it. Of those four, three of them got off for insufficient evidence, and if it hadn't been for the Terrorist Conspiracy Laws, the other one would have gotten forty days for disorderly conduct, instead of six years. In that time we've been picketed at five of our offices, we've had our Portland office fire-bombed, our Seattle office was blown up, our pipelines have been vandalized. . . . When you factor in repair of damaged facilities, delays from the opposition they stir up, legal fees, political campaigns, perception management, opportunity cost, what's it come out to? Thirty million? Forty million a year?"

"Or more. There's no question they've crapped all over the playing field. But you're lumping the violent extremists in with the so-called citizen groups."

"Our intelligence is telling us that the two groups are so closely related, you can't deal with one without addressing the other." He leaned back. "There's a lot of bad ideas in the air, Jim. And they affect moderates and extremists alike. We need to get more proactive."

I didn't say anything. We were getting close to the part of the pool where the water turns dark blue. "I'm not sure Water Solutions is really qualified to launch a war on bad ideas, Walter. Even with the mighty Whitehall on its side."

Although, if someone wanted to launch a war of any kind, Whitehall would be the one to turn to. Barrington had suggested we bring them in after the bombing at the Seattle office four months ago. Whitehall had assigned us Walter, a man about my own age who'd graduated from Duke, served in the Special Forces, and then spent two decades in the CIA in counterterrorism before being recruited into the private sector. He jogged every morning and still had a square military outline under his clothes. We shared an interest in Classical literature, and the first time I'd met him we'd gotten into a discussion about *The Iliad*. He favored Hector, doomed to defend Troy in a senseless war, while I was partial to Odysseus, the man of twists and turns. By the time our meeting was over, we'd begun a friendship, and every few weeks he'd bring in an article from *Classical Review* or news about a new translation of Thucydides. To cement everything, we had a mutual friend in Richard Boren, the former Secretary of Commerce, and the three of us would occasionally get together for a drink. Walter radiated warmth and competence, and after he fired our in-house security team and replaced it with his own men, everything seemed a lot calmer.

"Let me explain this strategically, Jim. Right now, these guys can take potshots at us at will, whether it's bombs, demonstrations, or legal actions. They can choose their time and place. Even if they're caught, they go straight to government custody, and the government has its hands tied by all their lawyers and their sympathizers. You can't run an effective counterterrorism operation with a bunch of pencil-pushers looking over your shoulder."

"So you want us to get more 'proactive.'"

"Yeah. We run our own program. Infiltrate their groups, neutralize their leaders, diminish their credibility through public education campaigns. We disrupt their operations before they happen."

I'd heard similar proposals put forth as wishful thinking after a couple of whiskies at various executive functions, and they always had a nasty ring. "It sounds like something I'd have to run by Legal."

"I already have. As far as the protest groups you were worried about, there're very few laws restricting private individuals from joining them. Government, yes. But we're not the government. At worst, you'd be risking some bad publicity. The big upside here is that most of the infrastructure for collecting intelligence is already in place."

"How so?"

His face lit up at the simplicity of it all. "Marketing data! For example"—he pointed to the composite photo—"we've got a picture of Randy Radical here. Let's say we infiltrate his group, Protect Our Water, and we get this guy's name and phone number. We log all his calls and use them to map his social network. Mix that with his credit card records, his health records, his travel records from the airlines. Before you know it, we've got a pretty clear profile of who this bozo is, who he knows, and how to get to him."

"A judge would say that's a violation of Randy Radical's civil rights."

"And *if* these people were law abiding, I'd be out there shoulder to shoulder with them, defending their rights. But they're not. They're the first to go squawking about civil rights when the government doesn't follow the rules, but what about John Polling's rights? What about your right to run your business without getting assaulted on your front steps or having a bomb go off in your office?"

Some distant part of me couldn't help considering Whitehall's angle on all this. Their business was security, and my safety—or rather, my fear for it—was another revenue source for them. On the other hand, some people said the same thing about the insurance "racket," then lost everything when their house burned down.

"Okay. But we're just a water company. Who's going to provide all that other data you talked about?"

"Jim." He spoke carefully, meaningfully. "There's a lot of other companies out there who have the same concerns we do. And I'd guess Uncle Sam's got more than a passive interest in this venture, too."

I looked out the window toward the distant Capitol Building, not knowing what to say. "Well"—he stood up—"you've got your CFO and his staff coming in five minutes. I'll leave these with you." The stack of photos landed on my desk with a soft slap. The picture of John Polling's body was on top.

When I got home that night the house had a strange fragrance, a powerful incense that went straight through my nose and into my brain. I floated there in it for a few moments, disoriented at the sudden mysterious transportation of that smell. I was no place and no time for a moment as a memory struggled to the surface. I recognized it. Sage. Wyoming. For just an instant it all hung there before me in a tawny sun-bleached picture far stronger than the dark wood of my foyer: the broad empty high plains, the dust plume of a pickup off in the distance as it churned across the Rosebud Reservation. I was standing on a rural route with my thumb out, looking at the clouds. A sense of freedom and openness so overwhelmed me there in the foyer of my house that I almost had to sit down. It was a feeling I hadn't had since I was twenty years old. Just as quickly it fell away, left me stranded there on an antique carpet made by long-dead Turkic nomads, with the Barrington Fund's foot still on my neck. I draped my coat over a chair and looked for Anne.

She was curled up in the library, as usual, so I asked the maid to bring me in a sandwich. Anne had a certain catlike way of sprawling on the couch in her black leotards and long silver hair that filled me with a mix of admiration and vague desire. She'd been doing yoga since we'd met thirty years ago, and moved like a woman half her age. Just over fifty, her mix of youthfulness and age fascinated people. She was on the boards of a dozen charitable organizations, and she had a constant stream of love letters from the elementary school kids she taught in the city. Now she was nestled into the maroon and blue stripes of the antique Bolivian manta draped over our couch, a Penelope to my Odysseus.

She looked up when I came into the room. "How was work?"

"Crappy." I loosened my tie. "This Polling assassination has Barrington freaked out, and they're tightening the screws on me. It was a difficult day."

"That's too bad, honey." She gave me a sympathetic look and then patted a space on the couch next to her. I knew better than to start in about the problems caused by John Polling's murder, since I'd never told her about my arrangement with John in the first place. And I didn't mention that "tightening the screws" meant actually putting our house on the line. That was all Water Solutions, and the company was something we'd agreed not to talk about, one of those unsigned, unspoken contracts a lot of married couples arrive at.

I'd met Anne at a board meeting of one of D.C.'s decrepit ghetto schools, where she was an apprentice teacher and I was doing a volunteer project trying to arrange corporate grants for inner city education. Hers was the beautiful white face among the dark determined features of the parents, and I suppose I was the young white guy who gave a damn. The parents themselves picked up on the obvious symmetry, and when I managed to get the school a sizable grant from an oil company, I almost felt they were offering her to me as a prize. We had a brief, wonderful courtship and then got married when she became pregnant with Tina. Not exactly fairy-tale material, but how the human race got made, and we joked that it saved us years of dithering. Right after that I got a job writing loans for the World Bank, specializing in third world water infrastructure projects. That was my introduction to the business of water.

"Have you been burning incense today?" I asked her. "I thought I smelled sage when I came in."

She leaned over and picked up a scorched bundle of dried green shrubs bound with ribbon. "Roger came and we did a little purification ritual."

Roger was her latest yoga instructor; part yogi, part Native American spiritualist, he came twice a week. The two of them always seemed to be purifying something or other.

"I thought that was what the six new ionizers were for." She didn't react, so I went on. "I mean, it seems a bit contradictory to be cleaning the air with ionizers at the same time that you're filling it with smoke. Doesn't it?"

That got her. She crinkled her eyebrows. "Looking for a fresh opponent, dear?"

I sighed. "I'm sorry. It's been that kind of day." I slipped off my gray jacket and slung it over the arm of the couch. "Do you mind if I put on some music?" I picked up the remote and started Bach's Cello Suites, the Yo-Yo Ma recording. The gentle sawing sounds of the string and the varnished wood poured out of the speakers like incense. It was my own purifying ritual, I suppose. I listened to it quietly for a few minutes as I sat on the couch by her feet. Anne listened to it, too. There was something indescribably sad about the pieces and their beautiful moaning.

"I was attacked today," I began. "Physically."

The shock registered on her face immediately and she sat up, alarmed. "What happened?"

"There was a protest outside our office, the same old crap about 'the people's water,' and when I pulled up, they attacked me with water balloons."

"Water balloons!"

"And one of them sprayed urine in my face." The amusement dropped from her eyes and she leaned toward me and put her hand on my cheek; then she reached around me and squeezed close, sighing. "That's horrible, Jim. Are you okay?"

"Yeah. It was a bunch of yahoos from Harrisburg. I thought I'd try to have some sort of dialogue. Silly me! I'm surprised Gary didn't tell you."

I could hear the distaste in her answer after I mentioned her bodyguard's name. "Gary and I don't talk very much."

"You didn't like the last guy, either."

"No, Jim, and I'm probably not going to like the next one." Walter had reorganized the protection regime for my family, and my wife had not been very cooperative. "They're creepy!" she'd said. My son had refused them entirely. Only my daughter had gone along without any resistance, always the good girl.

The maid brought the sandwich and a beer and set them next to me. "I'm really starting to hate those protesters. I'm tired of their shit. They need to take it up at the ballot box if they don't like it."

"You've already beaten them at the ballot box, remember? They won a referendum, and before they could get it implemented you got another referendum on the ballot and overturned them. That's why they're holding signs and throwing water balloons."

"Well, that's how democracy works." I took a bite of the sandwich. "Speaking of which, today Walter started talking about some new program he wants me to join, some sort of—" I waved my hand in the air, looking for the right words. "—counteroffensive against all these militant and civil groups. As if I needed things to get weirder."

"A 'counteroffensive'? What does that mean?"

I'd wanted to confide in someone about Walter's program, but I realized I'd chosen the wrong person. I backpedaled as best I could. "I don't know. . . . Some sort of public relations scheme the marketing guys at Whitehall dreamed up to bring in more revenue. Believe me, I'm letting this one go by."

"I certainly hope so." She closed her book. "You know, maybe your company should get out of water."

I'd been hearing that a lot from her the past couple of years. "Anne, I've told you: A company like ours doesn't just 'get out' of water. Water is ninety percent of our business."

"Can't you sell out, then? Do something else? I mean, all this with protesters and bombs and bodyguards . . . I've got a bad feeling about it."

I couldn't explain to her how precarious things were at the moment; the vultures would swoop in as soon as I showed weakness. "This protest stuff will blow over. Some people just don't understand that what Water Solutions offers really is the best product."

I didn't see agreement there, but she changed the subject. "Josh called today," she said.

I kept my voice even. "How much did he ask for?"

She got a little sharper. "Why don't you try 'How is he?' Or 'What's Josh up to these days?'"

"Okay. What is Josh up to these days?"

"Well, he's changing apartments. He wants a place with a lower rent. He said he wants to be more financially responsible."

"How's his Web-design business?"

"I didn't ask."

Joshua was our underachiever. Of our two children, he'd taken after his mother: light-eyed where I was dark, small-boned where I was broad. Our differences starting cropping up around his middle-school soccer games. It bugged me to see him making all the same stupid mistakes the other kids made, so I bought a dozen soccer balls and set up a net in the backyard. When I stood in the goal for him to practice his shooting, he'd methodically kicked each and every ball sideways. By the time we'd gone through all twelve balls, our relationship was in the toilet. He spent the next fifteen years kicking the ball sideways, failing his way through prep school and college. I rewrote his trust fund so that he'd have to stand on his own two feet. Every several years he would fly back to D.C. so he could fill me up with stories about friends of his who were going to cut him in on some brilliant Internet venture, or other cockamamie deals that would never come off, and I would do my best to pretend it was all real. I suspected he was borderline manic depressive. Our daughter, Tina, who'd made Dean's list at Princeton and now did commercial real estate in Boston, still adored him, and his mother went to visit him in San Francisco a couple of times each year. I hadn't spoken to him at length in half a decade—most of his adult life.

"So what else did Josh say?" I asked, as irked as after our last round of battles five years ago.

"He's coming to visit!"

"Great. What for?"

Anne sounded annoyed as she answered. "Because he's your *son*! Because he wants to *see* you. Is that so mystifying?"

"When? I'll arrange to be out of town."

"You know, Jimmy, maybe you two ought to try family counseling."

"Oh, please!"

"You're going on the assumption that there'll always be time later to fix your relationship with him. What if something were to happen to you tomorrow? Or to him? This is all very temporary." She swept her arm toward the walls. "All of this. It's an illusion."

I took it at first as more of her yoga mumbo jumbo, but as the melancholy string-tones vibrated through the room, I started imagining Josh's death in a car crash or a drowning. The phone call, the hands thrown helplessly in the air. I'd lost my father in an auto accident when I was twelve. Now that devastating recollection cut through all the annoyance I'd been feeling a few seconds ago. Whatever Anne's lingo about illusion, she'd brought home the point that in relationships there was pride and power, and there was love, and woe to the person who mixed up their relative importance.

She had leaned back into the stripes of the old Bolivian manta and was looking at me with an open face. She seemed to glow as she sat there. "You're right, Anne. Thank you. When did Josh say he's coming?"

"He said he'll surprise us."

Perfect! He'd drop in whenever he felt like it, and then I'd be the bad guy if I didn't clear my schedule for him! I felt myself balling up inside, then expelled it all in a long breath. Okay.

The music changed to a more uptempo piece and I tucked myself under Anne's legs and began rubbing her feet. She made little purring noises; foot rubs were one of her favorite things. As I worked my way toward her heel, my mind began drifting back toward my business situation. I had to counterattack the Fund, even if it was only a feint:

maybe putting out a few feelers to one of their rivals would bring them around. I didn't need to take their crap lying down. But to interest new money, we'd need to offer some assurances against the lawsuits and the terrorist attacks. I started thinking about Walter again, his idea of being proactive.

"Ooh!" Anne said softly. "Easy on the Achilles tendon." And then, "Perfect!"

She was lying there with her eyes closed, smiling. Always good-hearted, always supposing that everyone was as well-intentioned as she was. In that moment of simple happiness I recalled Walter's picture of John Polling's bloody corpse. Maybe Walter was right: It wasn't just my business at stake here; it was my life. And certain people out there didn't distinguish between the two.

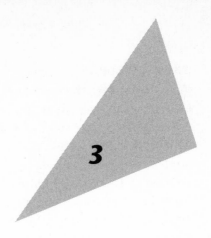

3

I've ditched the Young Corporate look and changed vehicles, clean as can be with my Mariners sweatshirt and a fresh espresso triple-shot speeding me down Rural Route 2 for my next rendezvous. I'm passing the empty strip malls of NASCAR America, eyeing all those cheap real-estate plays that went belly-up in the currency collapse. They crowded the edges of every little town in the precrash heyday, making Mom and Pop feel like Players with their own little tax-evasion scheme, just like the Big Guys with their fancy accountants. "Here, little people!" the Regime said. "Steal like the pros!" Except when the bubble burst, it was mighty hard to tell the difference between a tax savings and a huge loss, and now ugly unrented strip developments garbaged up the country with peeling paint and cracked plastic marquees. This is the road to McFarland's place.

I last saw McFarland eighteen hours ago at the apartment, when he'd been unpacking his .308 and setting up a little sandbag rest on the windowsill. If he'd been one of those pithy movie heroes, he would have said, "It's showtime!" or "Let's rock!" or something like that, but he was McFarland, so he said nothing at all, just rearranged the potted plants and checked the egress route to the basement door. The usual unspoken questions before an operation: Would the target show? Would there be inconvenient bystanders? But a bigger tension than that hung over us. We all knew that with the Polling operation we were crossing the line of the forgivable, and that added a weight to our little get-together that I hadn't felt before. I think we had the sense, McFarland, Joby, and I, that we were stepping into something much bigger, an eternal Civil War, played out in numberless countries by a succession of named and nameless men. Underdogs versus Overlords, world without end. Or maybe it was just me, because I find that thought strangely comforting. Particularly since I was the one to initiate the operation.

The word that John Polling had a girlfriend in Seattle had drifted over to us in a Starbucks wrapper. "Can you believe it! He's doing this girl who's young enough to be his granddaughter!" A friend who had a friend who was fucking America's most successful corporate con artist after her shifts at America's most successful corporate café, something that normally would have been like, "Yeah, what an *asshole*!" but in this case fell to me, who could recognize it as a useful piece of data.

I took it back to my crew, and we took it to McFarland, and the conversation turned to whether we might drop him. Up until then we'd only made some bangs and started some fires. McFarland was different, though. He was ready to go to the next level, and we had to decide if we were going with him.

We found out where the girlfriend lived and McFarland reconnoitered it. I checked the layout from high up in an adjoining apartment building and drew up a schematic. Hypothetical plans for a hypothetical action. We examined it in the back of a T.G.I. Friday's at the Bellevue Mall.

"Basic assumptions," McFarland began, cracking his long bony fingers. "He's got unlimited resources and so he's got unlimited security. I guarantee he's got twenty-plus people in D.C. changing shifts every two hours."

"But this is Seattle."

"That's right. And this is his girlfriend. That's what makes it sweet. See, he could handle it two ways. One, he brings six or seven guys and does a full-on protection regime, multiple cars, the whole bit." He took on a low, pompous voice. "'I'm John Polling and nobody can touch me!'

But that gets noticed. The other, he brings his top two guys and he dresses down: check shirt, Polarfleece. He slides in and out without anybody being the wiser. My guess is, he's number two, keeping it quiet. It's the 'none of this is really happening' trip. Because that's what's going on in the mind of a man who's cheating on his wife. It is happening; it's not happening. Basic human nature. Plus, we know his wife and her lawyers would tear him a new asshole if she found out."

We talked about some possibilities, a subject McFarland really warmed up to. There were a million ways to whack somebody. There was a nicotine phosphate pillow in their hip pocket in a bump pass, so when they sat down, it burst and went into their skin. Too much security for that, he thought. There was the RPG round as they parked the car, like the People's Revolutionary Army had used to take out Somoza in Paraguay in 1980. Hell, he said, in El Salvador the guerrillas killed someone by dropping a bucket of water on his head from four stories up. "Broke his neck, gave him a concussion—he died right there on the landing." McFarland was a regular catalog of great ideas. "We could rent the apartment next door and set a bomb off on the other side of the wall when they're doin' it. Or ambush him when they go shopping."

No, he finally decided, a sniper shot would be better, and it looked like some of the apartments across the way offered a perfect line of fire toward the front door. "I could use a fifty-cal," he said. A .50-caliber rifle shot a 725-grain bullet with a muzzle velocity of 2,800 feet per second. "That'll bring down an elephant. We get him anywhere in the body cavity and he's gone. Two rounds'll go through twelve inches of concrete."

"Doesn't that mean if the girlfriend's behind him, the same bullet takes her out, too?"

"And maybe somebody in the apartment behind them."

No good. He decided on a Remington .308, with a 180-grain bullet that McFarland would load himself. McFarland always loaded his own bullets. He hammered the serial number down with a ball-peen hammer, then resighted it at the range. The Word was becoming flesh a lot faster than I'd expected, but whenever I had doubts I just remembered Jeffrey Lansing getting kicked to death and John Polling walking out of court with a smile on his face. The lightning had to strike.

We got lucky and I found an apartment with a clear line of fire We rented it under a name we'd pulled off a canceled check and then built an identity on. I dyed my hair black, wore a fake beard, glasses, dark contact lenses: Hispanic Lando. In the apartment, I always wore cotton gloves, but just to be safe we collected combed hairs from a salon Dumpster and spread them around the apartment. Here, boys: here's some DNA for your database. McFarland pegged the range from the window to the front entrance at two hundred feet. Well within his capabilities. The front door would be the stopper: Joby would squirt in some superglue when Polling showed; then McFarland would get him as his girlfriend fumbled with the key. If they got through, Joby would be waiting. If they turned back or McFarland missed his shot, the spotter at street level would also be the plug: the plug would move in from behind and do the job with a pistol. That was me. I went to the range and practiced with my HK.

We bought a bunch of potted plants and put them in the open window; then we waited. We figured that Polling's security would check out the surrounding area before each visit, which they did. And they saw the window open all the time, and that thick row of greenery in front of it, soaking up the sun.

Our IT guys hacked into his mistress's phone account and started logging her calls. We put a friend behind the counter at Starbucks where she worked, to keep an ear out for her movements. It seemed they usually ate at a certain pricey French restaurant, and we caught her making a reservation for the following Friday. Sarah and Lilly shadowed her, saw her buy silk lingerie and a bag of delicacies at the market. Smoked oysters, expensive cheeses, twenty-year-old port—the kind of thing you nibble on after jumping in the sack. McFarland came into town with his .308.

Polling's security guy arrived beforehand and checked out the neighborhood. Our window was open, as always. The plants were there, as always. We let Polling go in and make himself comfortable. We knew he'd be back that night without his guards. They went out for dinner at eight o'clock. At 11:18, their date was ending. I was the bird dog, standing out on the street with a lapel mic.

"They're getting out of the car," I muttered. "He's in his blue fleece jacket. She's still in red. Locking the car. Coming up the walkway. They're alone."

"Got 'im," McFarland said. By now he'd have the gun leveled and sighted in on the target. I saw them get to the door, the girl taking out her keys, putting them into the lock. Polling stepped back a couple of feet and looked right at me.

I turned away; then I heard two loud cracks and a woman's scream. I didn't want to look, as if putting my back to it somehow made me not part of it. My knees went wobbly. There was a third report from McFarland's rifle, and I started walking away, forcing myself to walk at a measured pace as the girl's shrieks followed me. The adrenaline had no place to go but my brain, and everything slowed and crystallized. Every brick, every crack in the sidewalk seemed to jump out at me with some unintelligible significance, the scrawled secret words of a revelation. I struggled to hold my pace for the next fifty feet, seized with the fear that every apartment window was filled with witnesses taking my picture; then I cut between two buildings and bolted through the grassy darkness for my car. I eased the auto from the curb, sweat running down my ribs while my fake beard itched uncontrollably. I kept telling myself there was nothing to worry about, that we'd executed perfectly. We'd already cleaned the apartment, and I knew that McFarland would have dropped the rifle and headed out the furnace entrance in the basement. In twenty minutes I was approaching Tonk's apartment in West Seattle, where I cut my hair and uncapped a bottle of ashe blond Miss Clairol. The People had spoken. Justice had been done. I lay down with my eyes wide open and waited for the news to hit.

I'm eager to see McFarland now. I've got a new plan to get the Civils off their asses and onto the barricades, and I need McFarland's support to make it fly. I exit Route 2 and head down a two-lane lined with trees and open land, stretching between the failing towns of Sultan and Gold Bar. McFarland's mechanic shop sits at a crossroads with a convenience store and a bankrupt antiques shop whose cheap junk still fills the dusty windows. It's quiet out here these days; the oil shocks and the credit crunch are killing the outlying suburbs, covering the green-lawned landscape with FOR SALE BY OWNER signs and their hopeless tag-line: *Will Take Best Offer.* Except the best offer still sucks, and the up-and-comers in the new Service Economy are the repo companies, with their fleets of moving trucks and dirt-cheap resale warehouses. The Wal-Mart snake is eating its tail.

We first met McFarland's group staking out the regional office of America's foremost war profiteer. They were doing a street-person gig that Tonk made on the third day. Once he was sure it wasn't a brown-shirt, he went up to the phony bum and held out a buck. "Here you go, buddy. Take this and buy yourself a good book on surveillance." That was the beginning of our relationship. After a couple of weeks of sniffing each other's privates, we went up the chain to the man who called himself McFarland. A tall man with a sandy crew cut, he was slim but very fit, a martial arts nut that had a picture of himself smashing a foot-thick block of ice with the palm of his hand. He was a veteran of the Raq, the Ran, and the Stans, had seen his buddies wither away after the wars from a cocktail of depleted uranium and bad juju that the Regime refused to diagnose. "Call it Crybaby Syndrome," said one pundit. Benefits would not be paid to "victims" of Crybaby Syndrome. I think that put McFarland over the edge.

When the Accord rubber-stamped the president's pension theft, McFarland started getting organized, and when his county went to Internet voting, his group struck back. They torched the just-privatized Post Office and signed it High Plains Patriots; then they hit the Kent armory and made off with some goodies that made even me a little jumpy. I guess that he has between seven and fifteen men in his organization, guns 'n' ammo guys, experts at improvised weapons that he leads with Joby, his highly combustible second-in-command. They can make gunpowder out of dirt and shaped charges out of wine bottles. Throw in a soldering iron and a remote control toy, and you've got your own low-budget Pentagon.

Meanwhile, behind Door Number Two, us. Zero military background, no tactical training. An original core of zonked-out tree-spikers and soft-gutted white-hat hackers and crackers. But very fast learners with a background in social engineering. Why take down an armored car when you can talk the bank into wiring a million si-moleans to your bank account in Malta? Add a few turncoats from the entry-level corporate world and some rogue programmers, and bingo: You've got mail. Now credit companies keep sending us offer after of-fer for sky's-the-limit cards, and we keep accepting them. We've always got a fresh supply of new personas floating through the databases, with matching documents perfect down to the last wrinkle and tear. So when we suggested some cross-training, McFarland was all for it.

Up until then, we'd been tagging our operations with National Restoration Forces. We had about twenty comps that I knew of, sprinkled around Portland, Seattle, Eugene, and Olympia, sharing a byline more than anything else. We did a couple of joint operations with the High Plains people: a Wal-Mart, the Amibank offices in Seattle. Talk started to shift to the idea of a united front, and I suggested the name Army of the Republic. It had a nice Lincoln-esque ring.

I pull into the gravel yard of McFarland's garage and back in next to a rusted pickup. I close my eyes for a few seconds of buzzy rest, my version of sleep, then climb out. It's an Indian summer day, and the leaves have taken on that final hard green color that comes before they start to turn yellow. A couple of cows are drifting through a pasture across the road. The air smells beautiful out here, even with the faint trace of grease and gasoline that rises up from the gray dirt. Everything at this moment seems brilliant and precious—the America I'm fighting for. Into the moment walks McFarland.

"Lando! Look at you!" He claps me on the shoulder and holds out his hard oil-stained hand for me to shake.

"Mac." Mac hasn't seen me blond before: I was brown-haired before I went Latino. He takes in this new Lando for a few seconds, nodding his head.

McFarland hasn't done anything to change his appearance. In the daylight his long workingman face looks homey and warm, different from last night and all those shadows. He's wearing duck coveralls and a greasy SNAP-ON TOOLS cap. He's fifteen years older than me, joined the army instead of college. We put the hood of my car up and he checks the fluids, the reflexive kindness of a lifelong mechanic. "You're low about a quart of power-steering fluid."

He gets out the funnel and shoves it into an STP can. "Looks like the Army of the Republic is officially on the march."

"No shit. Did you watch KBX this morning?"

He grins down at the engine. "Sure did!" He turns to me. "We got a big kick out of that one. I think even Joby's warming up to you guys."

Joby's a short, barrel-shaped guy with the nerve-racking intensity of a white supremacist gang leader who got religion and went straight. That's how I imagined him, though McFarland laughed when I told him that. "Joby's a good boy," he said. "He's just protective." He never did say what Joby's background was, or explain the India ink tattoos crawling up the inside of Joby's arms. Still, Joby and I had done the Polling operation together. Till death do us part.

We go inside and McFarland pours me a Styrofoam cup of coffee that's aged to a dark olive color. It has an acrid, unpleasant odor. "Dude, I'm bringing the coffee next time."

"You Greenies with your fancy-assed coffee!" he says. The talk radio show was on, and we can't help listening as people call in about the operation. No phony sanctity here: most of them were jubilant. Bill from Bremerton weighed in: *My only beef is that nobody greased Polling ten years ago!* Next caller, from Everett: *I mean, I'm not saying I'm for this Army of the Republic or whatever they call themselves, I'm just saying, they did something that needed to be done!*

"This ought to get us a few recruits," McFarland says.

"Or better yet, copycats."

The next caller, with a high, wheezy voice: *See, when you don't got a Justice system, you got a justice nonsystem, if you catch my drift. It's a justice nonsystem!*

"Don't strain yourself, guy," I tell the radio. "That's some big thinking."

"I wouldn't knock it, Lando. They're usually bitching because the government hasn't shot us down like dogs." We gloat through a few more calls, then the host recycles the torture allegations that the government floated that morning. Doing his duty for his handlers.

"Listen to that bullshit!" McFarland says, but to our surprise, the next caller debunks the host, bringing up accounts from other news sources: *That's just good old-fashioned propaganda they're putting out! That's all!*

"There's still hope," McFarland says. He snaps it off. "What did those Democracy people want to talk about?"

I tell him about the meeting.

He's silent, thinking it over. "They want us to turn in our weapons, and all that crap?"

"No. But they do want a formal announcement."

I can see by the way his face hardens that the idea doesn't appeal to him. Maybe asking for a cease-fire sounds suspiciously like trying to take away his gun. "Now, who exactly are these guys again?"

"DNN: Democracy Northwest Network. They started out as a network of different groups opposed to the privatizations—environmental and social justice people, churches, labor unions. They fought a lot of crap off for years after it had already been instituted in the rest of the country."

"So we're talking about tree-sitters? Homosexual-rights types?"

"No, Mac, those guys all joined my group."

It's quiet; then he lets a long laugh go bouncing through the little office. There's a real light of happiness in his brown eyes, and for a moment I think, *This is how I want to remember McFarland.*

He shoos away the feeling. "Go on, Lando."

I pull myself back to the dirty glass panels and the orange NAPA clock. "I take these people very seriously. They can make telephones ring and they can put people in the streets. They're talking about shutting things down, and they feel like they can turn out the numbers to do it."

"Where?"

"Well, Seattle, I would guess. And she mentioned Boston and New York."

"Those are all on the coasts," he points out. "How many are they going to turn out in Peoria, Omaha, Atlanta, and Denver? You don't take the center, you're looking at a long civil war. Because that's where they'll draw their troops from."

McFarland is deeply into the popular insurrection matrix, but he does have a point. We need the center. We need those guys who drive around in little red cars at the Fourth of July parade.

"See, Lando, the force that can operate across a wide territory, and strike anywhere at any time, is the one that's going to give the Regime a run for their money. A few thousand people marching around on the coast isn't real relevant."

It sounds almost childish to me, but I respect the man and certainly his strategy has worked somewhere, sometime. Maybe Cuba, 1959. Nicaragua, 1978. But it won't work here, now. I try to figure out a gentle way to say it. "Most guerrilla wars are lost, Mac. You know that. Most revolutionaries die miserable deaths and you never read their names in a history book. To take these fuckers down we need millions of people getting involved, not just a few hundred engaged in armed struggle."

It annoys him to hear me stepping on his fantasy. "If you feel that way, why aren't you out there marching around with a cardboard sign?"

The caffeine starts knocking on my temple again, but I ignore it. "Because bottom line, what makes nonviolent resistance powerful is the threat that it might just turn into violent resistance. And that's where the Army of the Republic comes in."

His eyes widen slightly and there's a sudden barometric drop in the room. I've blundered into the scratchy, sketchy part of our alliance. "I didn't know you were the one making the decisions about where we came in."

We hear the grinding sound of a car pulling into the yard, and we both glance out to see a beaten green Ford F-150 come to a halt by the garage. A door slams and a short, wide man with thinning blond hair gets out and does a bowlegged little march over to the office. Coatless in the cool air, his black T-shirt shows a mushroom cloud sprouting over a map of Iran and the words THE FRIENDLY ATOM. Joby. Great.

The bell over the door jangles. "Hey, Jobes," McFarland says cheerfully, and I get up to shake hands. Joby nods at me with that malevolent glitter of his. "Cute hairdo," he says.

"Lando here's talking about a cease-fire, Jobes," Mac starts, and Joby's look seems to get slightly more hostile, if that's possible. I have to force myself not to shrink away; then he turns back to his commander for more explanation. Mac seems to have let go of the tension of the previous moment. He does a fairly neutral recap of the DNN and their Real Vote campaign.

"Buncha Patagonias," Joby says.

It's up to me now. I'm talking to a guy who has THE STRONG RIGHT ARM OF JESUS tattooed across his wrist, but if I don't put it out there in a way he can accept, the whole cease-fire could die right here, and my plan along with it. "I'm sure the Regime would like all of us to go on using those labels, Joby, because that works real well for them. Radical. Fundamentalist. Liberal. Christian. The Regime loves labels, because they divide people. Divide and conquer. As far as the DNN: Are you going to heist a Wal-Mart with these people? No. But they're as pissed as we are and they have tools we don't. A lot of them have already been gassed and clubbed. They aren't just going to be sitting around meditating on world peace."

He's hearing me, and I address myself to both of them now. "It's a question of mass. This Regime isn't going to fall without millions of Americans in the streets, and these people are all about that. My take is, we beef up the civil resistance by declaring a cease-fire, and let the Regime know we can be back in a heartbeat if they don't play ball with the surface organizations." I grin at them. "Let them bust their chops for a while. We're still calling the shots."

No words from Joby, but his stony red face has shifted from hostile to neutral, and he looks to his friend. Mac's gaze wanders over to an auto parts calendar and a color picture of Christ smudged with gray oil. Who would Jesus whack? "You're a smart guy, Lando," he says softly, in a way that leaves me wondering if it's a compliment or an insult; then he goes quiet again, reaches for some unnamable assembly, and wipes it down with a pink rag.

It's time to spring the plan I'd dreamed up after meeting Emily. "How about this," I say, unfolding a printout. "The so-called president's coming to Seattle on the fifth of December to do some back-slapping with his fellow crooks. The National Business Symposium. That's eight weeks from now. They shut down Seattle, keep the motherfucker off the podium, we'll get on board. If they don't, we do it our way."

A ballsy move on my part: How can I dictate to the DNN that they shut down Seattle on December 5? In my opinion, it's way past time for the Civils to give President Matthews a good crisp slap in the face, but besides that, I can see our guys aren't buying in without a show of strength from the "Patagonias."

McFarland's weary features seem to open up as he runs through the scenario. "There's a problem, though, Lando: We're just one group, and a cease-fire of just us doesn't mean anything. What are the other resistance groups going to say?"

I dig my fingernail into the Styrofoam cup as I think it over. There are blue notes all over the West Coast that I'm only slightly in contact with, and they have their own plans. "We need a meeting," I say. A few faces come to mind. Old comps from when I first went blue. Some other dangling threads I've never tried pulling. I'm seeing the first glimmer of a new machine here. "I can call it," I say. "I think I can get six or seven groups from the West Coast."

It surprises him. "In one room?" He becomes wary. "Who handles security?"

"We both do. Or you can be in charge. I have no problem with that."

That seems to ease things up all the way around. We chew over a few more details about the DNN, and then I put on my coat. An assassination, a cease-fire, a new network: It's been a busy day. "How much do I owe you for the power steering fluid?"

He laughs. "Forget it!" He and Joby follow me out to the car and he leans on the roof as I open the door. "I still say we haven't taught the enemy a big enough lesson yet," says Mac. "We need an operation that'll make 'em really value a cease-fire. Like you said before, a big bang with a big echo."

Silence as we all run down our personal lists of predatory corporations and corrupt politicians; then Joby speaks, and for the first time I realize there's more going on inside his head than Crackpot Fundamentalism honed on *Soldier of Fortune* magazine. With one word he hits on the nexus of everything hated about the Regime, and I feel a shiver of unease go through my stomach.

"Cascadia," he says.

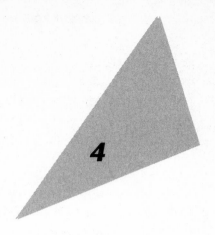

4

Mao said Revolution is not a dinner party, but this first meeting of West Coast militants tracks like one, with invitations engraved on encrypted e-mails or tossed out in person at furtive meetings in Bellingham and Portland. The season's must-attend social event for the blue end of the spectrum, convoked in a desperate-looking former chain motel on the outskirts of Tacoma and including some of the country's most elusive guests. We're thinking the Halloween festivities will give the cops an extra level of static to process.

Tonk and I get there first, joking about the miniature coffeemaker and playing with a set of Tinkertoys I brought. We've chosen this spot because it's near the intersection of two highways. The back of the room is separated from a rest stop by a hundred yards of woods and a chain-link fence; we've cut a hole in the fence and parked some vehicles by the highway in case of emergency.

This would be a choice grab for the Regime, a chance to draw crosses over the top leaders of most of the groups on the West Coast. None of the other groups will know the final location until they've met with one of our people at the local shopping mall, and from there they'll be watched as they drive the last wiggly miles to the motel.

Between McFarland's people and ours, we have a dozen *compañeros* with radios and phones in the area. For us, this is a big operation. Still, no meeting is ever completely secure, because your safety depends on the competence of everyone else.

I'm dressed for the occasion in a flannel shirt and a NASCAR cap, pumped up with a triple shot to keep me sharp. A whole lot of my recent history is set to parade into the room tonight. Comps I've met at direct actions and through friends, some of them before there even were any comps. I tree-sat in the Siskiyou with Earl E., demonstrated against privatizing the Post Office with Mark. Others I hooked up with through college friends that later formed the Jefferson Combine: Steve Sykes would message me an e-mail address, and we'd set up a rendezvous just to compare notes on document creation or new cracking tools. A risky business, but one that promised a distant upside someday. Maybe today.

The Portland guys show up first. Earl E. Warning used to wear his hair all the way down to his butt, but has cleaned himself up and sports a Portland Trailblazers sweatshirt and a Nike cap.

"Dude, I barely recognized you!" We slap hands in a high five and come together into a hug, where I disappear into his six-five, two hundred twenty-pound frame. Earl E., the not-so-gentle giant. I haven't seen him since Siskiyou. "I like the Swoosh cap. You make a great corporate shill."

"It's the new me, Lando. I worship the Corporates!"

"I'm lovin' it!"

"Speaking of logos, man: ever since you guys whacked Polling, the **A⊕R** crosshairs are all over Portland! Sweet!"

Earl E. has been underground for two years, since the courts ruled that all property damage in a political context constituted Terrorism. The feds had rounded up most of his posse in two days of raids, salting them away for six to twelve years for breaking windows in Berkeley the month before. Their cause célèbre finally buckled under the weight of the pervasive media attacks, and Earl. E. left Berkeley and regrouped in Portland with the resolve to break a lot more than windows. He'd gotten heavily into incendiaries; his crew has a dozen smoking ruins on their résumé. I get the feeling they're ready for more ambitious projects.

McFarland comes in from checking with our field people, along with Joby, who drags his crew cut glare around the room with the usual menace.

Tonk slaps him on his upper arm. "Lighten up, Joby, you're making me nervous! Are you still pissed because I outshot you?"

Mr. Christian Identity cracks a smile and mumbles something about sights.

"Oh, right, dude! Your sights. *Right!* I think you should e-mail them, Joby: *Dear Smith & Wesson, due to your defective sights, I was humiliated by some punk-ass Greenie—*"

McFarland cuts in as Joby turns away, grinning. "Don't argue with the boy, Joby. You'll just get in deeper."

The High Plains guys took a liking to Tonk after the Lynnwood Armory operation. They'd done it under the guise of a surprise military inspection. Tonk showed up dressed in a National Guard uniform and engaged the guard in conversation while the others moved in behind him. Because Tonk was a good actor, there weren't any casualties, just a couple of weekend warriors trussed up with duct tape. So Tonk was in, and had taken to doing some cross-training in improvised munitions out at McFarland's mechanic shop. But then, Tonk is always in. Tony Kerr, with his brown hair and his black T-shirt and his little beatnik goat-beard on his chin. Every woman's offbeat leading man fantasy, and my oldest friend on the West Coast.

The room's a strange mix of caution and camaraderie. Earl E. is describing a Wal-Mart heist they pulled outside some hollowed-out logging town.

"How much you get?" Joby asks.

"Eighty large."

"Shit! We did a Wal-Mart and got one-seventeen."

"Yeah, but we did it after they tightened up their security. We could have walked in and out of your Wal-Mart blindfolded."

Joby listens as Earl E. describes how they improved on our operation, infiltrating someone during lunch and hiding him above the suspended ceiling of the offices. "We reduced the Whitehall guys *inside* the office and egressed through the back door. We already had their authentication code, so by the time the guys outside got suspicious, we were halfway to Portland."

By now the representatives of nearly all the groups have arrived, bringing our number to twelve. In the corner, Katie from Olympia is sharing the terminology used by the Washington State Trooper bureaucracy, and the others are writing it all down or beaming it onto each other's handhelds.

Tonk comes up to me. "Where's the San Francisco guys?"

It's ten minutes after the hour, and ten minutes can mean anything.

McFarland looks over at me. "What's up?"

"I don't know. I'd expect them to call in."

The room goes quiet. For all we know, the feds are outside right now, moving in the Special Forces. "Should we scrub?"

"Hold on." I dial Kahasi, our Tlingit sentinel from up north. He traces his resistance back to 1803, when his ancestors burned the Russian stockade in Sitka. "Hey. We're still waiting to hear 'I Left My Heart in San Francisco.' What's up?"

"Nobody's called in a request yet."

"Okay, we'll wait ten more minutes—then we're turning off the radio. Why don't you check the other stations."

I close the line, nervous because we don't know where the San Francisco people are, nervous because if we scrub now, a lot of work goes down the drain. "No word. I vote we give them ten more minutes, then we scrub."

"I'm scrubbing now," Earl E. says. He puts on his jacket and I can see that he's carrying something heavy in the pocket.

"Just give it a few minutes."

He pulls the jacket over his shoulders. "Another time, brothers."

Three loud knocks at the door: heavy, FBI-type knocks. In seconds, everybody has ducked for whatever concealment they can find and has a pistol out and pointed just past my head. I move out of the doorframe. Tonk is at the back window, eyeing the woods.

"Who is it?"

"It's Mark. Trick or treat!"

I raise my hand toward all those little black circles facing me. "San Francisco."

The guns go away and San Francisco Mark breezes in with Jonathan, his partner who runs the show with him. Mark's medium height and slim, Armenian or something, with little black glasses and a dark face that always looks like he needs a shave. "You call that security? I just watched your contact person and followed the bread crumbs, man. You need to tighten up."

"Marcos!"

"Hey, Early."

Mark's the minor celebrity in the room tonight; his San Francisco group has pulled off operations that had wowed the country with their stylishness and their lack of casualties. They set off a pamphlet bomb on top of the Transamerica building that scared the living shit out of everyone and scattered leaflets over a two-mile area of downtown San Francisco. They also blew up Exxon, Citibank, and ten other corporate offices at the exact same moment on the morning of April 21, in what they tagged as the Earth Day Celebration. He could have made a fortune on the T-shirts.

Uneasy glances are going around. San Francisco Mark's breezing up to the door made us look like amateurs, and that's not a real trust-builder among this particular group.

"Let's get started," I say.

We're fourteen in the room now, representing maybe a hundred blue notes connected in turn to another couple hundred "friends" that support the cause with information or logistics. The group is crowded onto beds or sitting atop the dresser. Mark and Earl E. are cross-legged on the floor. I introduce each person by their war name and their area of operations. Earl E. Warning comes out of Anarchism. The Bellingham and Tacoma groups are former tree-spikers and GM crop-burners. McFarland and Joby are from the Militia movement, and the Eugene, San Francisco, and Olympia groups are a mixture of environmental and anti-corporate activists who started pulling some new tools out of the box after seeing the government methodically destroy every political gain they'd made in the past fifty years. Average age, excepting Joby and McFarland, maybe twenty-five.

"We're here to talk about two things tonight. One is to what degree we want to get networked. The other is a cease-fire proposal put to us by the DNN."

I start out with a short dissertation on networks, holding up a row of Tinkertoy rounds connected by long straight green rods. "This is a chain network, as in 'chain of command.' It's the typical military network, also used by smuggling operations and governments. Orders are issued at the top of the chain and come down to each node through a single link. For smugglers, merchandise moves along the chain from one place to the next. Advantages? Everyone's on the same page. Decision making is all done at the top. High degree of security. Disadvantages? Information transfer is slow, and it's extremely vulnerable to decapitation strikes."

I hold up the second construction, with rods radiating out from a single disc in the center. "This is a hub-and-spokes network. You can see that the node at the center is connected to all the other nodes. Information flows in from the periphery, through the center, and back out to other nodes on the periphery. Information flow is much richer than in the chain network, and any one node can be replaced without destroying the whole network. However, the core is still basically in command, and if the core gets destroyed or infiltrated, the nodes at the periphery can have a hard time regrouping."

They're all still paying attention, so I ask Tonk for the last network model, in which the Tinkertoys are arranged like a soccer ball, with connections going across the inside, too. It's a dense mass of green, red, and orange rods. "This is an all-channel network. Everybody's connected. There's no central command. Information transfer throughout the network is extremely rich and extremely rapid. So when *this* node, representing, say, McFarland and his group, gets information that might be useful to Mark over *here*, he can let him know immediately, and vice versa. Some nodes are militant cells, some are specialized task groups, such as Documents or Arms, some are individuals. Some nodes are in themselves chain or hub-and-spoke networks. Advantages: Extremely rapid information transfer. The ability to coordinate widely spaced actions in a matter of hours, or even minutes. Opportunities for cross-training and resource sharing. And extreme resiliency in case one node gets taken out. Since the knowledge is shared, it's easier to replace people."

"What about security?" says San Francisco Mark. "My group can be compromised by other people."

"There's no question that security is our biggest issue. If we decide to go all-channel, we'll all need to get up to standard with our encryption software and our security procedures. But there's a lot to gain. Think about the ability to pull in thirty competent militants for an operation, either on the operation itself, or just helping gather intelligence and compromise the target electronically. When it's over, they disappear again."

McFarland speaks up. "Which gets to my main question: Who's in command?"

"Nobody. If groups decide to coordinate, they can. If not, not. It's a network, not a chain of command. It's all by consensus."

Now we get into it for real, and it's obvious that everyone is torn between the desire to extend their power and the fear of losing control. We're the anti-CEOs discussing a merger. After an hour of debate, San Francisco Mark shakes his head yet again. "It still sounds like a security nightmare."

I can sense the crossroads right in front of me, like when I'd explained it to Joby and Mac a couple of weeks ago. I raise my voice slightly to get everyone's attention. "You know something, Mark? I'd be very pleasantly surprised if three years from now a third of the people in this room aren't either dead or drugged out in some maximum-security psych ward under a phony name. That's just how it is. Win or Die for America. Give me Liberty or give me Death. But we all know that somewhere in everybody's plan, there's that part where new recruits, flock to the cause, because without those recruits, you can't win. Well, this is the time where that fantasy starts to come true, and if we want to save this country, and save what's left of this planet, we need to take this opportunity. You want to design the security protocols, Mark? That's fine with me. I know how good you are. You want to network with some groups but not with others? That's okay, too. I'm not the boss and nobody takes orders from me. Ultimately, everyone still does as they see fit in their own eyes."

"Book of Judges," Joby pipes up.

I turn to him, surprised. "Thank you, Joby. I'm glad you're with me on that one." To the room again: "But let's move on here for a minute, because there's a related issue, which is the cease-fire proposed by Democracy Northwest."

I think of Emily: the toughness she showed in that conversation in the apartment, and also that soft little moment when we separated. I wish for a second she was here to catch my careful presentation of the DNN's strategy. I fill in any blanks she left and add my own discourse on the bloodless revolutions in Serbia and Prague. "Here's how I look at it: If we go along with them, we're basically linking up with hundreds of civil groups. So suddenly, instead of being a part of a network of a few hundred militants, we're part of a group of hundreds of thousands of activists. Or even millions."

"Hundreds of thousands of weenies," Earl E. said.

"They're talking about shutting down Seattle, Early. Can you guys shut down Seattle? Can any of us? Can we put fifty or a hundred thousand people into the street against the Regime? Can we organize and link up with simultaneous demonstrations all over the country?"

I let the question hang there for a minute, glance at McFarland before continuing. "There is *nothing* rulers fear more than when people go into the street. Because when people go into the street, it means they're paying attention, and rulers hate it when people pay attention. And when enough people go out there, and they refuse to back down, and it starts to spread, that's when dictators get on airplanes and presidents resign, because they know they've lost the test of strength. The Civils can make that happen." They're hearing me: we can all feel the vibration of the crowds and smell the tear gas. "I think of this deal as force multiplication against the Regime. We hook up our hard power to their soft power, and suddenly, there's more power on both fronts. More than we can get by blowing up a few corporate offices and whacking some bad guys."

It's quiet. Nobody wants to trample on that vision. Even Mark sounds a little timid when he finally speaks up. "I don't see how our force gets multiplied by sitting around doing nothing. We had years of doing nothing and the Regime just kept strengthening their grip."

"It's like this: We're the Bad Cops. The Regime and the Corporations start fucking with the surface political groups, we send them a little message that says, You don't like dealing with the Good Cops? Well, the Bad Cops are still out here, and we can disrupt your systems and ring your bell for a few million bucks anytime we feel like it. You fuck with the rights of the American People, we fuck with you!"

The silence gets crispy.

"Personally, I think that's the best-case scenario for our future as guerrillas. We need the Civils."

We dive into another round of irritable discussion. Interestingly, it's McFarland and his direct political opposite, Earl E. Warning, who haven't given up on being the spark that ignites the Revolution. Both think that increased repression by the Regime will eventually bring on a popular uprising. The old *foquismo* of Che Guevara. Mark's deservedly paranoid; others seem to have too much ego stake in their own gigs.

By one in the morning, though, everyone signs on to a loose all-channels network. We're surrounded by coffee cups and bit-up pizza crusts.

"Okay, people, closing arguments on the cease-fire. Let's try and reach a consensus. I'll start: I'm strongly in favor." McFarland backs me up with a surprisingly enthusiastic show of support, and as the oddball here—older, blue-collar, ex-military—his words have a particular density. Each representative weighs in on their group's inclination, and finally Earl E. sums it up for everyone:

"I'm with McFarland on this one, Lando: When I see tear gas in Seattle, I'm in. If not—" He gives an eerie smile. "—a hard fucking rain is going to fall."

Everyone leaves in ten-minute intervals. McFarland and Joby are the last to go, and they sit with Tonk, Sarah, and me and drink one last cup of fancy-ass Greenie coffee before making the drive back to the country. Tonk seems energized, like a golden retriever ready to go after the next stick. Never tired, never afraid. He just keeps burning. Sarah's focus has been worn to a brittle edge, the college girl who's been up all night studying for the big exam. Her hair's pulled back in a bun and her clothes are bulky and sexless, so she seems to be, on this critical night, exactly what she is: the hardest woman ever kicked out of Vassar College. Tonk and her have something going; she's too tough for me.

"Well, Lando . . ." McFarland crinkles a pack of cigarettes in his gray fingers. One for the road. "It looks like you got your network and your cease-fire. Pretty good for one night. Now we have to see what your DNN buddies are made of."

"They'll come through."

There's a little silence while he and Joby look at each other. "Have you thought about Cascadia?" McFarland asks.

Sarah throws me a suspicious glance before swiveling toward McFarland. She doesn't like being left out of the loop. "What do you mean?"

"Joby and I think we ought to take out Cascadia. It's a big show that'll leave everybody clapping."

Tonk, as always, in. "Nice!"

I wonder if they can hear the strain in my voice. "What about the cease-fire?"

Raspy, countrified Joby, with his Bible Belt belligerence. "The cease-fire comes in our time, bro. When we declare it."

"Joby's right, Lando."

I look at Tonk and Sarah and the other two. With the first heists it was written, with John Polling it was sealed. We're the network now. I can't go against my tribe.

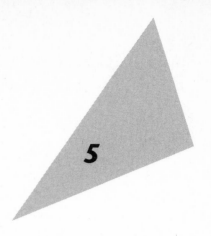

5

I watch for Emily from the front window of the 5 Point Café, a woozy bar with a cardboard Old Glory on the wall that sailed through the Great Depression and looks like it'll go on sailing through anything the Matthews Regime can throw at it, like one of those grizzled indestructible drunks who stays on his feet no matter what. Outside, a pigeon-speckled bronze of Chief Seattle holds court for the homeless and the unemployed who hang out in the little plaza. It's the intersection of Hip and Down, where the faltering gentrification of Belltown meets the whited-out storefronts of the Denny Regrade. The DNN rents cheap office space in a little null zone beneath the underpass. I trail Emily for a few blocks as she leaves work and walks to her tai chi class. She's wearing a chunky hand-knit sweater and khaki pants, and when I see her striding up the street with her brown hair hanging loose I feel the same wobbly feeling as when she'd gotten out of my car two weeks ago. For a brief second the old hunger hits me again and I have to clear my mind. I overtake her and address her without looking in her direction. I'm wearing an old sweatshirt and a stocking cap—a different Lando than last time. "Just keep walking, Emily. Don't turn around."

She jumps a bit as she recognizes me, not smooth at all, but keeps walking. I fall into step about five feet from her. "I'd given up on you," she says.

"I got tied up at the Space Needle." We'd hung a huge **A⊕R** banner from the city's number one landmark, and it took city workers half a day to remove it.

"I read about that. I'm impressed. But I'm kind of on my way to tai chi now."

"Yeah, and I have my anger-management session, but we need to talk."

On my instructions, she goes on to tai chi and ducks out the back door, where I am listening to talk radio in my fine Japanese sedan. The day's topic: why domestic terrorist scum aren't entitled to protection under the sacred God-ordained American Constitution. To my surprise, the "strap 'em down and hit 'em with fifty thousand amps" people are meeting some resistance from the *volk*, who are still talking about John Polling.

Don from Bellingham: *The fact is, these guys are citizens and they still got some rights. Nobody's talking about taking constitutional protection away from fat cats like John Polling or James Sands! I mean, who's the bigger criminal here? Huh?*

James Sands . . . the man who had steamrolled the opposition and privatized Seattle's water, now piling triumph on triumph with the huge Cascadia project. That familiar twist of anger shoots through me, and a follow-on dose of sadness at how things have turned out. I rub my temple, the old sleepless/caffeine headache crowding in at the hairline. I spot the cold dregs of a triple shot seeping through the seam of a paper cup on the dash, and I pour the bitter syrup down my throat.

"Do you really think someone could be following you?" Emily says as she slides in.

"I'm worried about you, not me. You're a member of a proto-terrorist organization; that makes it okay to spy on you. Believe me, they're all over Shar Simmons and Dan Schwartz. Especially since your voting campaign started."

"How do you know?"

"If I didn't know shit like that, we'd be talking through a sheet of Plexiglas right now."

We head out Aurora Avenue past a mile of abandoned car dealerships and fast food restaurants, a uniquely American wasteland of junk architecture and treeless pavement from back in the days when buying things and throwing them away was the number one form of entertainment. It's a landscape possible only with cheap gasoline, where nothing is walking distance. A world of dirty marquees and toppled garbage cans, LIQUIDATION SALES, FOR LEASE signs, and abandoned chain stores the size of airplane hangars still echoing with forlorn calls to now-extinct shoppers. All built ugly to a code that demanded ugliness, built wasteful to a code that demanded waste. Blind stupid America, living like there was no tomorrow. At last it had all collapsed and left this garbage like the plastic crap strewn along the high-water mark after a storm. "This is what we sent armies all over the world for," I say. "So we could build junk buildings with huge parking lots and drive around in big cars."

"I don't know," she answers. "I have a bit sunnier view. All this junk development has its roots in 1950s traffic engineers. We built an autocentric infrastructure without realizing how much energy it took to maintain it. Then it acquired so much momentum that we couldn't change it. Don't assume conspiracy until you've ruled out incompetence."

"God, you are such a Pollyanna! Haven't you ever heard of Greed? General Motors and Firestone buying up streetcar companies just to bankrupt them? Oil companies spending millions on propaganda to convince people they're not responsible for global warming?"

"Lando, the problem here is not Evil. It's ignorance." She sounds a little annoyed with me. "You're really into Us and Them. I'm not. I think we're all Us."

I swing into the Smorgasteria, a horrifying all-you-can-stuff-in-your-craw buffet with a wagon wheel out front and phony Boot Hill tombstones on the walls. Westerns play on big screens scattered around the vast room, and most of the scarce diners have their faces tilted toward the noisy rectangles. The fifty-yard-long steam table is like a massive TV dinner, with fried chicken, macaroni and cheese, an amalgam of foods that have been wrenched from the innards of some vast walk-in freezer and "cooked," or else slapped together from uncertain ingredients like Reddi-Wip or Jell-O.

"I personally go for the Salisbury steak, but the marshmallow salad's a winner, too."

Emily shakes her head slowly. "Why are we *here*?"

"There's lots of empty space, it's out of the way. And, I guess, there's a certain nostalgia factor. My father used to take me to a cafeteria like this when I was little. He hated it, but he knew I liked it, so he'd take me there when I visited him at his office."

"What did your father do?"

That sense of my father with his chair pulled close to mine, arm around my shoulders, smiling down at me from the vast heights of his shirtsleeves and tie. I cancel it out. "Oh, long story."

"I've got time."

"Long not-very-interesting story. Let's get some chow." I forget to mention one other reason I chose Smorgasteria: We'd taken an interest in the supermarket across the road and their daily cash pickup.

She ends up with only a green salad, and I sit us by the front window as the Whitehall truck pulls reliably into the parking lot across the street and circles around to the rear. I glance at my watch and memorize the time. There's nobody within forty feet of our table.

She looks at me funny and shakes her head. "Are you really going to drink all three of those cups of coffee?"

She takes a bite of salad while I cut the corner of a gray slab of ground beef. The classic cafeteria flavor; I'm back in the past for a moment, my father in his suit and tie, a piece of Salisbury steak on his plate. His secret favorite. "You know," I say, "if the Earl of Sandwich invented the sandwich, does that mean the Bishop of Salisbury invented the Salisbury steak?"

"I think you're overintellectualizing this a bit."

"Granted. So we'll cut to the chase." I glance around and lower my voice. "I managed to get a meeting together of representatives of most of the groups in the Northwest, which, I have to say, was not so very easy."

"Which groups?"

I identify the groups by their most famous actions: San Francisco Mark by the Earth Day and Transamerica operations, Earl E. the guy whose buddies were now doing six years for breaking windows at a demonstration. I mention a few city names, "and of course, us, the AOR. I wouldn't say they represent every single militant on the West Coast, but we got the majority of them. I pitched your idea."

"And what did they say?"

I lay down a preparatory sigh—a little expectations management. Brace her for the worst and then let her see there's a way out. I hate to play those games with her, but if I'm going to put ten thousand people on Pike Street, there's going to have to be a certain amount of misdirection. "It's a very tough sell. I mean, right now we have momentum. We've been collectively kicking the Regime's ass. On the West Coast, we've done twenty-eight operations in the last sixty days. We've only had two guys go down, and we managed to get them legalized before the Regime could gulag them. Most important, the public reaction has been good. Listen to talk radio for a few hours. Or look around Seattle: We're not the ones scribbling **A⊕R** all over the place. Success gives people the courage to resist. So when you ask for a cease-fire, a lot of the militants feel like, *Hey, I've been hanging my ass out there. Why should I give up something for nothing?* They want to know what your group has to offer."

Emily doesn't answer at first. "Well . . . We didn't think of ourselves as negotiating with you. We're just asking for your cooperation."

"I understand, Emily. Personally, I think you guys have the right idea. We're mosquitoes. We can annoy the elephant, but we can't bring it down. You guys can bring it down." That seems to lift her up again, and I go on to the crux. "So we like the idea of working with the DNN. But the bottom line is—" I put down my fork and look carefully into her chocolate-dark eyes. "—you need to shut down Seattle. Matthews is coming to town on Dec fifth to address the National Business Symposium. They'll be deciding how to carve up the rest of the country. You keep him off the podium, break up the meeting, shut the place down, and we declare a cease-fire within twenty-four hours."

I can see the surprise in her face. "What do you mean, 'shut down'?"

"Shut down, like . . . tear gas, rubber bullets, riot police. News commentators saying, 'Seattle came to a standstill today. . . .' Front-page photos of kids facedown on the pavement. Unarmed people getting pepper-sprayed on national TV. That version of 'shut down.'"

She sits back and folds her arms across her chest. "We can't just decide that fifty thousand people are going to materialize in downtown Seattle to face an army of police shooting rubber bullets at them. And, honestly, I don't think the DNN is going to let the militant groups plan its strategy."

"But you want to plan ours!" That singes her. "Look, I understand how you feel. I mean, you guys are the experts. You know what's doable and what isn't. You're not an on-demand riot service. But you have to offer us something!" She's staring at the puddle of oily water in her salad bowl. "Emily, listen to me. We've been watching the Regime neutralize groups like yours for eight years. It's always the same: If they lose at the ballot box, they beat you in the legislature. If they can't stack the legislature, they beat you in the courts. Steal a state election here, investigate an opposition governor there. You know the drill. We've had eight years of that crap. Look at Water Solutions; you fought the good fight. You passed a referendum and they slapped it down. Whatever you did, they'd throw a few more millions at it and undo. Now we're all happy consumers of private water delivered through a system we paid to build. Okay? We're in a position to send an unmistakable message to the Regime that we're not putting up with their shit anymore. We don't want to give that up to watch people march around in circles for another ten years." A big shoot-out begins on the television next to us, and bullets whizz past our table. Pictures, pictures, loud and empty, getting into my head before I can stop them. "The showdown's inevitable, Emily. If there's no showdown, there's no change."

Her face has turned into a hard white sheet. She punches out each word slowly and clearly. "We are *not* your tool!"

"And *we* are not a bunch of morons you can order around because of your superior intelligence and moral authority!" My heart's beating faster now. "Believe me, Emily, I want to do it your way—"

"Don't try and manipulate me!"

"It's bigger than just me! Don't you get it?" Ma and Pa seven tables away tear their eyes from the television to ogle us, and I lower my voice and lean toward her. "I am putting my ass on the line for you, and you don't even know it."

The elephant in my personal room: that we may pull off our biggest operation yet just before the demonstration we're asking for. Outside, the Whitehall truck comes trundling back and I look at my watch. Eighteen minutes. Emily's staring out the window without seeing it, still smoking after the last little exchange, so I toddle off and bring her back a bowl of Jell-O salad. "Peace."

She pastes on a wooden-nickel smile that disappears immediately, but I don't give up. "C'mon. Jell-O has always been a food of peace. It's yielding and accommodating, as opposed to—"

"The Bishop of Salisbury?"

I nod my head at her admiringly. "You've got *the Way!*"

She lightens up a little bit. We both know the substance of our meeting is over. She has to get back to her people and reach a consensus, and depending on that consensus, maybe we'll never see each other again. Still, I can't quite muster that last little rise to the feet. When I look at that long slim nose and angular cheekbones they seem sort of noble, even beautiful, and I'm surprised I overlooked that. I like her shape and she has a kind of mysterious sensuality that always underlies supercompetent women. What would she be like in bed? Reserved and remote, analyzing Article Three of the Bill of Rights while I'm stripping her panties off? Or some other person entirely? I wonder if she has a boyfriend, but it's a little awkward to say, *Yeah, we won't ice anyone for a while if you start a riot, and, by the way, are you seeing anybody?* Lando, Lando . . . You're thinking with the little brain now.

I wonder where we could go. My apartment? No. The car? An hourly hotel? Or even a whole night in a hotel. I could check in under my Rampton alias, pay with cash. For an enemy of the state the quest for shelter is constant—the shaky refuge of a safe house, a foreign country, a new identity, an altered face. I remembered that when the Montoneros needed a hideout, sometimes they would go to the hourly love hotels, which promised anonymity to lovers and urban guerrillas alike. On the other hand, one general became obsessed with the love hotels, and would raid them and then expose the cheating spouses to their other halves. He was quite the moralist . . . in everything but torture and murder.

We're still sitting there at our impasse, and it seems like she doesn't want to leave either. "Hey, umm . . ." I haven't been this nervous since we pulled the plug on John Polling. "In the interest of building trust in our professional relationship, do you want to go to a movie?"

"What's playing?" She sounds dubious, still pissed about the deal I offered.

"Let's see. . . ." I open up the newspaper that was lying on the table when we arrived. "At the Bellevue Miniplex we've got *All the President's Men, Missing, Z, State of Siege, 1984—*"

"Ha, ha, ha."

"Seriously? We've got a teen slasher movie with a masturbatable young heroine. We've got a corporate action thriller where an American mercenary rescues a kidnapped oil executive from Venezuelan narcoterrorists, we've got a corporate romance about two down-on-their-luck stock car fans who meet at the Daytona Five Hundred and realize that even without health care, a vote, a job, or a decent school for their kids, they can still be happy because they live in the greatest goddamn country in the world, and I think this other one's about a little girl who gets stuck in a well and the whole town pulls together—"

"Let me see that!" She pulls it away from me. "Jesus, you're scary. You should be doing movie reviews."

"So, unless you really want to find out what happens to the little girl in the well, I suggest we hit this one at the Pacific Place. It's the least offensive and we'll burn up less dinosaurs."

She rolls her eyes but we end up going with my choice, a cute romantic comedy. Guy meets girl, guy makes an ass of himself, guy gets girl. I'm still a sucker for those, but the movie's been sponsored by RapidMail, so there's a RapidMail logo in every other scene, a relentless inescapable advertising plug that I've paid good money for.

"I hate RapidMail," Emily says as we leave the theater. "When they privatized the Post Office they practically wrote the contract for it. Their former CFO was in charge of negotiating on behalf of the government."

"Don't get me started." I stop and scan the fake indoor mall street for a moment. A couple of brownshirts in front of the video arcade.

The usual bored plainclothes guy sitting at the snack bar. We've been compiling a list of all the security people we've made around Seattle to share with other comps. I feel a yawn coming on and try to choke it back. "You want to go for a drink?"

"Are you sure? You look tired."

"Can't be. I slept at least two hours last night."

I take her to the Toddle-In, an old '70s lounge-lizard bar that went arty. The lighting is heat-lamp red and art-student masterpieces pepper the walls. I like the Toddle-In because I can always toddle out the rear exit into the rear entrance of another building. Emily mentions she hasn't been to a bar in over a year. I tell her she needs to get out more.

It's a statement that invites comment about a boyfriend, and when she makes none, it lifts my spirits a little. We sit with drinks at a booth near the back door. I'm facing the entrance, eyeing the three groups of college students and the digital types clustered at the bar. Emily's looking smart and self-contained, as always. A minuscule gold bead in her nose, those dark eyes. "How'd you get into this, anyway? Being, like number three in the DNN."

"I don't consider myself number anything. We're trying to get away from that sort of hierarchy."

"You know what I mean."

"Well," she lets a little smile go, "you already know I was in law school. After I got out, I moved to Seattle with my boyfriend at the time. We moved into the Apex, and I was sort of casting about for where to begin. And I saw these little flyers on the bulletin board at the Apex that said 'Protect Seattle's Freedom of Speech!' At that time, it was illegal to put up posters on public property. So I went to this meeting, and, as it turns out, I was the *only* one who showed up!"

"Which made you—"

"Outreach Coordinator. And through that I ended up meeting Shar, and later she offered me a job at the DNN."

"And the boyfriend?" I ask as chattily as I can. Just us girls here.

The quick sideways glance; hint of a buried story. "He went back to Portland. He thought I was a little too committed to the cause." It takes a second for that little detour to settle out; then she freshens her position in the seat. "How about you: What do you think you'll do when this is all over?"

"Oh, I don't know. Get a house in the suburbs, raise ten or twelve kids. That sort of thing." I shrugged. "And you?"

She gets a gravelly voice and puts on a pretty good French accent. "When zis war ees over . . ." She laughs. "Sorry. This is so *Casablanca*. I don't know. I have this fantasy about joining the Corporate Fraud division of the Justice Department."

"And I thought my fantasies were outlandish."

"But seriously: What do you want to do?"

I try to remember my early college days, before the Resistance had become everything. "I used to want to be a journalist. Or maybe I'd go down to South America and trade with the Indians. Hang out in the mountains and eat San Pedro cactus. I don't know what I'm qualified for, to tell you the truth."

"I'm sure you're a great organizer. You have to be to do what you're doing. And you're certainly charismatic enough."

Charismatic, eh? That gives me a little charge.

"Do you want to dance?" she asks.

I haven't danced in four years, but I follow her onto the floor. I can't get the hang of the music and I feel awkward bouncing up and down eighteen inches away from her, but I'm enjoying looking at her, with her belly dancer build. She seems completely at ease, twists around and shakes her hips in a way that makes me think even more of bedding her. I can see why Seventh-Day Adventists outlawed dancing.

With another drink I can relax more and now I'm eager to be on the floor, to be away from Tonk and McFarland and Sarah and Joby and the security norms and the constant hunt for safety, for intelligence. I want for fifteen minutes to not analyze every face on the street and compare it to other faces, to not inventory parked cars, to not be Lando, or Henry Rampton, or whatever false identity I'd assumed at birth. I want to escape for one hour into that golden stream of innocent life that I've never really known: to order a milk shake, wear a letter jacket, hit a baseball, float on a sunny lake. To get the girl, lose the girl, get the girl, in an endless dream of teenage despair and ecstasy. There she is in front of me, no longer an attorney or my liaison with some political group, just a young woman near my own age hiding very promising-looking curves beneath a white T-shirt and all her other clothes of lawyerly manner and political distance. I lean over to her. "I'm sorry, but I might be arrested tomorrow, so I have to tell you that I'm thinking very seriously of propositioning you. Which I know would be extremely unprofessional."

It's juvenile and it's an attempt to backpedal even as I move toward her. In my entire life I've never spoken to any woman like that before, and I regret it immediately. She doesn't give me either a smile or a scowl of disgust, but with my confession the hidden purpose seems to have gone out of our dancing, and I feel hollow and out of place. She keeps her eyes down to the floor for the next ten seconds, still dancing, then says, "I want to go."

I can't believe how crass I am, how utterly a jerk. I want to apologize but I'm too fucking mortified, some part of me trying to pretend that it was all cool, all perfectly adult and modern that I'd come on to her. She says nothing as we collect our things and head for the door. Just before we get there, in the shadows at the entryway, she suddenly grabs my lapels and crowds me against the wall. "I don't know why I'm doing this!" she says in a low voice; then she puts her hands around the back of my head and pulls my face down toward hers. Her lips open and take me so by surprise that my knees almost buckle. I feel her tongue against my mouth, tasting that faint alkaline tone through which every bit of mystery and desperate urge mixes improbably. *You don't know me at all*, it says, *because this is the other me, the woman waiting to maybe wreck you or maybe take you to some planet you've never known before except in some porno movie you saw when you were seventeen.* It blows the top of my head off.

She pulls away. "Where do you want to go? It had better be someplace close or I might change my mind."

I stumble. "My car?"

She wrinkles her nose. "We're not going to make love in your car!"

We end up at one of the fleabag hotels a few blocks away, where transients flop and streetwalkers look determinedly to the side while their johns pay in advance. I remember for one flickering second the Montoneros and the general who pursued them, wonder if they had the same bald-headed desk man, the fluorescent lights of the lobby, the unused pigeonholes awaiting mail and messages that never come, the worn red carpeting on the stairs with their little unpolished brass rods holding it in place. Flat gray chewing gum, a sign about the fire exit, room 38, the scratched brown paint on the door, wooden table, broken lamp, tattered bedspread, the mirror, the delicious privacy while all the world outside hangs motionless.

I pull her over to me and run my hands down the small of her back as we kiss; then I slip my hand under her blouse and feel for the first time the warm liquid surface of her skin. I slip my fingers under the waistband of her sweatpants and down from there. My odalisque. Her hand grabs the hair at the back of my head to pull my face away for a few seconds, looking at me. "Who *are* you?" she asks; then I pull her mouth close again. I can see us in the mirror, and part of me tells myself that this isn't really happening, despite the two people in the mirror, because somehow it isn't me but Lando, the urban guerrilla, in the mirror, and the other me's looking on with wonderment. Then that feeling disappears and I'm back in my body, feeling all of her, feeling her breasts against me. Whoever she is. Her long face, viewed from so close, has become unfamiliar; her eyes are closed.

We untangle for a second to tear off our shoes, our pants. It's like coming up for air, but I don't want to come up for air. I want to stay under, away from all identity, free for an hour with this barely known woman and nothing else. I clamber on top of her and when I slip inside, all identity, real or false, floats away on that raft of warm delirious flesh. For a few minutes we know each other as intimately as two people can and at the same time not at all, as if we're no one, no place, with no past, no guilt. Free.

After, we look at the ceiling, quiet. I don't know what to say. To say anything would be to admit I had an identity, either Lando or Rampton or me, and I don't want to take back that mantle yet. I roll over and look at her profile, with her brown hair falling back from her face.

She turns to me, sounds worried. "Does this complicate things?"

I'm inescapably Lando again. "That's one of those 'there is no right answer' questions." She doesn't respond. "No—the right answer is: 'I kind of hope so. But God help us if it does.'"

She rolls over and puts her arms around my naked chest, and I see her breasts lie one over the other with the brownish pink nipples peeking out. She says, "We'll just have to be responsible about it, that's all."

"Yeah."

"That should be easy for you. You're already living under an assumed name."

"Who said it's an assumed name?"

"Most people with names out of a *Star Wars* movie are living under an assumed name."

"Didn't it occur to you that maybe my parents were big *Star Wars* fans and named me Lando?"

Her lips turn up at the corners and her voice becomes liquid with humor. "No, that didn't occur to me. What are your parents like, anyway? Besides being science fiction buffs."

My parents. My parents. I run my hand down her side and caress the hollow at her waist. She's like a Modigliani painting I studied in college, all sex and contour. "It would be a security breach to tell you about my parents."

"O-kay!" her singsong voice, from high to low. "New subject."

We end up talking about a trip she took to Guatemala a few years ago, where she saw a quetzal in the ruins of Tikal. We talk about that amazing view from the Temple of the Moon, across the plaza where thousands of people were cut open and sacrificed to the continuance of the world. I recite my bit about the Mayans' base twenty numeric system, how their calendar extended 142 nonillion years into the future and into the past, but she doesn't answer, just lies there close to me, and for a change there's no racket in my head pulling me to the surface. "I'm getting sleepy," I say.

"Mmm." She drapes her arm over me. "Me, too."

I try to rouse myself. "We have to get going."

"Why?"

"We just do. Because I'm blue and you're on the surface."

She wraps herself around me, her leg across my stomach. "We're safe. Trust me."

"You can't be sure of that."

"Shhhhh." She moves an inch closer and kisses my jaw, and I feel myself giving in as her breath moves against my ear. Her soft whisper: "We're not really here. We're in Tikal and we're lying on a grass bed a thousand years ago."

It's so nonsensical that I have no answer, and then the darkness comes flowing in and covering everything; the tilted lampshade, the tarnished mirror. John Polling dims and disappears, and the pursuers that I know are coming for me. My lies are far away in a future I don't have to claim, leaving just her warm nakedness and her gift of sleep. Miraculously, through some lost secret pathway, she's led us out of base ten into ancient jungled base twenty, where no one can find us, and everything adds up differently.

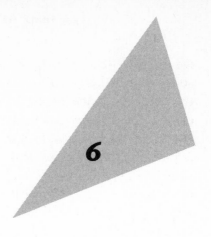

6

I kissed Lando good-bye at the metro station then went straight home to the Apex. The empty hallways had their usual faint smell of living—the tomato sauce cooked last night in the third-floor kitchen, the whiff of mildew coming from the slightly leaky bathtub in one of the bathrooms. A sign on the refrigerator had an arrow pointing to the floor. NOTICE: LOOK DOWN! MOUSETRAPS ARE ONLINE! PLEASE WATCH YOUR TOES. Beneath that was scribbled in smaller letters, definitely Dave's handwriting: *Vote Here: Peanut Butter or Cheese*. Yet another note had been taped up below the bait referendum: *Doesn't anyone know another method? This is really inhumane*. Finally, a business card–sized scrap of paper with a little fist on it that said SAVE THE MICE!

I poured myself some carrot juice then took a handful of dried fruit out of my cupboard. A little message from Dave fluttered out onto the counter: *Sister Emily, I O U 1 Guru Bar. Thnx, DAVE*. I rolled my eyes. Dave owed me a case of Guru Bars. I reached into his shelf on the refrigerator door and opened up a soy shake. *Thnx, Em*.

I took the snack to my room and closed the door. Heathcliff purred as I stroked his long black spine and looked out the window at the tin-colored drizzle of early morning. Whenever I made love with someone for the first time I had to retreat and think things over, to try to separate the excitement from vague feelings of remorse that came over me. I always flashed back to when I'd slept with the captain of my high school basketball team and gotten the cold shoulder from him the next day. Now I'd done it again; I'd made love with someone I barely knew, which was, on top of everything else, incredibly unprofessional. I wasn't sure why I'd let myself fall for him. He was a punk and a hero in a combination I'd never encountered before. Even if I hated his tactics, he was as passionate as he was cynical, and utterly unintimidated by the power of the government. Maybe it was the mystery. My college roommate Lori would probably claim that his being a fugitive meant he was safely unattainable, and so I had nothing to fear from him. I pushed those thoughts away. I'd responded to something real. There has to be a place for that in life, or what's the sense of changing the world?

I lay back on my bed and dreamed for a while, splashing around in the memories of Lando and our night together, the whole kaleidoscope of places and talk, and how we'd finally curled up and fallen asleep together. I'd woken up first and watched him dozing there, thinking how strangely boylike he looked when all the scheming and fierceness were drained away. He had a long, ropy rock-climber's body, and what looked like an appendectomy scar at his hip. He had pale gray shadows under his eyes. He was such an odd duck, with his insomnia and his constant espresso drinking. His accent was vague: somehow New England, maybe Midwestern, but I hadn't spent enough time back East to place it. It seemed almost put-on, like the way he implied that he'd participated in the Polling Assassination. No way he'd been tied up very tightly in that, however pompously he talked about it. He wasn't that type. He was like me, really, an organizer.

Which brought me to his proposal. He was trying to shove that demonstration down our throats; I could practically hear the gears turning as he maneuvered us into position. Even so, I had to admit there was a lot of truth in his slick diatribe. I was curious to see my colleagues' reaction. It was seven thirty now, late enough to call Shar. We arranged to meet at the Lilac Café, near the Market.

I changed clothes and washed my face before I left, but I couldn't help being paranoid that Dan and Shar would see how tired I looked and figure out that I'd done something very stupid last night. My eyes had that dark, puffy look that they always get when I don't sleep, and as I examined them I had time to worry, as usual, that my face was somehow too long. The first gray hair had come in at the edge of my forehead, and I'd been defiantly resisting the urge to pluck it. Now I yanked it out, thinking that without it I might look fresher.

It was a longish walk through Belltown and I decided to splurge on a bus. The rain was beading up on the windows as we rumbled along. Beautiful, lush Seattle. Most of the country was suffering from the drought, and in Eastern Washington the summer wildfire season was still going strong into November. In the Emerald City, though, the cool comforting touch of raindrops was never far away. It was easy to feel one step removed from the slow-motion apocalypse that seemed to hang over so much of the planet. I got to the Lilac first, and leafed through an abandoned Business section of the *P-I*. Real estate in the suburbs kept dropping and retailers were nervous about another weak Christmas season. It could have been the headlines of any November of the past five years. At least we still had rain.

When Dan and Shar got there I moved us to a little stall farther inside that gave us a view of anyone who might be watching us and didn't offer any long lines of sight. The erotic buzz of my encounter with Lando had worn off now, but the sense of paranoia hadn't. Lando had delivered a long monologue about directional microphones, lip-readers, foot surveillance, and electronic penetration.

"Assume you've been infiltrated," he'd told me. "Assume your office is bugged, your lines are tapped, and your car has a locator beacon in it. But most of all, assume you're infiltrated. Watch out for the eager beavers who come in and want to do everything, or the people who just don't feel right. They claim to be vegetarians but they eat hamburgers, or they talk about pacifism but want to start fights at rallies. Those are your infiltrator types. Also watch out for people who are angry because they don't feel listened to, or their girlfriend took up with one of your organizers, or they lost a power struggle: whatever. Those are your potential informers. Always beware the angry ex." He'd shaken his head and curled up the corner of his mouth. "You guys are wide open."

I repeated this to Shar and Dan, who seemed to silently rifle through the possibilities in their minds. Both of them had been activists for more than two decades. They'd founded Democracy Northwest and received tiny stipends more fitting for a college student, which Dan donated back to the organization anyway. Shar was the elder wise woman of our group, one of those postmenopausal women who'd gone beyond the coquetry and sexual politics that women my age couldn't escape. She had frizzy black hair going gray and two sons in their twenties she'd raised by herself after her husband died of snakebite in Mexico. She'd spent most of her working life as an emergency room nurse, the kind of person who could stay calm when the blood was on the table. She'd helped plan the Battle of Seattle, when demonstrators had shut down the city and put the issue of Globalism on the evening news. She had a firm, businesslike voice and no fear of confrontation whatsoever. She was our public face. I hoped that someday I would be as strong as she was.

Dan was the behind-the-scenes man, the politician who calculated which side everyone's bread was buttered on. He was bald and skinny, with a little potbelly and silver wire-rim glasses completing the picture of the ineffectual wimp. He was anything but ineffectual, though. He understood all the power relationships in every branch of city government, and he knew the city statutes intimately. Seattle had resisted the purge; a lot of city officials still opposed the Administration and hadn't been maneuvered into impotence yet. Dan was expert at cultivating relationships with the right people, and could convince the city to grant a parade permit or police protection after other people had been refused. Open and friendly, he didn't seem in the least threatening, and that was his strength. He could talk to the Unitarian Church or the Police Benevolent Association and end up smiling and shaking hands with everyone there. The story about him was that he'd made a fortune in the dot-com boom and gotten out before it all caved, and I'd seen him play that one very subtly in the right format. *Look, I'm smart. I'm rich. I'm a businessman. Listen to what I have to say!* He handled many of the liaisons with other groups and with the few governmental entities who hadn't been brought to heel yet by the Accord. Some people thought he was a bit weasely, a bit of a breast-starer, but over the years he'd come through.

"So besides your realization that everyone is out to get us, how did it go?" he asked me.

"Well . . ." The memory of our hotel room billowed up but I managed to keep a straight face. "I think it went well, but I'm not sure you'll agree."

I described Lando's Militant constituency in the same indefinite terms he'd described them to me, then got to the point. "The good news is, they're willing to announce a cease-fire. But there's a catch: They want us to shut down Seattle to prove we're serious."

They looked at each other. Shar was indignant. "We were shutting down Seattle when they were in elementary school!"

Dan broke in. "I don't like this. Strategy shouldn't be determined by the fringe. It's the tail wagging the dog."

"It's bullshit!" Shar added.

Dan went on. "They understand what they're saying, don't they? Shutting down Seattle means people are going to get gassed and clubbed and shot with rubber bullets. Or worse. They realize that, don't they?"

"They do. But let me finish, because it might not be as bad as it looks. They want us to demonstrate when the National Business Symposium meets to discuss the debt crisis on December fifth. Matthews is supposed to show up for the opening ceremony. They feel like fifty thousand people out there holding up signs calling for a real vote when the biggest Corporations of the world are watching will make an appropriate impression. And I have to agree with them. Matthews will be touting more privatization to reduce the debt he and his pals ran up, and people are angry. I think it will be a good way to focus attention on Real Vote."

They looked at each other again, and Shar raised her eyebrows. "It's not a bad idea. We wanted a presence there anyway. And shutting it down—" She tosses her wavy brush of black gray hair. "—that'd be an appropriate wake-up call."

I felt a little tingle of warmth as she agreed with me, but Dan wasn't signing on so easily. "This gets back to what I thought before we even approached them," he said. "Any whiff of collaboration and the Administration's going to use it against us. Especially after this last assassination."

"They're going to do that anyway if the East Coast Militants declare."

"That's true." He continued, already weighing the other side of the argument, working out strategy. I think he was always happiest arguing against himself. "Of course, if we've already announced the Vote campaign, and the armed groups *happen* to declare a cease-fire afterwards, that *would* give a sense of empowerment to people, the feeling that their actions achieve something. The government can accuse us all they want; a cease-fire still raises our stature in the public eye."

"I think we should do whatever it takes to bring the Militants back into the community," I said. "At least it's a step toward peace, and away from violence."

Dan lifted up his hands. "Hold it. This has to be decided on its own merits, not on how it relates to the Militants. Besides, we just got going on the Real Vote issue. If we try to pull off a major demonstration at the Business Symposium it could easily fizzle."

Shar spoke again. "But, Dan, think of fifty thousand people saying no to the privatizations, right in Matthews's face. That's a message. Especially if we shut the Symposium down."

"That's assuming we can turn out fifty thousand."

We were all quiet as we imagined the whole long organizing process, the meetings, the endless strategy, then the clumsy maneuvering of masses of people that would end with tear gas, beatings, arrests, hospitalizations. It was where the will of the People came flat up against the will of the State.

We talked for another hour. Dan was worried about jeopardizing his contacts in the city government with a head-on confrontation. "I think maybe we should do some polling. . . ."

Shar shook her head. "I disagree. You can poll till the cows come home, but actions are where people find their strength. We've been polite for a long time. If Matthews is coming here to preside over slicing up the spoils with his pals, maybe it's time to get rude. My vote is we shut them down."

"I vote we wait," Dan said. "We're not ready yet."

They both looked at me. I could think of three or four other people in the organization with just as much wisdom as me, or more, but I was the one who happened to be sitting there and I was the one closest to the Army of the Republic. My ears turned hot as I answered. "I think whether we're ready or not depends on us. On how well we organize." I couldn't keep from giving Dan an apologetic little smile as I finished. "So I have to vote with Shar."

Dan nodded slowly and gave Shar a long look. She tipped her head at him in some unspoken communication, and he turned to me. "Okay, Emily. Mark December fifth on your calendar. Because this Seattle project's going to be your baby."

In reality, of course, it wasn't just three people deciding. It had to go through the council and then to our affiliates. I always told new volunteers that organizing is like the process of imparting an electrical charge to hundreds of thousands of individual particles, except that they don't automatically line up, like iron filings near a magnet, but instead have to be stroked, and reasoned with and energized, one by one. It's a tedious process carried out with flyers, e-mails, speeches, press releases, Internet postings. Little by little, a few line up, maybe not pointing the exact same direction, but same enough to affect others, to write letters to the newspaper, to speak out, and to one day show up in downtown Seattle with a water bottle and some sandwiches to put their bodies on the line.

And what then? Civil Groups like ours acted in an escalating scale of confrontation, beginning with a simple letter to the editor or politician and continuing up the chain to boycotts, marches, sit-ins, blockades, and general strikes. At that latter end of the spectrum numbers became everything, because when the crowds got big enough, when the difficulties became constant enough, when it became clear to everyone that the opposition was not just a few scattered students or intellectuals, but truck drivers and grocers, teachers, clerks, carpenters, and mothers, that was the point where soldiers refused to fire on crowds and policemen refused to club them. When that happened, no regime on earth could stay in power. That was our ultimate goal: not to topple the government through violent resistance, but to massively demoralize it. The Matthews Administration would crumble without violence because they would have no one left to defend them. It had worked in a dozen countries around the world in the last two decades. It would work for us.

Whatever utopia you're trying to build, you always have to dig the first foothold in the unglamorous earth of the real world. My initial flurry of organizing conversations were with the heads of local groups. The idea was to set up meetings with their membership so that we could explain what the DNN was doing and why. I talked to

anyone who would answer the phone: the Lutheran Church Federa-
tion, the Seattle Education Association, Catholic Human Services,
the League of Women Voters, environmental groups, student groups,
the few remaining labor unions. I would go out to a church basement
or rented meeting hall and address a room of anywhere from five to
twenty-five people and carefully explain why we were demonstrating.
Each meeting resulted in more e-mail addresses and telephone numbers, more hits on the Web site, more money. When the time came,
we would be asking all these people to show up.

We put out our invitation all over the West Coast, with e-mails and
press releases and a four-page newsprint pamphlet that covered all
the Northwest hot spots: Seattle, Olympia, Eugene, Portland—even
down to Berkeley and San Francisco. Now was the time to say NO to
Privatization and YES to a Real Vote.

Our phones started ringing. "I want to come up and help organize," they'd say. "Can you find me someplace to hang?" *My partner
and I do nonviolence training. We want to help out.* Within a week, we
had rented a second office space and found housing for twelve out-of-
town organizers who were coming to Seattle. They showed up with
babies in tow and their own laptops, and in no time at all we had a
second network humming away. And still they kept calling. *Hey, I ran
an organic restaurant here in Santa Cruz for ten years. I can do food.
Hi . . . I'm director of the San Bernandino Street Puppet Theater. . . .
Hello, I heard about your action and I wanted to volunteer to help with
communications. . . .* Social Justice lawyers, Greenies, ex-Yippies with
hip replacements and canes, ready to make one last stand. I was
starting to think the Seattle Project was going to work. And when it
did, Real Vote! would hit the headlines.

Not that our ballot campaign wasn't beginning to gel on its own.
That the recent elections had been riddled with fraud was accepted by
all but the most delusional partisans of the Administration. The president's party was like a dishonest carpenter that used to work in my
father's boatyard: He had fifty ways to steal, and by the time my father
figured those out, he had fifty more. The Party did everything from
disqualifying suspected opposition voters to hacking into the computers that tallied the results. They had pushed tirelessly for paperless
voting, either through machines manufactured by Administration
cronies or directly over the Internet, and they could swing an election

with or without local help. In the end, the system had been balkanized into a county-by-county mess of paperless voting machines, Internet voting, old-fashioned punch cards, and mail-in ballots that was managed and tallied by the Administration's corporate clients. I'd ground my teeth through three elections, waiting for some sort of widespread reaction to what had become increasingly obvious. Now, at last, the Government's relentless "perception management" had begun to fall short. People were sick of rigged Government, and the Real Vote! campaign offered them a way out.

Five days after we announced Real Vote! with twenty-five other Civil Groups across the country, the Jefferson Combine issued a letter promising to refrain from violence as long as the democratic process could move forward. A half-dozen smaller groups followed suit, leaving only the Army of the Republic and the West Coast groups still waging their private wars. The series of cease-fires were news by anybody's standards, and they made the Real Vote! campaign impossible to ignore.

The Government's counterattacks began almost immediately. They were experts at using images to convey a deeper message. Television crews would do man-on-the-street opinion polls and choose the grubbiest-looking, most inarticulate pro-Vote person they could find, while the Government would always be defended by moderate-sounding, clean-cut Citizens. On the talk shows, one pro-Voter would face three or four detractors, because the idea was to show us as a minority, going against the common wisdom. Phony news pieces circulated by the Government featured 1930s file footage of crudely made ballot boxes and Ku Klux Klansmen. "Politicians used to steal elections with paper ballots," a think-tanker would point out. "If people feel uncomfortable about computerized voting, they need to monitor the voting, not try to go back to the nineteenth century." On the late-night talk shows, jokes about the voter movement turned up in monologues and in the patter between guests. The Hammer gave the voting issue a Hammer *down*. "Don't these loonies know this is the twenty-first century?"

And yet, something out there was beginning to resonate. I glimpsed it at the Renton Rotary Club. I'd had dozens of these presentations, usually with Church or Labor or social action groups, or even neighborhood committees. We'd gotten this meeting through a volunteer's father-in-law, and I walked shyly into the Comfort Inn conference room twenty minutes early and shook hands with the president, an engineer who had been laid off in the downturn and seemed to be scraping by with small consulting jobs. I'd taken the stud out of my nose and even re-dyed the purple streak as concession to the conservative crowd. My host showed no signs of sympathy toward the DNN, but set up a lectern and offered me coffee. He had a Rotary pin on one lapel and an American flag on the other. It was a whole different feel, and I was nervous.

"I don't know how many are coming," he said, "but you've got half an hour."

About thirty people showed up for the presentation on Real Vote! A few more drifted in after I started. They listened carefully as I went through the well-documented evidence of election fraud, most of which had never made it to the broadcast media. I laid it out calmly, trying to keep a neutral tone. When I finished, a man stood up to answer me. I could tell he'd been sent by the Government by the way he went through their talking points. He was the image of reason as he trotted out the paper-ballot elections stolen by Kennedy and Johnson, and the Chicago Democratic machine politics of the previous century. He sounded scholarly and patient as he brought these things up, dismissing the "circumstantial" evidence I had presented of voter tallies that didn't match exit polls, of voter registrations accidentally purged, of opposition districts hit by power outages on election day— the whole list. He spoke of "the President" with reverence, the way someone might have said "His Highness" or "His Holiness," and was launching into a soliloquy about how the present Administration had inherited all its problems. "If you look at the previous Administration—"

A small middle-aged man stood up and spoke out of turn. "That's bullshit!" he spat out. "That's bullshit, and you know it!"

The Government's man looked like he'd been slapped. "Excuse me, but I think I have the floor right—"

"You're a Government plant! That's all you are! I saw someone give your speech on TV last week! Word for word!"

Things got of hand as the Government's man tried to defend himself against a growing number of attackers who cut off his arguments with snorts of frank disbelief. It turned out that the man didn't even belong to the Rotary Club, but had supposedly been invited by a member who wasn't there, and at this his attackers became even sharper. My host gaveled the meeting to silence and the man hurried off without another word. "We're having a demonstration," I began again. "We've decided to confront the Government about the vote."

Afterward, I got names, phone numbers, and addresses for a dozen people, then apologized to my host for the ugly confrontation.

He hesitated, then gave a dry assessment. "It's a long time coming," he said. "And this is just the beginning."

When I got outside, a few snowflakes were falling and the air had a wet, fresh smell. I was puzzling out my crumpled bus schedule when two men from the audience approached me. One of them was a small sandy-haired man with a slippery, confrontational manner. He looked about forty, wore a carpenter's jacket and blue jeans. His friend was bigger, with a blue blazer but no tie. He stood slightly off to the side, watching us.

"That was quite a meeting you ran in there," the smaller one said. "You got 'em pretty stirred up, didn't you?"

I wasn't sure what he meant by it. "I just shared some information. If information about stolen elections stirs people up, maybe that's a good thing."

He gave a foxy little smile. "You sure were quick to get their names and numbers. You look like one of those Radicals trying to agitate against the government."

I hadn't been able to decide where he was coming from, but I wasn't going to back down. "I consider stealing elections radical. I consider bankrupting people's pensions and then using that as an excuse to sell off public assets radical. I don't consider talking about voting radical."

He turned to his large friend and laughed, watching me for my reaction. "She wants to change the world, don't she?"

I was nervous now, more nervous than I'd been at the meeting, but kept looking him in the eye. "You're right. I do want to change the world. With or without your approval."

He raised his eyebrows at his friend, then broke into a smile and held out his hand to me. "I'm Joe Simic. I'm here doing a little organizing myself."

I looked more closely, and as I recognized his face a little whirlwind of excitement distracted me for a moment. Joe Simic had ruffled a lot of feathers in the Midwest. Originally a Labor organizer in Detroit, he'd turned to organizing the unemployed and underemployed, forming them into a group called the Throwaways. His picketers were loud and rude, working class people without work. They had no problem with confrontation. Whiffs of sabotage and violence floated around his organization, but nobody had proved anything, yet. They waved the flag and traded on an ultrapatriotic anger that made me a little uncomfortable because it was the kind of anger that could go either way.

"Did you talk with Dan Schwartz or Shar Simmons yet?"

"An organization is only as good as its rank-and-file field people. I wanted to check out your operation from the bottom up. And I must say, I'm impressed by what I saw here today."

"They weren't exactly marching on Washington."

"That comes later," he said. "When the Rotary Club marches on Washington, it's all over. And with good work like yours, that day will come."

"Well . . . Thanks." I was at a slight loss for words. This man accused of inciting riots and blackmailing Corporations seemed more like a school bus driver than an organizer. "I'm Emily Cortright, Mr. Simic. Welcome to the West Coast."

With all of that happening, the possibility of seeing Lando seemed far away. He'd given me a secure cell phone number, but I couldn't think of an excuse to call it. I had to hide away the little gem of that night, telling no one and letting it gradually fade until it was just a quiet yearning. I was still ambivalent; I had slept with someone with whom I was supposed to maintain a professional relationship. I'd been too easy. Another part of me thought it was wrong to be working with militant groups that were, in their violence and lawlessness, just as bad as the Matthews Administration. Maybe it had just been a fling for him anyway, a chance to pick some low-hanging fruit, the way men do. Then my phone rang and I recognized his voice immediately. The call was coming over the Internet, probably from a café somewhere.

"Hey!"

"Hey!"

"Have you been enjoying the liquid sunshine?"

"I always enjoy liquid sunshine."

Liquid sunshine was the duress code he'd given me. I felt silly saying it, but if I answered negatively, it meant something was wrong, and he would get off the line and start taking precautions. We exchanged a few more sentences to set up a meeting, and two hours later he sidled up next to me as I came down the stairway of the metro station. I felt myself quiver inside when I spotted him next to me. It was a cold wet November day and he was dressed in a black rain jacket, his face recessed inside the big hood. He signaled me briefly with his eyes to make sure I saw him; then I followed him out and ended up next to him in a booth in the back of a nearby bar. When he peeled back his hood, it was like the sun coming out of the clouds. He leaned over and kissed me for a long time.

"It's good to see you. I've been thinking about you."

"Is that just code, or have you really been thinking about me?"

"I've really been thinking about you." He ran his hands down my side to my waist, beneath my jacket, looking me right in the eyes. *"Really."*

I took each wrist between my thumb and forefinger and peeled them off. "Down, Rover. I take it you have a professional reason for arranging this meeting."

"God, you are tough!" He leaned in again and whispered in my ear. "That's what drives me insane about you!"

I laughed and pushed him away. "Why don't you get on the other side of the booth for a while!" I had the feeling he'd called me up just to see me, which made me happy. He moved across and flagged the waitress, ordering a triple shot of espresso. I ordered tea. He leaned toward me when she left.

"So . . . I wanted to touch base with you. First of all, let me say that you are one kick-ass organizer. Almost every known Militant Group east of the Cascades has declared a cease-fire."

"It was a lot of people, not just me."

"Yeah, but I'm talking about you. I'm in awe of you. In a quiet way."

I felt myself blushing. "Thank you."

The door opened and his attention shifted to the people coming in, then back to me again. "We'll sign, too, when the time comes. But our guys wanted a progress report on the Business Symposium protests. I think they sort of consider me an informal member of your board."

I smiled and put my hand up. "Maybe you'd better just disabuse them of that notion."

He gave me that teenage-boy smile. "I've tried!"

"Right!"

"Well, how *are* things progressing? When's the revolution start?"

I told him about the progress we'd made on Real Vote!, that we'd enlisted some two hundred small local groups and more than twenty larger groups across the country. As for the Seattle Project, we'd already doubled our volunteer staff. "And we've been approached by Joe Simic, of the Throwaways."

That impressed Lando. "If he does in Seattle what he did in Detroit, we're going to have some sad little Corporates. Is he in?"

"He's cagey. He's being careful not to commit to anything until he sees where the weight is. Like your people." He didn't rise to the bait. "Anyway, we've already been granted a parade permit for the day Matthews is supposed to address the National Business Forum."

"That was fast."

"There's still a lot of people in the Seattle government that hate the Matthews Administration."

"Matthews *Regime.*"

I rolled my eyes at him.

"Excellent. Now that that's settled, how about dinner?"

He drove us to a Chinese place close by. I noticed that he'd pried the outside markings off his car so that I could tell it was a Toyota only when I saw the insignia on the steering wheel. When he got out to pump gas, I picked up a telephone bill from the floor of the car.

"Who's Henry Rampton?" I asked cheerfully after we started up again.

His mouth tightened. "I borrowed his car," he said, and then it was quiet for a moment.

I tried to stay breezy. "So what's Henry like?"

He didn't answer.

"I'm sleeping with you," I said quietly. "Who's Henry Rampton? Where is he from? What are his parents like? Does he have a girlfriend I don't know about?"

He stayed silent as we maneuvered through the kind of confusing and serpentine intersection that Seattle is famous for. "Henry Rampton is from Webster, Mass." He pronounced it *Websta*, and the *Mass* had that harsh New England flatness in the *a*. "He went ta school at Daniel Websta High and he layta graduated from Bawston University. His parents ah Phil and Dawna Rampton, but unfawtunately theyuh deceased."

It made me uneasy. "You're good."

"Thanks," he said in his nearly accentless voice again. "That's how I sound to most people."

I looked out my side of the car for a while, bewildered by it all. "Can I ask which is the real accent and which is made up?"

"I really wish you wouldn't."

Such a guy thing, at the bottom of it. Secret agent, if-I-told-you-that-I'd-have-to-kill-you sort of crap. As daydreamy as I'd been about this relationship, I also knew there was something very two-dimensional about it, and suddenly I felt ashamed that I'd fallen for all his lines. "You're right. I don't want to intrude on your privacy. You've got this whole thing about someone forming a profile of you, but you know what? That's what happens when two people get to know each other. They form a profile."

He kept looking straight ahead as we approached the Seattle Center. His silence made me angrier.

"Maybe we should end this right now, Lando. I mean, this whole thing is really unprofessional. It's dangerous for you and it compromises me. I can catch a bus two blocks from here that will take me right to my apartment. I'll show you where to pull over." We went through two more lights without either of us saying anything. "Let me off at that corner, please."

We swerved to the side and I turned and extended my hand to him, but he just sat there gripping the wheel.

"I've been blue about four years," he finally said. "I've been in Seattle for three. I'm not the best at what I do. I'm not the best planner, I'm not the best actor, I'm not the best technician. But for various reasons, I've been able to make a lot of connections with other groups. I guess that's my particular skill set. People trust me enough to talk with me. And as you know, that's a good person to have in a network.

"But that's politics. You want personal stuff. Okay. I had a girl-friend before I went blue. I haven't seen her since. I wrote her a Dear Jane letter and had a friend mail it from a different city. I went to college but I dropped out. My parents think I'm a failure. They're wondering what they did wrong."

"Do they suspect what you're involved in?"

"I think my mother's wondering, but my father's pretty much clueless. You know: work hard, fill up the little car with blue and pink pegs, and then retire to Millionaire Estates to see who's collected the most money. He's busy drawing the picture."

"How did you end up in the Army of the Republic?"

I could see he was weighing his endless Security considerations. "I was in college and . . . you know how it is. Every day there's a few more species made extinct, and less oil, and more greenhouse gases, and more forest and farmland being destroyed. And our guys just refuse to deal with it. They're too corrupt, too cowardly. It just started getting clearer and clearer that something needed to be done and we couldn't sit around waiting for someone else to do it. I kind of met people who felt the same way. Some of those guys later became the Jefferson Combine." He raised his eyebrows. "There's another puzzle piece for you.

"So," he continued. "Things happened. Some friends got popped. You have to assume in that situation that you're a suspect, too. Even then I was smart enough to build an alias. I put Henry Rampton together and was waiting to activate him. I guess it was the break I needed to devote myself fully to the cause. Groups like ours need people who are available twenty-four hours a day, because the struggle is going on twenty-four hours a day. You can't exactly say, 'Hey, I'll show up for surveillance when my shift at McDonald's is over.'" He smiled. "Unless, of course, you happen to be surveilling McDonald's. That's why we need people on the surface, too. Like you."

"Hold on a second—"

"Yeah, I was going to ask you. There's this package, and I wondered if you could drop it off at the Exxon offices for me. . . ." He grinned. "I'm kidding."

We called in our order to the restaurant and sat in the parking lot waiting for it while the windows fogged up. "I went to the West Coast.

That was when they were cutting down the last redwoods that weren't in their little tree museum."

"In Humboldt County. I remember."

"Yeah, well, you remember some logging trucks got burned?"

"That was you?"

"And friends. We were pretty amateurish, but we figured it out by the end. When the heat got too high, we left it to the tree-sitters, and you know what happened to them."

Everybody did. They'd cut the redwoods with the sitters still in them. The first outright murders sanctioned by the Matthews Administration, and widely applauded by commentators like Paul Wells and the Hammer. I think the headline in *Newsweek* was "Getting Tough with Ecoterrorists."

"It was a defeat," Lando went on. "In every way. We failed the trees and we failed our people. The only benefit was that it made us understand who we were dealing with. We couldn't pretend that the good old American way was going to come to the rescue, because they'd consolidated too much power and the system didn't work anymore. After that some of us came up here to organize. That was the National Restoration Forces. Then we hooked up with some other people, and we became the Army of the Republic."

He looked at me as if to see if that information would satisfy me.

"Congratulations," he said. "You've just become a high-value target."

It unnerved me a little. "So how do you feel?" I asked him. "Are you afraid?"

He tilted his head. He looked very fragile at that moment. "I have no illusions about this regime. Those guys in the security forces aren't in there because they're incompetent, and neither are the Corporates. The shakier the Regime gets, the more they're going to want to liquidate the opposition, and thirty percent of the country will be cheering them on." He shrugged. "So of course I'm afraid. But you have to have a vision of something better, and truer, even if everything in the world around you denies it. Because if you believe in it hard enough, you can make it materialize. Every good thing in human society was created that way." He smiled awkwardly. "I should check on that food."

I reached out and squeezed his hand, then hugged him clumsily there across the bucket seats. As he ducked out into the rain I had a notion that filled me with fresh resolve, even though I knew that the same notion had crushed a million hearts before mine and would go on crushing them as long as anyone tries to rescue a person or a country or anything else that's valuable and endangered. I thought, *I can save this man.*

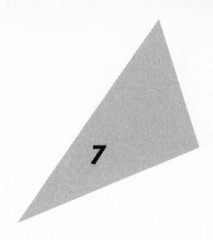

7

*I*t's large," Gonzalo says.

"Large is good. Large captures people's imagination."

Sarah's presenting the case for Cascadia in the private upstairs room of an I District Chinese restaurant. It's Sarah, so I know they'll all be good arguments. Whatever her prep school wardrobe and college-girl freshness, she's more relentless than any of us, the Joby of the far Left. I know they'll be logical and precise: she practiced them all on me yesterday.

"One, as we know, they're hated. In the Northwest, James Sands is up there with John Polling. Seattle hates him because of the privatization; Oregon fears him because of his plans for the Columbia River. They're condemning people's land for his right-of-way, and a lot of bankrupt little towns in the West are facing a new civil war about their water supply, thanks to him. He's the back-East city slicker looking to horn in on their water rights. An operation against Water Solutions would have very high appeal. I think we've got a solid yes on the first criterion."

A string of positive sounds threads around the table and I think of

Mr. James Sands. Like John Polling: somebody's husband, somebody's father.

"Criterion Two, can we do significant economic or moral damage? I think that's a very big yes. I've been researching them. They lost a lot of money when China nationalized them, and also when they got kicked out of Iraq. As omnipotent as they may seem to us little people, in their world, they're pygmies. Monsters like Bechtel and Halliburton are always trying to muscle in on their territory. I think the bombing of their office last November hurt them, too. Not materially, but in terms of risk-assessment."

"Whoah," Gonzalo says, "wheeling out the Corporate vocab. Now we're getting serious."

"Let me finish, Gonzalo, because it gets better. Water Solutions borrowed a lot of money from a particularly nasty private equity fund called the Barrington Fund. They specialize in buying into companies with insider status in their respective countries, particularly weapons and utilities, and then they work their connections to get contracts. I found out that they have a performance clause in their agreement with Water Solutions: If the pipeline isn't operative by a certain date, Barrington's loan turns into equity capital. And in that case, James Sands, one of our very favorite Corporates, suddenly gets demoted to minority shareholder."

"I'm liking the irony angle," Tonk says. "But doesn't that just help Barrington?"

"It's not about Barrington," Sarah answers. "It's about showing the Corporations that we can hurt them. *Really* hurt them. Then they can make a cost-benefit analysis as to whether it's time to pull the plug on this Regime, because cost-benefit is their only criterion for making decisions. Which leaves us with Item Three: *Is it doable?* Can we design an operation that will cause massive economic damage to the Cascadia project?"

McFarland answers. "A pipeline that long is completely vulnerable. We can set charges ahead of time and do simultaneous attacks all up and down the length." The prospect of an easy hit seems to buoy him. "If we whack the head honcho at the same time, that could pull down the whole house."

"Hold on a second," I said. Things are going off track. "I'm not sure this justifies whacking somebody. Polling was involved with killing an organizer. This guy"—the name feels strange in my mouth—"James Sands, is only guilty of being greedy."

"I'm just saying, if you want to send a message, attacking their pipeline *and* closing out the head guy will do it."

"And what's the message? That we're indiscriminate killers?"

Joby jumps in. "Nothing indiscriminate about it!"

Sarah raises her voice. "Boys, boys! Put your little toy guns aside for a minute and learn something. The key to the whole Cascadia project is their water-intake plant at the Columbia River. They've invested over a billion dollars in it, and it's about to come online. It's the control center for the whole pipeline. You can't rebuild it in a few days, like you can the pipeline itself. That's where we can do the most damage."

I can sense things taking shape in the happy little pause that follows her words.

McFarland, operational: "Any idea of the security there?"

"They've got Whitehall on board now," I say, "which means we'd be up against the first string."

"We kicked Whitehall's ass at Wal-Mart," Tonk says. "So did Earl E. Warning's crew. They're not invincible."

"Those were smaller operations," Mac answers.

"And we were smaller. We've got better resources now."

It's going a little too fast for me. "There's another question we have to ask. I don't think we can ignore the political fallout. Are we going to be jeopardizing the DNN's goals by launching a big operation?"

Sarah answers. "I've thought about that some more, Lando. We can schedule it for early December, just before the Business Symposium demonstration. We spank Water Solutions, then declare a cease-fire right after the demonstration because we want to let democracy take its course. The Regime won't even have time to mount a good propaganda campaign before we pull the rug out from under them."

"*If* they shut it down," Tonk reminds us. "That was the deal."

"If they shut it down."

McFarland is still more interested in the technical issues than in the political. "We'd need good intelligence. Have we got anyone with access?"

What we have is some good solid *maybe*s. An acquaintance who was cashiered by the Seattle Water Works when they were privatized. A sympathetic civil engineer who works for a Water Solutions subcontractor. Risky friends to pull in on a project this hot.

I look around at Sarah, Tonk, McFarland. These are my people. Their lives depend on me and mine on them. Win or Die for America. I blow out my anxiety with a big sigh. "I might have a source inside."

"Who?"

"I can't tell you that. I'll check it out if we decide to research this."

Kahasi beeps us twice, and then the waiter comes in to sweep away the dishes on a big brown tray. We start in again on the pros and cons. As the gung ho swells around the table, I'm off on my own for a second, in a perfect little world where I sit down with James Sands and just talk with him, convince him of why Cascadia was wrong, that water was the common wealth, that it belonged to everyone, not a corporation that would leverage it for maximum profit. Because if James Sands could be convinced, they could all be convinced. The John Pollings of the world could be isolated and diminished, and nobody would have to die.

But James Sands doesn't happen to be sitting in on this discussion. In twenty minutes the hands go up and Cascadia moves to the top of our list. Gonzalo will start probing their networks. McFarland will organize people in Oregon to start surveilling the water plant, two hundred miles southeast of us.

Lunch is breaking up, and Sarah looks at me. "Lando, can you talk with your source inside Water Solutions?"

All faces turn for my answer, like picture cards in a solitaire layout. "I'll see what I can do. Give me a week."

We crack open fortune cookies. I don't say anything about mine, just roll the little ribbon of paper into a ball and throw it on the floor.

A good son is his father's greatest happiness.

8

I usually sent a car for Joshua when he showed up at the airport,
but I decided to get him myself this time, even though he'd only given
us a day's notice. I expected to see him come hulking through the
airport with his backpack and his jeans; when he appeared at the
baggage claim in a pair of khaki pants and a button-down shirt, it
heartened me. His hair was short, and even though he'd bleached it
bright blond like a California surfer, it looked like he was actually
making an effort. Joshua had been born a month premature, and
from the time he was a baby, he'd seemed somehow precious and
delicate. He was surprised to see me waiting for him. His face lit up,
and he shambled into an awkward hug.

"Hi, Dad."

"Hello, son." I patted him on the back.

"I didn't expect you to be here."

"I had a break at the office."

He looked skeptically at my suit and tie. "You never have a break
at the office."

"Okay, I just wanted to get you myself."

That surprised him. "Thanks." He took out an NFL cap and put it on low over his face.

"Don't tell me you've turned into a football fan!"

He tapped his cap. "Irony, Dad."

"Got it. Irony." Same old Joshua. We chatted briefly about his mother and sister as we headed for my car, then threaded through the garage to the ticket booth. The flat concrete light underscored the thin dark skin below his eyes, and despite being so young, he looked a little haggard. I wondered about that as we accelerated to speed onto the highway; then my mind drifted back to my meeting in a few hours at the Barrington Group, the finer points of my plan to back them off. I'd need to drop the Japanese on them in just the right way, so that vague little piece of information would hit bottom with a soft but resounding thump. Make me sign personally! I'd send those weasels scurrying back into their holes.

Several minutes of silence had gone by while I plotted the afternoon's battle. "So what are you doing these days?" I asked him suddenly. "Got any new projects going?" I realized immediately that I'd stepped into a minefield by asking about his "career," but it was too late.

"I'm still plugging away with Web design." He hazily described sites for a restaurant and a preschool. "It won't get written up in *Fortune*, but it pays the bills. Money isn't everything, right?"

I wondered if he was making a gibe at how I'd restricted his trust fund. He'd never complained about that before, but that didn't mean he didn't resent it. An idea occurred to me. "You know, I'm not sure if you'd be interested, but I have an acquaintance who's launching a new online venture in the San Francisco area. Something to do with grocery stores and consolidating sale prices. He's looking for investors now. It might be, you know, something we could do together."

He didn't say anything, and I hated myself again. He'd been here fifteen minutes, and I'd already offered him a deal, like he was some sort of politician I was trying to finesse. I felt my old resentment cropping up. Now he would jump on me for my crass dollarization of our relationship.

To my surprise, his answer was relaxed, even warm. "I kind of like having my own gig, but I'll think about it. Thanks for considering me."

"Yeah." I cleared my throat. "You know, Joshua. Sometimes I try do the right thing in the wrong way."

"I know." He gave a little laugh. "Maybe that's where I get it from."

Gary waved us through the gate and said a few words into his walkie-talkie. "Who's that?"

"That's Gary."

"Yeah, Gary. What's he doing here?"

"He's just a bodyguard. After William Byzic was murdered we beefed up our security."

"Who's William Byzic?"

"Don't you read the newspapers?" I explained how he'd been murdered by ecoterrorists after some protesters had been killed in a confrontation with loggers on one of his timber holdings.

"Oh, yeah."

Joshua had had a brief fling with radicalism in his college years, but had become completely disconnected from politics by the time he'd moved out West. He seemed in harmony with his generation in that respect: thirty million kids plugged into a big pleasure machine that fed them a constant pap of songs, videos, fashions, and ideas that they effortlessly ingested and retained, as if consumption itself were some sort of achievement. They walked around with plastic earphones plugged into their brains and worried more about how to get free downloads than about the drift of the country. At least Joshua didn't have wires coming out of his ears when I picked him up at the airport.

We sat down to lunch in an alcove of the dining room that looked out on the duck pond and its willow. Even in mid-October, autumn seemed to be eluding us; it was still too hot to eat outside, and people were chattering about global warming as they always did at these times. Phyllis brought poached chicken breasts and au gratin vegetables, but I refused the wine. I'd already missed half the morning, and I hadn't fully prepared for the showdown with Barrington. I tried to get a peek at my watch when my son was looking at his plate, but he raised his head before I could finish.

"In a hurry?" he asked.

"I'm sorry. I have a meeting later this afternoon."

"Don't let me get in your way."

"No, no. You're not at all in the way. Our guys will brief me. I can be ready in five minutes."

"What's the meeting about?"

"Oh, company stuff."

"Like what?"

It was the first time he'd shown any interest in my company, and it made me take a fresh look at him. The accoutrements that had once seemed temporary—the bleached hair, the tiny goatee—things I had thought of as youthful affectations pasted onto my child's face, for the first time seemed like things that belonged to the face of a stylish young man. Women his age probably found him hip and handsome, regardless of whose son he was. "Well, as you may know, we've been working on a big pipeline that will go from the Columbia River, where there's plenty of water, down to the Southwest, where they need water."

"Cascadia. Of course I've read about it. I did think privatizing the rain was a bit harsh."

I shrugged. "That's just a lawyer thing. If we allowed people to collect and distribute rainwater it leaves the door open for another company or municipality to come in and undermine our system. Don't worry; nobody's going to be arresting people for getting a bucket of rainwater off their roof. Anyway, Cascadia is the biggest private public works project in the United States. It takes some significant capital, and when you've got interest at twenty-seven percent, the clock ticks pretty fast. I arranged to finance it with a private equity fund, but after John Polling's assassination, they've started jerking me around."

"John Polling . . . wasn't that the guy—?"

"He was murdered by terrorists three weeks ago in Seattle. The media had a good time with it."

"What's that have to do with your business?"

"This will probably sound weird to you, but we were bringing John Polling in as a limited partner on the Cascadia project."

His eyebrows went up and things became quiet. "Why him?"

"John had the money and the connections. As a matter of fact, I had lunch with him and the Undersecretary of Interior five days before he was killed."

Joshua was staring down at his plate, and I could sense the old disapproval lurking there.

"Look, he was actually a nice guy. Nothing like his public persona. The press only reports what suits them, but John Polling donated millions of dollars to charity every year. Not many people know that. He also set up a foundation to help children that needed plastic surgery. You know, kids that had been burned or had terrible accidents. Think of how he affected those children's lives. What's the net happiness gain when a child can go through an eighty-year life span with a normal face instead of horrible scars?"

"I thought he embezzled a bunch of money."

"He shaved it a little close. That's not grounds for a death sentence in my book." Joshua didn't seem to get it. "You want the straight scoop? John Polling covered his ass when things went against him, and that's a normal part of business. You don't throw away decades of work because somebody in your legal department gave you bad advice."

He started to answer, then dropped it.

"Anyway," I went on, spearing a piece of cauliflower with my fork, "we were already behind because of all those lawsuits and ballot initiatives in Oregon and Washington, and John's murder made the Fund tighten up. Which is exactly what the terrorists want, of course."

He hesitated before offering his next comment. "A lot of my peers think they're heroes."

"Well, they're not! They're fucking punks who want to do with bombs what they can't do with ballots!"

"Hey!" He held his hands up. "Don't kill the messenger! I'm just giving you a report on what the younger generation is thinking."

"It doesn't sound like they *are* thinking! You read about John Polling—they tortured him! What kind of people shoot a man in the knees and groin and watch him die?" Josh's jaw clenched, and he looked back down to his plate. "Sorry to get ugly, but it's an ugly thing." I hated playing the sympathy card, but I couldn't help myself. "And it could have been me, you know."

He gave me a look I didn't understand, a sort of reassuring, slightly smug look. "It couldn't have been you, Dad."

I checked my watch. I had another two hours until the meeting, which meant I should leave the house in forty minutes. I desperately needed to talk with my CFO, but for the first time my son and I were conversing like two adults, even if we didn't agree on everything. "Why don't you come into my study. I'll show you something cool."

In the study, a pile of blueprints was laid out on the table. I walked Joshua over to them. They always gave me a little rush of excitement when I looked at them, because they were maps that covered states instead of mere counties or cities. One of the largest private construction projects of the century, and it was mine.

"These are some of the elevations for the Cascadia project. Do you want to see the overview of the whole thing? I'll pull it off the server."

"Umm . . . Not right this second, Dad."

I tried to mask my disappointment. "Some other time. By the way, we have a few friends coming over for dinner tonight. We planned it before you told us you were dropping in."

"Anybody I know?"

It occurred to me he might have seen their names in the paper, and I watched his face for a reaction. "Howard and Connie Pettijohn, and Richard Boren and his wife." A flicker of something. "Richard Boren used to be the Secretary of Commerce."

He knit his eyebrows for a moment before he recognized the name. "Oh, yeah. Cool! Any chance we'll see the Kassels and the Werezewskis while I'm here?"

Old family friends we'd spent Thanksgiving and gone apple-picking with. "Josh, I haven't seen Kurt Kassel for about five years. And I heard the Werezewskis got divorced."

There was a pathetic tone of optimism in his voice. "Why don't you call Mr. Kassel up? Didn't he used to be one of your best friends?"

"You know, Josh, it's different when you're older. People get into their own orbits. Kurt's still teaching, as far as I know. Your mother runs into him once in a while. Maybe the three of you can get together."

My phone went off and I looked at the ID. "I'd better answer this." Our CFO: The legal department at Barrington had thrown a new curve at us. I hung up and put my hand on Joshua's shoulder. "Some things came up, Joshua. I've got to run. Will you be okay until Mom gets home?"

"Sure."

I felt a pang as I looked back at him sitting alone on the couch. For an instant he was eight years old again, and I was replaying the same mistake I'd made over and over again throughout his youth. I stopped halfway out the door and poked my head in again. "I'll be back in a few hours," I said.

He nodded. "Yeah, Dad. I know."

The meeting took place in a small conference room paneled with pale oak and stainless steel. A huge Motherwell canvas covered one wall; the moody leaks of dark crimson creeping down the picture plane lent a sense of foreboding to the room that probably hadn't been intended when it was purchased.

It wasn't a cordial meeting. I'd been in shock after John's assassination, and I'd let the Fund beat up on me a little. Whatever the numbers said, though, I hadn't built a two-billion-dollar company to be pushed around by a bunch of lawyers and accountants, and today was my turn. I'd been in talks with a Japanese consortium, and now, as we went over some of the new terms Barrington was trying to impose on me, I referred obliquely to a possible takeout loan that would free them from their risky venture. After all, with the Southwest in danger of drying up and blowing away, a water pipeline with all the permits in place looked like a pretty good investment in some quarters, whatever the risks.

It had exactly the effect I'd been hoping for. There was a brief surprised silence, in which I could practically hear the lawyers scurrying back to their cubicles. Barrington's lead man became suddenly friendly, larding the discussion with remarks about how far we'd come together and how committed the Fund was to the Cascadia project. He ended with a tactical retreat, agreeing to take some of the issues back to Brussels for further consideration. I thanked him graciously; then all Barrington's people left the room except for one of the VPs, who'd previously been silent. I would put him at around thirty-five, with blond hair and an overly handsome face that set me on edge somehow. I managed to glance at his card as he straightened his papers. His name was Denton.

He spoke in a pleasant baritone. "Jim, I know Water Solutions has had some security problems in the past. How is your security now? Are you happy with Whitehall?"

I told him we were very happy with them. We had instituted new protocols across the entire company and security incidences had been reduced by nearly 70 percent.

He smiled. "Walter's a great guy, isn't he?"

It caught me a little off guard that he seemed so familiar with Walter. "Walter's a prince. If you want to talk Thucydides or Xenophon, he's your man."

The reference escaped him. "No doubt. So"—his tone became less casual—"has Water Solutions embarked on any new initiatives with Whitehall?"

I knew what he meant, but I wasn't letting him crowd me. "Well . . . We submit our security arrangements to you quarterly, as per our agreement."

He nodded his head. "Yes. Of course." He looked at me carefully. "But what about *new* initiatives, maybe something that hasn't made it into the reports."

"I'm not getting your drift here."

He cocked his head and frowned, as if momentarily resigning himself to my obtuseness. "I'm sure you're aware that Whitehall is the leading private sector resource for counterterrorism and counterespionage. The Fund wants to know that you're listening to them carefully and undertaking any directives they suggest. It's our money at risk, too." He tilted his head and gave me an ironic, almost mocking smile. "At least, as long as we're holding the note."

I didn't take my eyes off his, and I didn't smile back at him. "As long as you're holding the note," I answered him evenly. He didn't push any further, and the meeting ended.

I thought about that exchange as Henry drove me home. There was something disturbing about Barrington being in on Whitehall's program. Were they getting something on the other side? Barrington was one of the more aggressive equity funds, with a membership list heavy with ex-politicians and ex-Intelligence people. I'd heard them described as "capital in search of a victim." I didn't like Denton, and

I didn't like the Whitehall program he was pushing. I'd learned some disappointing things about our Republic in the decades since I'd protested Oliver North and his shadow government, but I could still recognize that certain powers belonged only to the people, however ignorant or incompetent they might be. As for Denton's little stab at intimidating me: I'd hired and fired a dozen smart young fellows like him. I wasn't some small-town shopkeeper he could shake down for a donation to the Policemen's Benevolent Fund.

I'd come home early so that Josh and I would have time to have a drink together. Josh was sitting in the library looking through a book on Italian capitalism and its influence on Renaissance art. He had the book opened to a portrait of Cosimo de' Medici.

He looked up when I came in. "How'd your meeting go?"

"Don't ask," I said. "Things just keep getting weirder."

"How so?"

I waved it away. "Just . . . business weirdness. Creditors are happiest when they're coming up with new hoops for you to jump through. Are you ready for the best martini you've ever had?"

"I'm not a big drinker. But sure, power one up for me."

The ice was already in the bucket, and Phyllis had put out a fresh tray of cocktail shrimp. I moved the shrimp over to Joshua and started my bartender act.

"The key is the right gin and the right amount of olive juice. I use this ridiculously overpriced English gin—" I showed him the label and then poured out two jiggers into the mixer. "Now that the dollar's been taken out and executed, they keep it in a safe behind the counter."

I shook the mixer until my hand ached with cold and then poured it out into a thin cone of Baccarat crystal. Joshua hadn't said anything. "Extra olive?"

"Thanks." He took a sip and crinkled his eyebrows. "Yikes!"

"That's a neat book about art and capitalism, isn't it? If they were writing that five hundred years from now, it would be about the movie business."

He pointed down to a portrait of Cosimo de' Medici. "I'm not sure *Superman Returns* is going to hold up real well against Michelangelo and Dante."

"True, but cinema is still the art form of our time."

"No, Dad, cinema is the *craft* form of our time. Have you noticed how pathetically shallow most movies are? You sit there for two hours and when it's over there's nothing there."

"Yes, but a great image stands on its own. Like at the end of Kubrick's early movie, *The Killing.* I can't get that image out of my head. Sterling Hayden puts together this elaborate racetrack heist that he's spent years planning. It goes like clockwork and he's left with all the cash in this old suitcase at the airport, waiting for his flight out of town. It's night. The wind is blowing. The cops are all over the place but they don't know who he is. Then, as he watches, his suitcase falls off the baggage cart, opens up on the runway, and all the money blows away. And you just see him helplessly watching this whirlwind of dollars go sailing into the darkness."

"Harsh."

"Harsh my ass. Fucking *haunting* is what it is!" The martini was kicking in already. "I've got that movie! We can watch it tomorrow if you want."

We heard the front door open, and Joshua jumped to his feet. "Mom!" He rushed out of the room, and I stood up and slowly followed him. They were hugging by the front door and her eyes were closed with pleasure as she held on to him. Anne was wearing her favorite jacket, a beautiful piece made out of an old Tibetan carpet. Celestial blue and gold, on the back it had two dragons contending for a flaming pearl. I sometimes thought of it as her, me, and Joshua. I walked over to them.

"What do you think of your big boy as a surf bum?" I asked her.

"He's no surf bum. He's a rock star!"

"I'm seeing Billy Idol."

"*I'm* seeing Roger Daltrey!"

"Who are those guys?"

Anne and I looked at each other. "O-kay," I sighed, "that just aged me about a hundred years!"

Anne took off her coat and we all returned to the library. I made Anne her usual weak mixture of sweet vermouth and soda. "So, just as a reminder, the Pettijohns and the Borens will be here in an hour."

A look of distaste came over her and I saw her roll her eyes at Josh.

"Just try to be nice, okay, sweetie? I know Howard isn't your favorite person, but you like the Borens, don't you?"

"They're charming. Richard can regale us with tales of big contracts he let out to his friends when he was in the government."

Joshua laughed. It irritated me.

Anne glanced at him slyly, then back to me. "And I forgot to tell you: I invited Roger."

I turned away without answering. "Great," I said when I'd composed myself. "Maybe he can lead us in some poses."

"Why shouldn't I be allowed to have my friends over, too?"

"Who's Roger?" Joshua asked.

"My yoga instructor. You'll like him."

"I like Roger, too, but when you make a guest list, you usually try to have people who have something in common. This is like having Mr. Sulfur, Mr. Saltpeter, and Mr. Charcoal to dinner." I pointed at Joshua. "And don't you be Mr. Match!"

The Pettijohns were some of my wife's least favorite guests, but they always invited us to their parties and I felt obligated to have them over once each year. Besides, I liked Howard. He had an old-fashioned—some would say, *tribal*—sense of loyalty. He would deny his friends nothing, and go to elaborate lengths to punish his enemies. He was the kind of friend who would lie to a Senate Sub-Committee to protect you. Together, we controlled most of Appalachia's water.

The Borens arrived first and we retired to the library for a drink. Richard was tieless in a navy blazer and a pair of khaki pants—his official uniform since retiring from Commerce. It was a deceptively casual outfit for such an influential man, and maybe it underlined his real stature: he was always the one in the room who didn't have to dress up. He was slim and elegant despite being a little bowed by scoliosis, and he had a courtly Virginia accent that perfectly matched his relaxing manner. His passion was Colonial America, and he sometimes lectured on the subject at Georgetown. Jean was done up in a matching skirt and jacket, ever the Smith career girl. I liked Richard a lot. At sixty-six, he'd reached an age where the usual issues of midlife—money, troubled children, business rivalries—had all been overcome, leaving him free in the way I imagined myself in a few years. It hadn't hurt to get pieces of some very big projects after his tenure with the government, but what I envied the most was how his family had worked out. He had formed a lobbying firm with his son, and they sat each day in adjoining offices on K Street, meeting with some of the choicest clients in Washington. His daughter had married a marine colonel and had two children. His other son had recently been elected to the Houston City Council.

I'd just begun to mix martinis for Richard and Jean when Roger arrived, tall, well-built, and handsome in a magazine sort of way, wearing blue jeans and a pink sweater without any shirt under it. He radiated good health, with his black curls clustered around a complexion that glowed photogenically. A grown-up Botticelli angel. My wife told me he'd had a modeling career before he got established as, well, whatever he was. I hurried the martinis along, serving them just as Roger was going into an explanation about tantric yoga.

"So," I said as I handed the drinks around. I wanted to rescue Richard from the yoga discourse. "I have a question for everyone." They all turned to me. "Josh and I were talking about this earlier, but we didn't finish our discussion: What's the most important art form of our time? I say it's film. Josh thinks films are inherently shallow—"

"*Movies,* Dad. Not 'film.'"

"What do you think?"

Richard laughed good-naturedly. "Must I choose sides?"

Joshua took a step toward the center of the room and spoke a bit too loudly. "Mr. Boren . . ." I noticed his glass was empty. "In any civil war, sooner or later you have to choose sides."

Richard's smile faded a little. "I'm not sure I understand you."

"It's the war between Words and Pictures."

Joshua's strange vehemence silenced everyone in the room. I was sorry I'd pushed another martini on him twenty minutes before. Richard laughed, a good sport. "You're way ahead of this old man, Joshua."

"Okay. Think of it like this: Imagine America as a boxing match. Words are the skinny lightweight with glasses, spouting off logical propositions and complex thoughts, even after the round starts, when he should be swinging. Mr. Word can't stop himself, because that's his nature: Sentences propose ideas, paragraphs develop them. '*We hold these truths to be self-evident,*' '*When, in the course of human events . . .*' Now, wading toward him you've got Pictures: big, beefy, good-looking. Seeing is believing. Feeling is believing. Pure sensation.

And in a knock-down drag-out between logic and sensation, guess who goes down?"

Richard went quiet for a moment, then answered. "Well, I think you're not being entirely fair to pictures, there, Joshua. Television news is a fantastic tool for informing people—"

Joshua interrupted him. "No, on the contrary, Mr. Boren! On the contrary: It's a fantastic tool for giving people the *illusion* they're informed! People watch a thirty-second news spot and actually think they know the story. But it's only pictures, because that's what makes good TV. Not numbers, not complicated relationships. Just gut-level sensation. Little ideas on a big canvas. It engages people's emotions, not their minds."

It was the old Josh coming out, the snide little kid who'd kicked the balls sideways just to spite me. I couldn't resist answering him. "The last time I checked, Joshua, words hadn't disappeared! There's magazines, newspapers, journals, novels. Publishing is a multibillion-dollar business."

"That's true, but they're losing. Pictures shape everything. Seventy percent of Americans use television as their primary news source. Look at any major political speech of the last ten years: It's crafted to the television mind, with Freedom this, Liberty that. It's show biz, not thought."

Richard weighed in on his side. "He's got a point there, Jim!"

That irritated me even more. I ignored Richard and rolled on, louder than I should have been. "Come off it, Josh! You can't blame pictures!"

"I'm just saying . . ." He stopped and lowered his voice. I think he sensed that old hostile weather front moving in between us. Looking from me to Richard, he spoke softly and reasonably. "I'm just saying that in *our* country, in a democracy that depends on a well-informed public, it comes down to this: The Constitution was written words. Debilitate the written word, and all you have left is *America: The Movie.*"

No one answered. Richard raised his eyebrows, paused, then patted Joshua on the shoulder. "Joshua, thank you. That's the most interesting discussion I've had in a long time. And I don't want to hear any more of this 'Mr. Boren' stuff! I'm Richard, and my wife is Jean."

Josh looked contrite. "Sorry if I went off on you. It's kind of an obsession."

"It's a worthy obsession," Richard said. He looked over at me. "This is some boy you've got here, Jim."

"He's his own man." I smiled, and I relaxed. It looked like Joshua had finally learned when to quit.

The doorbell rang. "That's Howard," I said. "Shall we move into the dining room?"

As we left the library, Richard guided Josh through the door. "So you do Web design? I've been thinking about having a Web site made. . . ."

Howard and his wife already had their coats off when we reached them. He walked over and grasped my hand tightly. "Jim, I'm sorry I'm late. Why they decide to do roadwork at rush hour, I'll never know." He looked innocently up to the sky. "Must be those efficient government bureaucrats at it again."

Richard growled in mock anger. "Don't you start up with me again, Pettijohn!"

Nothing patrician about Howard Pettijohn. Short, with a slight paunch, he had black hair and sharp Appalachian features in a pallid complexion that was stippled with pink, as if he were always close to anger. His wife, Connie Sue, ranged a good five inches over him, a blonde in her twenties whose rare words were made lopsided by a strong mountain accent. A raconteur and a rascal, Howard was something of a showboat. He loved to appear in the news, and he reveled in the bad-guy image he'd acquired among the Environmental and anti–Free Enterprise crowds. Lately he'd achieved a little more notoriety than he liked. The usual "alternative" news venues were circulating allegations that he'd been some sort of intermediary between the government and right-wing paramilitary groups, and these reports irritated Howard to near apoplexy. "Now they want to legislate who you can have a drink with!" he'd sputter. Besides our joint ventures, he owned a small stake in my company.

We went into the formal dining room and sat down to dinner. Wine was poured, and the guests broke into little conversation groups. Roger was talking about Chuang Tzu dreaming of being a butterfly, while Howard was loudly declaiming to Richard, "If you want a real steak, I'm talking beyond prime, you got to go to . . ."

I'd seated Josh safely on my right hand, isolated from Howard and Richard by the wives. The wine was poured and we made a quick noncommittal toast to health. Josh asked for only a half inch in his glass, which relieved me. Phyllis brought out bowls of cream of chestnut soup, and I could see Joshua was pleased.

"I asked Phyllis to make the chestnut soup," I told him quietly.

He gave me a shy smile. "Thanks."

Chestnut always went over well; even Connie roused herself enough to ask tremulously about the ingredients. As the first glasses of wine disappeared, the conversation started to relax into the usual dinnertime chatter about movies or places. Richard mentioned his upcoming skiing trip to Jackson Hole, and as the conversation turned to Wyoming, the sensation of sage and empty highways billowed out of my memory for a moment. A long pipeline of dust behind a speeding pickup.

"Have you ever hitchhiked?" I asked Joshua.

"Only serial killers hitchhike nowadays."

"I hitchhiked all the way to California when I was twenty."

"You've told me that."

"*That* was freedom." I chuckled. "Did I ever tell you about the time I got picked up on suspicion of bank robbery?"

"Yeah, you did."

"One of those wrong place, wrong time deals."

"I know, Dad: *James Sands: the Outlaw Years.*"

I wrinkled my nose. "Ouch!"

The conversation at the other end of the table turned to Polling and the terrorists, and I felt Josh's attention shifting there.

"That was low," Howard was saying, "the way they tortured him first. It shows you what kind of government they'd run if they ever got power. They'd have concentration camps for anybody who ever made a profit."

"I'm not condoning their actions," Roger answered, "but the evidence doesn't indicate that they actually tortured him. I read the autopsy report online, and it showed a shot to the head and to the heart. Death was pretty instantaneous."

"Well, I'm not sure I'd trust everything I read online," Howard said with a snicker.

"Even if he died instantly, it's still murder," Richard put in.

"As I said," Roger answered, "I'm not condoning them. But the torture claims that the government has been making are false. I think we need to look at these people clearly and objectively, not vilify them."

"I think we need to just shoot 'em down like dogs," Howard came back. "You get the first couple, then the others'll think twice about what they're doing."

"It worked for Hitler," my son put in.

The conversation stuttered for a moment; then Howard answered. "I don't think you can compare Hitler to a democratically elected government trying to protect itself."

"Hitler *was* democratically elected. Personally, I think the man was a visionary. The Big Lie theory—can't argue with that one. War as an economic engine—that's still around. And what a management team! Göring, Goebbels, Speer, Himmler: those were guys who kicked ass and took names." He raised his palms reasonably. "I mean, you can doubt the guy's objectives, but you can't doubt his tactics."

Howard Pettijohn's face tightened and seemed to grow more florid. I looked over to Anne, hoping she'd somehow keep a lid on our son, but instead she seemed amused by him. "Well," I said quickly, "Politics and religion: two forbidden subjects at the dinner table."

"Politics *is* religion," Roger started in smugly. "It's all about faith in an idea, even if that idea is completely unrelated to the facts."

Howard misinterpreted Josh's attitude, glanced conspiratorially at him as he played on Roger's bombast. "I'll say! Like this whole Real Vote thing! What planet are these people from? We've got the cleanest, most technologically advanced voting system on God's green earth, and these loonies still go around crying that Americans don't have a real choice. They just can't face the fact that most of the folks in this country don't share their radical ideas!"

Roger came right back at him. "Actually, if you want to talk about facts, there's factual evidence of widespread fraud in every election in the past eight years."

"Has anyone been to that Motherwell exhibit at the Hirschhorn?" Jean Boren said brightly. "It's making me rethink abstract expressionism."

"I saw a Motherwell today," I answered.

Roger sailed on rudely. "But I really think that's the great accomplishment of this Administration! They've abolished facts and made belief in their illusion the highest form of patriotism."

"That's bullshit," Howard shot at Roger.

"You know, guys," I interrupted. "Politics—"

"No, it's not bullshit," Roger went on calmly. "Look at the invasion of Venezuela. Matthews insists that the Venezuelans came over the border and attacked our troops. He says it every time he opens his mouth. When he's done saying it, the other people in the Administration say it for him and then the media repeat it. Now over half the country still believes it. It doesn't matter that every other government on the scene says it's not true, or how absurd the idea is that Venezuela would provoke a war with the most powerful military in the world. They're believers. It's religion. They hang out with other believers who believe in the same so-called facts, and they're all happy together in their shared illusion."

Howard was squirming in his chair. "That's—"

"Excuse me, I'm not finished. The problem is, the further away from the real facts that their story gets, the more willing they have to be to discount other evidence that contradicts it, until they're living in a world where what most people would call objective truth doesn't exist. It's a social pathology, and that pathology is always present when countries go insane, like in Nazi Germany or China during the Cultural Revolution."

Pettijohn snorted. "I'm sorry, but I feel like I'm talking to some kind of Hollywood liberal. America-haters are always ready to equate this country with the Nazis. As I recall, the Nazis put people in gas chambers and burned them in crematoriums. Have we done that?"

"I didn't equate us with the Nazis. I said—"

"You did so! I just heard you. You said America was going insane, like the Nazis!"

"What I said was, the same social pathology is present here that was—"

"Don't try to back off it now! You equated this country to Nazi Germany, and I resent that! It's too bad you can't go back to Nazi Germany and get a firsthand experience of what the difference is! My father helped liberate those concentration camps, and by God I will never forget the things he told me. What was your father doing? Fighting for the Vichy French?"

Roger's eyes narrowed. It had gotten ugly, but I couldn't bring myself to interrupt it. Some part of me was enjoying seeing Roger's smug intellectual viewpoint be reduced by Howard Pettijohn. At the same time, I was waiting to see what he came back with. Roger looked flustered and angry. Howard was staring right at him. Roger dropped his gaze and inhaled slowly and deeply, as if centering himself with some breathing exercise, then looked up into Howard's reddened face.

"What you're trying to do is an excellent example. I was talking about two realities that don't intersect, and you insist that I was equating America with Nazi Germany, which is a *lie.*" A tiny loss of control at that word; then he went on in a low, tense voice in the silent room. "I don't know if you actually believe what you're saying, which would make you a pathological liar—"

"Did you just call me a pathological liar?"

"No. Personally, I think you know very well when you're lying. That's a cut below a pathological liar."

Pettijohn leapt to his feet and threw his cloth napkin in Roger's face. "Why don't you and me just step outside, pretty boy!"

It was absurd: the small paunchy Howard challenging Roger to a fight with that barroom cliché.

"*How-ard,*" his wife implored.

Roger didn't stand up. "We both know you're too much of a coward to do your own fighting. Hired guns are more your style, aren't they?"

Howard stood glaring at him for an incredibly long moment, then said, "I thought so," as if he'd just won a great contest.

My wife broke the silence, speaking quietly. "Howard, I'd like you to leave my house."

I held my fork in the air without moving. "I think we're all taking this a little too seriously. Howard and Roger are both passionate guys—"

"No!" Anne interrupted, giving me a hard glance before turning back across the table. "Howard, your manners are unacceptable and you are not welcome in my house! I'd like you to leave."

"Anne . . ." I could feel everyone waiting for my answer. My wife and I had been able to coexist because we'd pushed politics far into the background, especially at social gatherings. It was a truce we'd lived for many years, and it kept us whole. "Anne, Howard is my guest also."

"That's okay, Jim! I won't dirty the carpet of such a fine home!" Connie Jean rose beside him. He glanced back and forth between Roger and Anne, and then at me for an overly long moment. "It looks like you've already got enough cleaning to do! I'll find the door myself. Come on, Connie."

The rest of us sat there. It was as if a neutron bomb had been dropped near the dinner table, leaving all the place settings intact but killing everything in the area. Anne stood up abruptly and left the room, and the remaining guests floundered another half minute before excusing themselves. Richard and his wife shot me sympathetic looks as they backed out the door, while Roger slipped out after a quick apology to my cold stare. I went into the library to join Anne and Josh.

"Anyone mind if I put on some music?" I punched in a Tellenbach cello concerto and sat down on the couch. The calming music soared into the room, but I couldn't really hear it. My head was roaring. "That was quite a fun evening." Neither of them said anything and I couldn't help going on. "Thanks for calming the waters. Both of you. I appreciate that. I love driving my guests out of my house in a rage."

"What about the people who live in your house?" Anne answered. "What about their rage? Or are wives supposed to be seen and not heard?"

"Rage! About what?" I said sharply. "Just tell me what your rage is based on!" I began to imitate her. "'Boo hoo! I have a private yoga instructor who charges three hundred dollars an hour. Boo hoo! I have to live in this big house. Boo hoo! my husband keeps making large donations to the Waldorf School and the Children's Fund and every goddammed charity and environmental group I put in front of him and now he expects me to be nice to his friends for three hours a year, too! Boo-fucking-hoo!' You certainly have a lot to be outraged about!"

"You think the only thing people have a right to be outraged about is money!"

"I don't think they have a right to get outraged about some harebrained complaint they read about in a left-wing magazine or some theoretical people's rights to water or air or whatever kind of bullshit happens to be fashionable! You're always the first to sympathize with the poor oppressed masses, why don't you go out and be one of them?

Go live on your Waldorf teacher's salary for a while and see how you like that! Maybe Roger can give you a discount!"

As soon as it came out of my mouth, I regretted it. She stood up, and Joshua and I both watched her as she stalked out of the library, leaving the door open behind her. "Mom!" Joshua called. Her footsteps faded down the hallway, and then we heard the door leading out to the garage open and slam shut. The low rumbling of the electric door hummed through the house. Joshua looked at me with a stricken, childish grimace, and I felt first shame, and then a sudden rage at him.

"And you're the one who started it! With those stupid comments about the Nazis! Who made you a political scientist?"

"You going to start on me now, Dad?" he said calmly. "Maybe the Pettijohns and the Borens can be your new family."

"It's just . . . That fucking Roger! Parroting all that crap from the radical media. He'll never set foot in this house again! When your mother gets back that's the first thing we're getting clear on."

I looked for some assent from my son, but he merely watched me. "Where do you think she went?" he asked.

Various unpleasant images came to mind, some of them involving Roger. I threw my hands up into the air. "Who knows! She's capable of anything. Godammit!" I walked in a half circle. The cellist was still sawing away at the Tellenbach and it suddenly offended me. I turned it off and wandered over to my desk, sat down. "Why did you have to antagonize them like that? With that Nazi crap."

"Sometimes I like to mirror people's attitudes back at them."

"For what? To teach them a lesson? Do you think Howard Pettijohn is going to learn anything from you? You're a kid!"

He stiffened angrily and I was sorry I'd said it. "I didn't mean it like that. People like Howard Pettijohn aren't capable of learning anything you can teach them. Their world is graven in stone, it has certain rules, and nothing you say is going to change that. Whatever you show them, they'll rearrange everything until it fits in with a view that justifies them being exactly who they are and doing exactly what they do. They'll just write you off as a radical or a pointy-headed intellectual or whatever else works."

"And these are your friends?"

I sat down again on the couch, moving a silk cushion out of the way so I could lean back. "Now we really have come full circle." I smiled. "It used to be me who disapproved of your friends. I thought you weren't political."

He stood up, agitated. "You don't have to be to know who these guys are. I mean, Howard Pettijohn? Richard Boren? Come on! I'm apolitical, not comatose."

"They're my friends. I'm not going to drop them because you disapprove of them, any more than you did when I didn't like your friends. All those druggies and wannabe revolutionaries you hung out with in college. I'll take Howard and Richard any day."

"Dad, these people have been accused of terrible things! Huge public rip-offs, death squads—"

"Accused! That's not a conviction!" I waved it off. "Besides, that's all politics."

"Dad!"

I cut him off with a low pointed voice: "You are a very young man with a very narrow and naïve view of how the world works."

He flashed with anger; then, just as quickly, he relaxed. "I'm not going to rise to that bait anymore. You put people down to silence them, just like you did with Mom a few minutes ago. You silence them, but that doesn't mean you've answered them." He came over to the couch and stood above me. "What does it take, Dad? What does it take for you to learn?"

"Learn what? Oh, I get it: that I'm evil and crooked and going to hell. You've become quite the moralist."

"You said Howard's image of the world was graven in stone. How are you any different? All these people opposing you and Water Solutions—you think they're just cranks, or radicals."

"You're right!" I said sarcastically. "I can't understand how *bringing* them something is actually taking something away!"

"Get this, Dad: They don't want to be subjects in your empire. They don't want people like you or Howard Pettijohn controlling their water or their roads or their government. They view those things as the common wealth, not as a market to be exploited."

It was nothing new to me. I could only half-hear him, and I barely paid attention to my answers. I was wondering where Anne was, angry at her for her tantrum and her idiot friend Roger, angry at myself for not knowing ahead of time that my free pass with her was running out and that Howard was just the person to use it up all in one shot. She didn't know the kind of fight I was in, and now Joshua, his mother's son in every way, was choosing this moment to lecture me about how wrong I was and how I should change. Words, words, an endless stream of sanctimonious words! Now he was telling me that I had "incredible powers of organization and persuasion." That I could "accomplish a lot." I could accomplish a lot!

"I'm sorry you find a two-billion-dollar-a-year business so goddamned insignificant!"

"I'm just saying maybe it's time to move on."

"Move on? I'm getting that from a twenty-six-year-old who couldn't even finish college? What do you know about moving on? You've never created something you could move on *from*! And at the rate you're going, you never will!"

A waver like a heat mirage passed across his features, and a feeling of horror came over me. "I'm sorry," I said. I stood up and put my hands on his shoulders and squeezed them. He stared at the floor. "I'm sorry. That was a stupid thing to say, and I know it's not true. You're going to do something someday that makes me very proud. I know that. It's just . . . I spent fifteen years of my life building Water Solutions and when I feel like people are attacking it, I kind of lose it." He nodded without answering. "Look: I created a global enterprise from scratch. Can you understand what that means? It's me. My intelligence, my vision . . . I mean, maybe I'm a small person because I need something like this to show the world how damned clever I am. I don't deny that. Maybe if I could compose a great symphony or hit a baseball five hundred feet I'd be doing that instead, but this is what I can do, this huge intricate venture of thousands of people working together. And it's something very few others can do. I just wish you could respect that."

He finally sighed, and seemed to search for the right words. "I understand, Dad. I really do. But you have an illusion about Water Solutions—"

I became irritated again. "Yeah, I know, I tell myself it's a legitimate business when I'm really just a parasite on the public—"

"No. There's a deeper illusion than that. You think that because you created Water Solutions, you control it. But the reality is, it controls you. That's the fundamental illusion, and it's what all your other illusions come from. You've drawn this picture, and I'm afraid one day that picture's going to coming crashing down on you, and on Mom, too."

I thought of the Barrington Group, and of smooth, mocking Denton. "That's just what I'm trying to prevent."

He hunched over on the chair and tilted his head down, rubbing his hands across his temples as if he had a headache. He seemed under stress, and I felt bad that I was causing it. After a minute he stood up and crossed over to the elevations that were layered on the table.

"So, how does this thing work, anyway?"

I hesitated. Maybe he was trying to cheer me up. "Are you really interested?"

"Of course!"

I felt a little better. "Hold on, I'll pull the overviews off the server." As I pecked in my password I could feel him watching over my shoulder. The printer hummed and the big blueprint curled out onto the table. I began to explain the project to him, and he listened for a good twenty minutes before his attention started to drift.

"Hey!" he finally said. "Do you want to watch that Kubrick film you told me about?"

I thought of the stark black-and-white footage, the final scene with the money whipping away into the darkness. "Let's order a comedy."

Phyllis brought in the wreckage of the dinner party and we ate it as we watched the movie, but my wife didn't come home. She didn't answer her cell phone either. At midnight Joshua went up to bed and left me alone in the library, and in the silence, the anger came on again. My wife had humiliated and then condemned me, and was now in some unknown place, maybe doing things whose images tormented me. My son was becoming one of those hyper intelligent failures who make a lifestyle out of pointing out everyone else's stupidity, especially mine. Why did I have to put up with this crap? In the daylight world I was lauded for my genius, but here in the intimacy of my own home I was a fool. Thief. Parasite.

As the night dragged on, though, and I waited uselessly for Anne to return, I found myself adrift in those empty hours where there are no defenses against insurgent doubt. Why were they allied against me like that? Was it so wrong to build a great enterprise? Could I actually be as blind and stupid as they implied, an unwitting husband and incompetent father? These thoughts swirled around me and away into the dark expanses of my sleeping house.

I closed my eyes and tried to hold on to one peaceful memory of standing on a highway somewhere and looking at the stars. Business school just an idea then, everything still open. Maybe Anne and Josh were right; maybe it was time to close out this act, to get to the other side, where people like Richard Boren were. I'd created this business and I could leave it behind. The solution floated happily across my mind: I would finish this project as my final seal, then sell my interest and be free. Yes. That would solve everything at one stroke. The pipeline would be my exit strategy. No more creditors. No more protesters and weird counterinsurgency programs. The end of swarming details. Free.

I dozed off beneath the blueprints of my venture, dreaming of Cascadia and its long indigo progress across the Western states.

9

*A*lways strange to be back in the old manse; so much is exactly the same as when I lived here, but worse. My parents in an armed truce, my father's sleazebag friends taking up more and more mindshare. The smarter he gets, the dumber he gets—scrawling his password on a piece of paper taped to his computer and insisting he's got it all figured out. I wait up with him for my mother, watching his stiff upper lip sag as the hours go by. At midnight he looks so exhausted and so mortal that I get a lump in my throat, hug him, and retreat to my room to wait out the three or four hours before I can struggle down into herky-jerky sleep.

My room hasn't changed since the days when I was being expelled from boarding school and flunking out of college, other than my clothes not being all over the floor. The World War I biplane models are still zooming around the ceiling, the balsa racer I carved for Cub Scouts is sitting in front of its third place trophy. One of those father–son activities; I can still remember the excitement of teaming up with my father. He could use the hacksaw and drill straight holes, which seemed like the absolute height of godlike competence in those days. No matter how angry he made me, he was still the man who wore a business suit and went to the office every day, and that made him the standard to be lived up to. It wasn't until I went away to boarding school and had a girl ask me, "What's it like being related to the Antichrist?" that I realized I wasn't the only one pissed off at my father.

I lie back on the bed and pick up a copy of *Nefesh HaTorah*, a book I'd gotten from the Boston Lubovitchers during my Jewish kick. I'd gone with a friend to check out the guys with black hats and beards, a goof, really: I was only a quarter Jewish, and even that quarter had converted to Unitarianism before I was born. I skated in on the coattails of my paternal great-grandparents, beanie-wearing Poles I'd seen glaring out of black-and-whites from the 1930s but never thought much about until they became convenient that afternoon. The Lubovitchers did their best to blow that spark to life, even ignoring my earrings and my piercings except for one subtle reference by the rebbe to the Talmudic injunction against mutilation of the body.

We were a bizarre match in every way; they fled the world and its politics at a time when I realized that politics were what mattered most. For them, the ancient stories of the Bible *were* their politics, a world that interpenetrated our world and dragged us into its Edens and regicides whether we wanted to go or not. In their own mythology they were something between cosmic janitors and God's own Civils. When the universe was created it was unable to contain God's divinity, and it shattered, scattering sparks of godliness around our broken world. Their job was to patiently gather these sparks through acts of justice and kindness, repairing the world by creating the society God had intended in the first place.

An awesome vision, it went perfectly with my thoughts about political action. Where I got confused was with which methodology God wanted us to use. Were we talking God the creator of Eden, God who demanded we love our neighbor as ourselves? Or God the Smiter, God the Judge? The rebbe's esoteric textual analyses failed me there: I lost patience and moved to the West Coast to gather the sparks as I saw fit.

It doesn't seem any clearer tonight. The logic that leads from the Polling Operation to Cascadia is inevitable, but so is the commandment to honor your father and mother. I leaf through the *Nefesh* without finding answers, then get online and read the news of our ailing world until it starts to swim in front of me. The Regime's media bulldogs are ripping into a senator who'd dared to investigate military contracts, while climate change is starving out a hundred million Africans. In Borneo the last bits of rain forest are being cut down so Indonesian generals can sell palm oil diesel to American suburbanites. Estimated loss: seventy thousand species. I turn off the computer and lie down in the dark. Maybe the rebbe thought he had eternity to get it together. It looks to me like we're dealing with a much shorter time frame.

Mom shows the next morning, a little rumpled after a night in the nearby Faceless Motel. Whatever they say to each other, it's behind closed doors, but there's a truce in there somewhere, at least for the two days left of my visit. My father goes back into overdrive on Cascadia as if nothing ever happened, strangely cheerful after the drubbing of the night before. At seven in the morning he disappears into his car and at seven that night he drops in for dinner and some Lite conversation. My mother and I go to the National Gallery and talk about him as we drift from painting to painting. "It's like he's been completely absorbed by this business and these people," she says. "All his friendships have deals attached to them. He talks the way they talk, he argues their points of view." She rolls her eyes. "He even gets custom-made shoes from some shoemaker they all use."

"Dad needs a wake-up call."

"It had better come soon, that's all I can say."

An ominous line, more ominous than she knows. She steps away from it, makes it general. "This whole country needs a wake-up call. I don't know what it's going to take for us to get up off our cans."

"People are getting off their cans, Mom. There's supposed to be a big privatization conference in Seattle next month. You watch: Democracy Northwest is going to shut it down."

"Who are they?"

"They're a group based in Seattle, but there's organizations like that all over the country. Just get involved in one."

"I can hear your father already!" She tensed up again around the subject of my father. "We just don't seem to agree on anything anymore."

Staring down that long corridor of little squares on crisp white walls, I can't believe I'm asking the next question. "Is there something going on between Roger and you?"

She takes a step back. "Is that what you think?" Mom laughs. "Roger's got a girlfriend who's twenty years younger and far more beautiful than me. No. This is a problem your father and I have been sweeping under the carpet since before you were born." We amble down to the next picture. "You know, your father got into finance to help people, believe it or not. When we met, he was helping cities get loans for their projects. Public transportation systems, urban redevelopment. I really admired him. He was a very good man. He still is. Then, after the currency crash and all those municipal bankruptcies, along came *Garfield*."

She says it like Garfield's the kind of bad-penny friend who drags a guy into strip joints and all-night poker games. "Who's Garfield?"

"Garfield was a small town in New Jersey that was too bankrupt to get a loan to fix their water system. The water was awful, but he couldn't get them financing to fix it. So he put together some people he knew and bought out their water utility. Then they realized that it would be much more efficient if they also owned the system of the next town over. And that's how it started. I never thought it would end up the way it is now." She sweeps it all under the carpet one more time, turns on her heat-lamp smile. "But I want to know what *you're* doing."

For some reason, my lie synthesizer is running a little ragged at the moment and I hesitate. "You know, same old thing."

The heat lamp goes off, and her mouth is straight. "Don't give me that song and dance about Web design. I'm not your father. You're thin and you look like you haven't been sleeping. You never answer your cell phone and you never mention any friends. The biggest giveaway is that whole apathy act. You haven't been apathetic about anything since you were two years old."

I semi-surrender. "It works pretty well on Dad."

"These days he's gotten very good at believing what he wants to believe. What's really going on?"

She knows I was into things in Boston, and she's asking me about a lot more than my sleeping habits. "Well, Mom . . ." I swallow. I rarely see my mother anymore, and I may be seeing her even less. The paintings are watching us. A camera in the corner of the ceiling. Unlikely that there's listening devices. Not in an art gallery. Just her expectant face, sensing more acutely than any electronic device ever could. "Maybe I just spend too much time in front of the computer."

She looks at me and then turns away and fumbles around in her purse. I reach out and squeeze her arms to make her feel better. "Mom, there's nothing weird or dangerous. I'm really just superbusy and a little stressed out."

She dabs at her eyes with the little cloud of tissue. "Okay. You're a grown man. You have your personal life." She pulls out of it and becomes the parent again. "But Joshua, promise you'll ask me if you ever need help."

I promise, and it's typical of my mom that after five minutes she can go on as if there really is no undertow beneath her motherly happiness, as she's managed for years with my father. The eternal optimist. Maybe she clings to me more tightly this visit, and cries too deeply at the airport when she drops me off. I struggle to keep it together during the last hug, feeding my head a cozy history-less future where the whole family is kicking back with cups of coffee and crossword puzzles. I'm Lando again before I even let her go, gaming myself this time.

On the airplane I'm thinking about Cascadia. Sarah pegged it right, as she always did in that babe-with-brass-knuckles way of hers. James Sands is near the edge, and with just one big step back he'll go tumbling through space. We blow Cascadia, and Water Solutions crumbles, the country applauds, the all-powerful corporations start to realize the people still have the will to fight. Is it up to me to protect my father's schemes?

I tried. I made my best pitch about the common wealth and his answer was *"There is no common wealth! Only wealth created by individuals, and freeloaders who try to claim a share of it with words like 'commonwealth'!"* What could I do with an attitude like that? The man's King Saul, crazed with power in the Book of Samuel. But then I think of Dad, working eighty hours a week to hold together his masterpiece, a jerk who always gets it wrong with his son, his wife, but even so, redeemable.

Then there's my crew. For them, it's survival, not a big house and a private jet. Without my help, they might give up and move on to a new target, or they might try it anyway, in over their heads, and fail big. I wish I could bounce it off some confidant, but some decisions you have to just make and stop thinking about, because once you make them, the logic of your old life doesn't apply anymore. There's only the new logic, of the Revolutionary, the criminal, the Corporation, whatever you've chosen, and if you don't close your eyes and hold on tight, the dissonance will grind you to dust.

I very quietly approach Gonzalo with the password. Chubby Gonzalo, living on cola and corn chips, enemy of exercise and all that is wholesome. The hacker with the golden phone voice, he's that rare find: a guy who can not only write the programs, but also has the acting skills to impersonate a snippy auditor demanding an account number, or the helpful tech support guy who slips them a Trojan horse in the name of better computing: *Hey, you could just install this upgrade while I've got you on the line! Yeah, we're moving to the new standards next month.* Gonzalo can do more damage with a keyboard than most people can do with a bazooka.

"Holy shit, Lando. That's a gold mine!"

"Keep your shirt on, big guy." I stuff down one last twinge of regret. "Maybe we should hold off on it until we know we need it."

He shakes his black Zappa curls. "You can't hold off on this stuff. Their security protocol is going to call for him changing his password every few weeks, maybe every few days. We need to break in now and put in a back door. How'd you get this, anyway?"

"Would I tell you and spoil the myth of my omniscience?"

"Whatever. I'll cover our tracks by sending one of their people on a blind date. He'll be the first guy they arrest if they make us." He shrugs and moves on, enchanted by the possibilities. "We could score big on this! I could see moving a couple million through some bogus purchase orders. Maybe cook up a piping deal with a dummy company in Mexico, then move the money over to the Caymans and back here. I'll have to talk to my banking guy about this."

"Dude, this isn't about money."

"I know." He lets out one word in a rich, fantastic tone. "*Cascadia!*" He sips out of a black can. "They've got all those schematics online and fully downloadable to authorized persons such as ourselves. After all, they are 'The Future of Water.'"

"As they tell us over and over again."

"With enough poking around, I'll bet we can get a good chunk of their security protocols, too."

"Let's focus on the schematics. I've got a server number for you."

"Server number? I worship you!"

Not feeling so very upbeat about my new cult. It had been an exceedingly easy intelligence operation, seeing as I'd carried it out against my own father. I watch a little signal flag float across my conscience, disappear into a blue-sky void where everything happens because it must happen. The place where John Polling had his last appointment.

"Okay," I tell Gonzalo. "Drop it in."

The information flood isn't long in coming. All the schematics, all the elevations and blueprints. A set of pictures that didn't lie, courtesy of James Sands. We spread them out on Tonk's floor.

The pipeline's intake is above the Bonneville Dam, just east of the Cascades. The pipeline itself is two huge concrete conduits, eight feet in diameter, running underground at a depth of four feet. It has sensors every three hundred yards to track water flow and pipe integrity, and these sensors connect to the pipeline's nerve center at the intake plant—our target. Hundreds of millions of dollars of tubing and computers had been intricately assembled to control the flow of water and provide a communications hub for the entire line, and it was decked out like a concentration camp, with guard towers, razor wire, and probably tremblers to detect footsteps around the outside.

"Six guys can get in, blow it, and get out," McFarland says.

I'm crunching through a bag of chips: dinner for me. "What about the guards?"

Joby speaks up. "We can take 'em. We'll disarm 'em and neutralize them until we're finished."

"That's a lot of metal on metal. The last thing we want is for the news the next day to be all about some twelve-dollar-an-hour security guard with three kids that was gunned down by the Army of the Republic."

"Hey, you gotta break a few eggs."

"We're not talking about eggs."

Joby crinkles his eyes in disgust. "Well, maybe we can all form a circle around it and meditate until it explodes!"

Tonk cuts us off before things heat up too much. "Jobes? Your meditation idea? That's very spiritual and I honor that. I really do, bro. And Lando: I think it's awesome that you're willing to stick up for eggs. 'Cause nobody really sticks up for eggs in this world." He purses his lips for a moment. "However, both of you dumbasses are missing the really simple and obvious way to blow this Popsicle stand."

"What do you mean?"

He points to one of the diagrams. "It's a *pipeline*." We all look at each other and Tonk stares up to heaven to deliver him from these morons. "*Pipeline!* Engage brain, Lando! What does every half-decent boarder do tricks in? A half pipe. What have I ridden a hundred times? A half pipe. This is just a half pipe with a lid." He looks around at all of us then taps his finger on the stiff curl of paper. "You *ride* pipelines!"

After weeks of debate and intelligence work, the plan falls into place in five minutes. We decide on the day after Thanksgiving, something to cut through the pumpkin pie leftovers and cozy memories of helpful Indians paving the way for their own annihilation. By the time we leave, we're all smiling. Almost all of us, anyway.

By coincidence, when I get home a message is waiting for me on my machine in San Francisco. The esteemed head of Water Solutions has requested that I call him back. Then requested again the next day, and the next. I make myself a bowl of ramen and throw in a load of laundry I've been putting off for a week. I wash the dishes, leaf through a climbing magazine, sweep the floor, stack the newspapers, hang up the towel I left on the bathroom floor. Finally I sit back on the couch and steady myself, then dial his number.

"Josh!" The old Dad voice comes flooding through with all that messy cargo. "How goes the war between words and pictures?" He waits for a few seconds then says. "It was a joke."

"Laughing on the inside, Dad."

"Okay, I'm an idiot. I admit it."

I smile, sitting there at the coffee table in my living room in Seattle. "Don't worry about it, you don't have a lock on that particular quality. How are you and Mom getting along?"

"We're getting along." He's not too sure about trying to enlist me as a confederate. "We have some things we need to work out. I personally don't think she's completely in reality about our lives."

"What do you mean?"

"Oh, for instance, about the business and what I'm dealing with. To be honest with you—" He lowers his voice, and I imagine him sitting in his office in his dark blue suit. "—things have been a little precarious lately, with the secondary financing and everything. With John Polling out of the picture my creditors are just being a real pain in the ass. Don't worry: the Japanese are very interested in American infrastructure projects. Barrington doesn't know it yet, but they're about to go sailing out of this deal on their ass." His cockiness dissipates. "But right now I'm under some pretty intense pressure."

Back to my therapist role. "So Mom's not supportive and that pisses you off."

"You saw what's going on here. She has this attitude that Water Solutions isn't a legitimate business."

"I agree with her," I say before I can stop myself. "You're using political and economic leverage to sell people something they already own."

And of course, he snarls back at me, "You may not think Water Solutions is legitimate, but fortunately tens of millions of other people are finding it legitimate every time they need water! I didn't call you to get another lecture!"

"Then why did you call me?"

It seems to confuse him. He bites his first few words off until he can find the right tone. "Actually! . . . Um, actually, I'm going to Seattle next week to speak at a conference, and I thought I might come down to San Francisco beforehand and visit you."

Now I'm the confused one. He wants to visit me. I've still got my apartment there: I could go down and throw some eggs and milk in the fridge, grab some up-to-date magazines for the coffee table, and play it out. But even that charade is impossible, because my social calendar is already taken up with a previous commitment in Eastern Oregon. It's all a little too ironic, even for me. "What conference are you speaking at?" I ask automatically, trying to buy a little breathing space.

"The National Business Symposium," he says, failing to sound modest. "I'm supposed to speak right after the president."

"I guess they haven't talked to your equity-fund buddies lately." It's an autopilot comment that slips out of the brain-scrambling weirdness, and it pisses him off.

"Do you have to belittle everything I do?"

"I guess I learned from an expert, didn't I?"

Over the receiver, I can hear a faint sigh. "I can't change that now, Joshua. We can only go forward. I'd like to come to San Francisco and spend some time with you next week. A couple of days, maybe. Since you aren't coming home for Thanksgiving."

I feel that deep and hurting chord down in my chest. The man is pulling it out from further down than I can ever remember, and all I can do is shine him on while this sick feeling of inevitable disaster pours into me like wax into a mold. A lifetime of missed opportunities, and they just keep slipping further out of reach. No need for me to fake regret. I clear my throat. "I'd like to, Dad, but I'm going skiing this week in the Sierras."

"You are?"

"Yeah. Winter camping. Get up, freeze your ass off for twelve hours, crawl into your bag. Repeat. I've been planning it with some friends for a couple of months."

"Sounds fun."

"Yeah." I'm lost there for a second. "What are you going to say at that conference?"

"Oh, I'm going to talk about public–private partnerships. How we need to stop thinking of people as Citizens and start thinking of them as Customers."

Same old Dad, with another neat little package, honed down to the kind of one-sentence Mission Statement engraved on the company Training Manual. Customers, not Citizens. That's who James Sands *is*. I feel the calm coming back. "Well, Dad," I tell him after a few seconds. "It sounds like you nailed it."

Meanwhile, it turns out we're not the only ones gathering information. For the last six weeks we've had someone in the Seattle DNN office, very quietly doing her low-paid clerical job for the cause and looking to all appearances like an innocent young do-gooder out to gather a few sparks. She doesn't steal their files or plant bugs, but she gives us an idea about who comes and goes, and when she surprises another staffer after-hours coming out of Dan Schwartz's office, the little question marks start sprouting.

William Lee fits the profile perfectly. He stirred himself in a month ago when the DNN announced their Real Vote! project, and suddenly he was everywhere at once, working sixty or seventy hours a week, doing all the shit jobs no one else wanted to get saddled with. A sure ticket to upward mobility in a world where Volunteer Burnout relentlessly thins the ranks. His story is that he's some sort of trust fund kid with time on his hands and a disposition to Fight the Machine. Our girl gets his picture in a group photo and we blow him into an eight-by-ten. She plays the mutual friend game and squeezes out the name of his high school back in Philadelphia, and I give Gonzalo his information.

Gonzalo starts to run the checks, and the recent ones come out okay: driver's license, credit report, a few Web postings on bulletin boards. His references from a Philadelphia antiwar group check out. When we go back to high school, the first red flag goes up. I'm sitting there as Gonzalo makes the call: "Hi, I'm a friend of William Lee, and we're doing a little tribute scrapbook for his birthday. I was wondering what it would take for me to get a copy of his yearbook photo? Don't worry"—he smiles—"we'll try not to embarrass him too badly!" They're happy to comply, but unless Bill invested in cosmetic surgery, something is seriously wrong. The William Lee who graduated from Penn High School was Asian.

So they'd built an identity on William Lee, but they'd failed to backstop the yearbook. Not a major error when you're infiltrating an organization as slack as the DNN. We hold a small meeting: Gonzalo, Sarah, Tonk, and I. Do we tell the DNN and have them go public with it?

"We don't know who he's working for yet. Gonzalo—" Gonzalo flinches because his name always comes up and it's always followed by the words "can you—?" "—he brings his own laptop into work and logs on to the network. Can you maybe get a keyboard sniffer in there?"

Gonzalo's annoyed. "Lando, man, I'm up to my ass in Cascadia right now! You want to pull me off that to go after this William Lee character? 'Cause there's only one of me."

"What about Emil and Joey?"

He rolls his eyes at being asked to explain this lower order of tech people. "Yeah. I guess so. They can, like, monitor the data that comes in, as long as I supervise them. I know a guy who wrote a new sniffer that he claims is undetectable."

The sniffer will automatically send every one of "Lee's" keystrokes to us over the Internet. Gonzalo works out the technical details, finally settles on our girl dropping a file onto his drive from a memory stick when he's in the bathroom. A dicey thirty-second play that goes off just like in the movies. We sit back and watch the show.

He's reporting to a kind of electronic dead drop on a secure shell, where his handler probably comes by on the other side and downloads the communiqués. He's providing a steady stream of information on the doings at the DNN. Names, conversations, e-mails, whatever general strategy or organizational issues he's privy to. He's keen on giving estimates of the DNN's numbers, particularly important in the run-up to the Business Symposium demonstration. He dumps the membership database at regular intervals, and reports on everything from contacts with other groups to office romances, knowing that those sorts of domestic dramas can sometimes be exploited. In the '70s, the FBI used to send civil organizers anonymous letters saying that their husbands were cheating on them, or forge phony personal attacks by one group toward another. Just a friendly way to throw some sand in the gears. Our friend Bill Lee still liked these tactics, suggesting some sort of sexual harassment smear against bachelor Dan Schwartz, and recommending that more information be gathered on Shar Simmons's sons in case they could be used to get to her. I'm relieved to see that he hasn't got anything on Emily and me.

"So who's he working for, Gonzalo?"

"I can't figure that out. The IP address is in frigging *Moldavia*, and I haven't had time to hack it. And don't even think about asking! The Cascadia operation's two weeks from now."

"Got it."

"Let's just assume," Sarah says, "that anything he knows, he's going to share with the other security agencies."

"We need to tell the DNN. At the very least, they need to take precautions."

"Why don't we just steal his laptop, beat the crap out of him, and send him packing?"

We all look at Tonk. Sarah jumps in first. "Great idea, Tonk. Did you learn that at the Alley Oop School of Counterintelligence?"

Gonzalo shakes his head. "He's all over their LAN. If they sweep the network, it's going to tip him off. But at least he'll be out of there."

I'm thinking about Bill Lee, the stinking spy, the traitor. Some clean-cut youth my own age ready to fuck over the whole country for an attaboy from his bosses, a promotion, a slap on the back from the other rats. As much as I like the idea of sneaking up on him in some alley, that's playground stuff. "No," I say, "Tonk's got the right idea. But I've got an infinitely more effective way to beat the crap out of Mr. William Lee."

10

*L*ando sidled up to me as I approached the tai chi studio. "I have something I need to talk to you about."

I couldn't resist a quick glance. He was looking straight ahead in his long black overcoat, clean-cut and thin-skinned, like a smart young lawyer or junior member of the Chamber of Commerce. "Must you always grab me before tai chi?"

"Think of all that pent-up energy, waiting to be *released*."

"Oh, shut up! Where's your car?"

I went through the building and out the back way, then down the block to his car. He joined me a minute later. He got in and I leaned over and yanked him toward me, and we kissed with our bodies twisted across the seat. I could taste the bitterness of coffee in his mouth. "This is crazy!" I said after a minute.

He smiled. "You're the one who decided to enter the crazy sweepstakes. Don't complain because your number came up." He handed me the same floppy hat as the first time. "Lean back and enjoy the ride, madam."

I closed my eyes and we swung into motion. For a minute my

eyelids changed from tan to bright orange as the sun shifted across my face. I felt light and excited, as if we were going out on a date.

He said, "This is our six-week anniversary, you know."

"I figured that out, too, but I wasn't going to say it."

"Oh! So I have to be the sensitive communicator in this relationship?"

I let my voice get as cool as I could. "Who said it's a relationship?"

That seemed to surprise him. "Well . . ."

I felt across the seat for his thigh, then patted it. "I'm just helping you avoid the mistake of taking me for granted."

I felt the hat come flopping down over my forehead. The featureless landscape of my closed eyes turned dark brown. "So," I started, "it looks like those anger-management sessions have been working for you."

"What do you mean?"

I was elated, but I didn't want to be obvious about it. "No one's heard a peep out of the Army of the Republic since the last time we talked."

"Oh, you know how it is. . . ." His voice sounded a little strained. "It's the holiday season. Everybody's busy clipping turkey recipes and looking for that special little something to put under the Christmas tree."

"Hopefully something that doesn't go *tick tick tick*. You guys are really helping us by taking a break, you know. When all that stuff came out last week about the Administration selling off the National Parks, our phones started ringing off the hook. I'm sure Matthews was praying you guys would blow something up and take the heat off."

"Yeah . . ." There was a little silence, then a sudden deceleration, and an angry shout. "Jesus! Moron!" I felt him touch my leg. "Not you. I would never call you Jesus."

"Thanks. So . . . is this a de facto cease-fire?"

He took a little while to answer. "I guess you could say we're in an organizational phase."

"What's that mean?"

"You know: organizing, analyzing, strategizing . . . just, like, all the *-izing*s."

There was something underneath it. "For what?"

"Whatever happens."

"That's sort of a nonanswer, isn't it?" We were back to our first meeting again, where he moves the red cape every time I charge. He didn't answer me, and I felt us accelerating onto the highway. When we reached cruising speed he went into the same tiresome explanation.

"I can't tell you things about the AOR, Emily. You know that. They aren't mine to tell. I tell you, maybe some Whitehall guys pick you up and take you into the little room for a few days without anybody knowing about it. You'll talk. *I'd* talk. And then everybody's at risk."

"I think you're a little paranoid there. As bad as Whitehall may be, I don't think—"

"They will." His voice became fatalistic in a way that annoyed me. "They'll start with us and then they'll work their way down to you. The Corporates want to eliminate a whole way of thought, not just the guerrillas. That's how it works, whether you're an Argentine general or some medieval pope. You always end up trying to kill the idea by killing the vessel that holds it."

His apocalyptic view made me uneasy. He seemed so vulnerable. "That's not going to happen here. Because we're going to stop them before it does. The whole country's going to see Matthews and his cronies for what they are: greedy little men with no answers."

"Yeah, right."

I was surprised by his negative mood, and I felt like I had to prove him wrong. "For starters, we're going to close down the Business Symposium on December fifth."

"You're sure of that?"

"Yes. Do you want to know how?" I'd never described the whole plan to anyone before. Only Dan, Shar, and I knew about it. "First of all, the DNN is in touch with dozens of organizations and civil society groups, and that's who we're organizing for December fifth."

These were churches, labor unions, environmental groups, student councils—entities that had membership lists and held fund-raisers: the "respectable" side of the protest movement. They had people in charge and well-thought-out agendas. Many of them had set up teach-ins or rallies for their own particular environmental or civil liberties issues. "So we're arranging for everyone to converge at the Seattle Center on the first day of the Business Symposium, when Matthews is supposed to give the opening address. We're aiming for fifty thousand people."

"A nice sing-along at the Space Needle. That'll make Matthews sit up and take notice!"

"Do you ever stop being a jerk?"

"Sorry."

"Anyway, as I'm sure you're aware, the DNN has an evil twin—"

"I'm likin' that—"

"The Direct Response Group, and they've got their own plans."

The Direct Response Group really was Democracy Northwest's alter ego. The building blocks of Democracy Northwest were established civil organizations, but the building block of the DRG was the affinity group. An affinity group might be two people or it might be two hundred. They came together on their own and they made decisions group by group, springing to life for a particular action and then dissolving again.

The DRG had picked out eighteen strategic intersections around the Convention Center to shut down. Affinity groups would select an intersection and take responsibility for blocking vehicles and pedestrians in whatever way they chose. The traffic snarl would only be the beginning. With vehicle transportation halted, the delegates would have to walk, and once they were on foot, the affinity groups would link arms and meet them as human barricades. They would confront them in the streets and at their hotels, forcing the privatizers to face their intended victims in person. If anyone wanted to stop the affinity groups, it would have to be with clubs, tear gas, and brute force.

The Direct Response Group hadn't tried to keep their plans secret from the police. They had put their invitation out in printed broadsides, posters, Internet films, and on their Web site. The dilemma for the police was that the DRG's actions were scattered around the whole downtown core. The protesters would come at each intersection in small groups from every angle, like the millions of e-mails focused on a server in a denial-of-service cyberattack. It would take thousands of police to secure such a large area, which in itself would shut down the city. Besides, having all those uniforms around would send the wrong message. What the Symposium wanted, with its presidential speaker and its elegant trappings, was to communicate that their plundering of the country was right and fitting, and that the only people who opposed it were a tiny minority of freaks and utopians. But if the minority was so tiny, why would the National Guard be needed to stop it?

A key issue for us was how the police would react. There were two main security forces. One was the Seattle Police, headed by Chief Bennet, who Dan, ever the insider, knew privately hated the Matthews Administration and everything it stood for. The Seattle PD were charged with keeping order, but they also respected the right to protest.

The other force was the King County Sheriff's Department. Chief Tom Grundel, the King County Sheriff, had survived several investigations for police brutality and jailhouse torture. A vocal admirer of the Matthews government, he wore the accusations against him like a badge of honor, proof that he was an ass-kicking upholder of the law. If the King County sheriffs came early to the demonstration, it would be a very different situation.

"Okay," Lando said as we slowed down and began the stopping and turning that meant we were close to our destination. "The DRG gets rowdy downtown while you guys are speechifying a mile away at the Seattle Center. What if the blueshirts start with mass arrests right off the bat and clear out the affinity groups before Matthews shows up?"

"We thought of that. The DRG thinks they can lock it down with five thousand to ten thousand people. They'll start around three in the morning and they think they can hold out at least six or seven hours, probably longer, depending on how many people show up and how many cops are on hand. They figure the police can field about twelve hundred officers. Moving ten thousand people that don't want to be moved is just a hard thing to do. That puts us at midmorning."

"Okay. What happens then? Matthews isn't scheduled until two."

My stomach fluttered as I told him what only two other people knew. "Then thirty or forty thousand angry Americans march out of the Seattle Center."

"To the Convention Center?"

"Bingo. They flood downtown, block up all the streets, the police are surrounded, they've got thirty thousand new bodies to move and they can't even get their buses through to get rid of the people they do arrest. The streets are filled with tear gas, the delegates are scared to come out of their hotels. Matthews is left standing at the airport with his finger up his butt."

Lando laughed loudly. "Very cool!" I smiled beneath my blindfold. I felt him reach over and squeeze my thigh. "So," he went on, "nobody knows that the civil groups are planning to join in with the Direct Response people?"

"Just Dan and Shar. We haven't even told the Direct Response people."

"Have you put any of this in writing, or even alluded to it? Like in an internal e-mail or anything?"

"No."

"Good." His voice became sly again. "I like the head fake. In fact, you're kind of faking out your own people, too."

I was sensitive about that. "They'll have a choice about whether to go downtown or not. It's up to each individual."

"In that time, there was no King in Seattle, and every demonstrator did what was right in their own eyes."

It was his old Book of Judges line. "You've got this weird Bible thing going. What's that all about?"

He laughed. "How many ways could I answer that question?" He paused, thinking it over. "Here's one: I like the Bible because it's the original reality machine. It's what all those Corporates wish that TV could be."

"Oh-kay."

"See, the Bible it doesn't just tell a story, it borrows every beam of light, every tower of cloud, every mountain, every flood, every massacre, every crooked ruler, every imperialist war and interprets what it means. And if you're a believer, there's very little separation between the Bible and the world itself. That's what Channel America and the rest of them are aiming for—to be the new Bible and redefine the world just the way they want it, where the powerful get the goods and the meek get fucked over because it's part of some wonderful God-given order." His voice changed to his version of a gospel-hour crusader. *"And so His wrath must be called down upon these false prophets!"*

"You're freaking me out here, Lando."

He laughed. "Okay, I'm just kidding about the wrath part. I don't know. . . . Maybe it's because the Bible's a universe that's illuminated by Right and Wrong—" I felt the car go down a short steep incline and then come to a halt. "—and as you've probably figured out, I'm sort of a moralistic SOB."

"Not you!" I laughed with him and kept my eyes closed as he led me inside, then opened them to find us in the same apartment we'd met the first time. It struck me again how motel-like it was. An apartment without an identity, like the person who lived in it. "Is this your place, Lando?"

"Nope."

"I didn't think so. It doesn't feel like you."

He moved up behind me and I felt his hands glide along my waist. "You're catching on." He pushed my hair out of the way and kissed my neck. His cool fingers slipped under my sweater.

It was all so strange. I was intimate with a man I didn't know in a place where reality had been manufactured. The weird nothingness came up around me like a flood, and I had no choice but to swim in it, to try to grab any landfall that came to hand. I turned and put my arms around the person who called himself Lando. "You know, when we're apart, I feel like I'm making this whole thing up."

He moved his face close to mine. "Of course you're making this whole thing up. So am I."

He brought his mouth to mine and we kissed in front of the refrigerator for a while. He began to pull me toward another door, opened it, a bedroom, and I noticed the shoes on the floor and the blouses draped over the dresser. "I still don't even know if you're seeing someone else."

"No. Never, Emily. You are my one and only."

We began kissing again, and for a moment or two I wondered if that's what he was to me. And then I gave in and stopped wondering.

An hour after that he brought me some green tea and sat down on the couch with an air of seriousness. He looked almost elegant in his white dress shirt, unbuttoned at the cuffs, but he looked tired, too, as always. He produced a manila envelope and became businesslike.

"So tell me something," he said. "Are you sure no one knows the master plan for the demonstration?"

"You, me, Dan and Shar. That's all."

"Have you talked about it on the phone? Have you e-mailed anything about it?"

"No. It's all verbal. Like you told us to do."

"Good," he said slowly. "Because you've been infiltrated."

"What?"

"William Lee. He's an infiltrator." He pulled out some pages, topped by a yearbook photo of an Asian man. "This is William Lee. Or at least, the real William Lee."

I felt calm at first, a superficial kind of calm, as if this were something I was watching at a movie theater. "How do you know?"

"Just take my word for it. This is one hundred percent positive information. We've been tracking him for a month."

"You mean, you've been spying on us?"

"Don't get all indignant! We were tracking this guy from another angle, and we traced him to your office."

"That's just . . . William Lee seems like a fairly common name. You could—"

"Yeah, I knew you'd say that. Take a look at these. They're transcripts of messages your boy's typed into his laptop."

As I read them, a feeling of vertigo came over me and I had to sit down. They were reports of goings-on in the office that would have been impossible to forge. Conversations between Dan and Shar he'd sat in on, conversations between him and me. I thought of cute, bland-looking William as I read the analyses before me: *The DNN hopes to gain power by redefining the Administration as illegitimate and marketing itself as the organization most able to reinstate a "legitimate" government.* Our ranks were staffed by "armchair revolutionaries" and "fuzzy-logic college kids," who had "focused the dissatisfactions of mainstream people uncomfortable with recent economic changes." That was the overview, which could have been pumped out by any Right Wing think tank. It was the personal stuff that infuriated me. He mentioned Dan Schwartz in stating that we weren't dependent on our leaders' personalities, but that we were *still vulnerable to well-conceived attacks on the leaders' prestige and credibility. Dan Schwartz has never married and seems to have no lasting romantic relationship. He seems less homosexual than sexually inept. Infiltration by a female agent could produce a highly credible sexual harassment or assault charge which would be particularly damaging given the DNN's constituency.* I saw my own name, where he described me as efficient and work-obsessed. He noted my new relationship with Joe Simic, which

I'd stupidly told him about immediately afterward. He had his own sinister take on it: *While the DNN's organizational strength is growing, it could be neutralized by fostering a rival power base, such as the Throwaways or other protest groups, and using our influence within those groups to cause friction.*

Influence within those groups . . . So the Throwaways had been penetrated, too. I looked up from the pages. Lando was watching me. I shook my head. "This is so *vile*! Look at this!"

I ranted on about William Lee: always the first to damn the Matthews Administration, the one who always wanted us to push harder, to break the law. He'd volunteered for every shit job there was, and it had gotten him a hook in nearly every one of our operations: outreach, logistics, media, membership. Good-looking, an accomplished climber who claimed to have soloed the highest mountains in eight Western states. He seemed to fancy himself a ladies' man in an overpolished, slightly formulaic way. He'd even asked me out once, and I'd almost said yes.

"Who does he work for? The FBI? Homeland Security?"

"We haven't been able to figure that out."

There I'd been, living in the secure little reality that "William Lee" had helped create for me. "How could we be so damned stupid!"

He put his hand on my shoulder. "You weren't stupid, Emily. It gives you a bad feeling, I know. But your most important secret, about how you're going to turn the lights out on the Business Symposium—you've kept that safe. You did what you were supposed to. You did well."

I felt less like a complete idiot, but I was still angry. "We're going straight to the press. We're going to embarrass Matthews like he's never been embarrassed before. And I'm going to meet with Joe Simic tomorrow and show him this."

"No. Not yet."

"What do you mean?"

"Don't expose him. Use him."

"How?"

Lando seemed to have it all planned out. "First, you sideline him. Get him out of the office. Tell him you need him to put up posters in Timbuktu for the next couple of weeks. The Spokane Association for the Mentally Challenged needs help stuffing envelopes: whatever. At the same time, you complain to him about how bad things are going. Send Shar and Dan a few interoffice memos whining that America just doesn't seem to give a shit. Maybe you brief your three or four most important liaisons and set up a secure communications network with them outside the office."

"Can it be that effective?"

"Oh, they've got other sources. But you might be able to head fake 'em, give yourself another five or ten percent advantage. But five or ten percent could be decisive. The main thing is, you don't want two thousand National Guard troops sealing off the Seattle Center because they know you're making the Long March. After the Symposium, you go public. It'll make a good follow-on to the demonstration."

"I'd need to clear this with Shar and Dan."

"Of course."

We linger awhile longer; then he brings me back to Seattle. "Good luck with our friend. Remember, it's important that he thinks nothing has changed."

The next day I put on my best act until I could grab a bite with Dan and Shar. I brought the transcripts, and I could see Dan quaver at the part about him being sexually inept. I felt bad for him because at heart I suspected it was true and that he wished it wasn't. Shar was so angry about the part about her sons that for a second, I thought she was going to go into William Lee's office and rip his face off. I managed to calm them down, keeping them focused on the idea that using William would be the best revenge. We came up with a dozen tasks that would take him out of the loop and agreed on what false information we would plant in our interoffice memos. A week after our meeting, I got a call from Lando telling me that our little counterintelligence operation was working: the spy's latest reports reflected our sense of disappointment and said that the demonstration would attract only small to moderate numbers, even though I was starting to sense that we were stronger than ever. "You're a natural, Emily," he said. "Let me know if you ever want a second job."

The world was feeling like a pretty wonderful place these days. The

Seattle Project was going well, and Real Vote! was gathering steam across the country. Minds were changing one at a time, and each one was a victory. Soon the West Coast militants would declare a cease-fire, and the violence of the last two years would be behind us. It felt like winning was possible, now, after years of losing. Through all this, I kept the knowledge of Lando close and quiet and golden.

11

*J*oby pulls up in his pickup with the last few bricks of ANFO wrapped in neat black plastic under a load of horse manure and dirty straw. "New plan—" He grins. "—we're just gonna compost the fucker."

Amonium nitrate and fuel oil are the cheeseburger and fries of the Resistance. Joby sweeps off the overburden and shines a red beam of light over the black Visqueen blocks in the bed. I don't need coffee to keep me on edge right now. We're hunched down in a thick stand of hemlocks about ten miles from the intake plant, a lucky spot of coniferous cover with a big wide clear-cut running through it. In the middle of that mass of nuked brush and razored-off trunk is a gravel road with a tidy little manhole winking up at the night sky. Mac saws through the lock, then grabs the pry bar and levers off the metal disk. He shines the flashlight onto the rungs. It looks smooth and industrial down there, its own kind of nothingness.

"Tonk? You ready?"

Tonk climbs down with his backpack; then we lower down the pieces of the bikes and the cart. Tonk starts assembling them while

Joby hauls the last of the ANFO over from the truck; then he climbs down, too. We toss the ANFO down to Joby brick by brick, then carefully lower down the detonator. Mac had welded up a harness for the bikes and the cart, and in our practice sessions they'd been able to assemble the whole package in fifteen minutes. Now they do it in twelve, keeping the detonator apart until they reach the target. We've calculated two hours to the target and an hour to get back, with thirty minutes of insurance.

"We're clear down here."

"Did you paint it?"

"Shit!" We hear the rattle of a paint can and then a hissing sound. X marks the spot.

"Now we're clear."

A little pause. This is where we should say something inspiring. McFarland takes a stab at it: "There's a lot of folks depending on you two. Win one for America. We'll rendezvous at oh-three-hundred. Godspeed."

Joby twists his round red face toward me from the well of darkness, but all I can see is the glittery white flashlight shining from his forehead and a puff of white mist. "The jubilee's coming to Water Solutions."

The jubilee. Bible code for the great leveling. "Amen, bro. Tonk!" A second headlamp blinds me. I grin down at him, give a little nod. "Go big."

He puts his hand over the lamp so I can see his smile. "Can't wait to see it on TV."

Their beams swirl crazily around the gray tube as they climb on the bikes; then the cart of explosives slides away as they pedal into the underworld. We wait until the hole turns black, then McFarland slides the manhole cover back and looks at me. After the bright beams from below his face is indistinct, and I am looking silently into the timeless shadow of McFarland. He's barely there: like me, barely there, somehow dissolved into other places and times even as we're vibrating in the November darkness of a country called America where some few want to rule and others resist and it always turns out like this, sooner or later, two spirits in a dark wood waiting for a rendezvous. A lot of things I'd like to tell McFarland right now.

"We'd better get moving, Lando." He flicks on his red-tinted head-lamp and we follow it through the woods back to the vehicles. I'll take Joby's pickup and hook up with Gonzalo in the city. Mac'll wait on a side road until Joby and Tonk pedal up on their mountain bikes. They'll have four hours to get back to Seattle before the Water Solutions show comes on. Good Morning, Mr. Sands.

Not much in my little tunnel of highway to distract me from all the things that might go wrong. Unknown sensors, unscheduled maintenance, gear failure, bad luck, the possibility that they've somehow known all along and are waiting to spring the trap. Tonk and Joby wiped out, State Troopers up ahead with their cars whaled up across the road. I'm wearing out my watch on the drive back, mentally synchronizing the time they should reach the target, the time they're arming the bomb, the time they're out. Ten minutes to pedal in the dark to McFarland's Jeep. I cover fifteen nervous miles and then my cell phone rings once and stops. They're traveling.

Gonzalo's waiting at his cave in front of a bank of computers and televisions. Emil's with him, monitoring a couple of screens and hanging on the master's every word. Now the information operation begins. Out in America the world is flipping on the box for their daily dose of How The World Is, supplied in bite-sized images by helpful Corporates. They want pictures: We'll give them pictures.

At 6:40, Gonzalo clicks a file on his computer screen and a cell phone dials the Cascadia plant. "Security."

Our computer-synthesized voice answers him. "Your facility is under attack by the Army of the Republic. The building will be destroyed in five minutes. You have five minutes to evacuate. Water belongs to everyone. The People have spoken." By the time the voice finishes we're blanketing the media with e-mails, while Gonzalo's computer calls KINO to give them the scoop. KINO is the only station close enough to get a live feed up in time, and helpfully we provide their contact information to all the nationals. Big day in the sun for small-town folks. We hit our mailing list to let them know an operation is about to happen and put up our indictment of Water Solutions on the A⊕R Web site.

"We're getting hits," Emil reports.

We've said five minutes, a sleight of hand for the twenty they've really got. We need to give Big Media time to set up the megaphones that relay His Master's Voice, but not enough for Whitehall to sniff out the package. We watch the televisions. At one minute after the warning, America's fresh morning faces are still talking about diets and cars.

"Call the Dumpster in, Gonzalo. They think we're bullshitting."

Gonzalo dials a number, and two hundred miles away a small bomb explodes in a Dumpster across the parking lot from KINO. A bomb threat isn't news. An explosion is. Gonzalo's computer makes a second call. "Your station is not under attack, but the Cascadia pirate water facility will be destroyed in exactly four minutes. The people's water cannot be owned."

A sudden interruption on the screen. Cut to the situation room and a new actor holding a white piece of paper. Serious, so serious because now we're ramping up some *real* entertainment. "Ladies and gentlemen, we're tuning in to a rapidly developing terror situation in Eastern Oregon. We go to our affiliate station KINO in Hood River, Oregon."

The Brand X KINO guy, looking cancer-grim but no doubt totally digging the excitement. His anchorman scowl: ". . . has just exploded outside our studios and is apparently linked to an attack on the nearby Cascadia water plant."

"There you, go, hoss!" Gonzalo says, sipping from his black soda can, "I thought that'd get your attention!"

Within five minutes a half-dozen major markets are carrying live feeds of the facility. The big intake plant is viewed from a distance, doubtless cordoned off by Whitehall. Very dull television, basically a four-story structure with some tubes and a logo, no smoke, no bodies, so the commentators are desperate to keep people entertained until the main event, coloring in the history of the AOR and mixing up some crap from other groups and the voice-over of the "counter-terrorism experts" on their go-to list. They're pulling out all their best adjectives, the classic *shadowy*, the faux-compassionate *misguided*. *Violent. Extremist. Bloodthirsty.* The Polling operation is good for a quick rehash, and they pull away long enough to show Polling getting onto a jet, then to the same old rainy footage of police lines and blue-shirts and Polling's sheet-covered body. They're back in a flash, though, to that scratchy winter landscape. Gonzalo sends them a new threat, a little handholding so they know we won't let them down after they've so graciously interrupted their normal programming for us: Don't worry guys, we're there for you.

"We made NPR," Gonzalo says. Turning up the radio, that comforting reasonable voice: the soft side of the iron fist.

Emil checks our site. "Shit, man! Traffic's exploding."

My old friend Mr. Headache is rapping at my temple again, but I'm too busy to pay any attention to him. On TV they're going over the history of Water Solutions in the "neutral" tones cooked up by Corporate image consultants; then they connect our attack on Water Solutions to the DNN's Water Project, a four-second flash of demonstrators outside an office. Smoothing the way for the next crackdown.

I look at my watch. "Two minutes till it blows, Gonzalo."

"Okay. Let's try it."

He clicks on another file icon, and a blue band starts crawling across the middle of the TV screen. WATER BELONGS TO EVERYONE, NOT THE CORPORATIONS! FIGHT BACK, AMERICA! WWW.ARMYOFTHEREPUBLIC .ORG.RU. STAND UP FOR YOUR COUNTRY!

"Yes!"

Suddenly the message disappears again.

"Shit! There goes five weeks of work."

"Hey. You still got twelve seconds coast to coast."

"They saw it," Emil says. "We're getting a new spike on the site."

"Are they clicking through to the platform statement?"

A pause as he checks the stats. "Only about twenty percent, but they'll be back after the show."

So they're getting our word from the platform page: Sensible trade laws. Real environmental protection. Health care for everyone. Fairness in Media. Re-nationalization of all public functions and land taken over by corporations. Basic good government. Why do we have to blow shit up for this?

One more minute and the *if*s are really screaming at me. What if the bomb doesn't go off, or the charge is too small? What if Whitehall's sent a guy down to defuse it? A win either way for them: they get a hero or a martyr, and either one's a propaganda gold mine.

My armpits have gotten slippery and I can't stay in my chair. I jump to my feet, check my watch. Thirty seconds. Gonzalo and Emil are glowing in the luminescence of their screens, both with white cotton gloves on. Ready for the clean out.

At precisely seven the ground at the base of the intake plant dissolves into brown smoke, and then the lower section of the building seems to heave upward. An audible gasp of surprise is heard in the background of the camera, the picture wiggles slightly as the blast wave ripples through the earth, a wall of expanding smoke and a dull boom as the sound wave reaches the microphone. A general collapse sets in at the front of the building facing the camera: the façade slides down into the smoke like a calving glacier in a nature film. The off-camera crew fills the background with their cries of panic as a few bits of debris shower the ground nearby.

"Right *on*!" Gonzalo shouts, "Fucking *incredible*! Lando, man, this is so excellent!"

I feel a sense of fatal power coursing through me, covering over the dread that runs just as deep. We've done it. The whirlpool is spinning faster, and I can feel it tugging at my feet even as Water Solutions begins to descend into the funnel. Maybe it's the sweet black sludge I keep sucking down, or two nights without sleep, but a wave of nausea rolls over me and I have to sit down.

"You okay, Lando?"

My head's down in my palm and a sudden sweat slicks up my hairline. "Sure."

It's on all five screens now, with news actors and video clips, a whole picture show getting a massive share of a multimillion-mind market against our little Web site and its twenty thousand words. All negative, but that's okay: everyone has to knuckle under at first for propriety's sake. We condemn this. . . . We condemn that. . . . It was the afterburn we were looking for, that deep satisfaction inside twenty million people who wouldn't have their noses shoved into the corporate water trough. We could only hope for some tiny light to go off in people's heads. Maybe now they could stand up for themselves and say *"No!"* I push the nausea away and get on my feet.

"Let's clean it out, guys."

Gonzalo and Emil start powering down and pulling cables. The van's parked right outside the door, and when it's all packed up we'll haul it out and move on. I start bleaching the bathrooms and the kitchen, vacuum, spread some hairs around. In twenty minutes we're loading up and heading for Gonzalo's new cave, my brain burning along on some mix of caffeine, adrenaline, and pure amazement. We've just outwitted the baddest security outfit on the planet, and millions of dollars of carefully purchased influence has been blown away in three seconds. We can do this, I'm thinking. We can really do this.

12

I met up with Walter in midafternoon, West Coast time, when they waved me through the cordon of security surrounding the smoking bomb site. A cold wind was blowing and the smoke crumpled off to the side as it rose off the building. I'd forgotten weather existed. Walter pulled out an extra fleece jacket, thoughtful as always, and I mumbled a thanks and put it on under my coat. He toured me around the crater, sidestepping doors and office partitions and white ceramic fragments of a toilet that had avalanched off the building when it collapsed.

"They accessed the pipe through a manhole ten miles from here. We're getting boot and tire prints. It looks like they used bicycles to haul the explosive, and when we're done sorting through the debris I expect we'll find some kind of cart to move them."

I was too numb to ask questions. I'd never seen anything like it in real life. The blast had sliced off the side of the building and I could see half rooms still intact with dust-covered office furniture and gray-screened computers. Bats of pink insulation fizzed out of the walls, and high-pressure hydraulic piping was twisted toward the sky like crazed cannon barrels. I stood there for a while gazing at each torn-open office and hallway, as if I were looking at the cavities and ventricles of my own body. I supposed I should feel rage, but all I could feel was a deep incoherence. A small brief surge of consolation: At least I hadn't let them make me sign personally.

Our engineering supervisor approached us. "They're still stabilizing the building, Mr. Sands, so we haven't been able to go inside and see what's salvageable. As soon as we can do that, we can put together a time frame for repairs."

I didn't answer. The building was a teardown. Even I could see that. What was left of the computers and the physical plant was so damaged that the simplest solution would be to dig a big hole in the ground and push it in. So much for meeting the performance clause. Barrington had already summoned me for a meeting the next morning, and I was analyzing it from their viewpoint. As a going project it penciled out to a couple billion. As salvage value, there were rights-of-way and piping still worth hundreds of millions to Bechtel or Halliburton. The quick solution for Barrington. All they had to do was get rid of me.

Someone had brought in a silver-sided catering truck, and I wandered over there for coffee. The feel of the warm paper cup against my fingertips seemed more real than the destruction around me, and I stood in the lee of the truck and looked at the perfect triangles of white bread, the plastic tubs of coleslaw and potato salad. I hadn't eaten food like this in a couple of decades. The day's hot dish was Salisbury steak with mashed potatoes. I ordered it out of some weird nostalgia, but at the first taste an inexplicable wave of grief went through me, a sense of wasted effort, of wasted life, and I had to fight back tears. Walter drank his coffee and stared discreetly out at the landscape.

Neither of us said much until we were on the Gulfstream, headed for D.C. I wondered how much longer I'd have this jet, how much longer until I'd be flying commercial, like everyone else. We were heading East, away from the setting sun, and soon the portholes became flat obsidian inlays in the jet's walls. I was outside there, flapping in the empty stratosphere. Why was this happening? All my life I'd been able to sidestep any disaster that came at me, to go around my opponents, to outwit or outbluff them. Even in this case, I'd been set to close a secret agreement next week with a Japanese consortium that would get the Barrington Group off my back for good. But that deal was dead now. As dead as John Polling.

Walter moved over to the couch near me, offered me a glass of tonic water. It pulled me back into the little capsule of the plane, and I refocused on him as he began in calm, sympathetic tones.

"Jim, you know the story of Troy."

"Of course."

"One of the basic lessons of *The Iliad* is that if you don't have force, it doesn't matter how right you are. Troy didn't start that war: the Greeks did. But once the Greeks showed up on the beach, it didn't matter who was right anymore. If a society doesn't have the will to protect itself, that society will crumble."

I didn't answer him. I knew he didn't need an answer.

"Jim, when you've had enough, we'll make it stop."

Until now, the shock had been so intense that the anger stayed distant and cold, like a red glow on the horizon. As Walter started winding up, though, I could feel it drawing closer. "This is not the time for a sales pitch, Walter."

"This isn't a sales pitch. This is a conversation about the future of your company." He settled back into his couch. "And maybe of this whole country."

"Please don't tell me how this never would have happened if I'd signed on to Whitehall's counterterrorism program. In my opinion, there's a real question of negligence here."

"Jim, they could have attacked that facility any number of ways. They could have crashed a plane into it, they could have floated an explosive device—"

"I'm not interested in how many exotic ways they could have attacked it! I'm interested in not having it attacked! When I hire what's supposed to be the best security firm in the world and my most sensitive asset gets blown up by a bunch of punks, I expect a little more than a laundry list of all the ways Whitehall could have failed! What the fuck am I paying you for?"

He raised his eyebrows and turned away. He seemed to know that I needed someone to be mad at, and that was his particular cross to bear. "Look, I'm sorry about the intake plant, but I told you two months ago: You can't win playing defense. We either go after these guys or we give up and let them and their fellow travelers run the show. But be clear on one thing: If they're running the show, you're out of business."

"I can't talk about this right now."

"I'm sorry but we need to talk about it now, because Barrington will be asking about it tomorrow morning." I looked at him sharply and he raised his hands. "I'm just being straight with you, Jim. We're the designated security contractors and the Fund communicates with us as per their agreement with you. I'd be letting you down professionally and as a friend if I tried to sugarcoat things. And as a friend, I'm telling you—" He leaned a bit closer. "—this is the wrong time to piss off your creditors."

Below us, the lights of Denver spread out in a flat circuit. I thought of my previous meeting with the Barrington Fund, when they'd nudged me about Whitehall's new security initiatives. It looked like Whitehall and the fund had a closer relationship than I'd realized.

"Don't forget who the enemy is here, Jim. It's not Whitehall or Barrington. It's the Army of the Republic. And their allies. Fortunately, we have a strategy for going after them."

After the relentless psychological beating I'd taken that day, there was something very comforting in the idea that Whitehall could spread a vast mantle of protection over the company, over me. I at least had an obligation to listen. "And what strategy is that?"

"The Algerian model. The French developed it in the fifties. In the classic guerrilla organization, the members only know the people in their cell, except for one, who'll have contacts going up and maybe laterally, too. The idea is, you get somebody, and you find out who else is in his cell. You round those guys up until you get the guy who can lead you to the next cell. Every time you clean out a cell, you get the information you need to jump to the next cell. You keep getting their most experienced people, with the most extensive connections, and after a while, they're too debilitated to function effectively and they collapse. Then you just mop up the remnants so they don't rebuild. With enough defeats, the whole idea eventually just goes out of style."

It sounded like some World War II novels I'd read, but in those books, it wasn't the good guys using those methods. "The French lost Algeria, Walter."

"The French lost Algeria because public opinion in the mother country got in their way. That's not going to happen here. This is a fight for the homeland, not a colony. The same method was used successfully in Uruguay, Argentina, Chile, Greece, El Salvador. It works."

I recognized that all the places he'd mentioned—from Argentina to El Salvador—had murdered and tortured tens of thousands of innocent people, but it seemed somehow tactless to ask about it. We were exploring this intellectually.

"Let's get this straight. We track these guys down and arrest them—"

"We don't arrest: We capture."

"I'm not sure I understand the difference."

"Arrest is a legal process. Capture is a simple fact."

"And if they resist being captured—?"

"That works, too." He read my silence. "Remember, these are people who've declared war on the State. They've robbed, they've bombed, and they've murdered. They call themselves an army. You can't compromise with these people, Jim. They hate everything you stand for. And they want to hurt you."

I felt the rage welling up again. "They're little shits who can't build anything! All they can do is destroy what other people build! They're fucking sociopaths! They're fucking . . . they're just . . . motherfucking punks, goddamn them!"

A moment ago, I'd been fairly calm, but now my hands were clenched together and my chest was vibrating with the intense pressure that seemed to rise up from my stomach. The white ceiling flashed pink for a moment then settled back to its normal color. I took in a deep breath then let it out slowly. Walter was watching me. I wasn't sure how much time had passed. I decided that losing control was a luxury I wasn't going to allow myself again. I would deal with Barrington, and I would deal with the Army of the Republic. Right now I had to be cool, and that was all. I listened.

We needed an effort that wasn't hindered by the courts, Walter said, where information could be gathered without encumbrances and acted on quickly by competent people. This was an enemy that crossed all the normal boundaries of civil, criminal, social, and terrorist, and it would take a different kind of effort. "See, Jim, there's a whole range of groups out to take you down, from the Seattle Water

Projects and the so-called Democracy networks all the way to the Army of the Republic. At this point we need to ac vigorously across the entire spectrum, and if that means getting rou er than you or I would normally accept, then we'll just have to make t sacrifice. It's not just for Water Solutions: It's for the good of our wh e society."

It sounded ugly, but there was a certain comfort in t ness at the moment. It was a relief to stop thinking about the rights terror- ists and their sympathizers for a change and to consider t e oblem from a different, more professional viewpoint. "Have you ught about what's going to happen when the word gets out about t is cause it will get out. You're talking about forcibly detaining pe- That doesn't stay quiet."

He seemed unconcerned. "I suppose the public might think t there's a war going on between competing radical factions, or mayb between right-wing paramilitaries and radicals. There'll be plenty of evidence turning up in the media to support those theories. Either way, it's nobody's business, is it? If it comes back to Whitehall, we're govern- ment contractors. Take it up with the government. End of story."

I was feeling a little more balanced now, almost back in the game. "I take it there's a price tag attached to this."

It was an offensive way of putting the question and I could see his annoyance that I'd reduced a matter of national security to dollars and cents. "Unfortunately, yes. It costs a lot to hire professionals and keep them in the field. There's twenty-four-hour surveillance teams, undercover agents, computer specialists. You need people to effect a capture and to interview the suspects. You need secure places to hold the bad guys until you turn them over to government custody. It starts to add up. What we're looking for from associate businesses like yours is a sponsorship of two million dollars a month until the threat has been completely neutralized."

"I'm already paying Whitehall more than a million dollars a month for security!"

"That's a different mission. You want to go after the Army of the Republic? Whitehall will go after them for you. But we can't do it at our expense."

"What's my alternative?"

He was silent for a moment, then cocked his head thoughtfully. "You'll have to talk to Barrington about that."

He rose and fetched a tray of smoked salmon and caviar from the galley, then set it down on the coffee table and peeled off the plastic film. After that, he came back with a bottle of iced aquavit and two frozen cocktail glasses. "I know you too well. Here." He handed me the frosted drink, smoking with cold. "It's been a long goddamn day." He patted me on the shoulder. "Things are going to get better, my friend. Don't worry."

I took a sip, desperate to relax. The plane felt like it was holding still in a black void, eternally stuck somewhere over the Midwest. Tomorrow I had to face my creditors, and I hadn't yet figured out my position. I wasn't even sure I had a position to figure out: Barrington would be dictating my next move. I sensed that conversation would depend somehow on what I told Walter. I pushed a cracker into the black eggs and ate it, but it felt dry and dusty in my mouth.

"So when does this counterterrorism program end, Walter? How long am I paying Whitehall two million dollars a month?"

"Oh, there'll be predetermined criteria. You'll notice terrorist incidents becoming fewer and farther between. At a certain point, the president will declare victory and take all the credit. The so-called civil society groups like Protect Our Water will putter along, but they'll have to play by the rules, and those rules will keep them from creating too many problems. Don't worry." He smiled. "We intend to work ourselves out of a job."

I reached my house at one in the morning, and Anne was already asleep. Walter's words had faded away and left me dangling between the wreckage of my water plant and the impending meeting I had with the Fund tomorrow morning. I put on my pajamas, still wrinkled from the night before, and thought how innocuous I must look in them with my small belly and my graying hair. Why was I failing? I'd hired the best people and I'd planned and executed without fail for fifteen years, bold when boldness was called for, cautious when it wasn't. And yet here I was about to be pushed out of my own business by arrogant little bureaucrats like Denton.

My father had worked his whole life for the City of Chevy Chase, and though he was a kind man—loving to me and my sisters, a Little League coach—in his best year he'd earned just over thirty-two thousand dollars, and his death left us heartbroken and threadbare in our little suburban ranch house. I was the oldest, and I'd always felt it was up to me to redeem him somehow from his unintentional abandonment of us, to protect the family, and, when they no longer needed protection, to protect my own against all the devastating surprises the world could throw at them. Now, in my floppy pajamas, I'd somehow become a man who couldn't even protect himself, who'd failed even at the task of raising his son. Had I somehow wanted the wrong things? Was that my crime? I turned off the dressing room light and crawled into bed. Anne woke up and turned to face me.

"How are you?" she said quietly.

I sighed. I was trying to figure out how to answer her. "I don't even know anymore."

She put her arms around my neck and rubbed the knotted muscles at my shoulder blades. "Tina called. She wanted to let you know she's thinking of you."

"That's nice. How about Joshua?"

"I haven't heard from him."

"That's right—he's out camping. I'm sure he's having a great time."

"I'm sorry." She moved her massage up to the back of my neck. "So what comes next?"

"Tomorrow morning I meet with the Barrington Group. They inform me that since I can't meet the performance clause of our agreement that they have the option of turning their loan into equity."

"What does that mean?"

"They go from being lenders to majority stockholders. They can keep me around. They can force me out. They can sell the company to one of the big boys or break it up and liquidate it piece by piece. They're the ones with all the choices."

"You're an individual. You always have choices."

She was doing her best. "I'm sorry, Annie, but I can't Zen my way out of this. If I get into it with Barrington it'll be a bloodbath, and they've got a lot more blood."

She propped herself up on her elbow and I could see her face in the pink light through the window. "No. You always have choices. I understand what it took to create Water Solutions, and if you want to fight to keep it, I support you. But if it all goes away and it's just the two of us, that's okay with me. There are always new possibilities, and

I know you could do something really valuable, maybe even better than what you're doing now."

"I don't want to go out like this, to be forced out."

"That's ego, Jimmy. What do you have to prove to anyone? If you want to hold on to the company, I know there's no one craftier, or tougher or—" She smiled in the muffled light. "—more *devious* than you! The whole world knows that. But you don't have to hold on. You can let it go."

I was quiet as I thought about what she said, imagining myself on a sailboat, or winning a big grant for a bankrupt inner-city school again. Those parents had really valued me, in a way that no board of directors ever would. Before that, in Wyoming, being twenty, having everything and nothing. "You're right."

She moved her fingers up to my hair and threw her leg over mine, then began kissing my neck. We hadn't made love since that disastrous dinner episode a month ago, and her compact body felt surprising and familiar at the same time. As I ran my hands along her contours beneath the covers, all the wreckage of the day began to lose its structure and sink beneath the molten pool of darkness and touch. She rolled on top of me and let her soft breast fall into my mouth, and finally everything was far away, all the burdens of being James Sands flew upward like ashes, and I was back with the woman I'd been astonished by thirty years ago, that I had loved and somehow become separated from. Earnest, pleasing, she clambered up and sat astride me, her still-beautiful cascade of shoulders, waist, and flaring hips carved out in the gleaming shadows of our room, like smooth stones in a streambed. She was a swan, my mate for life, and for that small piece of dark eternity whirling through the night suburbs of Washington, nothing else mattered.

They put us in the Motherwell room again, seating me with Jack Mossberg, our CFO, while we waited for them to make their appearance. I stared over at the waves that seemed to descend the canvas in a mist of scarlet and maroon. It was like a sign I couldn't read. What had Motherwell meant by that strange undulating red space? "What do you think of that painting, Jack?"

"If they're in the market for more of those," he sneered, "my six-year-old's available." Jack was a fighter, and he'd come ready to fight because that suited him better than being ready to crawl, which was our more likely position. His idea was that if they tried a hostile takeover, we use the "crazy guy with a hand grenade" defense, ball up the company with lawsuits and debt so that everybody would lose. He had just the law firm to do it. I suggested we listen to what the Fund had to say before we pulled the pin. "Just lie back and sandbag them today," I said, bluffing my own man. "I've been in worse situations than this before."

A cohort of four men came in with laptops. The first to enter was young, blond Denton, who seemed to wear the same faint smirk as when he'd called me on the now-dead Japanese initiative I'd hinted at in October. I also recognized Bernhard Weitzman, who'd flown in from Belgium, and I moved to shake hands with him first. He was the senior of the group, looking very Continental with his stylish glasses and his aura of cologne. He was about my own age, though slightly shorter and rounder. A shining scalp rose from the gray fringe that remained at his temples. We'd gone out to dinner in Brussels about a year ago, before I'd known he might be my executioner. We'd finished the dinner with a glass of cognac, talking about our children. I tried to resuscitate that feeling now. "That Motherwell—" I motioned toward the huge postage stamp. "—do you know what it's called?"

It stopped him for a moment, and he looked it over. "No idea."

We took our seats and Bernhard relayed the Fund's sympathy and concern over the bombing. We murmured our gratitude back to him. "Very well," he began again in a crisper tone. "We're all adults here, so I'll get to the point. It doesn't seem that Water Solutions will be able to fulfill the performance clause of its contract. From the reports we've gotten, the Cascadia project is six months away from getting online now, at best."

"That's probably a good ballpark estimate." I thought I carried off the casual act well, considering that every person at the table knew that I had my neck in the noose and the scaffold was about to drop.

"This is a contingency the Fund foresaw, so we already have a decision on it. I'll be humanitarian and let you know quickly. The Fund *will* be converting our loan to an equity stake in Water Solutions. We could certainly cover ourselves with the salvage value of the pipeline and a few more assets, but we feel there's enough potential for the completed Cascadia project to help the project go forward. We'll provide auxiliary financing until the insurance claims are settled, which will also count toward equity."

So, we'd made first hurdle: They weren't going to break up the company for salvage value. They were going to take it over. They would now be the majority shareholders, and I served at their pleasure. I glanced over at Jack, who didn't betray either relief or curiosity. I suppose he still had his thumb on the pin of the hand grenade.

"I'm glad to hear that," I answered evenly. "We've all put a lot of work into Cascadia. The intake plant is just one part of it."

"Exactly. You're probably wondering what your role will be going forward. We realize that you're not completely at fault here. It's difficult to predict a massive terror attack like that, and unfortunately, it is inevitable that some of them get through."

"I would point out that we've been complying with all of Whitehall's security protocols as the Barrington Group specified."

Something flickered in Weitzman's face. He gave a half glance toward Denton then controlled the impulse.

"Yes," he went on. "Again, to be brief, we've decided to keep you on as the CEO of Water Solutions, James. And of course, we see no reason for you to change your management team. You built this company and you know your business better than anyone. However, we're going to have to insist that you sign personally. The Fund doesn't want to take on all this risk alone."

I swallowed. I was hanging by a thread now. I couldn't keep our personal assets out of it anymore. The houses, the real estate and stock: it was all going to be wagered on the company's success. "I can do that," I said quietly.

"Excellent," Weitzman said. "I'm glad that's finally settled."

A sense of deep relief flooded through me, like a flush of drugs into my system. I was still running the company. Even if I signed personally, even if I had the Barrington Group breathing down my neck, I still had a position I could maneuver from, and maneuvering was something I did well. Also, a change from loan to equity wasn't the sort of thing that made the business magazines, the way the dumping of a CEO did. After a few more minutes, Weitzman split off Jack and two of their numbers people to start looking at the financial aspects of the new arrangement, and excused himself from the room. That left me alone with Denton.

"Here we are again." He smiled.

"It does seem to keep turning out like that, doesn't it?"

"You talked to Walter last night, on the airplane."

"I did."

"Weitzman was easy on you. He likes you. But it's not my job to like people. Personally, I think if you'd given Whitehall the latitude it needed, as I urged you to do last time we met, this might never have happened."

"Whitehall had all the latitude it needed to protect that facility."

"The security arrangements for Cascadia were drafted by your people before Whitehall came on board," he insisted.

"Whitehall was free to make changes."

"They were your arrangements!"

I eyed him without answering: his combed, straw-colored hair and gym-trimmed shoulders made him annoyingly flawless. "Look, Mr. Denton. I'm sure you aren't here to defend Whitehall's good name. What's this meeting about?"

"I'm sorry. People accuse me of being tactless—"

I smiled thinly. "You *are* tactless."

He laughed. "Yeah. I think that's why they keep me around. It's like this: You're going to have to do what Whitehall tells you."

"You mean the two-million-dollar-a-month counterinsurgency program?"

"Bingo."

"I just got the full story last night," I said quickly. "I'd pretty much decided it was probably a necessary step."

That smirk again. "Well, now you've got one less thing to think about. Nobody needs these guys running around whacking people and blowing stuff up. They're a pain in the ass, and so are their sympathizers."

"I agree."

"Good. We're on the same page. As long as we're on the same page, you're the Man."

"Understood."

"And of course, it would be a very bad thing if anyone else knew you and I had this conversation. This is the kind of thing the media really goes to town on."

"I realize that."

"Good. Whitehall will help you set up payments for the program. They've got a whole department for that. It'll go through so many rabbit holes it would take an army of auditors to follow it." He gave a slanted little grin. "And I don't see anybody sending that army."

My mouth felt dry. I stared at him uncomfortably, feeling like the meeting was over but that I was trapped there in the room with him. He seemed content to stretch it out.

"I understand you're speaking at the National Business Symposium in a couple of days," he finally said.

"That's correct."

"Right after the president. Impressive. What are you going to talk about?"

"Public–private partnerships."

He nodded. "You might want to throw in some antiterror context, under the circumstances. You've hit the news cycle—you might as well make hay while the sun shines. Something about 'standing firm' always goes over well."

"I'll keep that in mind."

"Great." He stood up. "I'll try to catch your speech."

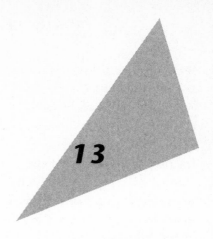

13

*T*here we go!" Dan said. "That's a happy man right there, Emily! Your buddies in the ski masks gave him the best Christmas present he ever could have hoped for."

The head of Homeland Security was on the screen in front of a flag of the United States, his square-jowled cardboard face urging Americans to "stand united against domestic terrorists and those who aid and abet them." Shar and I were in Dan's office to check on how the government was playing this. "Some terrorists, such as those who struck today, use the traditional weapons of violence and fear. Others hide under the guise of civil protest, and manipulate our democratic institutions to achieve the same ends."

"What do you think that's going to do to turnout?" Dan raged. *"'Hey, everyone, come downtown and help the terrorists!'"* He was starting to lose it. "These goddamned juvenile delinquents have done more to isolate us in ten minutes than Matthews has in the last three years."

"We don't know that yet."

"It's staring us in the face!"

I had no way to defend myself, and for the hundredth time I felt that wash of humiliation and anger at the way Lando had used me. He'd set me up perfectly, manipulated the entire organization into staging the Seattle Project, and now he'd made us look like complete idiots, especially me. To make it worse, I was expecting my period, which always left me ready to burst into tears one minute and whack someone with a frying pan the next. I'd spent the last twenty-four hours reliving every second of my meetings with Lando from a fresh new viewpoint: one where everything was phony. He was probably bragging to his buddies now about the hippie chick he'd seduced with his mooney-eyed talk about the Revolution, and now, the biggest laugh, fifty thousand people were headed for a showdown with the Seattle cops.

Dan turned up the television and leaned close to Shar and me. The fact that he was speaking in a soft voice didn't make him sound less angry. "We're not moving our people downtown to help the Direct Response Groups. I told the mayor we would stay put. I'm not going to squander a long-term relationship for the sake of some *maybe* deal with a Militant Group."

I was feeling even sicker now. I thought of Dave and the crowd at the Convergence Center. "Dan, we have an obligation—"

"We have an obligation to build a credible resistance movement! I don't know what got into your head about these militants, but in two years they're all going to be in jail or dead. I don't want the DNN to be buried with them!"

The shame of it all hit me with a slap. I felt my eyes tearing up.

Shar saw how paralyzed I was. "Back off, Dan. Emily's right. They never promised a cease-fire before the demonstration. Just because Homeland is making the predictable statements doesn't mean we don't still have a deal. And I'm not convinced what the militants did was so off base. This is corporate news we're watching. It's their job to show . . ." She glanced at the screen. "Hey! Speaking of the Devil . . ."

Dan scowled at the monitor. "And fuck you, too, Sands!"

The man we all recognized as James Sands, CEO of Water Solutions and Cascadia, came on the screen, with his usual smug executive façade looking sleepless and tense as a sympathetic interviewer lobbed him softballs about the bombing. He gave the company version of the noble Cascadia project and announced that reconstruction would begin immediately.

Out in the entryway, a group of staffers watching the same

broadcast sent up a flurry of angry comments. We still had a lot of people who had battled Water Solutions through the courts and the referendum process only to be outspent and outmaneuvered. They couldn't care less about the Army of the Republic's methods.

"I'm not so sure it's going to hurt turnout," Shar said. She gave him a pointed look. "Maybe we should just hold off on the recriminations until we see what develops."

I dragged myself back to my office feeling pretty beaten up, but I didn't have much time to wallow in it. In the twenty minutes away from my desk I'd gotten fifteen messages. Two were from logistics people reporting on sound systems and medical facilities. Four were affiliates reporting that their groups would be there. One was the tech person setting up the Direct Response Group's communications center downtown. Another was from the local ACLU chapter: Their head person was coming in for the demonstration and they wanted to reconfirm his spot on the podium to address the crowd. "Yeah, One P.M. between the Rasta Rockets and Tom Hayden is just great." They liked the billing, not knowing that by that time much of the crowd might already be facing off with the police ten blocks away. Or not.

The last message was a clear familiar voice with a vaguely New England accent. "Hi, Emily, this is Peter of the Wayfarer Pub. I wanted to let you know about our new happy hour promotion. Red Hook will be half price starting today at four o'clock. Now you can find the best beer in the Northwest at a great discount. I hope we'll see you here soon. Thanks."

So, he wanted to gloat! My stomach started churning as I listened to it again to get the information. The Red level of the Macy's parking tower, in the northwest corner. Okay. Let's see him gloat!

I walked over in a cool rage and rode the elevator to the Red level. Lando was waiting for me near the stairway in his overcoat and a stocking cap, wearing a silly-looking smile, like a puppy. When he tried to put his arms around me I pushed him with both hands and he went stumbling backwards.

"You lied to me!"

The smile went away. "I never lied to you! We said a cease-fire *after* the demonstration!"

"You used me!"

His eyes narrowed angrily. "Come on! It was a bright flash and a big noise! So what? You guys tried for four years to stop Cascadia and you failed. We stopped it!"

"At what cost?"

"What cost? In case you haven't noticed, there's a deep fucking sense of well-being out there that the Citizens of Washington and Oregon finally got some payback on their number one Corporate abuser."

"No! You're wrong! People are scared, Lando! And when they're scared, they go with whoever offers them safety." His face kept the same infuriating certainty. "What is it with you? Was this some ego thing? *Hey, look at us, we're the Army of the Republic! We can blow things up!*"

"Yes, Mommy, that was it!" He rolled his eyes. "Listen! We kicked the Corporates in the balls again so they'd remember what we can do if they start fucking with groups like yours. We had to show them the Boss-man can be reached. And you know what? America *heard* and America *saw*, and America's going to *show up* for you tomorrow ready to fight for their country!"

"Who appointed you Defender of the People?"

"My conscience! Just like you!"

I shook my head at him. "You think you're like us, Lando, but you're not! We are a mass movement! You and your friends are nothing but an arrogant self-appointed elite trying to game the system, just like the Corporates you hate. And you're going to bring a ton of shit down on your heads, and on ours, too!"

He looked confused. "Emily . . ." He opened his hands, then said weakly, "This is what it takes to gather the sparks."

I shook my head at the bizarre non sequitur. "What are you talking about?"

He pushed the whole idea away. "Forget it." He put on that cool façade again, like his version of a deal-making businessman: "Look, the bottom line is, we're declaring a cease-fire as soon as you guys shut down the Symposium. You need to stick to your original plan. March your people downtown, like you said."

"It sounds like you're the one who wants to be the Boss-man, Lando." He didn't answer, but I could see it bothered him. "Not that it's any of your business, but Dan doesn't want to do that anymore. He wants to keep everyone at the Seattle Center now."

"Fuck!" he exhaled. "What about Shar?"

"She's on the fence."

"Great. And where are you?"

I looked at him for a long time. Everything was all mixed up. "Where I am is thinking that our personal relationship was a bad idea and that it needs to be over."

He swayed backwards and was quiet for a few seconds. He said softly: "I didn't use you." There was a strange flutter of hurt in his voice. "You think I wanted Cascadia? You have no idea!" The little flicker of vulnerability disappeared, and he took on that infuriating certainty again. "This is what had to be, Emily. I've done what I had to do every step of the way, and whether you recognize it or not, shutting down the Business Symposium is what you have to do. It's time for the People to stand up to these fuckers." He tossed his head. "And if I had to help you figure that out, well, so be it. You ought to be thanking me."

"God! How did I not see what an arrogant manipulative . . . *asshole* you are? And I thought I was protecting you!" I took a step toward him. "Whatever happens tomorrow, the AOR is obligated to declare a cease-fire, as we agreed. And after that, *if* we have some reason to see each other, you and I stick to the issues, period!" Before I could stop it, I heard myself spit out one last command. "And don't go bragging to your buddies about how you bagged that chick from the DNN!"

He stiffened when I said that, nodded his head absently. His whole blustering guerrilla aura had deserted him, and I could barely hear him when he spoke. "I'd never do that." He made a little shuffling motion and half extended his arms, then dropped one and gave me an awkward pat on the shoulder. "Good luck tomorrow." He turned and walked across the oil-spotted cement before he stopped and threw one last line back at me. "Show them who you are."

I made it as far as the park across from the office before I sat down and burst into tears in front of the statue of Chief Seattle, a man who'd had his own sadness. How stupid I'd been—pining away for a romance-novel utopia with a man who wouldn't even tell me his real name! Like my old boyfriend had told me when he'd left: I always had one foot in a world that didn't exist yet, and never would, because once I got there, I'd have one foot in the next. I sat sobbing about the absurdity of my life for about fifteen minutes, until finally the tide receded enough for me to realize with horror that I'd been away from my desk nearly forty-five minutes and everyone was depending on me! I scraped myself off the bench and hurried inside.

I started listening to the nineteen fresh messages in my mailbox. The first was poor Will Lee, calling in from Spokane. "Yeah, Emily, this is Will. I really think my job out here is done and that I could contribute a lot more to the cause back at the office, so, please give me a call . . . ."

That made me smile. I dived into the frantic last-minute crises that had stacked up in my absence. Our child-care coordinator had a family emergency and we needed to replace her. Two volunteers were feuding about who would introduce the Rasta Rockets. The legal team had some pamphlets they wanted distributed and media people who'd been brushed off by Dan or Shar were asking to interview me.

I couldn't gauge the effect the Cascadia bombing would have on turnout. We had a good list of groups who promised to show up—environmentalists, public employees' unions, war veterans, retirees. As of two days ago, we were expecting at least three thousand of our core members. But the list of those not coming was long and worrisome: no Teamsters, no Longshoremen. No Christian Fundamentalists, no Throwaways. No Rotarians. Still not the kind of group that police would refuse to club. Not yet. They would do as they were told, and we would face them and there was no getting around that.

I worked until ten o'clock at night then decided to stop by the Response Commons, a warehouse downtown that the Direct Response Group had rented as their headquarters. It was buzzing with volunteers, most of them young, casually dressed in fleece or baggy sweaters, festooned with beards, facial jewelry, tattoos. Someone had stored an entire set of giant puppets in the main room, so there were twelve-foot-tall butterflies, bears, eagles, trees, and an effigy of Matthews with dollar signs for eyes. I saw a rack of Colonial soldier uniforms, pamphlets illustrating lockdown techniques or explaining about nonviolence, legal advice. Sheaves of placards leaned five feet thick against the wall, along with rolled-up banners on a white bedsheet. A few children were still tumbling around the child-care room, and a big pot of vegetarian stew sat on a table with a ladle and towers of paper bowls. It was an uplifting energy after a long day. I asked for Dave, and they pointed me toward a door with a white sign on it that said GONE FISHIN' PLEASE USE OTHER BATHROOM. I knocked. "Dave?"

He came to the door with a plunger in his hand. "Sister Emily!" Tall, with long pale hair that curled in every direction and an angular face balanced on a goatee. His style was unreconstructed Freak, but underneath his stoner flamboyance he knew exactly what was happening. He hugged me. "How's it going, my DNN coconspirator?"

"Good. I heard we got another mouse yesterday."

"Yeah. It was kinda sad, but he's on to something better now."

"Peanut butter or cheese?"

His look became slyly triumphant. "Peanut butter! That's eight for peanut butter, three for cheese. Check it out!"

"I actually came to see how things are going with you guys."

"There is no way we're not shutting this puppy down. Tomorrow the Empire hits a big rock, and that rock is called the People of the United States of America."

I smiled at him. "Will the rock be big enough?"

"The rock will be massive! Take my word for it. There's a deep spirit of resistance out there. We're turning out the lights on these white-shirts."

"What's the reaction down here to the Army of the Republic bombing Cascadia?"

He opened his arms wide. "Where do I sign up?" Looking reflexively to either side in case he'd been overheard. "No, most folks here aren't personally into destruction of property, but it's definitely one of the tools in the toolbox. Just like talking, and sitting around listening to music."

I knew who that was directed at. "Hey! We're going to have octogenarians out there. Just because they don't want to lock down and get gassed doesn't mean they don't count. Everybody's got their level, and they're all important."

"Yeah, yeah, I know."

"I don't get why Matthews is coming here, anyway. He knows this is enemy territory. What's with him?"

"Matthews wants to pimp on in here and stick his flag in Seattle's butt to show the world that nobody can stand against him. That's the deal with Matthews and his pals. Except it's going to play out different from the way he thinks it will." He pointed his finger at me. "And then you and I are going to go out dancing!"

"I told you: I'm a nun."

He shook his head and laughed. We'd played this game before. "Okay, Mother Superior. I've got to fix this toilet then go find housing for twelve anarchists from Iowa, if you can believe it. I didn't even know they'd invented anarchism in Iowa."

"A little heat lightning in the heartland."

"May it be so."

We hugged again and he hurried off toward a bank of landlines. Dave had spoken: The rock would be massive. I'd never known him to be wrong.

However Dave was calling it, the city of Seattle wasn't conceding anything. They wanted an orderly day, and had taken steps to make sure that the protest was nothing more than a distant rumble to the businessmen down at the Convention Center. They'd specified our "protest pit" at the Seattle Center park, a mile away from the Symposium, and would fortify the area around the Convention Center with hundreds of Seattle police. The King County Sheriff had added his own caveat, announcing, in a speech that was repeated endlessly on television in the days before the protest, that those who strayed from the designated protest area would be treated with maximum force. "They'd better bring some medical units," he said defiantly. "The People of Seattle will not be bullied by a bunch of Socialists who don't believe in Democracy."

We could expect eight hundred Seattle police backed up by another four hundred from the King County Sheriff's department. Auburn, Renton, Kent, and Tukwilla could send police, as could Tacoma. We knew that if things got dicey, they had a unit of National Guardsmen in reserve. Their strategy was to set up a perimeter of protection around the Convention Center with transportation corridors to the half-dozen nearby luxury hotels where the delegates would be staying.

The ironic thing about it all was that the whole "battlefield" was decorated for Christmas. I did a walk-through with Shar and a few other organizers near midnight, scouting just in case we decided to go downtown. The televised destruction of the Cascadia plant had put a scary militaristic tension on everything, and it jibed weirdly with the big plastic candy canes and red bows on the streetlights. At the Seattle Center, the police had put up orange barricades and chain-link fences to block off the entrances that faced downtown, where the Symposium would happen. A dozen or so of the police were standing around cradling black shotguns, and there were a few dogs.

"It looks like a concentration camp," I said.

"Give 'em a few years," someone said.

"They turned this half of the center into a cul-de-sac," Shar observed. "Anyone who wants to go downtown has to backtrack through the crowd and then walk all the way back around."

"Clever."

We greeted a few of our own people who were there to watch over the sound system we had set up for the following day's program then headed downtown along the route that protesters would follow the next day. Shar had chosen to spend the opening of the protest with the Direct Response Groups, and she wanted to survey the territory. A few police were at every intersection, talking to each other and eyeing passersby. Mounted officers were also on hand, looming above us on their huge animals, doubtless to convey a sense of what could be expected tomorrow. Orange barricades were folded up against buildings, ready to be deployed. And amidst it all were the reindeer and the wreaths, and the merry Santas lugging their red bags of surprises.

One of the other activists had a map where he'd been carefully marking the barricades and police presence. He'd upload it to the DRG's Web site, and then others would download the information. Within an hour, everyone would know the police preparations.

A flash went off as someone took our picture, and before I could move, several other flashes went off as a man dressed in a Windbreaker and stocking cap maneuvered to get close-ups of each of us. We kept trying to wave him away, but he moved in without apology or explanation.

Shar spoke up. "Aren't you a good American!"

He took another picture and we turned our back on him. As I looked around, I could spot three or four other men who seemed like they might be Security people, private or public. They were watching us intently.

"So they know we're checking them out," Shar said quietly to me. "That'll be used against us later."

"We're allowed to walk the streets," I answered. I didn't feel so confident. Who knew if or how the government would prosecute us once "our" demonstrators got involved. And that was part of their goal, of course: that fear.

Shar and I split off from the others so we could talk freely. She pulled out her map, and I indicated various intersections between the Seattle Center and the Business Symposium, our intended route. "So the Direct Response people are going to shut down this intersection at Ninth and Boren, all these on Pike, all of these on Fifth, these three on Union . . ."

Shar spoke as she looked down at the diagram. "What do you think of the idea of splitting into two groups, with one coming down Fifth and one down Seventh? If we come down, that is."

From what I could gather, it had become a pretty big *if.* "I think we should try to keep everyone together, because there's going to be a certain amount of splitting off anyway. That'll give us a big mass but also enough extra bodies off to the sides to keep the police from concentrating all their people in one spot. We can redirect people by phone once we get down here."

"You make it all sound so orderly," Shar said. "You know it's not going to be like that."

"I know. How's Dan about it?"

"He's still sulking." She gave a little snort. "He's comfortable with politics, but civil disobedience makes him nervous."

"It makes me nervous."

Rumors had been going around that the government was going to prosecute us under the Antiterrorism laws if property damage resulted, and that they were going to do a preemptive strike on the DRG Response Commons and arrest them for conspiracy to commit terrorist acts. Another was that the banks and other corporations headquartered downtown had brought in Whitehall thugs specialized in doing internal damage to protesters without leaving any marks, like the Chinese used.

Besides that, we had our own extremists to worry about, rogue activists whose juvenile agenda boiled down to "Smash the State!" They could leave a trail of shattered windshields and trashed storefronts, without caring whether the owners were small businesses, supporters, or even other demonstrators. These were the people who could whip the cops into a frenzy and then run away, leaving the rest of the protesters to deal with the consequences. I had friends who felt that way: They thought broken windows put issues in the news. Maybe they were right, but the peaceful groups hated them, and if they showed, the Media would make them our public face.

I went to bed at one in the morning and rose again at five thirty. I made a quick tour of the downtown area. Already, amazing things were happening. In the half light, protesters were scurrying past the light police presence and setting up lockdowns. They would converge suddenly on an intersection in groups of one to ten, from all four directions, and in the space of thirty seconds, a street that had been empty would suddenly fill with two hundred people. It happened too quickly for the police to respond; by the time they could call for backup, the protesters were locked together in the middle of the street, with an equally large group of supporters locking arms and sitting in front of them, like the soft flesh that protects a peach pit. They sat quietly with signs that said things like AMERICA: NOT FOR SALE! or DEAR MATTHEWS: THE AMERICAN PEOPLE CALLED. THEY WANT THEIR GOVERNMENT BACK! The police themselves seemed almost amused by it. The stood talking to each other and smiling, rocking occasionally as one told another a joke. I was relieved to see that they were Seattle cops. The King County troops were nowhere in sight.

I went to the office and started getting turnout reports. The Seattle Universalist Church expected 28 people, the Northwest Forest Alliance expected 412, the Renton Voting Rights League counted 18 who'd promised to show, while the Seattle Clean Water Alliance had counted 168, including children. The Seattle Transit Workers had commitments from 872 members to come to Seattle Center. I checked my lists and my mouth came open. Each of these groups had twice or even three times as many people as they'd expected a week before. A selfish feeling of power surged through me, and I couldn't help sitting back and enjoying it before throwing it away.

Dan was in an insufferably good mood. "This could be a big one." A meaningful little smile. "Things aren't as monolithic as you may think."

There were already a dozen indie videos posted online, and I watched the reports on television for a few minutes to see how they were playing it. The pictures were of young demonstrators locked together singing songs. One group was singing Christmas carols. Of course, the most colorful and extreme got the most coverage. Nothing about the Symposium or its agenda. The camera focused in on one belligerent protester whose sign made me uneasy. It said THE A⊕R IS MY DELEGATE. A great picture for the networks to amplify. Surprisingly, the police were still simply standing around, twirling their batons. I packed my things to go to the Seattle Center. Extra food, a water bottle, eyedrops, tampons. Aspirin. I didn't know when I'd be coming back.

By eight o'clock, several hundred people were already milling around the plaza inside the fenced limits of the Seattle Center. A low gray shell sealed off the sun, but no rain was expected, which would help turnout. Each gate had from a dozen to twenty officers posted in small groups. They seemed relaxed: this was probably the cushy crowd-control job of the day: just a bunch of everyday folks listening to speeches and complaining about the government, a gig that beat the hell out of babysitting the radicals downtown. They looked like a bunch of working-class guys who might just as easily be rerouting traffic at a construction site or installing a telephone cable. Some of our medical teams had already arrived, wearing red-and-white armbands and carrying bandoleers of saline solution for tear gas and pepper spray. They wore mountaineering backpacks stuffed with first-aid gear. The police ordered some to open their bags to be searched, forming little mounds of gauze and ointments on the pavement. Photographers were everywhere, either for the media or, I suspected, to add images to government security files for later prosecution. People on our side annoyed them by snapping pictures right back, getting badge numbers and faces to be posted on the Internet or used as evidence later.

I was getting reports on the confrontation downtown. The first phase of the lockdowns had gone well: All the chosen intersections were blockaded, and so far the Seattle Police were simply watching. Thousands more people seemed to be filtering in to the downtown core, and traffic snarls at the blockades had forced the police to close off all vehicles. At the Olympic Hotel they had clamped themselves to doors with U-shaped bicycle locks around their necks. The Hilton and Sheraton were having similar luck. At Eighth and Union, the protesters set up a giant tripod, dangling themselves twenty feet above the pavement, while a few blocks away on Seneca, demonstrators had inflated a giant nylon balloon of a whale and tied it down to traffic signs and fire hydrants. When I called Dave he was supporting a blockade at the Seattle Center. "The rock cannot be moved!" he said triumphantly. In the background, I could hear the chanting: *Whose streets? Our streets! Whose streets? Our streets!* I wondered how long it would be until the police contested that statement.

"Let me know if it changes."

Dan was standing next to me waiting for me to finish my call. Something smug about him. "The police are just watching, aren't they?"

"Yeah. Do you know something I don't?"

He looked to the sides, then leaned in to me. "We made a deal with the mayor. He hates Matthews. That's what I've been wanting to tell you: It's not monolithic. The Seattle PD's not going to step in and start arresting people as long as everyone stays cool. That's the deal."

"Wow. That's like . . . subversion. What's going to happen to the mayor?"

"In Seattle, he'll be untouchable. He already polled on it." Dan gave his insider smile. "I've been working on this the past five weeks, but it didn't come down until this morning, when the mayor realized that the Direct Response people had the numbers to shut it down. His cover is that a soft approach is the best option to keep things peaceful. It's a win–win. We'll shut the conference down and embarrass Matthews, he'll keep the peace. But our part of the deal is we don't send anyone downtown. We stay here. Got it?"

"I never signed off on—"

He put his hand up. "No. Don't even start. It's my ass on this deal. If we blow these people off, my word is dogshit, and so is the DNN's. Shar agreed to this, too."

"So I'm the last to find out?"

"I'm sorry. It all coalesced this morning. Your job now is to get across to the Direct Response people that they need to disperse at six tonight, when they're ordered to. Otherwise the cops are going to start making arrests."

"No one controls the affinity groups."

"I know. But at least we can influence them. There's still going to be some confrontations, but that's okay, too. There needs to be confrontation."

"Yeah, as long as it's somebody else's." He ignored the remark. Always the politician, he wanted to plod along as the safe, secure Moderate. Now he'd worked it out just the way he wanted. "What about tomorrow?"

"Tomorrow's tomorrow. What we're in for is two days here at the Seattle Center and then a day of forums and smaller demonstrations. We can make our point without starting a riot. Remember: we're still early in this struggle."

I shook my head and turned away from him. I felt like everybody's lackey.

The wide concrete expanse of the Seattle Center was beginning to be cluttered with people. There were groups dressed all in pink and groups wearing red, white, and blue. I saw at least a dozen Uncle Sam outfits, some of them towering above the crowd on stilts. A giant head of a grinning, venal President Matthews capered through the crowd, nodding and giving victory *V*'s with his fingers. The mosaic of signs formed an unequivocal text: "REAL VOTE! REAL DEMOCRACY!" "PAPER BALLOTS—REAL VOTE!" Other signs said "DON'T PRIVATIZE MY COUNTRY" or "AMERICA IS NOT FOR SALE!" The Raging Grandmas had showed up dressed in purple, and several hundred small children bannered as KIDS FOR DEMOCRACY came bubbling in with their faces painted with red, white, and blue stars. There was even a Santa with a sign reading "DON'T GIVE IT AWAY!" Along with the long-hairs and the young lefties were a surprising amount of men and women who looked like working-class America, people who'd maybe voted for the Regime in the last election and seemed a little puzzled to find themselves in their present company. On top of all that, though we'd tried to discourage it, were the other banners: A slogan of the Jefferson Combine: "2ND REVOLUTION NOW!" and "BULLETS OR BALLOTS: TAKE

YOUR PICK!" The red-slashed crosshairs of the **A⊕R** were speckled through the crowd like the season's latest fashion statement, like a Peace sign, but not about peace.

By nine o'clock the plaza was nearly full, and people kept streaming in. Drums were beating and people were dancing and singing in little groups. One of our organizers set up a device that would take photos of the crowd to provide later estimates, but we knew that the Seattle Center could hold 50,000 people and that we had nearly filled it already. The crowd was beginning to extend outside the gates.

Our first speaker got up: the former head of Seattle's public utilities union. He'd lost his job when the water system had been privatized. He was wearing his old uniform, and though he wasn't a dynamic speaker, he had a story and he had his anger, and by the time he'd finished recounting the privatization of the city water supply, the crowd was with him. "And I just want to say one last thing: I don't advocate violence, but by God, what goes around comes around, and on behalf of my brothers and sisters who are now either out of a job or took a big cut in pay and benefits, I want to say"—he shouted—"*it's good to see justice done in Eastern Oregon!* Thank you!"

A huge cry rose from the crowd and a chant began *"A-O-R! A-O-R!"*

"Great!" Dan muttered beside me. "There's five seconds of the evening news."

Our master of ceremonies quelled it and introduced the next speaker, Bonita Howard, a black woman with a turban who I knew from her work as a community organizer in Central Seattle. Her voice rang out majestically. "Just as this regime has made war on other countries, and made war on communities, they have made war on Democracy itself, and that is what we are here to address today!"

I checked the DRG Web site on my handheld: all the blockades were holding. None of the delegates could get to the Seattle Center, and the opening rituals of the Symposium had been officially postponed until eleven-thirty.

"SPD is still standing by," I told Dan.

He nodded. Behind the passionate speaking I could hear the ten o'clock bells ringing from a nearby cathedral. My phone vibrated. It was Dave, from the Convention Center. "It just got a lot more intense down here. The King County sheriffs showed up in storm-trooper gear. It looks like they're going to start making arrests."

"Have they made any announcements?"

"No, they're just forming up in front of us. They've got their shot-guns out and they're passing around CS cannisters."

"Thanks, Dave. Call me if it changes."

I looked at Dan. His phone had rung also and he was scowling into the little plastic wafer. "What about SPD?" he barked. "What are they doing?" Then, "*Whitehall? On whose authority? I'll call you back." He turned to me. "That was Shar, at Fifth and University. Something's happening. King County and SPD are moving in riot units. *And,* they're getting backup from Whitehall security troops. That's the freaky part. Let me see what's up."

He pushed a button and put the phone beside his face. A silence, then, "Yeah, Dennis! This is Dan Schwartz. It sounds like things are starting to get nasty downtown. I wanted to remind you that we are committed to a peaceful demonstration. Call me." He folded it up and raised his eyebrows. His thin, bony face looked gray. "Crap!"

He called two other numbers without success.

"Do you think the mayor changed his mind?"

"No. He wouldn't. You know what?" He stared intensely at me. "The mayor's not in control anymore."

Onstage our first band was tuning up, pumping an upright base and slapping fragments of bluegrass riffs into the sound system. I called the communications center for the DRG. "Hi, this is Emily from Democracy Northwest. Do you know what's going on?"

The dispatcher there sounded excited. Whitehall was at twelve blockades now, along with King County and Seattle riot squads.

"Is that legal?" I asked Dan.

"They'll make it legal post facto."

The bluegrass band launched into their first number, an up-tempo bluegrass version of the old song about John Henry. *John Henry told his captain, well a man ain't nothin' but a man . . .* I called Dave again.

"What's happening down there?"

There was a delay and I wasn't sure he'd heard me. "It's no jambo-ree, my sister. The Blueshirts just announced that we must disperse or they're going to start beating our asses. I believe the man said 'pain compliance.' They've got all their toys out now."

"Are you dispersing?"

"No. We are the rock."

His silly theatrics sent a wave of admiration through me, because I knew what was going to happen next. "You're a very courageous man, Dave. Is Whitehall involved?"

"They're kind of hanging back. I think they want to be the support troops, but I don't see any way the Blueshirts have enough guys on their own. We've got a lot of folks down here and nobody's talking about moving." I heard some explosions in the background and Dave's voice went up a notch. "They're gassing us. Gotta go!"

I turned to Dan. "They're dispersing them."

He nodded his head. We watched the musicians without saying anything for a minute. I noticed that the Seattle Police posted nearby had become warier. They weren't joking with each other any longer. I checked the television news on my phone. Nothing.

Dan's phone rang again and I watched his face. "They'd have to declare martial law to do that!" He listened some more. "Are you okay? Are you safe there?"

My phone rang. It was Dave. "We need some help down here. I've never seen them like this. They're beating the shit out of folks that are offering absolutely no resistance. Whitehall—" He coughed a few times, and I heard screaming in the background. His voice became tight and forced. "The National Guard just—" He coughed again. "We need help."

Around me, the crowd was smiling pleasantly at the music. People were dancing and children were chasing each other through the crowd.

Dan spoke first. "That was Shar. They've moved in the National Guard, which means they've declared martial law. She says it's getting pretty savage down there."

"I know. I just talked to a friend at the Convention Center. He says they're having trouble holding on. It sounds like the cops are coming down pretty hard on them."

"It's not just the cops," Dan said.

I went to the Direct Response Web site to check the blockades. One of them had been erased from the screen. The message said. "All blockades are under chemical and physical attack by the security forces. Affinity groups are needed at Fourth and University to retake the intersection." As I scrolled across the map, another message appeared. "Affinity groups are needed at Fourth and Union to retake the intersection."

"The blockades are falling, Dan."

He seemed unsure. "Let's get a quick consensus. I'll call headquarters and ask them to message all our affiliates with what's going on. We can get an idea of whether people want to go downtown."

I watched him call our number. He listened for a minute and then hung up. "Out of service. I'll try four-seven-seven." Again he called, and his face screwed up angrily. "That one's out, too!" We had five numbers at DNN headquarters. They were all out of service. "I can see Homeland's been busy. I'll message everybody from here and hope they get it."

He started tapping out a report on his device. It was ten thirty now, an hour until the Symposium was supposed to begin. Security forces had already cleared two of the Direct Response Group's blockades. If they cleared five or six they could open a passage to the Convention Center.

I called Bonita, who'd rejoined her group.

"Consensus? Sister, are we at the same demonstration? You're just going to have to get up on the stage and put it out there to the people."

"Will you go?"

There was a short pause as she queried the group around her; then I heard her warm, rich laugh. "We'll be in front!"

She was right about consensus. I had a list with fifty names and numbers. It would take me hours to poll them all. I turned to Dan. "We don't have time for this. We're going to have to make an announcement."

He kept texting without looking up. "Emily, there's a process and that's why we're a democratic group."

"We don't have time, Dan. They need help now!"

He glanced at me briefly and turned his face back to the little screen on his handheld.

I thought of Dave and the others downtown being beaten and sprayed. People were in pain and the barricades were falling, and if a few more fell, our deal with the AOR, and the cease-fire, would disappear. And meanwhile, Dan kept pecking away at his tiny keyboard. Peck, peck, peck, with his little owl glasses and his calculations. I reached over and took it out of his hands.

"Hey!"

"Listen! Those are our friends down there! We are not going to let them fail! Either you make the announcement, or I will! We're done making deals and we're done cooperating! This is where we show them who we are!"

For ten seconds he was in shock, then the surprise and indecision slowly drained out of his face, and he nodded. "You're right. I'll do it. It's my responsibility."

I watched him climb up to the stage and make a cutting motion to the bandleader. They snuffed the tune in midverse, and Dan fiddled the microphone out of its stand. "Hello? Hello?" His voice sounded tentative and thin. Balding and skinny, dressed in his gray pants and his navy blue Windbreaker, he looked bland and undistinguished. His wire-framed glasses had a brownish tint to them.

"Move it closer to your mouth," the bandleader told him.

His voice boomed out over the plaza. "Can everyone hear me now? I have something important to tell you."

The crowd answered that they could hear him and he shifted his weight. He was going to urge seventy thousand people to go downtown and get in the middle of a violent police action. His career as the moderate insider was drawing to a close now. He was about to trade in every card he had for a single gesture.

"People for Democracy," he began, speaking too fast. "Americans, hi, I'm Dan Schwartz. I'm a coordinator for Democracy Northwest." There were a few hoots and cheers from the audience, but people were puzzled that he'd stopped the music. "I have an announcement to make." He put the mic into his other hand, then shifted it back, uncomfortably. "As many of you know, the Direct Response Group blockaded intersections around the Convention Center this morning to try to prevent the Business Symposium from happening. They had intended a peaceful demonstration. Then, about forty minutes ago, in spite of the peaceful nature of the assembly, riot police moved in and as we speak they are violently attacking the protesters."

A cloud of *boo*s swept over the crowd, rising from all over the plaza. He motioned for quiet.

"Now, if these were all regular riot police, it would be disturbing enough, but these are not regular riot police. These riot police are backed up by the National Guard, and for the first time, by private riot police belonging to Whitehall Security. We still don't know by whose authority, if any, Whitehall's Security forces are operating, but it is absolutely confirmed that they are on the scene and they are participating actively."

The booing became more forceful, and the crowd became noticeably angry. Heads turned to comment to friends; brows hardened. Dan went on over the noise, speaking louder and more forcefully. "This opens a new chapter in the struggle between Corporate Power and the Citizens of this country! Our fellow Democracy activists can't maintain their blockades in the face of that kind of repression. They are being gassed and clubbed and attacked with chemical agents! If no action is taken, the Symposium will open for business and Corporate Power will have sent their message to America. And their message is this: *We make the rules now. We have our own army. And if you get in our way, you are fair game.* Because if they can brutalize us in the streets of Seattle, they can brutalize us anywhere in these United States. And that's something we need to stop right here and right now!"

I glanced over at the police at the nearest exit from the Seattle Center. One of them was on his walkie-talkie, while the others stood stone-faced with their legs apart, straddling the pavement.

Dan went on. "I am asking everyone here to lend a hand in this struggle. I am asking you to go downtown and intercede between the Security forces and the citizens who are peacefully assembled there. If you want to go, please go calmly and peacefully to the exits and make your way toward the intersections of Fourth and Union and Fourth and University." He gave more instructions as a low black troop carrier pulled up outside the nearest gate and a dozen riot police tumbled out of the open door. Three of the regular cops started toward the stage, but when they reached the stairs to the platform, seven or eight people blocked the way and refused to move. Cameras were hoisted into the air on all sides like weapons, all pointed at the police.

Dan glanced toward the ruckus. He knew he needed to set things in motion quickly. "For those who want to stay, there's no shame in that. Our program will continue here at the Seattle Center. For those who choose to go, let me be clear. I'm not asking you to fight the police. I am asking you to bear witness. By bearing witness, we will show that we will not be bullied, we will not be intimidated, and we will not stop until we have brought this corrupt Administration and its Corporate controllers to their knees! Ten years from now history will say that here, in the streets of Seattle, the Matthews Regime was defeated by an idea, and that idea was Government *of* the People, *by* the People, and *for* the People! It's time to make Democracy *real!*"

A howling cheer shook the air and made the whole plaza vibrate like a drum. It went on and on, deafening, and Dan wasn't sure what to do. "Thank you for hearing me," he said at last; then he turned toward the little knot of police and activists shoving at the foot of the stairs. "That's okay. Let them through."

A few seconds of indecision passed; then I started to note a strange granular movement toward the side streets, an agitation like rice in a pot of water as it neared the boiling point. Many started toward the gates, only to run up against people who were still facing the stage. Some were determined to leave, and pushed through, while others seemed to be carried along toward the thickening numbers near the gates. As the crowd began to move toward the exits the police tried to pinch off the multitudes who had never been able to enter in the first place and were blocking the entrance, but there were too many people, and the orange rope they tried to string up quickly collapsed in on itself. The thin barrier of blue-clad policemen retreated steadily backwards, no longer in formation, talking on their radios to figure out where to regroup. The regular police didn't bother using their clubs, but the newly arrived riot police from King County, maybe because they'd come fresh from the confrontations downtown, made a stronger stand. For no real reason except their own frustration, they began firing tear gas into the crowd.

At this, people began to move faster, and less calmly. The cries of the children being gassed gave a hellish tint to the growing chaos. The sound of gagging and choking started: an older woman a few feet in front of me had collapsed and was surrounded by a knot of people, one of them holding a moistened bandanna across her mouth and nose. "Need a medical team here!" he was yelling. "Medical team!" It had been a determined crowd before. It was an angry one now.

The crowds were flowing unstoppably out of the Seattle Center and into the streets that would take them downtown. I could hear drums beating simply and harshly, and keeping time to a deep belligerent chant: "Whose streets? Our streets! Whose streets? Our streets!" The newly arrived riot police were brandishing their shotguns and spraying chemicals directly into the faces of the front lines, but even so they were backpedaling, calling for reinforcements as they gave up their attempt to hold the line and melted off to the side. Cops with bullhorns were ordering people to stay where they were, but they were ignored or cursed at. The multitudes were moving toward downtown now and it would take more than a few dozen police to stop them. Now the chanting was becoming a roar, set off by the explosions of a dozen drums. "WHOSE STREETS? OUR STREETS! WHOSE STREETS? OUR STREETS!"

Dan was being calmly arrested. They had already put him in plastic restraints and were leading him off the stage. One of our legal people was with him.

He yelled at me. "Call Shar!"

"Okay!"

I dialed her personal number, but it was out of service. William Lee had accomplished something after all. I called Dave. I wasn't sure if he would answer, but to my surprise he picked up. He sounded on edge. "Bad time, Emily."

"What's going on?"

"They're making arrests and beating the crap out of anybody who catches their foot in a crack in the pavement. I've got about a minute before they grab me."

"You're going to have about twenty thousand reinforcements soon. We're coming down."

"For real?"

"For real. Can you hang on another fifteen minutes?"

"Me personally, no. But I'll spread the word. We'll get our support people to start jumping in. Party at the jail tonight! Woo hoo!"

I followed the crowd out and once I reached the open streets, I began trotting to get to the head of the group. We were mostly moving at a swift walk, with the bodies so thick in some patches that I had to be careful not to step on anyone's heels. People had brought their signs and even some of the huge puppets bobbed up and down above our heads. Some of the more experienced people had wrapped their mouths in water-soaked bandannas against the tear gas, and a few had put on goggles. The sheer numbers were amazing. The street and sidewalks were packed with people, and we stopped traffic at every intersection, flowing around the halted cars and moving through with only a brief glance at their astonished faces. Looking down the cross streets I could see that the next avenue over was as full as ours, and as we passed the clean orderly plaza of the Westlake Mall, the acrid bite of tear gas started to scrape at my eyeballs and my throat. At the cross street of Pike, a wave of a dozen protesters came running toward us, and when I looked down the street I saw one of the Whitehall's brown Humvees come racing after them. The protesters ran through the crowd and the Humvee's occupants piled out in their gray urban camo and their military haircuts and tried to push their way through, but then someone shouted to link arms, and in seconds we'd solidified into an impenetrable mass of people. Whitehall fought their way out and stood cursing us as we passed by.

The intersection of Fourth and Union had been retaken: it was packed with what must have been two thousand demonstrators, standing with locked arms, or hunched down beneath the onslaught of chemicals and gas. We squinted our eyes and moved through to Fourth and University, where the same scene was being repeated, and I headed toward the intersection near the Convention Center where Dave had been arrested. While I walked, I called two of our affiliates and asked them to bring people over there All around me people were hunched on the ground wiping their eyes, or having bloody red sockets pried open and washed out with water. Faces burned with pepper spray were being cleaned with mineral oil.

A few would-be delegates had been caught without their security in the middle of the crowd. Some twenty people were surrounding two middle-aged men in suits. "Why do you want to plunder our country? Huh? Why do you have so much contempt for America?" I felt sorry for the men, befuddled by the unanswerable questions being spit at them, but they didn't seem in danger and I moved on without getting involved.

It changed as I passed through the successive intersections. The police seemed to have retreated from the next intersection. There were police lines in front of us, but as we advanced they would shoot a few rounds of tear gas or rubber bullets and then retreat. They'd given up the streets; they merely lined the sidewalks to protect store windows and property. They'd lost, and they knew it. As I moved up Seneca toward the Convention Center, someone announced loudly that the Symposium had been canceled for that day, and the word spread quickly through the crowd. Hoots started rising up, and at the next intersection someone with a bullhorn was already giving a speech to rousing cheers.

I reached the entrance to the Convention Center. A huge mass of people was gathered there, with the police, soldiers, and Whitehall operatives standing by glaring at them. I asked around for Dave and was pointed toward an ambulance. He was lying there with his nose smashed and the blood running down over his mouth into his little goatee. His eyes were both blackening. "Dave!"

He lolled his head over to me, smiled dopily. I think he was in shock. "Emily!"

I felt myself tearing up but held it back. "We won."

His eyes shifted back to one of his support people and I wasn't sure he'd heard me; then he gave the tiniest nod and his smile changed to one of a deep and lucid satisfaction. "The rock cannot be moved."

PART II

THE WAR BETWEEN WORDS AND PICTURES

14

Watching the Civils give the National Business Symposium a major ass-whipping in the streets of Seattle made me wonder if maybe America was starting to come out of its coma. If most of the TV story that first night was about hippies and punk kids with nose rings, enough footage of brownshirts beating the crap out of people got posted that when the Corporates tried to restart on Day Two, a mighty host of pissed-off citizens came roaring in from the suburbs. Not just political types, but rowdy youths who wanted to fight and working-class people getting in touch with something that had been simmering a long time. Even the tacked-on pictures of Whitehall paramedics helping injured demonstrators didn't wash it clean. By midmorning, the only solid citizens left downtown were blueshirts, brownshirts, greenshirts, and sixty thousand angry protesters clogging the avenues and throwing tear gas canisters through plate glass windows. With the streets acrid and noisy with the sound of that prosperity, the Heroes of Free Enterprise decided to call the party off and do their deals in private. No Matthews, no presidential praise for these rescuers of our cash-strapped nation, no James Sands talking about "Customers, not Citizens." For the first time, the Regime stumbled.

The New Testament started rolling out immediately, making sure people took it the right way. One didn't want the sight of all those protesters getting gassed and clubbed giving folks the wrong impression. Instantly, the prophets began to tell us what this meant, ranting at their poisonous little water holes on the Internet and bellowing from their TV screens. Paul Wells, the fading "conservative," played it like another step in the decay of American Civilization. "The spoiled brats of the sixties are back among us . . ." And we realized it was all about spoiled brats with too much free time. *Newsweek* showed a bandanna-masked youth on the cover throwing a tear gas canister, and we realized these were unruly hoodlums. Their best guy by far: the Hammer, who stood up from his chair and gave the demonstration a Hammer *bleeping* down! "I mean, it's Tuesday, people! Don't these punks have jobs? Or did they all just call in sick?" In a sniveling, effeminate voice that he did pretty well for a guy in a death's-head T-shirt: *"Hi, don't forget to send me my sick pay while I'm down here saying how angry I am about the Free Enterprise system. Oh, I am just so, so angry."*

It was an expertly drawn picture, not by any one person, but by the entire machine, working disconnectedly and disparately, but eternally in its own shared interests. No irrelevant finger-pointing of how the common wealth had been squandered, or disturbing statistics showing how computerized votes were stolen. The demonstration itself became the story, as if it were a giant play put on by a cast of seventy thousand for the amusement of the country. The lasting coda: a picture of a banner saying MY TROOPS ARE THE ARMY OF THE REPUBLIC, showing up across all media. Pictures, pictures, pictures!

But as much as they can decorate the little room inside people's heads, too many jobs have been lost, too many houses foreclosed on. Suburbia's fresh out of money for school buses and crossing guards, and an unsightly parade of one-armed, one-legged veterans sends a chill even into the patriotic haze floating above schooners of beer at the American Legion Hall. Between Cascadia and the Seattle Smackdown, the Corporates took two solid hits on the chin, and if Emily is right that some slavish doglike part of the public psyche craves security above all else, that worn-down heavyweight part that's been getting the crap beat out of him for the last eight rounds finally staggered his opponent with a lucky punch, and a little lightning strike went off inside his head: *Hey! This fight ain't over yet!*

I called it in on a dime: We declare our cease-fire, and Democracy Northwest gets their Real Vote! signatures in less than a week. Ballot reform gets slated for a special election just after President's Day, and it's too one-sided to steal, coming in with an 80 percent Yes vote, even in the strongholds of the Regime out in Eastern Washington. No more Internet voting: We're going back to paper.

Emily's star is rising: When I see her picture in an article on America's Next Generation of Leaders it reminds me she's probably got no shortage of suitors these days, people she can be seen with in public and who aren't "arrogant manipulative assholes." *Hey!* I want to tell her, *your demonstration? This cease-fire? I'm the one who made it happen!* But all I can do is keep it hidden from Tonk and everyone else—another secret life within my secret life.

My father's afflicted by no doubt whatsoever. The day after the blast, I make my requisite condolence call, and the hideous stew of awkward silence and fake sympathy over the phone shows me he's plunging on, incapable of self-awareness.

I stay busy. Download a warehouse work schedule, snatch an employee directory from the King County Division of Elections, placate Gonzalo, message the Bellingham comps and tell them where there's some blasting caps waiting to be appropriated. Tedious bits of stray information that can be fitted together into one swift piece of booming clockwork. We watch and we plan and we track the Civils' progress. Two weeks after the DNN wins paper for Washington State, New York gets its Real Vote! referendum on the ballot, then Michigan. Election reform bills get submitted in forty-three states.

"So what!" Earl E. says. "What's that do for the Siskiyou?"

I'm not sure what to tell him. Maybe the Regime senses trouble ahead, but far from slacking up, they've picked up the pace, like the last looting of the palace before they flee. They sign endangered species over to extinction and slide no-bid contracts to their cronies without a squawk. It's a system that only anoints the corrupt and the pliable, and if you want to be Jesus Christ, you're going to be sitting all by your lonesome in the Senate cafeteria.

"They're going to nuke it, Lando. The whole Southern Cascades are going to be a fucking golf course!"

He's riled enough that I've hurried down to Portland to talk it over with him. We meet up in a beer garden down in the old warehouse district. Like a Hollywood set for conspirators: low, dim, with cheap plywood booths and a cut funk of spilled beers softening the air. My man's got an Oregon National Guard cap pulled low over his new crew cut and a flag waving on his chest above the slogan STANDING PROUD!

"Earl E., man, you can't just go bombing shit every time they piss you off."

"Why not? It sounds like a plan to me."

"I told you: We made a deal. We're letting the Civils do their thing."

"*We* made a deal, but in case you didn't notice, the Regime didn't sign on to *our* deal." He pushes his teacup aside and leans over the scarred wood table. "Lando, we can't replace the Siskiyou. When it's gone, it's gone. And a victory three years from now isn't going to bring it back."

I know the Siskiyou. One of the last uncut areas in the Northwest, legendary forest, with massive trees and thick moss that steams in the morning when the first sunlight hits it. Cedars that are seven hundred years old. Wild rhododendrons spraying purple blossoms over crystal-line streams. The kind of forest they use on posters with inspirational messages about God. Now some Corporate finally made good on a long string of payoffs and is ready to destroy it all to improve one year's bottom line. And for what? A bonus? A cheap homage in *Forbes* magazine? It's a question of whether a man like that deserves a bullet in the brain or pity, because only a truly pathetic human being could do that kind of destruction just so his fellow tribesmen will admire him.

"I agree with you, Early. But the civil groups can stop it in the courts. If they have to, they can go to lockdowns and tree-sits."

"Yeah, just like the redwoods."

Early and I had been on that one together, and we both remember how it ended. As to the courts, the Regime has placed their stooges well, and it's been two years since anyone had stopped a project on environmental grounds.

My colleague can tell I'm having trouble convincing myself. "See!

You don't even believe your own arguments, Lando! Listen . . ." In a cool operational voice: "The Louisiana Pacific branch offices are a couple of suites in a strip mall. It won't take—"

"And guess who's doing their Security?" I reach into the pocket of my hooded sweatshirt and pull out a press release I printed off the Internet, Louisiana Pacific announcing a shiny new relationship with Whitehall Security Resources.

He narrows his eyes and clicks his tongue. "So what! They're the dinosaurs and we're the mammals. We're faster and we're smarter."

I squeezed my forehead. I didn't want to dampen the esprit de corps.

He went on. "Lando, we can't let them destroy it. We need an armed campaign against the logging companies. Not killing anybody, just going after their tools. That could buy us enough time to get rid of the Regime and change the equation."

"You mean an armed campaign in the forest."

"Wherever Louisiana Pacific is. And, if necessary, against the contractors who do the cutting for them."

"Those are mom-and-pop operations."

"So what? Should I bow down to them because they listen to country music and put flag decals on their truck? Fuck them! They're part of the machine!"

"That's irrelevant here," I answer. "As soon as you burn the first truck, they're going to have some guy in suspenders and cork boots on the evening news complaining that the Radicals won't let him feed his family."

He looks at me with disgust. "When did you become a PR guy, Lando? Because your new gig isn't working for me." He slants toward me. "Do you really think if we kick back and do nothing, they're not going to try and liquidate us? Bullshit! We're the only ones with a cease-fire here, thanks to you!"

Now I'm getting angry. "We told the Civils that if they shut down the Symposium, we'd lay off. Well, they did! They left five hundred Corporates with their fingers up their ass. Now they've mobilized the whole state for this election reform—"

"Reform my ass! Voting in this country is like going to the theater to watch the worst actors in the world, and then applauding them like they're fucking De Niro!"

"These people are trying to fix it! But they need more time!"

He washes the room down with his gaze, maybe worried that he's been too loud, then goes on, still pissed. "If you don't want to go in on it, Lando, that's cool, but my crew wants to slap some hands."

"Don't do it, Early."

He glares down across the scarred little no-man's-land. I forgot what a big boy he is: eight inches taller than me with an easy seventy pounds. "You don't have the authority to tell me that."

"I'm not telling you. I'm asking you. On behalf of everybody."

"Everybody? Do you speak for everybody?"

The challenge makes me swallow, but I answer him with the simple truth. "I'm all the everybody we've got."

He picks that one up and examines it for a few minutes. It seems to drain off his hostility, and he's the same Earl E. I was crawling through the woods with three years ago. "I'll take it back to my crew and see where they stand."

I run the meeting by Sarah, McFarland, and Joby in a truck stop on I-5. Not so many big rigs around these days. The huge half-empty parking lot harks to the days when you didn't have to rob a convenience store to fill your gas tank, and the reigning vibe of the place is reflected in the bumper sticker GAS, ASS, OR GRASS: NOBODY RIDES FOR FREE.

McFarland pushes aside what's left of his cheeseburger and shakes his head at Earl E.'s plan, looking tired and irritated. "He takes 'em on in the woods he's going to get creamed. Whitehall's going to run a military operation. They're going to put their best recon units in to hunt him down. When's the cutting supposed to start?"

"Late June."

"He won't make it to July."

"He grew up in hiking in those woods. He feels he's got a moral obligation to defend them."

"What about his people? What's his obligation to them?"

We all clam up as the waitress brings a pot of coffee over. The ERP's urban guerrillas got wiped out when they went rural in Argentina. Che's little band got chased down and liquidated by elite troops in Bolivia. But sometimes it worked. The Karen held out for decades in Burma. The FARC rang up fifty years in Columbia, and we only need a couple.

Sarah cuts in just as I'm getting on a slightly more hopeful riff, trampling my buzz with that New York certainty: "It's a loser on every level. The media's going to play it as Greenies versus the working man, not Greenies versus the Corporation."

"I know." I sip my thin coffee and nibble at a sticky bun, too nerved-up to eat. "But I understand him, too. Those trees are five hundred years old. They deserve to be defended."

Joby twists up the corner of his mouth. "They're just trees!" I can feel his frustration. Before the cease-fire, he had the luxury of not giving a shit about Earl E. Now we're in the network.

McFarland taps a cigarette out of a cellophane packet. "Why don't you get help from the Democracy people?"

"Do you mean—" I look over at Joby. "—the *Patagonias*?"

He hears me. "Don't start in on me, bro."

"Mac's right," Sarah says. "If the Civils focus on it, they can probably slow down the process. Maybe the Regime will sacrifice Louisiana Pacific to try to gain back some of the credibility they lost in Seattle. That'll get Earl E. to back off."

We decide I should approach the DNN and try to persuade them to protect the Siskiyou and buy some more peace. I've been thinking the same thing, but I haven't been out front with it because it means contacting Emily, an assignment I'm dreading and pathetically eager for. I'm glad to have their authority on that mission. *I didn't really want to see you, Emily, but I had to.* "Meanwhile," McFarland says, "I'll try to keep Earl E. focused on Rock the Vote."

Rock the Vote's our backup project, one I'm hoping won't be necessary. It's big and it's loose, and it means the Civils failed. McFarland has a different name for it, one that encrypts and unencrypts in communiqués from the Midwest, the South, the Rocky Mountains. The grand, heroic version that'll make the history books, if we write them: the Strategic Counteroffensive. It's the chapter where the Good Guys win.

15

Now, up here in New England and New York, you've got the Jefferson Combine. And we think that they've got a splinter group down *here*"—circling his pointer—"around Philadelphia." Walter was in my office showing me his map of the country speckled with red explosions and their attributions. In the South and the old Rust Belt were the New Confederate Army and the U.S. Revolutionary Militia. Moving westward in little pawprints of flame: the Forces of American Resistance, the Constitutional Revival Party, *Unknown,* the Colorado Patriots, the Idaho Patriots, *Unknown,* another *Unknown,* the Montana Freemen, a half-dozen other *Unknowns,* the Anarchist Front, the Earth Day Group, the High Plains Patriots, and finally, in the far northwest, the Army of the Republic. It gave me the disturbing sense of an early-stage civil war.

Walter snorted. "They wish! I wouldn't even call this an insurgency. I'd call it 'civil unrest.' Remember that some of these groups may be only one person. That's all it takes to set a bomb. And ideologically, they're all over the place."

"But nothing new since the National Business Symposium ceasefire."

"Nope. That's all part of their strategy. They'll use the civil groups for the next phase. Let me show you what we've got on that front." He put another chart up on the screen. "This is just the Pacific Northwest, because that's where we've been taking the most hits, and that's where the Army of the Republic is based."

I had come to enjoy these briefings, but this latest chart took me by surprise. Dozens of color-coded boxes were scattered across a map of Oregon and Washington, larger or smaller depending on the size of their membership. Local civil organizations such as Democracy Northwest were represented by blue boxes, while regional branches of national labor and environmental groups were represented by green. These, in turn, hosted constellations of smaller boxes around them that included offshoot groups or chapters in smaller cities. In the smallest boxes were the little one-issue civic or neighborhood groups, people who were fighting to save the whales or preserve a neighborhood park. On a separate index Walter had listed each group's leader and, in some cases, their entire staff.

"But this map is six weeks old, from before the Seattle riots. It's ancient history." He changed the picture again. "This is what we think it is currently. Again, this is just Oregon and Washington."

Even after the spectacle of the riots, it shocked me. I'd always felt we were fighting a small vocal minority who had a disproportionate impact. This chart made it look like their influence was spreading. All the original civil groups were there, but now nearly every inch of the map was crowded with small boxes and tiny print, their connections sewn down in dotted lines or slim blue threads that spiderwebbed over every inch of the map. The urban areas from Seattle to Eugene were filled with names that at first glance seemed almost surreal. The Bellingham Episcopal Church was there, as was the Green Portland Society. The Eugene Public Land Trust, the Renton League of Women Voters. There was even a Rotary Club.

I took a breath. "So . . . we're at war with the Rotary Club?"

"Oh, don't worry. That's just one club that happens to have a Leftist president. It's the few-bad-apples syndrome. We get rid of him, and the Rotary Club comes off the map." I must have seemed unconvinced. "Jim, don't forget that until Cascadia, these citizen groups were costing you a lot more money than the armed ones. Besides, we talked about that: The lines are blurry. It's the classic pattern: You've got your terrorist arm, your political arm, and your social arm, so that sometimes you've got an organization that's running a legal clinic during the day, setting off car bombs at night, and giving milk to schoolkids the next morning. As I said before, you've got to engage them across the spectrum, militarily and ideologically. That's why you've got McPhee/Collins."

McFee/Collins, like Whitehall, had been another Barrington "suggestion." The Fund had concluded that Water Solutions' negative image was evidence that I needed a new force behind my public relations effort, and McFee/Collins was their only choice.

I'd heard of McFee/Collins over the years, as had everybody in Washington. They represented a wide array of powerful clients and a roster of A-list speakers drawn from the highest circles of government and academia. When a foreign government needed to improve its image in the United States, McPhee/Collins was the one to call, or when a company needed to correct all the media hype after a toxic release or criminal accusation, it turned to McPhee/Collins to pepper the airwaves with a soothing harmony of credible experts. Walter told me that before the Venezuelan invasion, McPhee had created the Bolivar Resistance Council out of a group of wealthy Venezuelan expatriates in Miami, fabricating "brave freedom fighters" out of businessmen simply by issuing press releases and setting up photo ops with world leaders. "If they're good enough for the Pentagon, they're good enough for us."

They invited me up to their New York office to pitch me. I took the company plane up with my Director of Communications and our Vice-President of Marketing; then we were picked up by helicopter and brought to a conference room on the eighty-fifth floor. Hovering there in the rarefied atmosphere of the glass towers I could feel the strength of the entire corporation beneath me, of thousands of minds working ceaselessly toward their unseen end.

The presentation was made primarily by my future account exec, Danny. He was surprisingly young, one of the company's hotshots with master's degrees in Corporate Communications and Psychology. He had a thin face and black hair slicked to salon perfection, and one of the McPhee people let it drop that he was the son of a famous newspaper columnist. Though his gray suit and burgundy tie blended in with the decorum of the firm, his youth and pedigree made him eerily compelling, like someone in touch with the latest mechanisms of culture that an older person like me hadn't yet caught sight of. As I compared his neat haircut and elegant clothes with Joshua's casual contempt, I felt an unexpected wave of anguish about my under-achiever. Joshua was smart, but he paled before this peer of his, already on the way up in an important company, a player in the mechanisms of society that Joshua could only criticize from afar. It took a certain boldness to rise in a company like McPhee/Collins, a quality Joshua hadn't exhibited any place other than his words.

After the introductions Danny got out of his chair and stood next to the blank screen that covered one wall of the room. He spoke with that absolute lack of doubt that belongs particularly to young people entranced with the purity of a new idea.

"Mr. Sands, Ms. Kopaceck, Mr. Reardon—" He shifted his eyes back to me. "—you're here because Water Solutions is a company at war. You've been picketed, you've been sued, you've been physically attacked, you've been bombed. That's war by anyone's definition. But the real war you're engaged in is a very special kind of war. It's a war of realities. And that's the war we have to win."

An interesting beginning. Maybe they'd pulled my college tran-script and noted my minor in Philosophy.

"Now—" He smiled. "—not to get too epistemological on you, Mr. Sands, but one thing about Reality is that the part we can directly experience, that we can know, is limited to a tiny fraction of a much bigger world. So the rest is going to be created, both by us, and for us." He began to lose his formal tones and become more conversa-tional. "For example: What do most people know about water? They know it comes out of their faucet and they get a bill every month. That's all. That's the Reality of water systems for ninety-nine percent of the population. Any reality beyond that, such as water quality or relative costs, is whatever somebody tells them. It's all created. And the picture created about things they can't know is what shapes their thoughts about what they do know. The only question is, Who's going to create that picture? You? Or the other side?"

The curtains slid silently closed and the lights dimmed. "So far, it's been the other side." A bar chart appeared on the screen beside him.

"We polled a sample group drawn from four of your markets. Less than one in five people has a positive image of Water Solutions. In the Pacific Northwest, one of your primary markets, that drops to one in seven, and the negatives are over sixty percent. The words most commonly chosen by our focus groups in the Northwest to describe Water Solutions are *opportunist, political,* and *predatory.* Interestingly, most rate their actual service as good to adequate. So I think we can safely say that right now Reality is being created by the other side: the Water Projects, the Democracy Northwests, the Protect Our Waters, and so on."

I could see my Communications officer squirming.

"That's the bad news," he concluded. "The good news is, we can change all that."

Now he went into a critique of our previous efforts, pointing to charts he'd had made of our expenditures and the media we'd used. Our communications had been print-heavy and too filled with facts and figures. "That's all thinker stuff. You want to influence thinkers? Fund some studies. Form an industry think tank and have them issue press releases. That sort of presence helps create a reality among thinkers, and we'll do all that. But be clear: Our real job is not to make people think. It's to help the broad majority of the general public *feel* that your company is a positive part of their community. When we rebrand Water Solutions as a fair and reliable caretaker of water supplies, your opponents will come to be seen as the goofy fringe elements that they are. And at that point, people will stop opposing you and move on."

It was going to be expensive. Their budget allocated 70 percent toward television, and we were soon on the air in the markets where we'd met the most resistance. Our commercials were heavy on pictures of wilderness cascades and children playing in summery swimming pools, bathing in the clear water we had brought them. Actors portraying the common man and woman praised us in well-scripted testimonials, and I marveled at all the little touches that were used to give the actors that authentic, I'm-not-a-professional-actor clumsiness. Within a few weeks McPhee/Collins began providing me with video clips of think tank fellows or public officials who spoke on behalf of utility privatization on television and radio, as well as the usual magazine snippets. We hired an actor who'd played a kindly doctor on television to be our spokesman, and along with that, McPhee decided to meet my own poor public image head-on with a series of appearances in friendly media venues. One day Danny called me in a particularly buoyant mood.

"Hey, Jim. I've got great news for you. We got you a slot with the Hammer."

"The Hammer?"

I liked to watch the Hammer occasionally. It was like going into a strip joint and telling yourself that you're an impartial observer doing some sort of anthropological study. He fascinated me, with his tattoos and his long hair and earrings. He had a certain simplistic grasp of the political reality, bolstered by economic and policy data that his staff provided. His figures were incomplete and one-sided, but even so, the references to GDP and interest rates and debt ratios lent a weird credence to his otherwise simplistic and jingoistic statements. He was famous for his interviews with members of the government or business establishment. He would usually pair them with sports figures or NASCAR heroes, and they'd bandy about laughably simplistic analyses and solutions to the problems of the day. Showing up on *The Hammer Show* was a mark of importance; I'd been in more than one CEO's office that had a picture of its occupant shaking hands with the Hammer. Even the president had appeared several times.

On a level below politics, though, he was the Hammer of Truth, the embodiment of the deeply satisfying idea that Truth was always simple and that those who disagreed were either stupid or evil. It was Truth in the religious fundamentalist sense, and the Hammer would occasionally throw out a few prayers over some sick child or injured soldier just to keep everybody feeling properly righteous. When an opposition figure came on, the Hammer was withering. He cut them off and he called them liars when their facts didn't match his own. He would kick them off the set and as they left he would point his finger as if it were a pistol and he was putting a round into them, complete with realistic recoil action. The kids loved it.

It wasn't my particular taste, but I suppose it served a purpose. Like it or not, The Hammer had become a leading political figure, with some of the highest ratings on television and an entire spin-off industry of books, CDs, and highly paid public appearances made in a scuffed leather jacket and black T-shirt. His taste in pets, music, liquor, and women was the constant fare of the tabloids, and he was often photographed at Washington parties and NASCAR events. The Hammer was a business unto himself, and his product was "Truth." He didn't sell it cheaply.

"It's going to cost eight hundred thousand, with half up front and the rest after the show airs. We got you a special agency rate."

"You mean I have to pay to be on the show?"

A stupid question: I wasn't a movie star or even a well-known politician.

"It's less than an ad in the Super Bowl. Think of it as four and a half minutes to show forty million viewers what a nice guy you are and how hard your company works."

"Okay."

"Now, the angle that we pitched was as part of the counterterrorism effort. Specifically, how the terrorists hurt working Americans by slowing down the economic recovery."

"Okay," I said slowly.

"You're newsworthy now because everybody saw the attack on the intake facility, and that's brought your company into the national spotlight. The other guest will be an exotic dancer named Tiffany Love who has a movie coming out next month. You might have heard of her."

"Tiffany Love?"

He laughed. "It keeps 'em watching. Your part of the show is the one they're worried about."

"Thanks for the confidence builder."

"Come on! You're a consummate public speaker; you'll just be working a bigger room here. And the Hammer is a master. If you were a deaf-mute sitting there in a wheelchair, he'd make people think you were Dr. Xavier from the X-Men."

They took me into the studio and put my makeup on. The first part of *The Hammer Show* was his monologue, where he commented on news of the day and took phone calls from the public. I listened to him recount little bits of news and give it the Hammer Up or Hammer Down. Wetlands regulations being eliminated to allow more jobs: Hammer Up. United Nations protesting the liberation of Venezuela: Hammer Down! Danny came into the green room to sit with me. He leaned over. "One thing: try to use the phrase 'enemies of freedom.'"

"What do you mean?"

"It's a public diplomacy thing we're doing for the government. It'll make you some brownie points. And don't forget 'quasi-terrorists.'" He clapped me on the shoulder. "Be a player!"

I raised my eyebrows. "I'll try."

"The Hammer's been briefed already. He's read our materials. Don't be fooled by the earring and the motorcycle jacket—he's a professional."

During the commercial break, they hustled me to the edge of the set. They'd dressed me business-very-casual: a white and blue striped shirt, no tie, blue jeans. Your friendly neighborhood CEO. The Hammer came up a few seconds later, his frizzy dishwater blond hair falling to his shoulders and his pale beard frothing out beneath his chin like mist. He was tall and bulky, wearing a faded black T-shirt with an American eagle on it and ripped jeans. He didn't smile as he entered, but flashed me a peace sign. "James Sands?" We shook hands. "I'm going to call you Jim. You cool with that?"

"Sure."

"Cool." He glanced at the clock that counted down the minutes until airtime. "We're going to talk for about four minutes about the problems your company's having, then we bring on the eye candy."

"Tiffany Love."

"You got it. Cool. Hang loose, Jim. This is gonna be fun."

He took his seat and the last few seconds counted down. The intro of electric guitars came on as the technicians signaled him to begin.

"Right on, right on!" he shouts, suddenly animated. "It's time to introduce our first guest. He started with a thousand dollars and a secondhand computer fifteen years ago, and he's built it into the number one supplier of water in these United States of America. Awarded a gold medal by the Environmental Foundation of America, he's also been on the front lines in America's fight against terrorism. Let's hear it for the C-E-O of Water Solutions, Jim Sands!" A few bars of the national anthem came over the speakers, and the Hammer put his hand over his heart during the "Oh say can you see" part. The music stopped. "Jimbo, you've had to go hand-to-hand with the terrorists, and we're going to talk about that, but first, how'd you get started?"

Steven had already briefed me on the script: This was where I polished the company hagiography for fifteen seconds. "Well, Hammer, we started out in a small town called Garfield, New Jersey. They had an old water system that showed high levels of lead and mercury in the drinking water. And you know, that stuff's not good for people. The problem was, they didn't have the money to bring it into the twenty-first century."

"So we've got Old, Run-down, and Broke. Classic Government."

I crinkled my eyes in mock surprise. "That's harsh, Hammer!"

"We're into Raw Truth, here, Jimbo. Blast away."

"Well, we solved their problem, the people loved it because it took a load off their taxes, and then the next town over, Sandhaven, wanted us to manage their system, too." It hadn't been exactly like that, of course; we'd had some people on the inside in Sandhaven who'd manufactured enough support to get things in motion. It had been a sixteen-month dogfight to take over the system.

"And now you've got . . . how many systems?" He looked down at some notes on his desk.

"We're serving forty-four million Americans in this country and another seventeen million abroad."

"Whoa . . ." Hammer seemed taken aback, and as a round of canned applause came over the loudspeakers some of the audience members started clapping mechanically.

When the applause subsided Hammer looked thoughtful, almost intellectual. "So Jim, when you go to make these upgrades, there's usually some whiners, aren't there?"

"Hammer, there are always people who are afraid of change. And I understand that. That's human. I mean, I'm a risk-taker, and so are you. But there are a lot of really good folks in this country who just aren't, and they want things to stay the same. And then there are other people who just don't like the free enterprise system."

"Let's talk about them a little. I understand your company has been having some problems on that front. Look at this photo, people." The screen filled with a picture we'd supplied of our Seattle office. "This is your Seattle office after it was bombed last March."

"That's right. They used a fertilizer bomb, similar to the one used to kill all those people in Oklahoma City in 1995."

"And you've had to duke it out with them up close and personal, haven't you?"

Another picture of demonstrators outside our headquarters. "Yeah, those are the quasi-terrorists. They physically attacked me on my way into work one day. They threw fake bombs at me and did a sort of mock assassination. It got ugly. Unfortunately one of their people ended up with some injuries."

Hammer laughed. "Shit happens, don't it? Check this one out, people."

Now the screen filled with video footage of our intake plant tumbling into a mist of gray dust. It went all the way through to the frightened voices of the camera crew as bits of debris showered around them. That clip had been deeply disturbing to me before, but now I was concentrating on my performance, so it didn't really register.

"Jimbo?"

"That was part of our Cascadia pipeline project. We'd been asked by the cities of Las Vegas and Phoenix to bring them water from the Columbia River, but a terrorist group that calls itself the Army of the Republic had their own agenda. Luckily, we managed to evacuate the building before anyone got killed."

A picture of John Polling's dead body came on the screen. "This guy wasn't so lucky."

"No. That's John Polling. He was assassinated by the Army of the Republic last May."

"They said Polling was a crook!"

"That's bullshit!" I was warming up now. "And even if he was a crook, do we leave it up to some self-appointed radical group to try, convict, and execute him? I mean, who elected *them*? What if they sit down one day and decide you're a crook, Hammer?"

He stood up and pushed his chest out, like an animal trying to make itself bigger. "Bring it on, fuckers! That's all the Hammer's got to say. Pool cues, ashtrays, bombs: whatever you got." He turned back to me. "I had a guy once who came after me with a jar of Slim Jims. Look at this. C'mon, look!" He pulled his hair back and pointed to a smooth expanse of forehead. I saw nothing. "That's called a Slim Jim jar upside the head, right there!" I frowned at the blank spot, as if I was examining a scar. "So bring it on! I'll show you what America's made of!" A round of canned applause came over the loudspeakers, and the audience complied by clapping their hands. He sat down again. "Jim, my friends in the intelligence community tell me that these nut cases are working with the so-called citizens' groups. What do you think about that?"

"I don't want to lump all the civil groups in one boat, Hammer. Civil groups are a part of the democratic process. But there's no question that people who share the same beliefs tend to hide behind front groups and use different tactics to achieve the same goals. Let me connect some dots for you. . . ." I quickly linked the Water Project, the DNN, and the Army of the Republic, tying the Cascadia bombing to the December riots in Seattle and the "cease-fire" that had immediately followed.

"So these people are pretending to be about Freedom, but they're really enemies of Freedom."

The Hammer had beaten me to it, but I piled on, eager to please the invisible people in the Administration Danny had referred to. "Yes. I'd call them enemies of freedom."

The Hammer turned to his sidekick, a huge biker-type named Shino. "Remember when we had that Democracy Northwest guy on, Shino? I'd like to bring him back so I can kick his ass again!"

Shino said in falsetto, *"No, Hammer! I came here to confront you in the arena of ideas!"*

"Then I had to bitch-slap him. Let's see that clip again."

A scene came on the monitor of a skinny intellectual type mouthing off about vote-stealing to a sullen-looking Hammer, and then suddenly Hammer reached over and backhanded him. The replay ended without showing the victim's reaction, and Hammer, Shino, and the canned audience burst into laughter. "Bap! Was that classic, Shino, or what?"

"Classic, Hammer."

The Hammer turned to me as if we were drinking buddies in a bar. "Then instead of standing up and fighting like a man, he goes crying to his lawyer. *'He bitch-slapped me! That mean man bitch-slapped me!'*"

Now the canned laughter was even more uproarious. The Hammer was shaking his head. "I tell you. I don't know what America's coming to!" He was suddenly addressing the studio audience instead of me. "But I do know what's coming to America! And to tell you the truth, I'm not sure America's ready for it!"

The brassy tones of "Big Spender" rang through the studio, and the small stunning assortment of curves that was Tiffany Love came on to talk about her movie. She preened and arched her back as she gave vapid answers to the Hammer's half-insulting questions. She did a cleaner version of her stripping act for the television audience, and on cue I stuffed a twenty-dollar bill into her panties. At that, she surprised me by plopping down onto my lap and launching into a series of grinding motions that pinned me against the chair. Hammer and the rest the audience loved my embarrassment: It was the first bit of uncanned laughter in the entire show.

Finally I moved offstage and out of the nervous energy of the lights. Danny walked me down to the dressing room and sat with me as they took off my makeup.

"Jim, you nailed it! You're a natural. Didn't I tell you it would go well? You're on the A-list now, big man. You'll be doing a lot more of this."

"To be honest with you, Danny, it feels a little weird."

Patting my shoulder lightly. "You're still nostalgic for facts and figures, aren't you? I told you, it's not about facts. And frankly, Jim—" He gave me a knowing smile. "—the facts don't support you."

My expression of surprise made him laugh, and even the makeup artist paused, listening as Danny continued. "My sister lives in Harrisburg, and she's a very smart woman. She made her whole case to me, with all the facts and figures and percentages, and you know what? She's right! You guys *are* screwing them over. But that's irrelevant to what we're doing here." He gave a merry shrug that explained it all. "She's not our audience!"

As I boarded the limo and airplane that took me home that night, I felt like a piece of wood being carried along a bubbling stream. I'd nailed it. I was A-List. Walter called to congratulate me. So did Denton, from the Barrington Group, and Jack Mossberg, our CFO, whose job depended in part on my performance. I thought of the things I'd said: *enemies of freedom*. Nodding at Hammer's nonexistent scar. It was acting, and even though I wasn't a professional actor, I'd carried it off and gotten the message out. If the message wasn't 100 percent accurate, that was no crime, because we were dealing with broad strokes here, with the essential truths that underlay the details. A greater good was at stake.

There was only one critic I was worried about facing.

Anne had told me she'd support me if I wanted to fight for the company, but in fact, she hadn't really made good on her promise. Things had cooled between us as I turned my focus back to business and the new role McPhee/Collins had ascribed to me. After that exquisite moment of harmony the list of topics that were off-limits to us had grown. Yoga and Roger were a loaded issue, and with the Water Solutions situation so abruptly stabilized, there was little to discuss there. I knew better than to bring up my media appearances, or the Program. That morning I'd mentioned I was going up to New York for a meeting and would get back late, but I hadn't said why.

When I came in the door the house was silent, and I went immediately to the library, relieved to find her reading on the couch. I noticed an empty highball glass on the table next to her.

"Thanks for waiting up."

She looked at me without a word, and I knew immediately that she'd seen the show. My embarrassment made me laugh. "The lap dance thing was totally unexpected!"

"That was sickening!"

The day had been too long and too weird, and I was tired of her silent disapproval of everything I did. I put my hands up in front of me. "Don't start! You don't know anything about it, so don't give me any crap!" I said it with all the finality I could muster, as if Hammer were whispering in my ear, *Show some spine, Jimbo!* I could tell from the look of outrage in her eyes that I'd made a stupid mistake, but I was beyond retreating. "What? Am I supposed to just sit back and let these people walk all over me? Let them spray me with piss and bomb my company?"

"This is that Whitehall thing, isn't it? The one you said you wouldn't be part of."

I didn't answer her, remembering Denton's admonition to keep it quiet.

"Answer me! Is this Whitehall's program? Is that why you're on television spouting all that propaganda and letting some stupid bimbo mash herself into your crotch while the whole country laughs at you? Is that what this is about? Did Whitehall tell you to do this?"

"You think everything is so simple—"

"I take it that's *yes*! Who else? That bunch of vultures at Barrington that—"

"—Good and bad! Right and wrong—"

"I've just lost all respect—"

"You are not my boss!" I yelled at her. "You don't dictate what I say and do!"

"No!" She threw her book aside. "Evidently that's someone else's job. I've had all I can stand, Jim." She began gathering up her reading glasses and her sweater.

I felt the panic coming into my voice. "You said if I wanted to fight to hold on to this company you would support me. Well, this is what it takes! We're . . . We're fighting a war here and I'm part of it, whether I want to be or not. Don't you understand that?"

She stood up from the couch, and I became frantic with the thought that she would run out again. I rushed to stand in front of her, and suddenly my anger at Barrington, the terrorists, at the whole sling my ass was in hardened into an iron sense of purpose. I made my voice flat and icy.

"Listen to me, Anne! Let me tell you how this plays out: I do my part and I bide my time. A year from now, when all these terrorist punks are in jail and my company is whole again, it's my turn to fuck Barrington. They fucked me; I'll fuck them. When that time comes I will kick Barrington and their goddamned program out on its ass so fast and so far they'll need a fucking compass to find my office! I'm playing the game, Anne, and it's a game you don't know anything about. You might want to consider that before you start judging me."

"You think this is all about you and your business—"

"And my family!"

She stepped back, shaking her head. *"Don't you dare!* Don't you *dare* use your family as an excuse! This is your ego, Jim."

"Maybe I'm doing this country a favor! Did you ever think of that? Bombings, murders, angry mobs in the streets . . . People like you just sit around hoping it will all go away by itself. Somebody's got to take action!"

"You don't believe that!"

"How do you know what I believe? All you care about is your school and your yoga and—"

"I can't live with this." She stepped around me and I watched her stride toward the foyer. I knew Anne, and I knew if she walked out this time it wouldn't be just for a night. I yelled across the house at her, *"That stripper thing wasn't my idea!"*

She opened the closet door and took out her coat. The incoherence of the day was spreading and deepening despite everything I said. "You don't get it!" I shouted. "I go along with them or I'm out the door! You understand? I'm out! We're both out!" I motioned toward everything around us. "The houses, the plane, your collection of Tibetan carpets. It all goes away!"

She opened the front door and turned to speak in a voice thickened with anger. "Then for God's sake, Jim. Let it *go!*"

16

"The keystone to lasting reform in this country is the Corporate charter," my date said. "They've taken that charter and parlayed it into a grant of complete impunity. If we scale back those charters and make officers personally responsible for the actions of their companies, and then punish companies who break the law by suspending their charters, you're going to see a whole new kind of Corporation emerge. One that can run its business without being a predator."

I nodded. The idea wasn't new to me, and, in fact, none of the ideas we'd talked about over our dinner at this posh Indian restaurant were particularly new. I'd agreed to this date partly because I'd gotten tired of the nickname the Nun and partly to convince myself that I could have a relationship with a real person. I suppose neither of them were particularly good reasons, and now my earnest young date was struggling to strike something up between us. I'd worn drab clothes and put my hair in a tight, unflattering little bun so as not to be too encouraging. I should probably at least pay for both our dinners. I'd just have to skip lattes for the next five weeks.

I hadn't heard anything from Lando since the demonstration three months ago. I still felt bad about how we'd left it—especially since he'd been right about the turnout, and the AOR had declared a cease-fire as they'd promised. I missed Lando. I loved his spirit and that he was willing to risk everything for what he believed in. But rationally, our relationship was more dream than substance, based on a few fugitive hours and my silly daydreams about an unattainable future. In the here and now, Lando and I had obligations to things that were bigger than ourselves, and those obligations would always put us at odds. As much as I wanted to call his secret number, I stuck to my decision and focused on my work.

Fortunately, the lull in bombings and arson had lowered the temperature a bit around all the Militants. Even though the Administration tried to vilify them, people didn't fear them the way they feared the foreign terrorists. The foreigners hated us and aimed for horrifying mass casualties. The Militants, on the other hand, had killed exactly two people, both of them corporate/political criminals who'd beaten the system in big public ways. As Lando had predicted, no one in the struggling lower and middle class had felt much sympathy for Water Solutions and their wrecked plant. In fact, there was even a kind of Guerrilla Chic sweeping the country.

"How'd you like Franklin Seven's press conference?"

"Lando!" I felt a fluttering in my chest, and I had to remind myself what had happened between us. "What are you doing here?"

He'd sidled up to me outside the bathrooms while my date waited for me to come back and order dessert. I noticed that his hair was longer and he looked less tired than before.

"You said you didn't want me cutting into your tai chi time."

He wore his young Chamber of Commerce outfit—navy blue blazer and nicely polished loafers at the bottom of his khaki slacks. I looked up and down his outfit in the narrow hallway and fingered the American flag pin in his lapel. "You are too much."

He nodded, but he wasn't quite so cocky as before. I could tell he hadn't forgotten our last meeting, either. "Not a peep from our side," he said. "Did we make good, or what?"

"You did. It's appreciated." I glanced nervously back toward my table. My companion's back was to me. "How have you been?"

"Just great. You know, turning the wheel of World Peace." A toilet roared behind me. "I need to talk to you," he said quickly. "It's serious. Ditch your boyfriend and walk down Sixteenth Street to Prospect after you leave here."

"He's not my boyfriend." It slipped out on its own, and I tried to cover it up immediately. "Not that that's relevant. This is important, right? DNN business?"

He looked at the ceiling, annoyed. "Down Sixteenth to Prospect, at Volunteer Park. See you in the next hour."

The door of the women's room opened and an Indian woman made space for me to pass. Lando was gone when I came out.

The rest of the dinner moved slowly, and when we finished the cardamom ice cream I wrestled him for the check. He seemed disappointed that I insisted on paying, and I suppose that prepared him for when I said a quick good night and left. I walked past the big porches and wide yards of Capitol Hill. At nine o'clock, the old residential streets were quiet and I could hear my footsteps on the sidewalk. I knew someone along the way would be watching me, maybe from one of the lightless windows in a house, or from behind the trunk of one of the old trees. It had rained that night and the air had that heavy refrigerated feel of impending snow. The weathermen were calling for one last little blanket before spring came. Near the end of the block, a station wagon pulled up next to me and the door opened.

"Hop in, Emily," the driver said. He looked about my own age, with a Seahawks cap pulled down to his eyebrows and a sweatshirt hood that covered the sides of his face. Big black-rimmed glasses made it hard to see the proportions of his eyes and nose. "Just keep looking straight ahead, please."

I did, but I could see out of the corner of my eye that he was looking at me. "So you're the famous Emily Cortright," he said. "You guys kicked ass at the Smackdown."

"Thank you. I think things are going to turn out okay."

"Yeah," he sighed, "someday we're all going to play ourselves in the made-for-TV movie."

I couldn't help smiling. "Lando's joining us, right?"

"Don't worry, your boy's all over it. Right up—" We turned another corner, heading back toward the restaurant. "—*here*."

Lando came out from the shadows of an evergreen bush and joined me in back, directing things before he even closed the door. "Next block is good."

The driver pulled over and got out of the car, leaving it running. Lando went over to him and gave him a brotherly hug. "Thanks, Tonk."

"No biggie."

Lando moved up to the front seat and pulled away.

"Old friends?" I asked.

"Years in the movement are like dog years: Every one is like seven. So yeah, we're old friends." He was quiet for a short time; then he pulled over and turned to me. "I want to say something before we get started, Emily."

I braced myself.

"I know you're pissed because you feel like I manipulated your group into shutting down the Business Symposium. I'm sorry I wasn't straight up with you. But I guarantee you that without a DNN victory, I never could have sold your cease-fire to my people. Not in a million years."

"The Jefferson Combine didn't—"

"That's the Combine. I'm talking about the people out here. I told you, I'm riding the tiger. And if the tiger wants Cascadia, I can't stop it. That doesn't mean I used you. It's important to me that you know that."

I sensed even without his earnest gaze that he was telling the truth, in his own way. Which didn't mean he wouldn't pull some other caper if he thought it was necessary. I might have to sort out my loyalties myself someday. "I guess that's just the way it is with us, Lando."

He looked at me a little longer, then nodded and started driving again, buoyant as if we'd left the whole matter at the curb. "So, give me a progress report. What's up with Democracy Northwest?"

A wisp of my old resentment came up, and he caught it.

"Hey: I may be an arrogant, manipulative asshole, but we're still on the same side."

I let it pass. "Okay. I guess you should know that your cease-fire isn't being wasted." I launched into an overview of what the DNN was doing. He was impressed that we were now connected with three thousand organizations across the country, all of them active in the Real Vote! campaign. In the Pacific Northwest, over four hundred affiliates had formally joined the Democracy Northwest Network. "That's six times as many as we had three months ago. We've got everybody from senior citizen groups to high school student councils."

"How about the Shriners? I'm not declaring victory until we've got the guys in the little red cars on our side."

"Hmmm. The Syrian Shrine Temple in Tacoma *might* be on the fence. I'll have to get back to you on that."

Dan had insisted we put particular focus on municipal employee unions, who'd been beaten up for a decade by the ruling party. Bus drivers, city bureaucrats, transit system operators, water workers, garbage collectors. Add in a few Teamsters and the Longshoremen's Union . . .

"Sure does make a general strike easy, doesn't it?"

"Funny you should notice that! We've even liaisoned with the police. Not to enlist them, but just to let them know what we stand for."

"I wouldn't get your hopes up. Cops and soldiers do as they're told."

"Until they don't. And that's when governments fall."

He gave a dry little chuckle. "Inshallah, baby. What's up with the Throwaways? Your Web site lists them as an affiliate."

I shrugged. "We work together on some issues. They're being coy."

"They weren't coy last week at Wal-Mart. It looked like they were ready to torch the place, if you can believe the videos. Even Whitehall backed down."

"Yeah, that surprised me."

"Oh, there'll be a massacre yet. They're just waiting for the right victim. It looks bad on TV if you shoot a bunch of people whose jobs have been offshored. Too many others out there are worried about the same thing. So tell me about the American Reform Party. You think they can win?"

"Well, coincidentally, the man you referred to as my boyfriend actually works for the American Reform Party. He says they've already got over two hundred potential candidates for the fall elections in Washington State, and they have a very good chance of putting a lot of them in power."

"The Accord can't be liking that. Their whole 'lesser of two evils' three-card monte doesn't work too well if all three cards aren't fake. But tell me, what'd you really think of Franklin Seven's press conference?"

"I thought it was brilliant."

That had been one of the boldest moves by the militants. Four days ago, Franklin Seven, one of the leaders of the Jefferson Combine, had arranged a secret press conference. He'd shown up in a Yankees cap, the team that had won the previous World Series, and he'd maneuvered that cap, above his ski-mask-covered face, onto magazine stands and TV shows all over the country. Even *People* magazine had given him a cover—FRANKLIN SEVEN: "I ALWAYS ROOT FOR THE YANKEES."

"I thought it was effective, too. He spent the whole first five minutes talking about the Yankees and their free agent situation and the last five talking about paper ballots and Thomas Jefferson. Now he's hotter than Che. He's trying to fight the picture war. Good luck!"

"What do you mean?"

"He knows TV's not going to address the real issues, so he's hoping that some good pictures can get people to rethink the little bits of information that do make it through. He's the photo, you guys provide the content."

I felt the old sting of his previous manipulation. "Thanks for letting us be part of the plan."

"The good news is, he's too big to kill now. I think as long as we keep the cease-fire, they won't go after him."

It sounded a little optimistic, but there was a certain logic to it. "So, what's this really about, Lando? I mean you and I, being here, the whole thing. You said this was serious."

"I need your help."

He let that statement stand there on its own, its simplicity reminding me of how I had asked for his help, and he'd given it. At the same time, I could tell by his tone of voice that it wasn't going to be an easy request. "What is it?"

"Maybe the Regime smells a change in the wind. Maybe they know they're on the way out and they want to get it while they can. You know what I'm talking about: privatizing the Golden Gate Bridge, parceling out the IRS to the big accounting firms—"

"I know."

"Some of that crap's reversible, and some isn't. They just let out contracts to cut the Siskiyou Forest, in Oregon, which was supposedly protected. It's one of the last shreds of old growth left in the Pacific Northwest. That's not reversible."

I took a deep breath. I knew where this was going.

Lando slipped into his cool, distanced political operator voice. "See, some people, not me, but some of our people aren't going to kick back and watch while Louisiana Pacific pads their annual statement with one of the last treasures we've got left."

"You're saying they'll break the cease-fire?"

"I'm saying it could turn out very badly for everyone."

I sighed. "And you want us to stop it."

"At least temporarily."

It irritated me. Not because it wasn't a worthy cause, but because we were buried in worthy causes, and I resented it. "You asked us to shut down Seattle and we did—"

"That's ancient history!" He caught himself. "What I mean is, the situation is fluid. I can't control it. Our people are pissed, and they have good reason to be. Can you really say you want them to sit back and let the Siskiyou be clear-cut without raising a finger? Honestly? Is that the moral thing to do? Be passive and let them destroy things they can never replace?"

I stared out the car window. I could list Dan and Shar's objections without even having to talk to them. "Aren't the environmental groups mobilizing around it?"

"Sure, but they're environmental groups. They don't go to the streets. We need a full-court press, like with Real Vote!"

"That's different. The Siskiyou is an environmental issue."

"Last time I checked, the Siskiyou was a National Forest that belonged to all the Citizens in the United States. It's a Privatization issue."

"I'm just telling you what Dan and Shar are going to say. They're going to say that we're a pro-democracy group and that we can't dilute our message."

There was an uncomfortable silence. "When you asked for my help, I put my ass on the line for you. And I wasn't the only one. I know you don't like to hear this, but we took a big risk just holding a meeting to discuss your cease-fire proposal. A lot bigger than 'diluting our message.'"

"I understand that."

"And I'm also talking about me, personally. I made your pitch for you and I backed it up with all my credibility. I didn't just throw it out there to die. I advocated for you, because I thought you were right, and because, well—"

"You wanted to get in my pants."

He laughed. "Hey! That's only fifty or sixty percent of it. No, seriously: I knew that on the big level we're in this together and that the DNN needed our help to succeed. And now we need the DNN's help. For everybody's good, because if certain people go to war in the Siskiyou, Franklin Seven isn't going to be showing up on the cover of *People* magazine in a Yankees cap."

"I'll do my best, Lando. I really will. I realize what's at stake, and I hope Dan and Shar will, too."

"Thanks. Hey . . ." His voice became a little awkward. "I wanted to take you someplace special."

"Where?"

"It's a surprise."

"Like the Smorgasteria?"

"No."

I felt a little awkward. "Um, we can't do anything, you know. I'm on DNN business." I tried to sound firm, but at the same time, I think I didn't want to be too convincing.

"Oh, of course! Lean back and close your eyes, okay?"

We arrived at the back of a small wooden house that could have been in any of a dozen different neighborhoods of Seattle. He led me in the back door and turned on the lights.

We were standing in a '40s-era kitchen with black and white octagonal tiles on the counter and cream-colored wooden molding with edges softened by endless layers of paint. It had the faint musty smell of shady kitchens in a damp climate, an older gas stove, not very clean, a few pots and pans hanging from hooks in the walls, a plastic colander in the sink with a few strands of dried-out spaghetti sticking to it. It was strange to see that he had a real eating, drinking, sitting-on-the-toilet life outside of the few hours we'd spent together.

I wandered ahead of him to the small dining room, where a scratchy wooden coffee table was surrounded by big pillows, Japanese-style. A bowl with grains of brown rice sat there with some smudges of black beans and a crust of salsa. In front of the bowl sprawled an electronics catalog and an empty Red Hook bottle.

"Last night's dinner?"

"Um, that was three nights ago."

Along the wall, below a poster of the Red Sox, were bookshelves made of cinder blocks and boards. A half shelf of worn software manuals, a primer on basic accounting, thriller novels, thick biographies of John Adams, Thomas Jefferson.

"Couldn't this revolutionary literature make you suspect?"

"Keep going."

"Morning in America: the Reagan Legacy."

"Now you're talking."

"The Laffer Curve and the Miracle of Supply-Side Economics." I looked up at him and raised my eyebrows. "The fantasy section?"

"You got it."

There was a sofa with an old wood-bodied television serving as an end table, complete with a speaker console made of gold-flecked fabric. A 1960s transistor radio molded in baby-blue plastic. A couple of catalogs with little white address stickers that read HENRY RAMPTON OR CURRENT OCCUPANT. On top of the television was a portrait of two older people.

"I take it these are your imaginary deceased parents."

"Phil and Dawna," he said in his Mass accent. "May they rest in peace."

"How come you get all the cool stuff and that other person has romance novels?"

"I won the persona lottery. Actually, there used to be three of us here, but the other two have their own places now." He moved very close to me. "So we're alone." For long and electric seconds the silence dissolved everything that existed except for us. Without saying anything else I reached for him and we began kissing. It was on again.

It had been three months since we'd been together, and that had been only the second time, so it still felt almost like kissing a stranger. I pulled away, suddenly puzzled.

"Why did you bring me here? Isn't this a violation of your Security stuff?"

"Officially? I told you, the Siskiyou problem."

"But we didn't have to come *here* for that."

He looked at the floor, then at me. "I guess that's the unofficial part."

Maybe someone else knowing is what makes things real in some way. We all need someone to form a profile of us, to understand us, and in love, when you let the barriers down, you want it to be a real profile, not fake one. He led me up a narrow stairway to a small attic bedroom beneath the eaves. The pink city light slanted through the back window and picked out pieces of furniture, a wash of floor. He clicked on a tiny lamp beside the bed. It was a simple, lovely room, all painted white, relieved by the rhythm of the tiny black cracks where the wooden wall boards had dried and shrunken away from each other. A white chintz bedspread covered the mattress, next to a small table with a Bible on it. Little signs of disarray: a pair of gray socks crumpled on the floor, a silvery puddle of nickels and dimes on the seat of a wooden chair. At the far end of the room an ironing board leaned beside a closet filled with suit jackets and shirts. He stepped over and closed it, as if he didn't want to admit their existence.

"Lando, does anyone know about us? I mean your friends."

He said emphatically, "No! But don't worry about all that—we're in the White Room now. It's where I can be me."

"Whoever you are."

"Whoever I am."

We sank down to the bed, which was oversoft in a wonderful way. He unfastened my hair and spread it out around my shoulders. We did everything very slowly at first, like we were moving through honey. I told him what I wanted and he told me how good it felt. It was the middle of the night by now, so everything happened in that druggy atmosphere of being really sleepy and really filled with desire at the same time. Afterwards we curled up together and disappeared.

When I woke up the next morning, he'd thrown a flannel bathrobe on and was sitting beside the bed with a blue ceramic teapot. Almost like a real boyfriend. "Good morning, beautiful. What do you want for breakfast? I've got eggs, yogurt, toast, oatmeal."

"That all sounds wonderful."

"One of everything. I'll be right back."

I propped myself up on the bed and sipped the tea. The usual winter haze had lifted, and a skewed rectangle of white sunshine reached across the wall beside the back window. I could see the branches outside were covered with a crust of snow, and I felt a little thrill of happiness. During the night Lando had thrown a burgundy-colored afghan over the bed, and I felt for a moment like I was in one of those perfect country homes from a housewares catalog, a never-ending morning of snowy sheets and steaming mugs, where the dog is somewhere downstairs and the fireplace is magically burning and no one will come to your door or call you on the phone to trample your peace. I held the cup below my nose and basked in the lemony vapor. We could just stay here for a while. All day. A couple of days. It was a weekend now. Maybe it would snow again. I had a right to disappear beneath the snow. Even the earth itself did that sometimes.

I felt a light winter chill on my shoulders and breasts, and I started searching the floor around the bed for the T-shirt I'd pulled off the night before. I came across something hard and angular, and glanced over the edge. It was a pistol. I'd never held a gun before. I picked it up carefully.

It was so dense and black, while the room was so airy and pale. Something dark and heavy seemed to billow out from it. I remembered how callous Lando had been when he'd talked about John Polling's assassination. I heard his footsteps on the stairs; then he was standing at the top of the stairs with a tray in his hands, looking at me.

"A gun and a Bible," he said, "the two things every real American has at his bedside."

"Do you really know how to use this thing?"

"Of course. It's an HK thirty-two. Eight in the clip, one in the chamber. You squeeze the grip and it's cocked. But don't."

My question came from out of nowhere, a joke that wasn't a joke. "Did you kill John Polling with this?"

A shadow passed across his face; then he gave me a look of good-natured condescension. "John Polling was killed by a .308 Winchester. That's a hunting rifle. What you're holding is a semiautomatic pistol that's not accurate beyond about fifty feet. Twenty feet if I'm shooting it."

"Why do you keep it by your bed?"

He answered with a tentative lilt at the end of his sentences, as if he were speaking a foreign language and trying to get the grammar right. "Because there're people who would kind of like to capture me? Then torture me until I tell them everything I know? So they can grab my friends and torture them, too?"

I swallowed but I kept smiling. It was all so strange in this wonderful white room. "You mean you'd never let them take you alive? C'mon! This Administration is bad, but they're not—"

He cut me off with an unpleasant intensity. "They haven't been challenged yet."

"What about the Symposium Demonstration? That was—"

"That was a bump in the road for them! Wait till you go after Corporate charters! Or make a serious run at the military-petroleum axis—that's when you'll see what these people are really like. When they go down, they'll go down in a rage!"

The whole weight of everything fell on me all at once, destroying the perfect morning in a few seconds. I felt my eyes tearing up.

He put the tray on the bed and sat down next to me, put his arm around my shoulder. "I'm sorry."

I heard the high whining complaint that had come into my voice. "You don't have to be so goddamned apocalyptic about everything!"

"I know."

"Why do you do this to me? It's scary enough without you slamming me against a wall every time I'm starting to feel like . . . like there's something precious here."

"I'm sorry. You just have to ignore me sometimes."

I wanted to reason away all the danger, to somehow normalize the things he'd done. "I mean . . . It's a process! If it takes ten years to make things right, then it takes ten years! It doesn't all have to happen in six months. And it doesn't take shooting anybody!" He held himself closer to me without saying anything, and I had the horrible feeling that he didn't think he had more than six months. I didn't want to live in that world he kept pushing me into. I flopped backwards on the pillow.

Lando put his hands around my waist and kissed my lips and looked into my eyes. "You're so beautiful. I'm sorry to load you down with my fears."

"Why don't you get out of this, Lando? You can't win."

He sighed. "It's your nature to want to save things and save people, and I need to honor that, because that's the higher impulse. But you're wrong about this. The People need us, and we *can* win. We're already winning. Now, please . . . Will you eat something?"

He climbed in next to me and we balanced the tray on our knees. I spread strawberry jam on the toast and crunched into it.

I was in love with this person I knew absolutely nothing about, except that he was so fragile that even when I was with him he didn't seem entirely real. When I wasn't with him I felt like I'd created him with my imagination—a cute, funny, fantasy guerrilla, just like so many people had created a fantasy President Matthews the way they wanted to see him. Even now, lying next to him in bed, there was still so much that was disturbingly elusive about him that I just started talking. "My father is a shipwright. Did I tell you that? He lives in Port Townsend and has a small shipyard there."

"What kinds of boats does he work on?"

"He used to work on a lot of wooden fishing boats, but that's all over. Now he works on yachts and sailboats. Lots of rich people in Seattle take their boats out to him." Lando kept listening without saying anything. "He's funny. He'd take in stray boats the way other people take in stray dogs. He'd find some old wooden Columbia River double-ender or fifties-era Chris-Craft on the beach, and he couldn't bear to leave it there."

"A champion of languishing causes: Gee, I wonder what happened to that strain of the family?"

"Very funny. He must have reconstructed seven or eight wooden boats with his own time and money. Our money. Finally, he bought this huge eighty-foot seiner from an old Norwegian fisherman from

Alaska. I think it was built in 1917. It had a motor as big as a twin bed. Just this massive wooden hulk, which my dad renamed the *Happy*. He decided he'd fix it up and we'd live aboard it and travel around the Northwest Coast repairing boats and living the life."

"Sounds great! Did you?"

"It burned to the waterline about a week after he got it. I always suspected my mother."

"Really?"

"I think she'd had enough. She's Greek. Never make a Greek woman angry."

"The underlying theme of many classic plays. Are they still together?"

"Yes. Once the *Happy* sunk, they could actually *be* happy. Figure that one out." He laughed and I chattered on. "My mother actually used to be a professional figure skater. She still coaches skating at the local rink. And I've got two little brothers. One works with my dad and the other's still in college. He's studying journalism." I sighed, running out of words. "And I'm telling you all this so that maybe when we're apart I'll feel like we have a real relationship that extends beyond great sex and some shared politics."

"I'm okay with great sex."

"Oh, shut up! Can't you be serious for more than two minutes?"

Things were quiet for a while. He poured me some more tea. Then, to my surprise, he started talking. "You'd like my mother." He leaned back against the pillows. "She's great. She's a teacher, and she's into yoga and all that stuff. And she's very smart. You two are kind of similar, actually."

"Thank you, Lando. That's a really nice comparison."

He crinkled his eyes. "Wait a second, this is getting all weird and Oedipal."

"You're not worming out of this."

"Okay. So, then, I have an older sister, the kind who always gets things right. She's very responsible, everything a big sister is supposed to be. As I've been hearing all my life."

"What about your father?"

His easy speech dried up. He glanced up at the ceiling, deciding whether to take on the question. "My father is one of those people who always wins at games. When you play Monopoly, he ends up with the Oranges and Boardwalk. In Risk he's always your ally and then your enemy. Right now my father's really absorbed in his game."

"What is his game?"

"I can't tell you that. Someday you might be an anonymous guest of the System."

"Do we have to live everything as the worst possible scenario?"

"No, we can make dumb mistakes that get me killed."

"That's a convenient trump card."

"I'll tell you this: My father is Big Corporate. And I mean Big *Bad* Corporate, not widget-makers or airlines. Arm-twisting, Government-buying, election-stealing, Disinformation Corporate."

"Seriously?"

"Yeah. He's one of the predators." He suddenly became nervous. "No one else knows that. Not even Tonk."

"Lando, if your father is some sort of big Corporate insider, then he could also do a lot of good. Think how much credibility he'd have if he talked about how things really work. It wouldn't just be coming from the opposition."

"Yeah, I used to think that. The pathetic thing is, he really believes in what he does. See, when you're one of those guys, you draw the Picture. First, you do whatever you have to do to make it big: screw who you have to screw, neglect who you have to neglect. And once you're up there, hauling in the big bucks, you draw the Picture. Donate money to charity, maybe help out some Salvadoran maid with free legal work, or pull some strings to get her family into the country. Drink wine with your Mexican gardener. And that's the Picture: You're a big generous guy who really loves to help people, not some conniving SOB who'd chisel a million dupes and lie about it if it made his company a few extra bucks. You happen to be rich just because you're so damned clever and hardworking. And anyone who's not rich just doesn't work hard enough. They don't deserve good health care or good schools. Color that in with some charitable donations and some puff pieces in the business magazines, and you start believing it yourself."

"You sound really angry at him."

"I love my father. But it's frustrating. He's a smart man. He's not Evil. But he's invested so much of himself in his little self-portrait that anything that doesn't fit, he just distorts until it falls into line. Some part of him knows that, but I don't know what it takes to break him out of his stupor. I keep looking for the words, and I keep not finding them." He gave a bitter little laugh. "It's human. Look at America: Matthews steals their pensions, and thirty percent are still cheering him on. Partly because they think he's going to show punk Radicals like you and me that he means business."

"But people can learn."

"Yeah," he said. "They *can* learn. If I didn't believe that, I wouldn't be doing what I'm doing."

We made love again on top of the toast crumbs, and as I lay there staring at the white ceiling, the warm slippery buzz began to fade away and leave the invisible questions hanging over us. I dragged my watch from the night table and looked at it. "Eleven o'clock."

He'd been lying with his arm across my stomach, but now he rolled onto his back. "Crap! I have to be somewhere at noon."

"So . . ." I didn't really want to be back in the world, but I had no choice. "I've got to talk to Dan and Shar about the Siskiyou. How long are we supposed to stop it for?"

"I don't know. A month or two? Whatever it takes to muster enough pressure to reverse the contracts."

A month or two. "I'll try."

"I need you to succeed, Emily. I'm afraid of what's going to happen if you don't."

The conversation with Dan and Shar went exactly as I'd known it would. I made all the arguments: that it was a Privatization issue, that the Siskiyou couldn't be replaced. I felt like Lando was standing behind me the whole time, and I made them as convincingly as I could, but they were adamant that we couldn't daisy-chain into an environmental issue. Even the prospect of a broken cease-fire just made them angry instead of convincing them. In the end, they agreed to run the issue by the board members at the next meeting.

I muddled through the rest of the day then went home early. Dave was waiting in the kitchen and could sense that I was down, but I passed quickly by and went into my room. At eight o'clock I finally borrowed a friend's computer and called Lando with the news. He listened as I bumbled through the explanation; then there was a silence that left me wondering if he'd hung up. "Lando? Did you hear me?"

"Tell Dan and Shar I'm glad they're keeping their brand pure," he said coldly. I heard his long breath come through the metal cable to the receiver, and a tone that sounded tired and final. "I love you, Emily. I'll do what I can."

17

*T*he Siskiyou's the one little shred of unmowed lawn left in Oregon. The loggers did a pretty thorough job in the twentieth century, reducing the Great North Woods into a jumble of tree farms and little stands of old growth as they cut themselves into bankruptcy. Still, as long as there was one big tree left, they wanted to cut it, go on living that fantasy of the limitless bounty of God's Country, where God promised to fill up your gas-guzzling pickup one more time if you'd just do him the favor of destroying His creation for him. The Siskiyou hangs on as three islands of wilderness in a sea of clear-cuts, roads, and burnovers. It's home to fifty-three thousand species and the world's oldest living form of azalea, with five of its rivers classified as Wild and Scenic, Government language for *We'll be back to cut you later.*

The sale breaks every law of economics Adam Smith ever wrote. The Government will spend more than eighty million dollars on road-building and planning, then sell off the timber rights to Louisiana Pacific for a total of about two million. The logs will be shipped to China in the round, then sold back to us as finished product. Nothing remotely free market here: more than anything just a chance for the Regime to spend seventy-eight million dollars of taxpayer money to show Greenies where they really stand.

Earl E. spent a lot of his teenhood in the Siskiyou, climbing the eight-foot-wide tree trunks and riding the wind in the canopy. Up there alone, the tree starts talking to you, reaches into your heart and becomes part of you, all its seven hundred years of rainstorms and fires, numberless sunny days and blowing snowflakes. After that, when you see them come down and become deadwood, ripped to pieces by men eager to knock them down and move on to the next stand, it makes a hole in you. So I understand Earl E. only too well. I sit back with the others and hold my breath, hoping he'll lay off. Hoping he won't.

The mere destruction of the last remaining forests doesn't count as news in Big Media, so we have to follow the Siskiyou Project Web site to get the blow by blow. At first an action alert goes out to their network, warning that all their appeals have failed and that the only course left is to buy time with direct action. Various defiant-sounding proclamations, maps, contact numbers, links to other sites hosted in Canada or Europe with instructions about how to rig up a tree-sit or a technical blockade. A few days later they start posting the visuals: loggers versus longhairs, little clusters of college-age Greenies chained to logs on muddy roads with nothing around but a few sheriffs and some angry-looking men in yellow hard hats and overalls. Same old story: loggers and Lefties fighting over the scraps while the Corporates back at headquarters take long lunches and wonder about when to cash in their stock options. It's unfailingly gray and rainy, the protesters look sodden and tired, not able to go home at night, but instead shitting in the woods and sleeping in musty tents that smell like mildew and dirty socks. It's lonely and boring, like any war, sparked by a few moments of extreme confrontation. A picture of a drag-assed Greenie makes it into the Seattle paper, but the networks look the other way.

"No direct action yet," Sarah says. "Maybe Earl E. decided to lay off after all."

I don't answer her, because Earl E. hasn't responded to my messages, gone deep blue for reasons better left unthought.

A brief flicker of hope as the Greenies start slowing things down. But after a few days the Forest Service and Whitehall seals off the area to try to crimp their logistics. Feeding several hundred people gets a lot harder when you have to carry everything in on your back, through the woods, and the hated FS takes the next step of rooting out the Greenie campsites and hustling them off to jail in Cave Junction and Selma, isolating the blockaders. The blockades keep falling, and then it's down to tree-sits. Images of big trees with bright red or yellow ropes webbed around the top with nylon-colored bivy sacks suspended like the cocoons of giant butterflies. Louisiana Pacific's contract cutters fell the trees around them, leave the big ancient ones standing naked in the middle of a grotesque stump field, isolated in the open, without anyone to bring them food or fuel; then they move on to the next stand. Maybe they've designated them Wild and Scenic trees. *We'll be back to cut you later.*

Not looking good for the Kalmiopsis Wilderness. America slumbers on, of course: if it's not on TV, it doesn't exist, and this one's not going to make the Stupid Machine until something explodes. Which doesn't take long. Earl E., or somebody else, decides to lob a picture their way. Four big logging toys go up in smoke the same night, with a .30-.30 round fired through the windshield of a pickup truck just to add an exclamation point. A joyous clashing of symbols arises from the Lie Machine.

A unilateral cease-fire declared nine weeks ago by militant groups came to a violent end today.

"That's just one group!" I spit at the screen.

Militants opposed to a timber sale in the Kalmiopsis area of Oregon—

"It's the Kalmiopsis *Wilderness,* you fucking liar! It was designated *Wilderness!*"

—have bombed four timber harvesting sites in an effort to halt salvage logging efforts by local loggers.

We don't have to look at the Web site to get this one. Channel America's plastered it jubilantly through their morning stories. A flaming high-line rig, a sad-looking foreman, scratching his head as if he were really engaged in some legitimate business, rather than a taxpayer shakedown that the interviewer forgets to mention. The Picture is Greenie Terrorists. The Picture is Hardworking Loggers Trying to Support Their Families. They work some kids into the shot, hiding behind their dad with little Stihl Saw hats. God bless America, where the last few species of Workingman can always be rolled out for marketing like the smiling pigs on a pack of sausages. The red, white, and blue panic logo AMERICA UNDER ATTACK! revives the old slogan they used before the cease-fire. Over and over again they show the bullet-webbed windshield of the logging truck. The prophets get busy: "There's a seamless connection between so-called mainstream environmental groups and these ecoterrorists," says one commentator with sketchy security credentials. "When a Democracy's standards are under attack, you can't let people hide behind the Constitutional guarantees they try to take away from others."

The last line delivered, stunningly, by my father on *Washington Challenge*, one of those Channel America "discussion" skits where four Right Wingers shout down a Centrist in a parody of debate. There's dear old James Sands, seated next to America's Leni Reifenstal, a neo-Nazi babe with long blond hair who smugly suggests that the governor of Oregon declare martial law and shoot to kill anyone left in the woods after twenty-four hours. Dad nods along.

Sarah's sitting next to me on the Blue Wave while it plays. "McFarland was right. We should have iced that prick."

He looks younger than in real life, hale and healthy with makeup, then I look closer, and the more I look, the more he seems like a corpse made up for viewing. He smiles, then appears thoughtful as the MC phrases his question: Did he think domestic terrorists are entitled to the same constitutional protections as other U.S. citizens? "The short answer, Bob, is, I don't think people are entitled to the protections they would try to deprive others of."

I can't stop my voice. "And what about governments that try to deprive people of their protections? What are they entitled to?"

No irony on this set, though. The three Fascists are bobbing their heads approvingly and even the guy playing the liberal gives him a thoughtful-looking gaze, his wimpy spectacles two little ovals of glass respect.

"I've been the victim of terrorism," my father dribbles on, "and, let's be honest: It's such a heinous crime that when a person resorts to it, they're excluding themselves from the Community of Law. They're Enemies of Freedom in the worst sense."

The crap piles up for another ten minutes, with my father smiling and listening, as if this were a real conversation. When I split from

Sarah I can't resist calling him, route it through my San Francisco number. At his office they put it through to him right away, still a son's prerogative.

"Joshua! How are you? I've missed you!" His voice sounds so happy at getting a call from me that for a moment I lose track of my anger, just want to talk about how Mom's doing, my sister's wedding plans, the weather in D.C., even his company's latest antics. I brace myself and try to associate the warm fatherly voice on the line from the man whose pictures had just injected a little more poison into the world.

"I saw you on TV an hour ago."

"Oh." A funny, deflated sort of sound. Subdued now: "They aired *Washington Challenge,* didn't they?"

"Yep."

Dire silence over the line. He goes belligerent on me. "I don't owe you any explanations!" When I don't answer, he gets nervous. "Joshua?"

"I'm not even sure what I wanted to say to you, Dad. I just felt . . . disgust."

That sets him off. "You have the luxury of feeling disgust, Joshua. Because you're sitting around as a spectator. I'm on the front lines! I didn't ask to be there and I can't say I enjoy it a hell of a lot, but as long as I'm here, I'm going to do my part! You think democracy is just something you can have a cozy feeling about and it'll be there. Well, it isn't! It's use it or lose it! There's a battle for hearts and minds going on in this country—"

"Have you got a few more clichés you can justify your life with, Dad?"

"I don't have to justify shit to you!"

"Yeah? What did Mom think? Did she see it?"

He doesn't answer, but I'm too angry to stop.

"What about Kurt Kassel? He was Secretary of the Virginia ACLU, wasn't he? What'd he say? 'Right on, Jim. That's showing 'em!'"

"I told you I haven't seen Kurt Kassel in five—"

"I know, you run with a better crowd now. Listen to me, Dad. You may think you're playing them, but the bottom line is, you don't play them. They play you! You're going to find that out someday."

I imagine him shifting the phone to his other ear. He sounds like my dad now. "What is this? You call me at the office to tell me you don't like what I'm doing? You didn't even ask how I am! If that's all you've got to say, then let's just drop it, because I'm too busy—"

"You've always been too busy!"

That stops both of us for a second. Finally he says, "You're not rational!" and I hear the line click down in my ear. I stare at it dully. You've always been too busy! Where the hell did that come from? Is that what this is all about? Some poor neglected Freud-child showing his anger at Daddy by blowing up his toys? I consider it as I make a cup of tea. Life sure gets trivial when you play the childhood card, as if every act you thought of as Free Will can suddenly be ascribed to being forced to stay at the table and finish your vegetables. Do I have some issues with dear old Dad? Sure. But I have bigger issues with the dear old Regime, and this weird nostalgic love for America the way it's supposed to be and maybe never has been or will be ever again. Maybe it's all the same thing, redeeming our fathers and redeeming the country. You reach a certain age and suddenly your parents' faults become obvious: their weakness, their dishonesties, their selfishness, the things they shouldn't have done and the things they left undone. All that burden of an imperfect world left on our doorstep one morning and no choice but to pick the brat up and try to make it better.

Not that those fine issues matter right now, as the pictures stream over television and Internet. The guerrillas are on the loose, and *You* might be their next victim!

"Fucking Earl E.!" I say.

"It could have been Volunteers," Tonk says, at Sarah's place. "Anybody with a milk jug and some gasoline could have pulled those off."

"They had timing devices."

Tonk shrugs. "So they had timers! Do you think we're the only guys who ever took apart a clock?" He stands up and walks in an irritated circle, then taps his fist against the wall a couple of times. Tonk's not a strategist, but he knows this isn't good for us.

Sarah's all business in her usual outfit of gray sweatpants and a T-shirt. "We need a statement." My guess is that Tonk stayed the night, but she doesn't seem any mellower for having had a good roll in the hay.

"How about, 'Let's stop cutting down trees and start cutting down CEOs'?"

She's annoyed, her perpetual mood. "I was looking for something a little more conciliatory, Tonk. The Jefferson Combine already disavowed them. So have the Gettysburg people."

"That's easy for them; they're two thousand miles away." I get up and wander into the kitchen to swirl the last dregs of the coffee into my cup, then rattle the icing-caked cellophane of a pack of Danish pastries. "Maybe instead of disavowing them, we should get across the idea that when Corporates own the Government, direct action is the only option left."

"I don't think that's going to fly, Lando. The whole reason we declared a cease-fire was to strengthen the Civil Groups. If we want to preserve that, we need to put some distance between what's happening in the Siskiyou and our cease-fire." Her voice softens as I come back into the room with my breakfast. "I hate to say it, but Earl E. has to come off like some sort of crazy splinter group."

I think of the people out there, whoever they are. Trudging through the soaking woods, eating cold food and staying under cover during daylight. By now the logging assets are all under guard and people are out hunting them. The tree-sitters are fighting hypothermia and the blockaders are all in jail. There'll be dogs and trackers, and Whitehall is definitely in the building now, doing flyovers with infrared and night-vision goggles, waiting to nail some Greenie heads to the wall. If they're smart, they made for Route 199 before the checkpoints went up, or maybe humped it thirty miles to I-5, where it's harder to clamp down. But that would mean retreat, and letting them finish off the forest. "Those are very brave people up there, Sarah. Whoever they are. We can't just turn our back on them."

She's not letting me off so easy. "Hold on a second, Lando. Remember the big meeting last fall? Remember the Civils shutting down Seattle in exchange for a cease-fire? Which *you* pushed for? If we're going to have a policy, we've got to be consistent."

"And turn against our own people? While the Civils are doing nothing, they're out there fighting the machine. At least they stopped the cutting."

"For how long?"

"Sarah, part of me thinks we ought to be down there ourselves."

"Yeah, the 'I'm under arrest' part."

"Look: Earl E. brought it to me and I said no, for all the very good reasons you've mentioned. But I can't help but wonder if we'd all gotten behind it, and attacked before they even got into the woods, it might not have gone this far."

Sarah listens and shakes her head. She's graded it not worth discussing. "We need to talk with McFarland and the High Plains guys before we put out a statement. They've got a say, too. But I think we need to do it soon, before someone gets caught. Once they're caught, it makes us look like we're capitulating."

"They were stupid to take it to open country," McFarland judges between funnels of gray smoke. We're sitting in the Pinsetta Lounge of the King Bowling Center, drinking plastic cups of mass-market beer. The room is dim and empty in the midafternoon. We could be in France in 1787, plotting the overthrow of Louis XVI. Words about recession and extinction slither across the bottom of the screen, but the football game blaring above them lets us know that none of that is really important enough to pay attention to. A couple of lanes are in use, and every now and then the muffled explosion of a strike erupts through the door like a breaking wave. "They're sitting ducks."

I feel like I have to defend them. "They couldn't choose the ground."

"This is a half-assed campaign, and half-assed campaigns get people killed for bullshit. Is it Earl E.?"

"We don't know. We haven't heard from him. Have you?"

He shakes his head. With his hollow cheekbones and brown eyes: the haggard workingman's saint.

"Nobody else has either. San Franciso Mark told me Earl E. contacted him about three weeks ago and asked if he'd be up for some operations against Louisiana Pacific, but that's all."

Mac nods; then the place goes too quiet as the jukebox runs out. I go up to the bar to get change and the bartender glances down at my T-shirt and gives me the thumbs-up. "Damn straight!"

It's the one with the flag and the motto THESE COLORS DON'T RUN! A good accessory for my fake USMC tattoo, which matches his own.

"Where'd you serve?" he says.

"Bolivia," I tell him. "The Chapare. They sent me home with malaria on my second tour." I give him a nod. "Later, bro. *Semper fi.*"

I put some loud choices on the jukebox and go back to McFarland, who'd caught the exchange.

"You're the skinniest marine I ever saw."

"Dude, I had malaria! Besides, I'm one of those psycho guys that lays out in the jungle for weeks eating bugs."

He rolls his eyes. "So about this statement Sarah wants to make. Do our other people want to back off from it, too?"

"They're mixed. They want to keep the cease-fire, but it makes them sick to watch them wipe out the Siskiyou. My guess is they'll sign off on whatever we decide."

"I'm not that worried about the Siskiyou, but I don't want to turn on one of our own." He went silent for a few seconds. "Maybe we can split the difference. Wait and see. Maybe they've exfiltrated already and the whole thing will die down."

A wonderful hope, but an exploding one, as those kinds of hopes turn out to be. Sarah calls me at Henry Rampton's house the next afternoon, just as I'm about to dig into a bowl of ramen. "They got one of Earl E.'s crew."

"Don't tell me that!"

"Turn on KFX."

The set goes on and I hear Earl E.'s voice sounding thin and weird and badly recorded against a still-photo of a burning high-line rig. ". . . wounded and captured by Whitehall mercenaries two days ago in the Siskiyou Wilderness area. We demand that his arrest be legalized and that he be treated in accordance with the Geneva Convention."

"Holy shit!" I said over the phone. "That's him."

"He didn't even scramble his voice. They're going to tie it to his old Anarchist Front days and come out with a photo."

Whitehall's spokesmodel shows up in front of the flashing cameras looking daisy-fresh in her navy blue dress. "It's true that we are serving as security consultants to Louisiana Pacific and its subcontractors, but any claims that we're running around shooting people or arresting people are just false. We have no record of a Michael Arliss, and anyone apprehended trespassing in closed areas of the Kalmiopsis timber sale would be turned over immediately to the Douglas County authorities."

Now it's the Douglas County Sheriff, short-haired and thick-necked, with the great seal of Oregon stamped onto the set next to an American flag. Officer Blah Blah earnestly denies that Michael Arliss is in custody. "We're still trying to get to the bottom of this story. We have received several calls that the suspect has been sighted in the last twelve hours, and we're proceeding on the assumption that he is still at large and should be considered armed and dangerous." To a muffled question he smiles and answers, "I wish we did have him, because I'd certainly like to ask him a few questions."

Now they flash a high school yearbook picture of Michael Arliss, a kid with a long face and curly blond hair wearing that uncertain yearbook smile. Rumors that he's been seen in Eugene six hours ago. *Anyone sighting Arliss should call . . .* My only question is whether it's Whitehall calling in the fake sightings or whether the blueshirts completely made them up. Look ma, no prisoners. Next a talker pops up: "Bill, I think what we're seeing here is the information war being played by the terrorists. If they can use the media to spread fear and suspicion . . ."

Right fucker: and you resent that because that's *your* job. I turn off the Stupid Machine and call Sarah back. "Do we know Michael Arliss?"

"One of Earl E.'s guys, evidently. Earl E. says Whitehall wounded him yesterday and has him squirreled away somewhere for interrogation."

"What's Michael know about us?"

"Whatever Earl E.'s told him."

The implications cascade down over each other. I've got a layer there: Earl E. knows me as Lando, which is the only way anyone but Tonk knows me. But he also knows Mac's home base area, all the passwords and authorization codes, enough to give Der Homelanders a running start at cracking the network. It all feels very shaky all of the sudden.

"Has anybody heard from Earl E.?"

"Not yet. I talked to Gonzalo. The comps are nervous."

I don't blame them. Nervous because this wasn't in the script, nervous because they've captured someone who might have information that leads, however indirectly, to the rest of us. Nervous, too, because if what Earl E. says is right, and I suspect it is, Whitehall's moving America into a brand-new phase, the phase where Corporates kidnap with impunity, and from there, it's one more very small step to death squads.

"Let's scrub the old network. I'll tell Gonzalo to issue a new set of codes to everyone but Earl E. Each group needs to redo their access information."

"Do you think we should relocate?"

Relocating means we change our apartments and maybe even our identities. But Earl E.'s never been to any of our safe houses, and he's met only me and Tonk. "Not yet. I think all they'll get from him is that there's a group in Seattle and that we're starting to network, which they know already. I'll check with McFarland."

McFarland did some cross-training with Earl E. fifty miles away on an unplanted farm, but other than that he's clear. Still, it's a chilly wind. One little thread leads to all the other little threads, so we're changing all the old connections and leaving Earl E. out of the web. I'm pissed at him, but I feel sorry for him, maybe still in the woods getting wet and cold, fighting a battle he can't win, abandoned by the gods, abandoned by us, his *compañeros*. I decide to keep my same phone line for a few more days, just in case.

I'm finally getting back to my lukewarm bowl of noodles when Emily calls. I've been so stressed out and busy that I haven't bothered to eat, and, stupidly, I give Emily a crisp "hello" to let her know how pissed I am about the DNN ducking the Siskiyou issue.

It seems to hurt her a little: she drops back into business mode. "I need to talk to you about something. We got a call this morning from someone who claims to be the group that just burned that logging equipment in the Siskiyou Forest. He says one of their people was captured by Whitehall and he wants our help to get him legalized."

"What did you tell him?"

"I told him it wasn't that simple."

Maybe the lack of wholesome meals is making me twitchy. "Why not? You're the Democracy people, aren't you? In the old American democracy it used to be illegal to grab someone and hold them in a secret prison."

She's trying to straddle here. "Technically, the police should be investigating this as a kidnapping."

"I'm sure they're all over it. They've probably got the head of White-hall in the back room under a desk lamp right now, sweating it out of him."

"Lando—"

I don't want to cut loose, but I can't help it. "You guys thought you could duck this whole Siskiyou thing to hold on to your Brand, but now it's just dragging your asses in deeper than before. This is exactly why I asked you guys to take action on the Siskiyou!"

"That's not helpful." She keeps her voice calm. "Of course we'd like to get this person legalized if he's been captured, but we need to know more so it doesn't blow up in our faces and get used against us."

"Anything you say can and will be used against you! They make that promise at the end of every cop show, and this country's one big cop show now!"

"For goodness' sake, Lando, calm down! I'm on your side, remember?

I hesitate. "Sorry. It's low blood sugar."

We're back in neutral again. "Anyway, I called you to try to check this person out before we make a decision. Do you know the man that they claim Whitehall is holding?"

"No. But I recognize the voice they're broadcasting. Yes, he's a real Militant, and I'd be very surprised if he was making this up. Have you tried calling Michael Arliss's family?"

"We haven't gotten through to them yet. Dan and Shar want to leave it to the Human Rights groups until we know more. They're set up for this sort of thing."

"Here's my advice: You want Michael Arliss legalized? Put people in the street and make a big deal out of it! You duck your head on this and you'll have three more Michael Arlisses next month."

"We can't call people out for demonstrations every time something bad happens! We need to focus on our core issues."

"Is that what you're going to say if they ever grab me?"

"That's not fair, Lando!"

I hear the fear in her voice and I wish I hadn't unloaded on her. "I'm sorry." A recurrent theme today. I take a breath and start over. "I'm sorry I went off on you. You guys didn't create this problem. Neither did we. It's the Regime and their buddies, and it's not going to end until they're gone. Do what you have to."

We hang up, leaving me pondering all the intimate, affectionate things we didn't say.

Fucking Earl E.!

The Siskiyou Project Web site states that there's three tree-sits left, and the company's threatening to send up climbers after them. The loggers are going back in the next day to resume cutting. If I were Earl E., I'd find it hard to stay away.

And he does. The news comes in on the Stupid Machine when I'm riding the Metro home to my place. *Ecoterrorists killed one logger and injured two more today in the Siskiyou. An improvised explosive device shattered the morning calm in the troubled Oregon woods today. . . .*

Visuals of the bent-up flatbed, an ambulance. The brownshirts have cameras in the carriage so I display no emotion, meanwhile thinking stupid stupid *stupid* Earl E.! Killing some guy with a lunchbox and a yellow hat, who, though not exactly innocent, was still so very far away from being a Polling or a Byzic, men who had corrupted entire systems. To which Earl E. would tell me, "It's the machine we're fighting, Lando. And they're part of the machine."

Right or wrong, it's bad strategy. The Pictures are lighting up all over, with Louisiana Pacific and the Regime swinging into high gear as defenders of the blessed victims. Some poor logger's worth a thousand times more dead than he ever was alive, when they stripped him of his pension and his health care. The dead guy gets sanctified from a million different angles: family man, disappearing vestige of the Old America that wore hard hats and did real work. Gonzalo runs across the Oregon court records that list six domestic violence complaints, but that doesn't make the hagiography. It's a straight story here: Honey, we got us a martyr.

By morning there's a crowd in front of the Southwest Oregon Conservation League howling for blood, and the cameras are loving it. A Louisiana Pacific front group has sponsored this particular show, but you have to go to the Internet for that information, and who has time for that? The picture is "Wrath of the Martyr's Friends!" and you don't even need a voice-over to know it's the fault of these stinking Greenies for lending aid and comfort to the terrorists. Shots of muddy logging roads show blueshirts with dogs and State Trooper cars with brown spattered fenders. Helicopters zoom overhead. Whitehall mercs in full camo pimp around with guns and grenades. America at work, doing the work it does best. Whitehall's the law in this little patch of the USA, but you have to read the fine print to get that, and the only print in this picture is the baseball scores. We have to come out with a statement now.

At four the next evening we issue our statement, just in time for the evening news. It goes out by e-mail and on our site also. "We, the Army of the Republic, as well as other unnamed groups in the struggle against this illegitimate Regime, want the People of the United States to know that we had nothing to do with the tragic death of Hilliard Benson this morning. As we have stated before, we condemn such acts of violence while Democratic means of change are still allowed to happen. As long as the People are allowed to work for change peacefully, we will not resort to any acts of violence."

Unable to completely abandon Earl E., we followed it with an addendum. "At the same time, we demand that any prisoners held by Whitehall be turned over to the proper Government authorities, and that the kidnapping of Michael Arliss be immediately and effectively investigated."

Our statement goes out verbatim in the papers, but paraphrased on the television underneath, ridiculously, a photo of the letter. In classic style they bury its one minute of content with hours and hours of twisted interpretation. Michael Arliss has been forgotten now, pushed down the list by poor Hilliard Benson. The security experts weigh in: *Bob, the type of explosive device indicates to us that these people may have received some training from our enemies overseas. It's possible that foreign terrorists inside our country have joined cause with these ecoterrorists.*

No, fellas, that was good old American know-how he got from McFarland, a connection I made a year ago and promoted as the brand-new stage of guerrilla operations. Somehow I didn't quantify a dead logger in there. Wife-beating, forest-killing Hilliard Benson, maybe not a perfect man, but not a man whose death I can justify. It's like a mess of divine sparks just went skittering off into the night.

My secure line rings at 3 A.M., just when I'm falling asleep.

"Judas!"

"Early! Where the fuck are you, man?"

"You shut me out of the network!"

"I'm sorry, Early. Your guy got grabbed and we had to take precautions in case he yard-saled on us."

"You fucking *condemned* us! Condemned us for fighting *your* battle. You goddamned coward!"

"I can't argue about this over the phone!"

He suddenly sounds close to crying. "How could you do that, Lando? After all these years? Man, I am out on the line here!"

"You're over the line, Early. Why'd you kill that guy?"

"We were just trying to disable the vehicle! That's all! Somebody had to make a stand." Acid in his voice again. "So we acted. While you sat on your ass with your one-sided cease-fire!"

It cuts me. There's no answer to something that bitter. He was 80 percent right, and the 20 percent that made him wrong was all about strategy and PR and the kind of crap that didn't mean much in front of a dead logger and all your friends slamming the door in your face. I wonder where he is. He wouldn't be in the woods now: it would be too easy to pick up his phone signal.

"What's your next move?"

"I need your help, Lando."

"What do you need?"

"I need money, and a doctor, and a place to be."

I have about twenty grand in cash around, but it's not mine to give him. "Don't you have some safe houses in Portland?"

"I'm not in Portland, goddammit! And they got Mike Arliss. Didn't you hear that on the news? Did you think I was just bullshitting about that? Whitehall's had two days with him. He knows our safe houses."

"All of them?"

He gets angry. "How many fucking safe houses do you think we have? I'm sorry, we aren't the Grand Army of the Republic, with its all-channels guerrilla infrastructure. I can't sit here and argue with you! I got a comp with an infected bullet wound in her calf. She's got red stripes going up to her thigh and she's got a fever. They know they hit her: guaranteed they're watching every hospital in a thousand-mile radius. I need a doctor, or she isn't going to make it."

"What if you leave her someplace then call her in?"

"She doesn't want to go that route, and I have to respect her wishes."

Win or Die for America. I don't know any doctors who'll treat a fugitive. Maybe Sarah does: she had a doctor boyfriend for a while. "Are you in Seattle?"

"No, but I can get there in an hour. Even some antibiotics would help." A silence, then his panicked-sounding voice. "This is fucked up, Lando!"

"It is fucked up, Early. But you and I didn't start this fight."

He gives me his numbers and I call Sarah. "No! Early's a moron. He went out on his own and now he's put everybody in danger and undone a lot of what we accomplished. We are *not* getting involved in this."

"If we don't, his comp's going to end up either dead or in the hospital and then probably go straight into one of Whitehall's private prisons. And you know they'll make her talk."

"That's not our problem. That's Early's problem."

"Shit flows downhill."

"Then step out of the way."

"Did you hear what I said? If we don't do something, either this person is going to die, or she's going into custody."

"Well, it sounds like our friend Early has some very important decisions to make." She ended the discussion with a statement I didn't believe. "I don't know any doctors."

"Love you, too. Good-bye."

Sarah's a hard woman, and hard women survive. In a way, I can't blame her, but it's not like Early had anything personal to gain from this. He was trying to protect one last beautiful little scrap of old growth when nobody else would, and he's smart enough to know that he'd probably lose. On some level, we all owe him. On some level we're all guilty, and so was Hilliard Benson.

I call McFarland, but I'm saved the embarrassment of asking for his help when he doesn't answer. There's still Gonzalo, Tonk, Lilly, Kahasi, but I feel like Sarah's already shut the door on our group. I dial Earl E.'s number. When he answers his voice sounds sickeningly hopeful.

"I can front you some cash and some antibiotics. That's all I can do."

"I need a doctor, Lando. It's not pretty here."

"I tried, Earl E."

There's a long silence where I have all kinds of time to ask myself how hard I really tried.

Earl E. breaks it, maybe wondering the same thing. "Well, fuck you!" When I don't answer: "How much cash?"

"Twelve large. That's all I've got here. And some amoxycillin."

His voice doesn't soften. "Where do I pick it up?"

I set up a dead drop a couple of miles away then call him back with the location after I've stashed it. I know I'll catch shit for this later. I wish him luck, but he's beyond all that. His parting shot: "Thank you, Judas."

We wait for the news to hit the media that the heroic blueshirts have picked up another "terrorist" at the county hospital, or that a body's turned up. Nothing shows. I scan the Internet, flip a few channels. Stale footage of wrecked industrial metal, the clean fresh sight of happy loggers standing next to buzzing fans of sawdust in the naked torn up understory. The Siskiyou is coming down, providing those great "Timmmm-berrr!" shots of big trees smacking the earth. No sign of the tree-sitters, as if they never existed. The triumph of the will.

And still no prisoners. Maybe she got better. The Siskiyou bombing is starting to run out of drama, despite the updates on the loggers' families and a spiffy documentary called *When Dreamers Kill!* Finally, just when it's reduced to little factoids on the crawler, Earl E.'s face zooms up on every monitor and every newspaper, some long-haired smiling oval cropped from a snapshot and blown up into absolute recognizability. WANTED FOR MURDER. The perfect résumé for any youthful job-seeker: Terrorist. Bomber. Arsonist. Murderer. Fucking Earl E.!

". . . Jonathan Blust. Not only that, they've got the Anarchist Front, his Earth First stuff. They go all the way back to kindergarten on him."

I listen to Sarah trundling out the damage report. It's a long one. From Earl E.'s point of view, everyone he ever knew is now dead, or too dangerous to touch until Judgment Day or general amnesty. I remember meeting him on that tree-sit in Ukiah, the long-haired crusader who had just a little less fear than anyone else in the crowd, and he's always been Earl E. Warning. I'm having a hard time reconceptualizing him as Jonathan Blust. I mean, what kind of name is that for a revolutionary?

The answer comes right back at me. The worst kind. The kind that comes with a face.

18

*T*his Siskiyou thing's a gift," Walter said. We were drinking bourbon in my office in the early hours of the evening. "Not the guy getting killed—that's bad. But the fact that they popped their heads up and gave us a shot at them . . . now we'll start flushing them out."

Since Anne had left, Walter and I had been spending a fair amount of time together. He'd been through a couple of wives himself, which was why he lived in a modest apartment in Alexandria. "They got everything, God bless 'em!" We would schedule our weekly briefings for the late afternoon, and that would turn into a couple of drinks and sometimes a trip out to a barbecue shack Walter knew about, or the latest spy thriller, where Walter would analyze all the security and military aspects for verisimilitude. It spooked me a little, because these were such middle-aged bachelor kinds of things to do. I didn't want to end up as the high-rent version of Walter, a man with four children by two wives and little apparent connection to any of them. But Walter was a good companion, and over the whiskeys he would give me the real scoop.

"So this guy that they claim Whitehall captured . . ."

"Michael Arliss."

"Yeah. Did we really grab him?"

"You know, I'm not authorized to go into detail about that stuff." He cocked his head. "I'll just say that I'm sure Michael Arliss is safe and sound."

"Is he part of the Army of the Republic?"

"He's part of a network that was originally called the Anarchist Front, which was mostly broken up after they got out of hand at a demonstration in Berkeley."

"I remember that. There was some hand-wringing when they put them away."

"That's right. Evidently, a few of them escaped and reconstituted their organization in the Portland area and started fire-bombing everything that looked at them cross-eyed. Those days are done, though. They overreached themselves with this Siskiyou business."

"So will this lead us to the Army of the Republic?"

He glanced off to the side. "Affirmative. We're working our way up the food chain."

There was something very satisfying about knowing the truth. Joining the Program had brought me into a secret brotherhood of men who understood that beneath the window-dressing of society, its laws and rights and democratic principles, were the real mechanisms that held it all in place. We were the ones making the decisions that mattered, beyond the puffery of politicians and lawyers. Society's hard hand, its fundamental meaning since men had first banded together to build walls around their villages: force.

Walter retrieved a can of cocktail peanuts and put it between us. "So what do you hear from your wife? Has she changed her mind about having protection?"

"No."

That worried him. "She may be pissed off at you, but that doesn't necessarily matter to someone who wants to get at you. Or to get at your money."

"Nobody's been kidnapped yet."

He looked at me pointedly. "Do you want her to be the first?"

"When you start talking like that, I reach for my wallet."

He laughed. "When do I get to meet that son of yours, anyway? Dick Boren tells me he's quite the character."

"Joshua's a character, all right."

"Dick thinks very highly of him. Said he's one of the smartest kids he knows."

"He's got his moments. He doesn't seem to be getting a lot of traction, though. Careerwise. I think his mother spoiled him when he was little."

"He's in Web design, something like that?"

"Something like that." I added quickly: "I put some restrictions on his trust fund until he learns to stand on his own feet. I don't want him to be one of those rich kids who floats through life living off their father's work."

"Maybe you're too hard on him, Jim."

"Hey: he's a lot harder on me. He's so damned Old Testament about everything." I laughed at the thought that bubbled up in my head. "Actually, he reminds me of my grandfather."

"Your grandfather?" Walter raised his eyebrows in anticipation.

"My maternal grandparents were both Jews. Old school—when my mother married my father, my grandfather held a funeral for her and didn't speak to her for twenty-three years."

"That is old school."

"No kidding! Can you imagine wasting twenty-three years of life with your child to show your disapproval? They finally made up a few years before he passed away, so I got to know him a little near the end there. He never accepted that I'd been raised Unitarian, and he had a crafty way of making me study the Old Testament with him. He was pretty much blind by then, and he'd ask me to read it to him. Of course, he had the damned thing practically memorized already, and he'd start rattling off all these connections and parallels for me, staring around the room. Like all those palace intrigues and miracles were written all around us. It was a weird sensation."

"I had a great-uncle like that," Walter said. "But he was a Southern Baptist."

"Well, we didn't raise Josh and Tina as anything, but when Josh went to college in Boston, he got in with these Lubovitch Jews, the ones with the black hats and the sideburns. For a couple of years he was really into it. He'd come home and go off on the Book of Judges or Saul and Jonathan, whatever. A lot of moralizing, usually about me. But the strange thing is, in his own way, he has that same sense of things his great-grandfather did. Like the world is really this giant holy book where everything we do is weighed."

"'In the beginning was the Word.'"

"I guess so." I sipped my drink. "Of course, with literacy dropping like a stone, maybe he'd better start looking for a new metaphor."

I hadn't talked to Joshua since he'd called me after my *Washington Challenge* appearance. I'd wanted to tell him then that Anne had moved out, but he was so busy attacking me that I didn't have a chance. Anne had probably told him by now and he undoubtably blamed me for everything. Our daughter, Tina, had been a lot more understanding.

Anne and I had met for lunch a couple of times in the two weeks since she'd left. There was no talk about lawyers or anything, and she didn't seem to have anyone else—I asked in spite of myself. We talked about the kids, her classes, the new show at the Hirschhorn. If she'd caught my latest TV or radio appearances she didn't give any indication. With so much off-limits, though, we kept running into these scratchy silences. Sometimes I wanted to tell her I missed her. Other times I went out of my way to prove that I was doing perfectly well without her. The old "Who needs you, baby?" attitude that I'd last employed after being dumped by my high school girlfriend forty years ago. Anne called me on it and we both had to laugh. "I can't believe that at the age of fifty-eight I'm back to being a teenager!"

In some ways, of course, things *were* going extremely well. The reconstruction of Cascadia was moving faster than expected, and our stock was beginning to rebound. Most of Cascadia's planning and contracting had been done the first time around, and Water Solutions cruised forward almost without me. I was content with that; other people could manage those details. These days I'd become far more involved in what Danny called Operation Big Picture, a change in roles that the Fund encouraged.

I began to work more closely with McPhee/Collins to try to take away the false sense of glamour that the armed radicals and the citizen groups had acquired. This required a lot of the public diplomacy that McPhee/Collins specialized in, and sometimes I'd have four or five media appearances in a week. I made a credible spokesman, since

I'd personally been a victim, and as much as I tired of seeing those clips of myself being hit with water balloons and urine, they helped us reach people on a gut level about what we had now firmly identified as quasi-terrorism. Part of my job was giving people a vocabulary to work with: there were terrorists and quasi-terrorists, radicals and armed radicals, sympathizers, appeasers, and, to leave some space for people's relatives and friends, the WIFs, or well-intentioned folks. On our side were the doers and the risk-takers, the wealth-creators and the stakeholders in the American dream. Half my appearances were representing the Terror Victims Association, an alliance that McPhee/ Collins had formed of business figures and families of people killed in terror attacks by foreigners.

We also responded more forcefully at a local, tactical level to the protesters who'd dogged our operations in Harrisburg and other places. Every time they showed up, McPhee/Collins plastered the local media with commentary that established them firmly as quasi-terrorists, and a few locals could always be relied on to chime in on our behalf. This made the WIFs quiet down and dulled the chorus of approval the radicals played to. Denton, from the Fund, had called a couple of times to express his contentment.

The attacks on the Siskiyou had opened up some opportunities on a national level, too. A campaign was mounted through Big Picture to force all the radical groups to condemn what had happened in the Siskiyou. As Danny explained, even forcing them to condemn it associated them with the terrorists in people's minds, and any groups that tried to make an issue of the logging itself or the government's supposed corruption could be attacked as sympathizers. For a while the paper-ballot groups and everybody else were falling all over themselves badmouthing their comrades in arms. When another bomb went off in an airport in New York, even the terrorists wouldn't claim it.

Or, better said, they claimed it and then tried to disclaim it. The bomb had gone off in the middle of the night, so no one had been killed, but the torn steel and shattered windows slid across every screen in the country, giving already-twitchy New Yorkers plenty of opportunity to reflect on what terrorists could do. The Jefferson Combine claimed it immediately; then, a few hours later, seeing that the reaction wasn't what they'd hoped, they called in and said that it was a lie, that they'd been framed. "We state categorically that we had nothing to do with the bombing at JFK Airport."

The more they protested, the guiltier they looked. "Of course they deny it," summed up one security expert. "That way they get the destabilizing effect of mass terrorism without getting any of the blame." The usual conspiracy theories played across the Internet, accusing the government or even Whitehall, but polls showed that support for the terrorists was dropping, and McPhee's private polls showed that support for the radicals was dropping with it.

Now, other tidbits of information were starting to come back to me as a sponsor of the Program. Three weeks after the New York bombing, an e-mail from Walter was waiting for me when I arrived at work. "Too Bad for Him" was the message, and there was a link to a news article. Madison Twelve, a long-sought lieutenant of the Jefferson Combine, was run to ground in Boston and killed in a shoot-out outside a Chinese restaurant. According to reports, armed men had tried to hustle him into a car and he'd been killed trying to escape them. Some eyewitnesses claimed there'd been an exchange of shots; others said the shooting had been one-sided. The head of Homeland Security appeared under the crackling flashes of the media photo corps: "Our evidence indicates that this was an internal struggle between two splinter groups."

Now the splinter group experts had their hour. "What we're seeing is a classic power struggle within the terrorist organizations," said one commentator. Another pundit claimed to be in touch with members of an ultraradical faction called JC 1776, which condemned the Jefferson Combine for straying from its revolutionary ideals. There were experts fat and thin, tough-looking ex-military and bespectacled academics. Foreign, national, government, or think tank. I wondered how many of them came from McPhee/Collins's client list.

Walter had very little comment on the Madison Twelve affair. He said that his area was the West Coast, not the East Coast, and that he didn't really know what was going on in New England. I took that to mean that he wasn't authorized to talk about it, and I understood that that sort of vagueness would henceforth be our mode of communication about the Program. The whole thing spun around in the media for about four days, and then was pushed out of the way by the beginning of baseball season. Still, in a distant way that I tried not to pay attention to, it bothered me.

Six days later another militant was killed. This time in Chicago, when his apartment was raided by the Chicago Police. Again, the death came during a shoot-out, but the group involved, the Forces of American Resistance, denied that their man had fired back and challenged the police to show any exit holes from bullets coming out the door. When the police produced the door, complete with exit holes, they claimed it was a fake.

"These people refuse to acknowledge basic facts!" Walter complained. But I couldn't help noticing the similarity to the Fred Hampton murder by the Chicago Police back in the '60s, a case I'd studied in college, when I'd been something of a quasi-radical myself.

Reports about missing persons started cropping up, mostly on the East Coast, and I watched the short-lived swirl of media coverage that attended each one. Often family members would sound the alarm and the radical groups would pick it up. At that point, the police or security forces would sometimes admit that they had the person incommunicado, as was their prerogative in terrorism cases. Other times, nothing was said.

I'd known this was coming, but as I watched it unfold, it made me uneasy. I took the long view, telling myself that this was simply the way that societies responded when they were attacked, from the days of the first nation-states. Other times I reasoned that the Program was a necessary evil that the terrorists had brought on themselves, and that the sooner their groups had been dismantled, the sooner we could put the whole thing in the past.

The scope of the events, though, made me wonder who else was in on the Program with me. Who were the originators? Or was this spread out over so many men doing little pieces of it that no one really had ultimate responsibility? I wondered what Richard Boren knew about it.

I arranged to drop by his office on K Street late one Friday afternoon. It was a classic Washington office: a big antique wooden desk, maple paneling, a green leather couch, the flag and the pictures of him shaking hands with three different presidents. It had an aura that couldn't be faked, and I always felt like a tourist there, son of a middle-class civil servant that I was. He welcomed me in and offered me a beer from a small refrigerator. As soon as I was seated a look of concern crossed his features.

"How's Anne?"

"She's okay. Enjoying her privacy, I suppose."

"Not to pry, Jim, but what the hell happened? I could see you two had different politics, but for goodness' sake!" He tilted his head inquisitively. "You fall for the secretary? That happens. People stray. On both sides. It doesn't have to be the end of the marriage."

He certainly remembered the dinner with Roger. "Nobody strayed."

"Then, good gracious, go fetch her stuff and bring her home! You two are too old for this shit! And it's not good for the kids, either, no matter what age they are. You don't think they feel grief?"

"I know they do, Richard. Thanks."

His message delivered, he was eager to change the subject. "How's your son? I sent him an e-mail a while ago but I never heard back from him. He still making war on pictures?"

"He's making war on me. Doesn't like my business, doesn't like my politics . . ." I stopped short at saying that he didn't like my friends. "You've probably seen it before."

"You raised an iconoclast, Jim. In the literal sense of the word. Let him have his head. He'll come back to you when he figures it out. I've got a lot of faith in him."

I had about fifteen years' worth of reasons to not be so sanguine about it, but I didn't see much point in belaboring Richard with them. I'd come for a different reason, anyway. It was hard to bring the subject up because it was a secret. Our own accountants didn't know where the payments were going: we'd created a subsidiary in Peru to route the money through. But I knew that Walter and Richard were friends, and I had a feeling Richard knew. He'd always been more connected than me. It was how he made his living.

"Richard, have you ever heard of a private counterinsurgency program?"

He was still laid back, but suddenly his posture became a bit straighter, pale eyes a little more intense. "Whitehall's program. You're in it."

I was glad he'd said that. He'd opened the door. "Who else is in it?"

"Jim, even if I knew, I couldn't just tee off on a question like that. That involves other people's privacy."

"C'mon, Richard. I'm not one of the peons. I've already forked out eight million dollars on this. I'm entitled to know who else is in the club."

"What did Walter tell you?"

"I haven't asked him."

He glanced away and tapped absently on his desktop while he thought about it. Finally he looked back at me. "There's at least fifty other entities in the program, but don't ask me for specifics."

That startled me. It was bigger than I'd imagined. "Is Howard in it?"

He tilted his head. "You know Howard."

I named three other big companies whose CEOs I was acquainted with and who used Whitehall for security. "You could be warm," Richard answered, and, "There's a good possibility," and, reluctantly, "That would be logical."

He was getting more reticent and I could tell it was time to back off. I shrugged. "Well, I guess we're doing the whole country a favor by nipping this in the bud. The longer it goes on, the more people are going to get hurt."

"That's how I feel," Richard answered. "These groups may be misguided idealists, but you can't sit back and let them run wild."

I didn't want to be impolitic, but I felt I could talk about my doubts with Richard. "What bothers me is the overlap with the legal groups. I mean, I've heard Walter's speech about networked terror groups transcending traditional boundaries and all that. But I grew up in the seventies, and I guess I'm a child of my era. It seems a little . . . undemocratic."

Richard's blue eyes seemed to harden for a fraction of a second; then he gave a soft snort of amusement. "You know, Jim, as I've matured, I've gone through a long evolution in my thinking. I used to be young and idealistic. One man, one vote. I believed in democracy, and I still do. But in a different way."

I settled into my chair, listening.

"You see, people are born as babies, and as they grow up, they learn about the world. They become more knowledgeable and more capable, because they have to. Well, in politics, they don't really have to. Things keep rolling along whether they know about government or not, and so most of them stay adolescents. They don't understand the issues, and frankly, they don't really care. My plumber can tell you a whole lot about the Redskins offensive line, but you'd never catch him putting that effort into learning about tax structure or foreign policy. He's just not interested! Now, the man's a great plumber! But does he really deserve to steer this country if he's too lazy to learn how it all works? I say, let children be children! Let them enjoy their lives and do what they're good at. Making the decisions is our job. That's what we get paid for. That's why you have your houses and your jet, and I have my things."

He looked at me for agreement and I thought it over for a few seconds. "I'm sorry, Richard. I missed the part where you still believe in democracy."

He laughed easily, rocking back in his chair and looking in my eyes. "I see where your son gets it!"

"No, really! I'm not saying I disagree with you, but exploring this intellectually: If we're making all the decisions, where's the democracy part come in? Nobody voted for us to represent them."

"Jim, if they didn't want us to represent them, couldn't they vote in some radical to get rid of us? Besides, they still decide certain things. Social issues, local issues: that's okay. They need to feel engaged. But some things are just not on the table. For example: You want us out of Iraq, okay! Bang on the table long enough, and we're out. But you're *not* going to starve the military. We'd be doing a disservice to the American people if we let that happen."

Maybe he sensed my ambivalence. "It's always been like that, Jim. In every society. Until it ends, and a new ruling class takes power. But I don't intend to let that happen on my watch."

It wasn't the picture-perfect America of 1776, but I didn't have anyplace else to go with the argument. At any rate, Richard had stuck his neck out and answered some of my questions, and I appreciated that. Still, it left me wondering about Howard Pettijohn, my cosponsor of the Program. As expected, he didn't have quite the nuanced approach that Richard did.

"The hell with it! They can lock up the whole lot of them radicals as far as I'm concerned, and kill anybody who complains. We need to use a stronger hand in this country, then we won't have the kind of crap we had in Seattle!"

I'd spent a good part of that day with Howard in the lobby of the

Olympic Hotel, watching him foam at the mouth as we waited for the demonstrators to be cleared out. At one point he tried to convince me to borrow our bodyguards' sidearms and go out into the street, so that we could shoot anyone who got in our way. It would be straight-out self-defense, he claimed. He wasn't much mellower sitting on his houseboat on the Potomac.

"You're goddamned right I'm in the Program!"

"How much are you paying?"

"Seven hundred thousand a month."

That stung me. "I'm paying two million!"

He lifted his bourbon. "You've got all those operations on the West Coast, where the Reds are thickest. It's quiet in my neck of the woods." He leaned toward me. "They got one of those New Confederate Army guys last week. I got to watch the interrogation through a two-way mirror."

"What was that like?"

"Oh, this was some twenty-three-year-old hillbilly kid that went up to Lexington for college and got his head filled with big ideas. He looked pretty rough when I saw him—they said he resisted arrest, but you know how that goes. They'd had him for a couple of weeks already, so they were in a different phase. They usually squeeze 'em pretty hard for the first three days. Get the information while it's fresh. After that, they have more time to wear 'em down and make sure they didn't miss anything. This guy was pretty out of it. Didn't seem real clear on where he was."

I couldn't help going slightly off-key. "Didn't you feel sorry for him?"

"Good Lord, *no*! It's not like they were sticking hot pokers up his ass. They were just, you know, asking him questions. They had him standing up, and he kept wanting to sit down. At one point he pissed himself. There was a lot of shouting."

"Good cop, bad cop?"

He considered it. "I didn't see any good cops around. These guys knew what they were doing, though. They'd been with Whitehall overseas during that whole Afghanistan thing. It was actually pretty interesting."

"Where was this?"

"I'm not supposed to talk about that stuff, but hell, we're both in the

Program. They have a detention center out in Rappahannock County. They cleared out the old county jail, retrofitted it with all kinds of electronic surveillance equipment and stuff. All confidential, single source, no bid." He smiled mistily. "Wish I'd had that contract."

We were alone on the houseboat and it suddenly felt insufferably intimate. I tried sipping my drink to normalize things, but it tasted like paint thinner and Howard's bulging eyes and scarlet-veined nose had taken on a rodentlike cast that I couldn't get rid of. He went on talking, now about a new group in Wheeling that was opposing our water utility there and how we should deal with the people that were making all the trouble. A grin, a little shake of his head: *Oughtta be a couple extra cells in that facility in Rappahannock! Don't you think so, Jimbo?* I nodded at him and didn't disagree. After all, he was my partner.

19

With Earl E. ID'd and his crew getting cut to pieces, July's shaping up to be the hottest on record. The weeks pass, though, and the Army hasn't been touched, giving me the occasional surge of chest-swelling hubris. Maybe we're just a little sharper than the Jefferson Combine. Maybe Whitehall isn't all it's cracked up to be. I don't hear the first few footsteps until I call my voice mail to check in on Joshua's world. It's Barry, the guy across the hall from my San Francisco apartment. He thinks I'm on a long-term contract with a software developer in Portland.

In the first message he sounds intrigued: *Hey, Josh. An old friend of yours came around here looking for you. About our age, blonde, definitely worth knowing. Like, where were you, how often did you come home: that sort of stuff. She said she wants to surprise you, but I wanted to give a buddy a heads-up. Call me if you have any questions.*

The next message is from the following day: *It's Barry again. Listen, um, did you say someone could stay in your apartment? Because I came home early yesterday and I heard noises. I thought it was you, so I knocked, and then that woman came to the door. Call me, 'cause it's creeping me out.*

A last brief try the next morning: *Barry here. Please call me as soon as you get this message.*

I'm thinking, hmm, someone's getting interested in James Sands's failure son. Probably Whitehall. The Homelanders would have sent some suits, somebody with an ID to flash. Maybe they've been watching the apartment and got curious as to why I've barely been there in the last three years. Maybe they figured out whose password got used on the Cascadia break-in and want to ask me a few questions about Dad's computer. At least I know they've been around, which counts for something.

My mother's been leaving messages for the last week, too, but with the Siskiyou operations going on, I just don't have the extra energy to call her up and lie to her. *Sure, Mom, everything's great. Business is booming.* She leaves about six messages in two days, so I finally call her up through my San Francisco phone. I'm actually kicked back on the couch at Henry Rampton's place, pretending it's my couch in San Francisco. I settle in with a tub of guacamole and some chips and crunch into one as her line rings.

"Hey, Mom. I'm sorry I didn't get back to you sooner. I was up in Portland doing some contract work."

She sounds like the usual Mom at first: that harmonious voice that wraps me up and hugs me close to her. How am I? The latest about Tina and her great job and sleazy boyfriend. I listen to her as I flip through a sports magazine, idly checking out the Red Sox stats. Then she starts in with her warning about bad news, and as I'm tensing up she delivers: She and Dad have separated.

The magazine fades away, along with the rest of the room. "That's ridiculous!" Stupid thing to say, but it just pops out. I pull myself out of the cushions and put down the chip in my hand. "Look, Dad's an idiot . . . but you can't just give up!"

"I'm not giving up."

"What'd he do? Did he, like, yell at you? Get in your face about being a teacher again?"

"No. It wasn't one thing—"

"Have you gone to see a marriage counselor? Because I've heard they can really help. Dad needs an objective outsider to show him what an idiot he is. Because, you know, he just gets confused about things!"

"These don't seem like marriage counseling issues. Your father hasn't done anything wrong. It's just a difference in values. Things that have been growing for a long time."

Wanting to just hug her, hug my father, pull them both close to me like I used to do when I'd crawl into bed with them, and meanwhile, that agonizing feeling of being so far away from those cozy warm sheets, the snow fort in the front yard of the old house, from everything that was innocent.

"Look, Josh, it's very hard to talk about these things over the phone. I've been trying to reach you to tell you I have a teacher's conference in Seattle next Monday, and I'd like to come see you this weekend."

I consider it for a second: a quick trip down to San Francisco, a few days in my fake residence. But there's the matter of my new blond friend. "This is a bad time."

"You sound like your father."

"I mean, I'm really busy these days. I'm up in Portland working on a design project."

The hope comes back into her voice: problem solved. "Well, I can meet you there for the weekend! My friends rave about Portland."

"I'm sorry, Mom. On this project, every day's a weekday."

She knows then, because she knows I'd never turn away from her like this when she needs me. "Josh!" Her voice dives. "What's going on?"

"Nothing's going on! I'm just . . . I'm on deadline and I've got a lot of other people that are waiting for me to finish." The silence from her end tells me she doesn't really buy it, but doesn't want to believe her only son is giving her a load of crap when she's just told him that her marriage is breaking up. I feel ashamed. "I'll have to call you back, Mom. I love you. I'm sorry. Let me look at my schedule and see what I can do."

I close the phone, lie back on the couch. Mom's taking a hike, Dad's probably full-steam ahead on his propaganda crusade, barely noticing she's gone. And Whitehall or someone else is tap-tap-tapping with their little white cane, like Blind Pew looking for Billy Bones and his treasure map.

I never do call my mother back, feel like the world's worst son. Instead send her an e-mail talking about Portland and how much I'd love to see her. Tina will come to the rescue, I think, in her usual cool and helpful way, taking my father's side. *It must be you, Mom, because Daddy never does anything wrong.*

It takes me less than thirty seconds to find her conference: "Failing Literacy: Teaching Strategies for the Digital Age." It's at the university, and I have no trouble spotting my mother on the first morning, with her long gray hair bouncing gently with her teenage walk. I have to hold myself back from rushing up to her. I'm in student garb, but with sunglasses, a ball cap, and a fake goatee that makes me a little harder to spot. I know she's refused Whitehall's protection, but they could be here anyway, could even be one of the conference participants, if they're really serious about it. I watch her from the edges for most of Monday, changing outfits twice and sweating in the August heat. I follow her chats with colleagues, walk alone to her hotel, wait an hour in a café across the street for her to come out, then hurry to fall in behind her when she leaves the hotel to go to dinner. I'm zooming from a couple of double espressos, and the little cookies they gave me aren't providing much ballast. She goes into one of the fancier restaurants on the Ave and I watch for five more minutes to see if anyone follows her in or parks themselves outside. It looks clean, so I suck in my breath and push the door open, wave myself past the hostess. She's sitting by herself at a four-top, lost in the menu. After nine hours of surveillance, I'm finally next to her.

"Is this seat taken, madam?"

It has the desired effect. She nearly falls out of her chair and her mouth opens wide. "Joshua! What are you *doing* here?"

"I came up from Portland to surprise you."

"That's . . . so sweet!" She stands up, and tears start to streak down her face.

"Mom!"

"I can't help it: I'm so happy to see you!"

We hug each for a while: she won't let me go, but at last she manages to sit down and wipes her eyes with a corner of the paper napkin.

The problems with my father must have disturbed whatever magical force has kept my mother so ageless all these years. She seems noticeably older than when I saw her six months ago, and I wonder what the correlation is between happiness and time. She wraps me in her familiar aura of flowing gray hair and organic perfumes and for a few seconds my whole Lando life winks out like a far-off star.

"You look thin!" she says.

"You always think I look thin."

"I'm still measuring you against that baby with the chubby little thighs, that's all. You look very handsome, though. A sports jacket! I don't think I've seen you wear a sports jacket since you got out of prep school."

"It's the new me."

"I like the new you!" She tilts her head to the side, smiling. "But I liked the old you, too."

I drop my gaze to the table, a happy eight-year-old again. I've even got a little rash on my chin, courtesy of my artificial beard and the July heat. "What do you hear from Tina?"

"Tina's doing *great*! She loves her job, loves her life."

"How about her scummy boyfriend? Is he still defending pesticide makers against class-action suits?"

"I think she's starting to wise up about Mark. He's a little boy looking for a substitute mother, and I think she's figuring that out."

"What about: he's totally amoral?"

She laughs. "Oh, Josh!"

Another menu appears and we look it over. It's one of those where vitamin-sized servings are described by novel-length menu entries. I'm starving, but as the first joy of seeing my mother wears off I start feeling nervous—my back is to the front door. I scoot around to the seat beside her. After we order I go to the bathroom and scope out the exits: like most restaurants, the bathrooms are near the kitchen, the kitchen has a service entrance at the rear of the building. Okay.

I sit down and the waiter sidles up with a dish of olive oil and vinegar spattered with bits of leaves, surrounded by a crown of crunchy bread crusts. A nice change from ramen, rice, and frozen burritos.

We start talking about Dad, who, according to Mom, seems to have been completely absorbed by his James Sands persona. "And after I saw him on that sickening *Hammer Show*, I had to draw the line. I couldn't stand it anymore."

"He was on *The Hammer*? Impressive. I thought *Washington Challenge* was his big moment. That's where I saw him."

"What did he say on *Washington Challenge*?"

"Oh, you know: Blah blah terrorists. Blah blah quasi-terrorists. Blah blah terrorism crossing the boundaries of civil and criminal. The same old crap. He's one of their foot soldiers now. Knowing Dad, he thinks he's one of their generals."

"*The Hammer Show* was worse." I could feel some heat. "He appeared with some . . . stripper, and then she took off her clothes and sat on his lap. It was degrading." She looks down at her plate. "It's all part of some program he's doing with his security company."

I forget about the bread crusts. "What do you mean?"

"I don't know much about it. Last September he let it slip that Whitehall had some sort of corporate counterterrorism program they were launching, and I realized that the reason he was making so many media appearances after the Cascadia bombing was that he'd signed on to it."

"He admitted that?"

"Basically."

"Mom, that's . . . That's terrible." A new step down for Dad. Before, I at least believed he was acting on his own initiative. Now it turns out he's part of a little professional hate club. And who knows what else they might get up to besides propaganda. I remember the infiltrator "William Lee." The unsolved Madison Twelve killing. "You should go to the press, Mom."

"I don't know very much. And besides, that's up to him." She spots my doubtful look. "I'm trying to give him a chance to redeem himself."

I sigh. "Everybody wants to redeem Dad. Except for Dad." I crunch into another bread crust.

"You know, Josh, he's not the same as he used to be. After that Cascadia bombing, he lost control of the business." She explains the bit about the Barrington Fund's loan being converted to equity, something Sarah had lined out before we'd blown Cascadia. "And now, from what I can gather, he's being forced to take part in this campaign that Whitehall and Barrington are involved in. He feels like he has to go along with it to keep his place in his business."

"What else does this campaign do? Is it just public relations, or is it more? Are there other companies involved, too?"

"I don't know, Josh. He doesn't like to talk about it, and I haven't pushed him."

"For Christ's sake, Mom, push him!"

"Don't tell me what to do!" That backs me right off. "I'm sorry. There's a lot of bruised feelings right now, and a lot of distance between us. We're trying to build on our strengths." She takes a sip of her water and leaves a smudge of lipstick on the glass. "When you've invested most of your adult life in a relationship, you're not so quick to go smashing it up. I left your father after a lot of agonizing, but I haven't given up on him. Have you?"

And it occurs to me then that maybe that's exactly what I should do. One of my reasons for helping with the Cascadia operation was that it would shake him up, and instead it pushed him deeper into his own little construct of James Sands, poor little rich Corporate. Maybe that's just who he is. But as I think of that, I remember him taking me to that cafeteria for lunch every once in a while, sitting next to me in his suit and tie. A gas-engine model airplane we put together once that I crashed to bits the first flight, and instead of getting mad he laughed, and picked me up and told me it was the best crash he'd ever seen, a really outstanding crash, and that we'd build one even better, though we never did. One of those little pieces of unfinished business that came wavering up to me once in a while. "No," I finally say. "I haven't given up on him."

The food comes and she decides to talk about me, asking about my contract in Portland, my recent work, why she can never get me on the phone. I bat plausible answers back to her while I check out a middle-aged guy with one of those square cop haircuts who maneuvers himself to a seat with a clear view of us and has a habit of glancing over at us every fifteen seconds. Wire glasses, blue blazer with no tie. He could be an operative; he could be an accountant. Maybe it's my mom he's looking at—by old-guy standards, she's definitely still got it. I'm evaluating him when my mother's voice floats in again: "But what about you? Any special lady friends on the horizon?"

Special lady friends. That's a delicate way of putting it. I think of Emily, our four "dates" together: the White Room, her long accurate analyses of the incredibly complex forces behind the mass movement. That run-on sentence about her dad and her family, all to try and somehow get us to be part of the same family. "Oh, there's sort of one out there. But I don't want to talk about it."

"Come on! Out with it!"

"I don't want to talk about it!"

"Just tell me what she does. How old is she?"

"She's a lawyer and she's about my age, and that's all I want to say, because it's in the formative stages and I don't want to jinx it."

"A lawyer! You and Tina really go for lawyers."

"Mom, I said a lawyer, not a pimp! No, really, this woman is . . . megasmart. Strong. A good sense of humor. She's devoted to helping other people. You would like her." Also built for comfort and very sexy, but Mom doesn't really want to hear that, does she?

"When do I get to meet her?"

"Let's just see how things go. Maybe next time you come to San Francisco."

Mom treats, as usual, and by now wire-rim cop-hair has turned his attention to a couple of women sitting a few tables away from us, so I'm feeling relatively relaxed. We head out and it's time for my mother to go back to her hotel. I've told her I'm staying with a friend, leaving for Portland again early the next morning, and when I refuse her invitation to come back to the hotel with her to talk she looks for a moment like she's going to start crying.

"Let's walk then," she says. "There's something we need to talk about."

I lead her over to Ravenna Park, still dusky in the long summer evening.

"Josh," she says, her voice no longer that mother-to-son voice, but rather, an adult speaking to another adult. "What are you into? Really."

"What do you mean?"

"Stop. It hurts my feelings when you aren't honest with me. I can never get you on the phone. You're always busy, but you're never very clear about what you're busy with—"

"I'm in Web design. I showed you that site I did—"

"That was over a year ago!" Her voice becomes softer. "Just tell me, Josh. I'm not going to condemn you. Are you into drugs or something?"

"No." I'm wanting to just let go, to tell her I'm part of the Resistance, a cofounder of the Army of the Republic, yes, *that* Army, that judged John Polling and judged Cascadia. Maybe she can absolve me of that guilt that settles on me when I'm tired and the furor of the Cause goes away for a while. "Actually, Mom, it's kind of political. I'm working with a group that's trying to get rid of the Regime."

I can still make out her fear in the dim light. "One of those Militant Groups?"

I back off. "No, Mom. It's more like an affinity group." I draw her a picture of me handling the IT for a loose group of political activists, nameless because they want to stay under the radar. Basically educators, really, like her. By the time I finished, I've even got them paying me a small salary "depending on how donations are that month." She listens to it all with only a few questions. "But whatever you do, don't say anything about it to Dad. You have to promise that. I don't want his Whitehall pals dropping in." I shrug. "And for that matter, being James Sands's son isn't a big bragging point in this crowd, either."

We're on the sidewalk that runs along the park now, in the dark under the trees. The first few leaves of autumn have given up and are crunching under our feet. She stops, turns to me in the faint light. When she finally talks she seems to barely believe herself. "You *are* one of them!" she says, and when I don't answer she throws herself against me and holds me, sniffling at first and then letting out a long catlike mewling sound that turns into a sob. I feel her trembling against me and I squeeze my arms around her. "Mom!" I say softly, not even sure what I'm talking about. "Mom! It's okay. It's all going to be fine."

"No, it's not!"

For some reason I'm all out of explanations. *No,* I think, *it probably won't be fine.*

"You have to get out of this, Josh. You have to stop."

Lando kicks in again. "Mom, I'm just doing little stuff for the Resistance. Nothing violent, nothing dangerous. I'm not going to get sent to jail. These are good people. They're not terrorists."

She tells me I may be in over my head, then spatters me with questions that I can't answer. She doesn't want to let me go. We walk until that time of morning when the big quiet comes over everything, when the traffic lights look lonely and you can hear them click as they change colors. We have an early breakfast at a buzzy chain diner where the last dregs of the bar rush have collapsed into their coffee cups. We puzzle out a final good-bye a block from her hotel.

"I'm proud of you, Joshua," she says, "I'm proud of your courage and your principles. But for God's sake, don't take part in anything violent, because that just leads to more violence."

I can't explain to her that John Polling is already buried, instead try to fight off the sinking feeling of the damned, say, "I've already told them: If it involves violence, I'm out." And then, "But don't mention any of this to Dad."

"I won't."

"I'm serious! Promise?"

"I promise, Josh."

A last hug, I watch the stab of light cross the glass door of her hotel when she opens it. By the time I reach the train the sky is turning the color of cement. The first few morning people are waiting along with me with their paper cups of coffee, all of us shocked and highly entertained by the news parading across the monitors on the platform. Franklin Seven has been shot to death.

The methodology of the hit isn't quite clear at first. They float the suggestion of a robbery on local TV, but it grows out of that fast. Franklin Seven was hanging in a safe house on Long Island when the bad guys came through the door at 4 A.M. with flash bangs and tear gas. I imagine he went for his handgun, a chance he probably got because they wanted to take him alive, but after the first shot they took him out with rounds to the chest and then the head, the famous "double tap" that means negotiations are officially over. The Jefferson Combine comes out with a statement honoring their fallen man. Patriot, hero of the second Revolution. Steven Sykes, age twenty-six.

No news on who actually got him. It must have been that pesky splinter group, or just clever Commander-in-Chief Matthews, playing it close to the chest. Channel America is beside itself: Hail the leader! America has been saved from a great peril! But it hits people funny: They still remember the Yankees cap, and it's a little freaky to kill a

Yankees fan. By midday, things take a turn for the ugly—a neighbor comes forward with pictures of a young woman in a T-shirt and panties being led out with a baby in her arms. Steven Sykes's wife and daughter, crying, shoulders hunched, surrounded by black-clad men with no markings on their outfits. A little different picture from the death-cult shoot-out Channel America's selling. Hard to celebrate having the Madonna and Child watching Dad shot to death in front of them. The image reaches people on some crucial level of uneasiness, and that detail, along with the pictures someone found of the pretty wife, sent all over the Internet, starts a rumbling in the suburbs. This was a frigging Yankees fan, for chrissakes! A loose consensus forms around a few placards outside the Malvern Police station: We want the wife and baby back, alive. The Malvern blueshirts deny having her. The Government denies it, too, and that puts people in the street outside the Federal Building in Southhampton. Office managers, housewives, clergymen and their flocks, students. We want them back. She has a name, Kristin Oldacre, her baby's named Liberty, and the pictures come down off the Internet and get blown up onto posters with the words WE WANT THEM BACK ALIVE! The Civils get off their asses and start energizing their networks. By nightfall they've got a thousand people outside the Federal Building and crowd control has to be called in. The neighbor starts showing up on television with his story: the low road is too juicy to pass up, and even though Big Media blankets him with commentary debunking him, missing baby Liberty keeps kicking the life out of their little party.

Damage control moves in the next morning. A freshly minted group of Right Wingers steps forward to take responsibility, the Patriotic Guard. They're rough; they're tough. They're going to save this country. By coincidence they happen to use the same tactics as the crack anti-terrorist squads trained by the Government, skill sets perfected overseas, now brownshirted out to the highest bidder by Whitehall and the rest of them. The PR tanks are everywhere at once: Is it a backlash from the Right? The internal struggle of a fragmenting Jefferson Combine? On TV and the Internet a thousand putrid flowers bloom, swamping the facts beneath a gushing sewage of commentary. It's Russian Mafia. It's Chinese tongs. It's an elaborate fake. A suicide. A drug deal gone bad.

In this America, anything is believable but the truth.

I knew Steve peripherally in college, stayed in loose touch with him through mutual friends in the Resistance. After he showed up on the cover of *People*, I carved out a happy little safe house in my head, where Franklin Seven was too popular to kill, and I think I had us all living in that house. His murder means I was wrong, that they can kill any of us with impunity, and I can tell by the fear in my mother's phone messages that I'm not the only one who's figured that out.

As the news sinks in, I sit at home and watch his murder unfold from a greater and greater distance, as if the screens are far above me, up where people can still breathe. I've been here before, many times, that airless hopeless place where time slows down and all escape routes are closed off. Franklin Seven's picture war has failed; they're too strong for us to wrestle with on that front, and maybe too strong on the military front also. We tried to match them metal to metal, and now they'll snuff us one by one, notching our deaths on their gold fountain pens and laughing at us for being stupid enough to give them the opportunity. As night comes one idea closes in on me and wraps its hands around my throat: There is such a thing as Justice and I'm on the shit side of it. I'm going to be punished for killing John Polling, for turning on my father. I'm going to bring a shit storm down on everybody's head, just like Emily said. Me, self-anointed executioner and defender of the People.

I sink into damaged sleep, hide in my bathrobe all day stalking the Internet, incapable of going to meetings or even returning messages. This house in someone else's name, vaguely my own but mostly belonging to an imaginary person and a phantom group: It's like I'm already underground, far away from the world of sunlight and air, like the ghost of a pharaoh banging around in his tomb. The messages on my phone get more and more irritated, tell me to snap the fuck out of it, but I just keep fluttering further and further down into the well, paralyzed.

Tonk finally comes over to pry me loose, listens as I blubber out my hopelessness for all of us and our doomed strategy. Tonk, sitting in my living room as I go on for a half hour about all the reasons we're fucked, why we can't win. He's quiet for a change, his good-natured face clouded by all my arguments. I'm frightened then, because I've done my best to destroy his faith in us, and at the same time I'm desperate for him to still believe. He nods his head a few times, his eyes turned down to the floor; then he looks back at me and speaks without any ambivalence.

"You know, Lando? I'm here to do something. I'm here to free this country. And I may do it wrong, and I may fail, and I sure don't want to end up like Franklin Seven. But it all boils down to one question." He shrugs. "How do you want to live? That's all. How do you want to live?"

And then he just sits there, and gradually things start shifting, and the sense of doom and stupidity starts falling away. Evil is always intimidating. It always has the advantage and it always tries to bend you to its logic of selfishness and fear to make you cooperate. Steve Sykes never surrendered to Evil. Neither would Tonk. Neither would I.

Tonk finally stands up. "Dude, let's roll," he says. "All your bullshit's making me hungry."

20

My radio went off at five thirty, and the first thing it told me was that Franklin Seven had been killed. I'm one of the earlier risers at the Apex: All the low-flow showerheads in the world can't ensure a hot bath there after seven. Even so, I stayed in bed for another half hour after the soothing voice of NPR broke the bad news. I cried a little bit, because when I imagined Franklin Seven I saw Lando, and also because even if its methods were wrong, the Jefferson Combine still represented the desire to reclaim an America that had slipped away. Dave was already at the kitchen table with another of our roommates.

"Did you hear about Franklin Seven?" I asked.

"Screw them!" Dave said. "They are *murderers*!" I was surprised by his rage. I'd never heard him sounding any more than annoyed, even after the King County riot squad broke his nose against the curb. Nobody had claimed the killing yet. "This isn't even the Government! It's fucking Whitehall or somebody like that! They faked that airport bombing, and now they're trying use it as an excuse to exterminate the Resistance. Are you guys planning anything?"

"Dave, I haven't even been into the office yet."

"We need to do something, Emily. If we let this go, we're next on their list!"

I suspected it was going to be a complicated day. By noon, when the news came out that his wife and baby were missing, the phones started ringing. People looked to us for action, and the murder of a young man and the abduction of his wife and baby moved people deeply. Of course, some were happy to see a "Bad Guy" rubbed out, but despite the propaganda effort to link Franklin Seven with the Polling murder and the recent airport bombing, which they'd denied, it was hard to make them out as bloodthirsty fanatics. The Combine had never killed or even hurt anyone, and most of their targets had been Corporate assets that symbolized their dominance. But more than that: The unclaimed murder and kidnapping, smacking so suspiciously of the security services, disconcerted Americans who always looked at death squads in other countries and reassured themselves that it could never happen here.

So there was a strong desire among our affiliates to make a showing, which Shar and Dan felt we should honor. A candlelight vigil was planned at the Federal Courthouse for eight that evening, and I began to switch my efforts from our poll-watcher campaign to organizing the vigil. Around six I was told a woman wanted to make a donation, and could I please talk to her. Most of the other staffers had gone to dinner, and evidently it was one of those situations where a certain gratitude is called for. We couldn't just say, "Hey, drop a check off with the receptionist."

I went out to usher her into my office. She was in her fifties, elegant and well-kept, with gray hair streaked with black, which she wore long. She was dressed professionally in a medium-length corduroy skirt and a white blouse that she transformed with a marvelous saffron-and-rust-striped silk shawl pinned across her shoulders. Her silver earrings and dark brows made her brown eyes look arresting and wise against her mane of hair. She reached out to me with her smile as soon as I approached, and took my hand for a moment.

"Hello, Emily. I'm Anne Sands."

"It's a pleasure, Anne." I turned to usher her into my office, saying, "That's a beautiful shawl."

"Thank you. It's hand-woven silk, from Laos. I got it at the Textile Museum."

"Here in Seattle?"

"In Washinton D.C. That's where I'm from. I'm in Seattle for a teacher's conference. Before the school year starts."

I picked up a stack of magazines from the chair in my office and piled them on my desk. "I'm sorry. We're a little pressed for space here."

I tried to move quickly through the meeting. I still had another ten people to call, and the vigil started in two hours. I wasn't looking forward to another dinner of raw carrots and a Guru Bar. "I understand you want to make a donation. That's very kind of you."

"Yes." She looked uncomfortable explaining herself. "I heard about that poor man in Long Island—"

"Franklin Seven? Or, I should say, Steven Sykes."

"Yes." Her voice started rising. "It was just so awful! Killing him in front of his family . . ." Her eyes suddenly started watering. "I feel like I have to do *something*." She shook her head, dabbed at her face with a tissue. "This is America!"

Her reaction made me uncomfortable. We were all sad about Steven Sykes, but for this woman it seemed almost personal. "A lot of people are feeling the same way you are, Anne. There's been a steady stream of Militants killed or kidnapped, and the danger is that the public will start to see it as an acceptable part of the landscape. The only good thing about this murder is that it might be horrifying enough to wake people up."

She composed herself, and a quick, slightly embarrassed smile crossed her face. "Sorry. At any rate, I wanted to make a donation to your group. My son is, I suppose, something of an activist, and he told me Democracy Northwest is one of the best groups. You were the ones who stopped the National Business Symposium, weren't you?"

"We helped. And thank you. I appreciate your thinking of us."

She took out a checkbook and began scribbling out a check, then tore it out and handed it to me. It was a rather fancy green check drawn on an investment bank in Washington, D.C., and she had filled it out with a neat graceful cursive. The amount was roughly twice my yearly salary.

"That's . . ." I looked up at her. "That's very generous of you."

"I know you'll do good things with it."

I looked her in the eye. "We will be tireless." I was about to draw on my well-honed vocabulary of pleasant expressions of gratitude when I noticed the name below hers on the check.

"James Sands?"

She gave a tense smile. "Yes. That's my husband."

The discreet thing to do would be to take the check and say nothing, but I couldn't help it. "Is that *the* James Sands, of Water Solutions?"

"Yes."

The size and source of the check made me giddy, and a welter of thoughts bumped against each other as I tried to absorb it all. Could this be some sort of trick by James Sands? To buy us off? Or blackmail us? Was she trying to wash away a feeling of guilt about her husband's business? She seemed sincere. I should shut up about it. She could still ask for the check back. "I'm sorry. I'm just a little surprised."

She smiled easily. "I know you've had your differences with my husband. So have I. He was a very different person when I married him. He actually started his career with the idea of helping third world countries solve their financial problems."

I couldn't believe it. "What happened?"

She answered wistfully. "The same thing that happens to a lot of people, Emily: He got an opportunity. That brought him other opportunities and new friends, and the people you have around you become your frame of reference. People admire you for your success. Your cost of living goes up. It all starts to seem completely normal." She smiled with half her mouth. "Nobody ever sees anything wrong with something they're making money at." For a second she seemed nostalgic. "Believe it or not, he's actually a good person."

I wasn't sure how to respond. After a certain point, people had to be evaluated by their actions, not by how they'd been thirty years ago, or how they treated their inner circle. "I don't mean to put you on the defensive, Anne, but why is he a good person?"

"Because he can still be brought back. Some of those people—and I'm saying this not as someone who reads about them in the paper, but as someone who's had them over for dinner—some of those people, they can't be brought back. They're sociopaths. You have to take away their power or put them in jail. Period. But my husband isn't like that."

I was still finding it hard to make the distinction. James Sands was regularly attacking the Militants and the Citizen Groups in the most devious way possible, purposely associating us with the extremists, trying to destroy the public's faith in their own advocates. He had dedicated himself to spreading lies. Yet she still thought he was good, that he could change. "Thank you. I'll remember that."

She shifted in her seat. I noticed that she had twisted the fringe of her silk shawl around her finger. "To be honest with you, Emily, we're separated now. He appeared on *The Hammer Show*, and frankly, that was too much for me."

I felt sorry for this elegant woman, confessing these things to a complete stranger. I was starting to see James Sands differently now. I didn't hate or resent him. I saw him as a person whose intelligence and drive had presented him with a set of temptations that intelligence alone couldn't prepare him to resist.

She looked awkward for a second, then went on. "There's something else your group should know. It might be related to this latest murder." She took a breath. "My husband told me that Whitehall was starting some kind of counterinsurgency program against anyone who opposes the Government or business interests. I think they might be the ones killing these people."

I just looked at her for few seconds. Her statement was so simple and disturbing that it swept all the other thoughts from my mind. I'd heard the same thing from Dave this morning, but this time it wasn't coming from a long-haired freak. I spoke slowly and carefully. "Do you mean a campaign against the Militant Groups?"

"The Civil Groups, too. Groups like yours."

She told me a short strange story about her husband being approached by Whitehall with some sort of proposition, and that her husband had refused it until after the Cascadia bombing, when his creditors at the Barrington Group had pressured him to join. I'd heard of the Barrington Group: ex-Military and ex-Government people hooked up with big capital to make a killing on their connections.

"So you're saying Barrington is involved, too? How many entities are in this?" She wasn't sure, but she named McPhee/Collins, a well-connected PR firm in Washington that did a lot of Administration propaganda work.

My scalp was tingling now: I'd never been this close to something so big and evil. We'd all suspected there was some sort of campaign directed against us. The alternative media had floated a few inconclusive stories in the last couple of months, but none of the Corporate venues would pick them up. If she had real information on it, right from an Administration crony like James Sands, it could be a major blow against the Matthews Government. I tried to stay lawyerly and critical. "Why do you say it might be connected to the Franklin Seven murder?"

"I just get this feeling . . . There's this rationale that they're fighting a war, and when men have that rationale—" Her voice caught. "—anything goes."

It wasn't the conclusive statement I'd hoped for, but I knew that she was the one whose life was coming unraveled, and I had to respect that. "Anne . . ." I went on as gently as I could. "You know that if Whitehall is managing some sort of illegal counterterrorism program that involves kidnapping or killing people . . . that's something the whole country needs to know about. Because that's the only way to stop it."

"That's why I'm telling you."

"I appreciate that." I tried to figure out how to go forward. "You mentioned that your husband resisted joining Whitehall's campaign at first. So he must have reservations. What would it take for him to go public about it?"

"You mean to be hated by all his colleagues? To possibly lose his business and be at the center of a controversy that would make headlines all over the world? Look at it from his point of view."

"I know, it's hard. But if you could get him to speak out, or at least to share concrete information—" I hesitated, trying to decide whether my next phrase was overblown and then realizing with a shock that it wasn't. "—you could save lives."

She looked down into her lap and sighed. Finally she met my gaze and nodded. "Let me think about how to approach him."

We were done, but I was connected to her now. "Anne, we're having a vigil at the courthouse in a couple of hours. We're asking the Government to step in and find Steven Sykes's wife and child. Would you like to come with me?"

Somewhere between one and two thousand people showed up, quietly holding candles and listening to a few short speeches about civil rights and America. Placards with the picture of the kidnap victims swayed above the crowd, along with posters of Franklin Seven in his Yankees cap. Along with that were Second Revolution banners, and a good number of Army of the Republic insignias, scrawled in red with the *O* and *T* merged together into a gun sight. There was some anger, but the overall feeling was of sadness, a sense of loss for the family that had been annihilated and for the country that was so quickly disappearing. Anne and I stood and chatted. It was the first demonstration she'd gone to in twenty-five years, she said. I introduced her to Dan and Shar when I caught up with them, and she left at eleven o'clock with a promise to stay in touch. I got back to the Apex near midnight, still thinking about the paradox of having James Sands's wife as one of our biggest supporters. I wondered what her children were like. One was an activist, she'd said, but didn't want to say more. The other worked in commercial real estate. I pictured teenage arguments turning into shouting matches at the kitchen table. The Good Child, the Bad Child. As I lay in bed, I couldn't help recasting them in the mold of my own unconventional household and it made me imagine James Sands like my father, building the *Happy* piece by piece, only to have it burn down to the waterline.

Aside from the darkness cropping up around the Militants, our work was going well. In Washington State, the new American Reform Party was coming on stronger than we'd ever expected, and many of their candidates had a good shot at winning their race. Their yard signs had gone up all over the state, and they ran on a platform of SMART SOLUTIONS, and CLEAN GOVERNMENT. The feeling was that the public had tired of its diet of magical patriotism and was ready for a new era. Matthews's party had never been strong in Washington State, and it looked like they were about to get voted out in a big way.

At the DNN, my job had changed from advocating for paper ballots to ensuring that our election reforms were put into place. I was in charge of building a network of citizens to oversee the new laws all over the state. It was grinding, uninspiring work, with clouds of minutiae that had to be explained over and over again to dozens of different volunteers. I wrote information pamphlets for our own people and for the public. E-mails went out by the hundreds of thousands, and scores of canvassers stood on street corners to inform people about the new laws. I got a perverse satisfaction out of this quiet community-building. We were changing the world one mind at a time, the only way it really could be changed.

Much of my work involved the Division of Elections, whose rank and file was welcoming, but whose Commissioner, a loyal Matthews supporter, did everything he could to impede us. He had the heavy body and florid face of someone who ate too much beef. At our single meeting he was cold and uninterested in my suggestions, and I left knowing that we probably hadn't heard the last of him. He quickly proved me right. One of our tasks was to oversee the rollout of new scanning machines that could count the mail-in ballots that would replace paperless Internet voting. The Commissioner did everything he could to slow the arrival of the new machines, as well as making frequent changes in the training protocols, so that we kept having to start the process over again. Voter registration roles kept being purged and then rebuilt, until the only thing we could be sure of is that a lot of prospective Reform voters had been "accidentally" eliminated and that we now had a new task of trying to locate them and get them reregistered. Meanwhile, he told everyone who would listen that we weren't ready to hold the election without Debarr's old corrupt Internet voting system, and that the Citizen Groups were screwing up the whole process. We came right back at him, exposing his sabotage to the public and making it clear who was trying to undermine their reforms.

Now, though, as we tried to cope with the Commissioner, an even more sinister kind of sabotage started to crop up. One afternoon I was talking to our receptionist when she answered the phone. I watched as her face clouded over. After five seconds she hung up. "He said there's a bomb in our office and it's going to explode in twenty minutes."

We evacuated and spent the rest of the day watching the bomb squad comb through our crowded little cubicles.

"They're probably planting a few bugs while they're at it," Shar muttered.

"That's sarcasm, right?"

Three days later another bomb threat came in, and between the evacuation and the long series of questions the investigators asked afterwards, I lost most of that day, too. The detective, a plainclothes man of about forty, seemed sympathetic to us, as did the uniformed police who had come to assist. We offered them coffee and they gave us their cards and said to call anytime we felt threatened in any way. A sergeant with a square face and a crew cut beneath his blue cap gave me his personal cell phone in case he wasn't on duty. "You just call me." He looked right and left, then lowered his voice. "I'm on your side."

Now the threats became more directed. A call was routed to my office. The voice on the other end was deep and cold. "Emily Cort-right?"

"Yes. And you are—?"

"How are things at the Apex?"

"What do you mean?"

"The Apex, where you and all your Radical friends hang out."

"Who is this?"

"See you around. Or maybe I should say, I'll *feel* you around. I hear you Radical babes love to fuck."

He hung up, and for a second, a mild nausea came over me.

"Don't let them rattle you," was Shar's answer. "It's a game for them." I called the detective and he took my testimony on a handheld. He was sympathetic, but it was clear that Seattle PD had bigger fish to fry than a nasty phone call. When I mentioned what we'd heard about Whitehall's campaign, he refused to be swept over the border of Crime into the treacherous realm of Politics. "Right," he said slowly. "We'll have to see if a pattern develops."

It happened twice more, ugly insinuations delivered in a flat conversational tone, always with a hint of sexual menace in them. Even though I didn't want to, I found myself glancing over my shoulder in the streets now, and felt a little surge of anxiety when I left the Apex each morning and stepped onto the sidewalk. Dave started walking me to work each morning.

I'd never stopped worrying about Lando during this time, and every time a Militant was killed or a disappearance was reported, it sent me into a little spiral of dread for a few days. I'd talked to Lando after the Franklin Seven murder, exchanging updates about our progress and his own reports on the status of the Militants. He sounded demoralized after the Franklin Seven murder. And he didn't believe the Patriotic Guard was acting alone.

"They're a front group," he said. "I don't think some dumbass group of wing nuts could find Franklin Seven after the Government's spent three years looking for him. Same with Madison Twelve. Or maybe they're a real group and the Regime's feeding them the information to make the hits, like the FBI did in the seventies, with the Secret Army Organization."

"One of our members thinks Whitehall is behind it. She has firsthand knowledge that they've mounted some sort of corporate counterinsurgency program."

"How does she know?"

"Listen to this: She's James Sands's wife! She told me her husband is part of it. Isn't that wild?"

There was a long silence on the other end, and when he answered he sounded far away. "Yeah. That's wild."

"Anyway, I'm not intimidated. I'm going to see all these people go to jail someday."

Maybe I'd gotten a little too bouncy about something close to him. He knew some of the Jefferson Combine people; Franklin Seven and Madison Twelve may well have been friends of his, not just names in the newspaper. I changed the subject. "When are we going to get together again?"

He sighed. It was strange to hear him sound so exhausted. "I don't know. I probably shouldn't even be talking to you."

"I really miss you, Lando. I wish all this were over."

He didn't say anything for a while. "It will be. You guys are turning the tide. Crazy people like me will be obsolete."

"You won't be obsolete. You'll just be repurposed as my personal plaything."

The sound of his laugh made me feel good. "That's one gig I think I can handle."

We hung up, and as I stood there staring at the food court of the Westlake Mall, thinking about what it would be like to be together someday, I felt a heavy weight come down on me and my vision got blurry and wet. I just didn't see how that was ever going to happen.

21

*T*he Franklin Seven assassination is a chance to introduce the Regime's new special guest act, the Right Wing death squad. Politics with a Latin beat. The Patriotic Guard is nothing but an audio file at first: *Newsweek* has to fake-up a black-clad model with a shadowy face to give them a more substantial feel on their cover. An expert job that works all around: Suddenly the Matthews Regime doesn't look so bad. "Now is the time for Americans to rally behind the center," says their editorial. "Radicals may have issues with the Matthews Administration, but the alternative could well be chaos." Majestic, flag-draped oaths from *Der Homelanders* about going after this new menace. *We treat all lawbreakers the same, no matter what their politics.* Right. To top it off, Matthews does a heroic spin on prime time to announce that "secret negotiations" have freed the wife and child. She'll still be held incommunicado, of course, and her terrorist baby, too, but at least America knows that the Franklin Seven story has a happy ending after all.

Nobody's clapping louder than the Patriotic Guard, ever ready to provide a sequel to the feel-good drama of the season. The New York Ballot Reform office in Manhattan shudders and burns, courtesy of the Patriotic Guard, and suddenly the new fashion sweeps the nation. The Tulsa office of the Oklahoma Voting Project goes mysteriously up in flames, as does the Save the Redwoods storefront in Ukiah. A very specialized virus chews up the computer systems in the New York headquarters of the Democracy NY Network, and the same nasty little bug wipes the hard drives in three other branches in New England. The official Media chalks it up to fringe players acting alone, but when an activist in San Diego gets shot through the window of her apartment, the local PD embarrasses everyone by accidentally catching the perpetrator, a neo-Nazi who claims he was acting with material and intelligence support from a man who worked for a little company called Whitehall. A very poor way of showing his gratitude to his handlers. The FBI moves in to "investigate" the issue, debunks him so thoroughly that he stops believing himself, recants and apologizes for soiling the name of the great security forces of the United States. TROUBLED LONER, proclaims the story in *Time* magazine, with the perfect iconography of the Alleged One taking his shame into the courtroom with cuffed hands and bowed head. Even worse, he's condemned in the higher court of the Hammer. "I say the man's a traitor. If he's going to take a shot at some Radical, so be it. That's a personal choice. But to then go blaming Whitehall when he gets caught, like some little punk-ass hiding behind his mama, that's some shit I do not accept. In other words, the Hammer comes *down!*"

But most of these are from actors who play journalists on TV. In the dying world of newsprint, words come back in a torrent, picking at all the little threads that lead to Whitehall. Rumors of secret Corporate slush funds bubble to the surface from interviews with unnamed sources in the security services, and a midlevel accountant with General Avionics comes forward with tales of money laundered through Pakistan for the disruption and destruction of anti-Government, anti-Corporate networks, both terrorist and "quasi-terrorist." He goes quiet again and no evidence appears, but I know it's real and that my father's part of it. I want to call him up and say, *Dad, why are you trying to kill me?* Except that it would only lead to another set of questions coming from his side, and he'd screw it up somehow, and then they'd be all over me and everyone I know.

The comps keep dropping. In the East, where the Jefferson Combine has consolidated most of the guerrilla groups north of Georgia, they're falling with regularity. We're into a new phase now; killing the "sympathizers." Henry Rosenberg, a lawyer for the Jefferson Combine, gets shot to death by unknown assailants on Cape Cod. It seems he was taking a little vacation time when they motored up to his sailboat between Woods Hole and Martha's Vineyard and invited themselves aboard. The locals played it as an accident at first, but then the Coasties dived to two hundred feet and recovered the body, looking suspiciously not drowned with a bullet hole in the chest and the temple and the bilge cocks opened. Imaginative hypotheses with pictures of the well-to-do family in better times. Jealous husband? Payback by the Combine for services not rendered? The number one rule in these cases is always smear the victim.

The next to go is a Combine spokesman, Phillip Weitzlauf. He takes a dive out of his sixth-story office window in Manhattan. The Patriotic Guard picks up the tab for this one, but the check's still on the table for the sudden run of disappearances, which, according to BringThemBackAlive.org, now numbers twenty-four in the last eight weeks. It's morning in America, and there's a brand-new feeling in the air: fear. Out in the heartland the sick sensation is starting to take hold that maybe everything isn't going to just be okay.

"It's time to rock it," Tonk says.

Tonk's not the only restless one at this meeting in Sarah's apartment. The country's in a deep drought, and the only thing resembling raindrops is the steady fall of comps back east.

McFarland is calm and commonsensical: "We need to go back on the offensive, Lando. If we keep waiting, we might not be able to pull it off."

"Besides," Joby says, "all this law-abiding crap is breaking us."

With the cease-fire declared, we've held off on the scams and robberies that keep the coffers full, and after eight months without any income, our expenses are starting to catch up with us. We have rent to pay on five apartments and groceries for a dozen blue notes, and the cool stuff that goes *pow* isn't cheap. Still, I'm feeling like armed resistance is our worst bet right now.

"I know where you're coming from, Joby. But believe me, there's nothing the Regime would like better than for us to break this cease-fire. The scary terrorists are their best prop."

Sarah jumps in to the rescue. "Lando's right. The longer this goes on, the worse the Regime looks. Especially with the attacks on the Civil Groups. Our sources say that every time they get attacked their membership grows."

McFarland speaks with an unusual intensity. "You and Lando think the Civil Groups have some sort of righteous aura, but I'm telling you the Regime's got all the resources they need to strip that aura away. They can twist you around until you love your oppressor and hate the people trying to save you. You watch! They're just warming up!"

Everybody storms out that afternoon, and for the next two weeks I'm patting myself and Sarah on the back, watching things play out exactly the opposite of how Mac and Tonk had said they would. The handwriting moves to the Midwest. When the Ohio Secretary of State trumps up a legal challenge to the new balloting reforms, a mob of ten thousand people goes Cecil B. DeMille outside his office in Columbus, strings a mannequin up on a sort of Port-A-Gallows then pulls it down and kicks it to pieces. A few of the municipal unions pile on with a work slowdown, and when the Governor tries to show them who's boss it lights the fuse on a half-dozen wildcat strikes that power the Buckeye State down to "standby" mode. *If we don't vote, we don't work.* Most notably, Joe Simic marches the Throwaways through Akron and a few scuffles turn into seven blocks of broken windows and burning Dumpsters. It's the first time the rabble throws down for voting, and I'm sure that gets noticed in the Imperial City. The National Guard's called out, guns on Main Street again. The Regime's man resigns. The dollar sinks a few cents against the yuan, Treasury bonds rise a quarter-point, ballot initiatives crop up in two more states. It looks like the middle 40 percent is starting to move.

Now, though, the Regime decides to show that the Civils aren't the only ones who can close things down. Evidence of contacts with the Jefferson Combine turns up in the Boston office of the New England Democracy Network, and that opens up Operation Wavelength, where the Homelanders cut loose with simultaneous raids all over New England, and on sister organizations in New York, Chicago, Ann Arbor, and Portland. Hard drives get confiscated, pictures of organizers being fingerprinted and booked flash a hundred times a day in the magazines and televisions of the Republic of Stupidity. No matter that charges get dropped a month later—a month is a past so distant that it might as well be written about in the encyclopedia. In the silly present, the Regime kicks up the volume on their information operations. No need to call them Utopians or WIFs. Now they're America Haters and Traitors. The Leader himself steps up to reassure us in his low raspy voice and his fake rural accent. "Now, some would say that America is a sinister place. They try to deceive us with False Gods of Lost Constitutional Rights, and to confuse the brave men and women who protect our freedoms with those who would take them away. We must stay *strong*"—he clenches his fist with fake strength—"before our internal enemies."

September comes, and the rumbling in the Network is getting louder. Bellingham signals that they want to resume operations, and the Portland and Eugene crowds are also impatient. Even San Francisco Mark wonders, "What's the point of a unilateral cease-fire that isn't recognized in the media as a cease-fire? The Regime's fighting this war without us." Even Tonk's beating the war drum. "We're the Bad Cops, remember? That's how you sold the cease-fire last year. We're supposed to stick up for the Civils."

A bomb blows up a Greyhound station in Philadelphia, a useless target for any guerrilla group, but very useful for pinning on the Gettysburg Contract, and laying it on so heavily and constantly that nobody seems to hear their denials.

Mac is losing patience. "The cease-fire's broken, Lando, without our side even breaking it. It's over. The Rocky Mountain groups feel the same way. It's time to launch the Counteroffensive."

I can tell he's walked with me just about as far as he's going to. "Okay. If the consensus is to resume operations, I'm in. All I'm saying is, let's wait." I'm reaching for another landmark, but there's only one big one on the horizon, and it's two months away. "Let's hold our fire until after the elections." His face starts to close up and I go on quickly. "That'll give us a good indication of whether the Civils can face the Regime on their own." He sighs and looks off to the side, annoyed. "We need to hang tough, Mac. We need to have faith in the People."

That becomes my line: *Wait till the elections . . . Faith in the people.* I work it to the bone with the other members of the West Coast network, traveling down to Oregon and San Francisco for meet-ups, and when I paste down a shaky consensus, I start selling it to the Jefferson Combine, who's heartsick from watching their comps go down and the civil groups get attacked. Encrypted e-mails slash across the country.

Postpone the softball tournament until after the MVPs have been chosen.

Easy for you to say. We are losing players and team spirit is low.

At three the next afternoon I get a call from Emily. There's an unfamiliar freak-out feel to her voice. "Lando!"

"What's up?"

"Something's happening at the DNN office! They sealed off the building and seized all the files and computers! They arrested Dana and Shar, and I think they're after me, too!"

Bad news, but good news. At least they'd grabbed all of them. If they'd only taken Emily, that might mean we had something to worry about. I pull over into the parking lot of a bankrupt furniture store. She's calling from a WiFi hot spot downtown.

"What are the charges?"

"Aiding terrorists. All that." She's panicking now—I can feel it. "But what if they know about us?"

"They don't."

"But what if they do? Can you hide me?"

What a sweet prospect that is: Stashing her at my house, in the little White Room in the attic, she could be my sex slave and I could cook her long elaborate breakfasts in bed and give her massages. All the time in the world. I rub out the beautiful dream. "No. Then you'd have one more thing to explain when you surfaced."

I've never heard her whimper before, but now she does. "I think they know about us!"

"Just calm down a second. They don't have shit on us. If they did, they would have picked you up first. This is the same crap they've been pulling all over the country. It's all about intimidation and propaganda. They're going to hold you for a few days and then drop all charges."

"How can you be sure?"

"Listen, it's all going to be okay. Are you listening?"

A little vacuum on the line, then a tiny "Yes."

"Stick to your story. That's rule number one. You're a Civil orga-nizer. Period. Don't embellish. Don't try to manipulate them. That's their game, and they're better at it than you. They're going to ask you if you've had contacts with the guerrillas, and you'll say no. They're going to hit you with the timing of our cease-fire, and you'll say there's no connection. They may tell you that Dan or Shar already squealed, but you know that Dan and Shar won't. They may lie and say they have evidence, but they don't. They're going to get your story over and over again from a million angles and see if you change it; then they're go-ing to haul out their worst accusations and try to break you. Stick to your story. And don't say anything without a lawyer present."

Her voice has a little smile in it. "I am a lawyer."

"Oh, yeah. Well, get some backup. And remember one thing: You're innocent. You have not done anything wrong." I got most of the spiel from McFarland, who seems to have his fair share of experience with arrest and interrogation.

She sounds in control again. "Okay."

"So call your attorney, go down to the newspaper office, and then call the cops and make them pick you up there."

"Okay."

"I want a copy of your mug shot when you get out."

"Sure thing."

"And don't stick a shiv in anybody in jail."

She laughed. "I love you."

"I love you, too, Emily. Be stronger than they are." We hang up in a good mood, considering she's about to be arrested. At least it's legal, instead of some private Whitehall prison. It pisses me off, though, in a way that it didn't piss me off when they busted the East Coast groups. I'm driving in from shooting video of a warehouse in Renton, and the more I think about it, the angrier it makes me. The Regime's decided that dragging their feet on voter reform isn't going to be good enough. They need direct action: Get the files, fuck with the leaders, gradually normalize the idea that the Civil Groups can be treated like criminals, because if they're treated like criminals, on some level it reinforces the idea in Joe Public's mind that they *are* criminals. Right now Regime stooges are going through the files, scanning the mem-bership lists to connect all the dots and screen out this one for a tax audit, that one for phantom violations on his driver's record. That's the easy stuff, doable by a couple of guys and a computer. More distinguished Civils can get Uncle Sam's special treatment: the sexual harassment frame-up, the kiddie porn planted in a work computer, nasty crap they'd pioneered in the '70s and are rolling out again for the greater good of America. These people have no intention at all of ceding power. Not by the ballot box, not by the will of a fat and sleepy People who get more outraged about an actor who cheats on his wife than a politician who cheats on a whole country. People should be in the streets about this, but instead they're snoozing in front of the television, sopping up their Lazy Man's Bible and ducking their heads in the hope that somehow things will just get better all by themselves. I'm almost feeling like it's time for the lightning, for the loud noise that wakes them up in the middle of their nap, but I keep up my inner pep talk about strategic discipline, about letting the Civils strike a blow at the ballot box, the true decisive way to discredit the Regime. Then, to my amazement, Governor Cox takes a step that defies all my arguments. He cancels the election.

The announcement comes out quietly in a press release Friday afternoon, trying to duck the news cycle. The Washington State Commissioner of Elections regrets that due to the heightened security risks to polling places caused by the terrorists and the difficulty in instituting voter-mandated changes in the voting system, the election will be temporarily postponed.

At first it seems like satire. There hasn't been a guerrilla action on the West Coast for ten months, and it's Governor Cox himself and his lackey in the Division of Elections that have been steadily sabotaging the changeover to paper ballots. But what would once have been considered outrageous is now considered merely bold, and Cox isn't stopping at bold. According to his Attorney General's interpretation, the wording of the ballot initiative implies that it'll expire before the postponed election takes place, and will thus have to be resubmitted and voted on all over again. It's surreal, but any legal argument still has to work its way through the judicial process, and with a state Supreme Court and Federal Circuit court that's been stacked with Party lapdogs, what should be open and shut is instead headed for a long slow trudge through the legal system.

The network lights up all the way from Boston to San Diego, and even though I know the Regime's blundered, that the Civils can make mincemeat out of this, my "wait for the elections" battle cry has been shot to pieces, and I'm running out of answers.

I get McFarland on his secure cell Saturday morning.

"You know that Cox canceled the election?"

"I do. But I've got something else to tell you. Meet me at the Hog Ranch."

The Dairy Queen in Bothell was a place we'd used before, with good views out the big glass windows and a crew of very unsuspicious teenagers behind the counter. At ten thirty in the morning it's empty. McFarland walks in after scoping the lot, his face looking drawn out. Something's more immediately wrong than the Regime's political maneuvers. He skips the intro.

"We lost a Friend last night."

A chill goes through me. "What happened?"

"They came into his house at four A.M., five or six guys in black fatigues. He was armed, but he didn't want a gunfight with his wife and kids around. He went along without a shot."

I thought, *So much for the heroic gun owner making a last stand against the Government,* then the horror of it washed over me, made even worse because I'm not reading about this on the Internet, but getting it directly from a shaken, almost fearful-looking McFarland, a man I've always thought of as unshakable. "I'm sorry to hear that, Mac."

"The thing is, he's hardly even done anything. He works at Department of Transportation, and we've been keeping him on the surface in case we need intelligence. He cued us in to some blasting caps about two years ago. That's it. He started getting a little paranoid last summer, so we sidelined him, and we figured that would be it." His voice falters a little, a rare sign of weakness. "Guess we were wrong."

I think about it. In the typical repressive regime, they arrest you and then they arrest everyone in your address book. The question is: Is McFarland in that address book?

"No. His only contact was the guy who recruited him, and he just went on an extended hunting trip."

"Okay. So . . . is this guy going to talk?"

McFarland looks directly at me. "Most people talk, Lando. Some take five minutes and some take five weeks, but there's very few heroes once they start putting it to you. I know, because I've put it to 'em. That was my job overseas: Make 'em talk. Any way we could." He looks out the window, far away. "The rule is, guilty until proven innocent. Except in the end, you want to beat all the innocent out of them. Because if you beat 'em and drown 'em and drug 'em and fuck their minds up, and they're still innocent, what does that make you?"

For a second McFarland becomes a different person to me. There's a sense of the damned about him, a vague repellent evil that makes me uncomfortable in his presence. I realize that he may feel that same repulsion every day.

In that moment, I understand the way that the noblest yearning for duty and sacrifice can be mixed up with all that is savage and shameful, like in the Bible, where a just and merciful God tells you to kill everyone, kill the children, kill the livestock, kill John Polling, leave nothing alive to sully this pure and just world. Except when it's all done you find out that wasn't really God after all, just some politician, or maybe it was God, but he taps you on the shoulder and says, *No, dude, that isn't what I meant,* and leaves you sitting in a Dairy Queen in Bothell with blood on your hands and no further orders. Mac seems to feel my sudden distance; he gives a cockeyed little smile and turns back to a long stare out the window. "I guess that's something I needed to tell you," he says, still watching the road, the lot, the infection of run-down strip malls around us. "I don't even know why."

He falls into silence for a half minute. He sounds fatalistic and depressed, like he finally hears the footsteps. I think I understand McFarland now: why he took up arms when so many others did nothing. His anger and his disillusion is far deeper than mine. When he speaks again it's final: "We need to strike back, Lando. They're bringing it to us and we can't run away."

I'm sick of convincing people, of convincing myself, but I also know that once I say yes, it leaves only Sarah holding back consensus for our group, and that means we'll turn, then San Francisco will turn, and Portland and Bellingham and the others. There'll be no more restraint on the Jefferson Combine, or the New Confederate Army or the Forces of the American Revolution or anyone else, and ten months of planning will suddenly explode into action. It will probably happen anyway: I'm not a commander and I have no troops. The guerrilla will be unleashed. Maybe that's what it takes to remind Americans where the center really is: not with the Regime, but with the Civil Groups, and their outrageous demands for fair elections and rule by the people rather than the Corporations.

"Okay," I say. "Let's rock it."

It starts in Boston, where at four in the morning the office of the country's largest health insurance profiteer goes sky high on two hundred pounds of ANFO, while simultaneously, in Sudbury, Framingham, Tewksbury, and Belmont the branches of Citibank burst into glorious flame. In Springfield, a dust bomb blows apart the RapidMail sorting station, and in three other small towns in the state "vandals" with sledgehammers, pickaxes and Molotovs take out a healthy scattering of automated teller machines. That's just Massachusetts. One minute later bombs start going off in Maine, Vermont, and New Hampshire, in cities and in small towns, like giant footsteps marching across the landscape of America, tapping toes in New York and Pennsylvania, doing a little jig in Philadelphia, where the Gettysburg Contract is strong, more sporadically in Atlanta, North Carolina, then through the Midwest, touching down in Cincinnati and Columbus, in big strides up to Chicago, to Minnesota, then going high, wide, and handsome in Texas, the evil seed of American corruption, where a dozen municipal warehouses leap into flames and the headquarters of one of the vote-stealing software companies is stylishly taken out with a homemade rocket launcher. Adios, paperless voting machines.

The giant is stomping on Corporate assets and crooked voting hardware all over the country. He walks gingerly through the Midwest, then more heavily across the Rockies in Boulder and Denver, where four warehouses holding a total of 720 voting machines go up in smoke. Once he gets to the Sierras and the Cascades time has spun back to midnight. McFarland's group takes out five targets, icing the Division of Elections headquarters in Olympia with gas bombs, ANFO, and sodium chlorate for extra bang-power. We take out four, with one dud, but Gonzalo drops his virus masterpiece into the Internet voting software they've been using to control the Evergreen State, and that takes paperless voting off the table in the old hometown. Eight bombs go off in other parts of Washington, and in Oregon the giant's foot comes down seven times across the state, a showing that surely would have been stronger if Earl E. wasn't out of the network. Northern California does well, too, as San Francisco Mark combines a few explosions with a major computer attack on the state election authority. Even little Juneau, Alaska, gets its licks in, adding insult to injury by including a big case of rotting pink salmon in the explosion. In two minutes the whole thing is over, and the smell of smoke is hanging all the way across the country.

Not all so clockwork, though. Fires destroy nearby buildings, and a neighborhood health clinic gets blown up by mistake. A couple of comps get popped and quickly disappear, incommunicado. In Colorado, a responding officer ends up dead in a shoot-out, earning the Media Martyr award. His only crime was upholding the status quo, a crime two hundred million other Americans could be tried for. Father of three, volunteer fireman. Inevitable when the metal starts piling up—we all know that—but however many times I tell myself that I still keep hearing that faint voice in the background saying, *No, dude, that's not what I meant!*

Several days later, the DNN prisoners are formally processed and set free. They're back at work, and so are we. And I can't help thinking this was what the Regime wanted all along, to have their enemy back, their beloved internal enemy that makes all things possible, just as Emily and Sarah and I said all along. Now it's our bombs and words against their endless lying pictures that turn Matthews into Moses, make Jesus out of John Polling. They're creating their country and we're creating ours. The cease-fire is over. We're back on the path of armed struggle. Win or Die for somebody's America.

PART III

TARGET AMERICA

22

I'm not in the least bit worried, Jim. This so-called counteroffensive is just the last spike of the fever before it breaks."

Walter and I were alone in one of the semiprivate rooms at his club near the Pentagon, sitting in brown leather chairs and listening to the news jabbering softly in the background. It was an institution for retired army officers, and its oaken interior, along with the pictures on the walls of great generals and warriors of ages past, lent it an atmosphere of classical dignity where the sacrifices of his predecessors could be appreciated without too much ambiguity. By now my ice cubes had melted into tiny little windows in the rust-colored whiskey, but I still hadn't broached the subject I'd come to talk about. It was a subject that had been increasingly on my mind ever since hearing Howard crowing about the torture session he'd witnessed.

"Walter, this is a bit awkward for me, but I'm a bit concerned about these killings and disappearances."

He raised his eyebrows thoughtfully. "So am I. It's ugly." He raised his hand and finished my thoughts for me. "Let me guess: You read about all this violence and you're wondering about the

Program, because you're not the kind of person who'd sponsor some sort of death squad."

It was an unexpected relief to hear him go straight to the point. "Basically."

He smiled. "Rest easy, my friend. You have nothing to worry about. What you're paying for is monitoring and responding to groups that are hostile to your interests. It's all legal, and you're not doing anything that the Seattle Water Project or Protect Our Water didn't do to you first. *They're* running public education campaigns—so are you. They're trying to collect information and disrupt your operations: You're doing the same to them. You're not guilty of anything except protecting yourself."

"That's ducking the question, Walter. What about these supposed kidnappings?"

He seemed a bit put off that I didn't accept his initial answer. The leather of his chair squeaked as he shifted his weight. "Don't forget that we're federal contractors. The things you're talking about fall under our government contract, not yours. Are we capturing and interviewing? Yes. Are we holding terrorism suspects incommunicado? Certainly. That's our job."

"They threw a man out a window, Walter. I think that's going a little too far."

He nodded heartily. "It's way too far! But that Weitzlauf deal was the Patriotic Guard, not us. Jim . . ." He seemed to struggle for a reasonable way to explain Weitzlauf's murder. "These terrorists set loose a chain of events. It's action and reaction. Now, you and I don't control what that reaction is. Weitzlauf pissed off the wrong people and they went after him. We're not responsible." He half-smiled. "Look! If it was us, we'd have kept the guy alive!"

Walter was lying to me. There were probably good reasons for it; he might even feel that he was doing me a favor by giving me deniability. But having it cross over from the realm of necessary vagueness to outright lying took away some of the insider cachet that I'd relished in earlier days. As much as we were friends, Walter worked for Whitehall, and that was going to color any relief to my conscience that I tried to wring out of him.

The idea that I was contributing to a program that might be killing people was working on me in a way that it hadn't when my anger at the terrorists was fresh and everything else was hypothetical. The execution on his sailboat of the lawyer Henry Rosenberg had made the murders suddenly stark and personal, despite Walter's intimations that Rosenberg had been into things far deeper than what was reported in the media. Maybe because I used to like to sail myself, and I kept visualizing the bloodied fiberglass and flapping sheets. Maybe it was because being killed on one's own yacht meant that even a rich middle-aged man with a family wasn't immune.

In addition to that, the political turmoil in the country was growing, rather than shrinking: In a recent briefing Walter had classified different areas where we operated as either "loyal" or "uncooperative." Wyoming, Utah, and Nevada were "loyal." Oregon was "uncooperative." The state of Washington was loyal, but the city of Seattle was "uncooperative" toward the federal security agencies and, by extension, Whitehall. Whatever we might have accomplished with McPhee's public diplomacy, the Matthews Administration undid with its arrogant and ham-handed treatment of anyone who disagreed with them. In Washington State their idiotic cancellation of the election had turned that issue into a flashpoint for opposition groups across the country. It was a mess. Walter admitted as much, obliquely blaming the Administration's stupidity for the problems. "Politicians!" he said, shaking his head. "Sometimes I wish we could just put 'em all on a big cruise ship, send 'em out to sea, and then sink it."

Although I didn't want Walter or anyone else to know it, I'd lost my appetite for the Program. There was something degrading about chairing meetings of terror victims whose bodies or families had been mutilated, while my principal gripe was that they had cost my company some money. I was tired of defending viewpoints I only partially believed in. The clandestine powers behind the Program had seemed seductively omnipotent at the outset, and I'd felt privileged to become one of them. But hadn't I actually been forced into this by the Fund, by Denton? As each new death sifted through the media the demands of being a player began to wear on me, and the fact of Denton began to crowd out the rationales I'd seized on before. The brutal truth was that I had knuckled under and joined the Program to keep my place as a figurehead at my company. I wasn't a player. I was a patsy.

Mine was an opulent failure, invisible to most, but no less biting by the fact that I confronted it alone. With Anne gone and the business on a steady course, I had plenty of time to contemplate my actions with a deepening sense of uneasiness. With each new death or disappearance I convened an imaginary jury of my peers and argued my case: Walter, Richard Boren, and John Polling if I wanted to be found innocent; my old colleagues, my wife, and son if I was prosecuting. I even found myself defending my actions to my maternal grandfather, who admonished me with Yiddish-tinted commandments salvaged from the wreckage of Eastern Europe: Do Not Lie, Do Not Murder. The sentiment of this strange court wavered back and forth, but by the end of the summer it fixed itself with sickening certitude on the verdict: I was guilty, a fraud, a murderer by proxy. I knew then, with a clarity I hadn't felt since I'd first listened to Walter's pitch in my office, that I had to get out of the Program.

Nobody was going to make that easy for me. I was Barrington's boy now: They'd boot me out of Water Solutions at the slightest hint of disloyalty. My best bet was to boot the Fund out first, a delicate and dangerous leveraged buyout that would be even more difficult to put together than when I'd tried it a year ago with the Japanese. I still had the second largest block of stock and knew the company better than any man alive, and that gave me a fighting chance. Howard Pettijohn owned 4 percent of the company: I approached him confidentially and offered to buy him out at a healthy premium. Meanwhile, I quietly contacted a consortium of Russian oil people I'd met a few years before: They knew pipelines and they were accustomed to unorthodox deals. We arranged to meet at a conference in Vienna and several days later they sent me the message that they could raise the necessary money. We would form a partnership to buy Howard's share, and that would again give me a controlling interest in the company.

We set up a timeline of six weeks. Everything had to be done in complete secrecy, even from Whitehall. My CFO, Jack Mossberg, was my main ally, stealthily putting together the numbers we needed, flying to London to work out the details with a City investment firm. For the first time in many months I felt good again, like the man who'd built the company instead of a lackey. The Fund had outmaneuvered me; now I'd outmaneuver them back. Whitehall and its Program were about to become someone else's problem.

In the midst of this Anne called me to set up a date. "There's something we need to talk about." It had a foreboding ring to it, but she wouldn't go into it over the phone. I wondered if she was going to lower the boom on me once and for all. We'd been in a stalemate for a while: We got together a few times each week, chatted on the telephone in between. I invited her over to the house for dinner the coming Friday night.

In the past few months I'd tried to imagine splitting up with Anne. There would be lawyers and a property settlement, and that would probably be complicated but not necessarily toxic. Anne wasn't a vindictive woman. She wouldn't go to war over money, though her lawyers would make sure they earned their fees. We'd probably have one of those amicable divorces where we stayed friends and got together every few weeks or months. Joshua would blame me. Tina would refuse to take sides. After a while I'd start dating women twenty years younger than me.

That wasn't an acceptable resolution for me. When I looked at her I saw the young woman I fell in love with, twenty-four years old, and the woman who held our babies and looked down into their eyes as they nursed. We'd always laughed a lot, in bed and around the house, and it wasn't until my forties, when I was increasingly involved in the business and she was less so, that we stopped laughing and everything became more workmanlike. We fought over how I treated Joshua. Sex became less frequent and less joyful. Outings with the kids became things we did one at a time, rather than all together. For my part, her crusading had worn me down over the years. I was tired of thinking about mass extinction and the gap between rich and poor.

And yet to give her up had something deeply disturbing about it. It would be saying that the business of life—the house, the bank account—was somehow superior to the life it supported, that people were interchangeable if one had sufficient property and sangfroid. There was something so shabby and sad in that notion, so much of Walter sitting alone in his apartment with his military history books, or Howard Pettijohn with his uncomprehending bimbo wife.

Anne arrived for dinner in her Tibetan jacket, with her long straight hair framing that serene oval of a face, red lipstick, a glitter of silver earrings. Her perfume swelled briefly over me with its indefinable cargo of exotic places. "So," I said after I collected myself, "how does it feel to be home?"

She took in the foyer and the living room in a long look then gave a light, noncommittal smile. "Same old house."

I tried not to let her reaction weigh me down. She slipped out of her jacket and hung it from the big wooden ball on the end of the balustrade so that the two golden dragons were facing me. She looked very alluring in a cream-colored blouse of that kind of silk that pours over the body like liquid, and she turned to me and suddenly we came together and closed our arms around each other. I just held her for a while. She felt so slight and so substantial. We finally separated and after the little aura of feeling dispersed, I smiled.

"I cooked dinner myself tonight."

"You didn't!"

"I did!" Leading her into the kitchen, I caught her glancing around at the surroundings. "There's a late run of king salmon on the Chilkat River, in Alaska, and it so happens that our main IT guy has a brother who lives up there. So I had this flown in for you." I showed her the perfect orange filet, now marinating in sesame oil and ginger, and she smiled approvingly. "Accompanied by wild rice, the last few pieces of fresh sweet corn in the state of Maryland, and for dessert—" I lifted the cover from a glass platter. "—an apple tart made from the first ripe McIntoshes of the year. Okay," I confessed, "Phyllis made the tart."

"I'm still impressed."

"Phyllis is visiting her sister this weekend."

"Hmmm. Is this all a plot to get me alone and compromise my virtue?"

"Am I that transparent?"

She rolled her eyes without letting on where she stood in the compromised-virtue department, and a little thrill of lust went through me. We moved into the library and sat down on opposite ends of the couch. We talked about Tina's new job for a few minutes: A Chinese company had hired her to help look after their portfolio of commercial properties in Manhattan. The boyfriend situation was still problematic: Mark the lawyer had been stringing her along for years without any commitment, and we both hoped that this move would make her reassess things. "I just talked to her yesterday," I told Anne with authority. "I think she's getting ready to pull the plug." I was glad I had the latest on it; I talked to Tina every three or four days. I hadn't talked to our son since he'd called to criticize my appearance on *Washington Challenge*. "What do you hear from Joshua?" I couldn't keep the sarcasm out of my voice. "Richard wanted to know if he's still fighting the War between Words and Pictures."

She glanced down and then up again. "I wish you two would work out your differences."

"Hey, I have no trouble working out my differences with him. He's the one who can't work his out with me."

"He loves you more than you know, Jim. You're his idol." I couldn't help bursting into a loud laugh at that. She went on. "He was very upset when I told him we'd separated."

"Yeah? I tried to tell him but I didn't get the chance: He was too busy laying into his 'idol' about appearing on TV." I sighed. "Let's talk about the kids later. Okay? I'd like to just enjoy a few hours with you without any conflict. That's a fair request, isn't it?"

The timer went off, and I came back to the library wheeling a cart with the dinner dishes on it and a bottle of Barolo. "I thought it would be a little cozier in here."

The fish was even better than I'd hoped, and the luscious taste of it, along with the wine, filled me with an exhilarating optimism. We talked about the news and the situations in Venezuela and Saudi Arabia, which we agreed were both disasters, and about the latest movie starring the latest star, which we also agreed was a disaster. It was very civilized, but at the same time there was a certain glossiness to the conversation. Sometimes I caught her making a sideways, uneasy glance, as if she were waiting for the opportunity to broach something larger. I had the disturbing sense that she might be about to ask me for a divorce.

When the remains of Phyllis's apple tart were finally scattered across our desert plates, I could tell she was ready. I braced myself and said, "So, you have something on your mind."

She straightened herself in her chair and took a breath. "I need to talk to you about this Whitehall thing you're part of."

I was startled: I'd been expecting a request for divorce. I sat back in my chair, unsure. "What aspect of it?"

She had none of that air of the concerned wife, or the indulgent ally. She was distant, inquisitorial. "I want you to tell me about it. Everything you know."

I realized that this might be my last reprieve, and I had a choice to make. I could either go defensive and keep her in the dark, or I could open up to her, and be on the same side for the first time in years. That would be a different side from Howard or Walter. I thought about Howard's description of the secret facility in Rappahannock, and of Rosenberg's body eerily hanging in the dark submerged cockpit of his sunken yacht.

"I'm getting out of that Program." She kept her reserve, as if I might be trying a new ploy. "I didn't want to be in it in the first place. They kept pushing it, and after—"

"Who kept pushing it?"

"Whitehall and Barrington. There's some sort of relationship there. I kept ducking it, but after the Cascadia bombing I was in shock, and all I could think about was holding on to the company and getting revenge on the punks who blew it up." I tossed my head. "I know—It's a bullshit excuse, but Barrington was in control by then, and they made it clear that if I didn't go along with the Program, I was out." Her expression didn't soften. "And as you could probably tell, I kind of bought into it. For lots of stupid, self-serving reasons, I bought into it. I lied to other people and I lied to myself." I threw my hands up and let them flop down again. "I'm sorry. I'm really sorry."

Her expression softened a little, but instead of feeling relief, I felt another wave of doubt. I'd been working people so long I almost wondered if I was working her, too, telling her what she wanted to hear. "This is probably hard for you to believe, but actually, I'm already taking steps to get out. I have been for the past few weeks."

Now I felt a compulsion to tell her everything, as if each word put more distance between myself and what I'd been a part of. We moved over to the couch and I spent the next hour explaining everything, starting with my efforts to get John Polling to invest in Cascadia. I explained the Fund had pressured me into putting up all our belongings as collateral, and how McPhee/Collins had redesigned our public diplomacy efforts with me as the centerpiece. For the first time, I could actually talk about how strange it had been to appear with the Hammer, with his neo-Fascist rhetoric and his fake stories about bar fights. In fact, I confessed, the whole PR thing had become shameful and disgusting.

"But it's not just PR anymore, is it?" she asked. "All these murders and disappearances . . . that's part of the Program, too, isn't it?"

Now I hesitated. "That's where it gets hazy. I suspect some of those events are the government, some may well be real right-wing groups."

"And the others?"

"It's complicated. Whitehall does corporate security, and they're also a federal contractor, so they can play it both ways. When it comes to penetrating civil groups, they're private citizens. When it comes to capturing and imprisoning people, they claim they're under government contract. Realistically, that's all window dressing. At this point they're all one entity."

I saw a little grimace scurry across her features. "Who else is involved in this Program?"

"I'm not sure. I've been told there's over fifty companies paying in."

Her hand moved toward her face then lost momentum halfway. "And they're killing people?" She sat silently for a while, stricken, then said resolutely, "You have to stop it, Jim."

"What do you mean?"

"Call the *Washington Post* and tell them you have information for them. If it becomes public they'll have to stop."

It seemed crazily idealistic, almost childish. "Anne, wait a second. I know where you're coming from, and it's a good place. And I agree with you; that's why I've already started working my way out of this. But it's very delicate." I went over the machinations of regaining control of the company, including its dependence on Howard Pettijohn's goodwill. "Once I do that, I am totally out of this Program and I'll have the freedom to do whatever I want. We're talking about three weeks. A month, tops. But if I stir things up now, it's going to set off a very unfavorable chain of events."

"Such as?"

"Such as me being fired, Howard telling me to go fuck myself, the company being dismantled, and you and I losing most of what we have."

"So?"

"*So?*" I was getting irritated. "So, you don't flush a two-billion-dollar company down the toilet because you can't wait three weeks."

"You don't flush someone's life down the toilet, either, Jim. They just threw that man out of a window! Another man was forced into a highway underpass! What's going to happen while you wait three weeks?"

"Anne . . ." I struggled to flatten my voice out. "Think this through. *If* and *when* I go public about this, both sides are going to want my ass, and we're going to need resources to protect ourselves. There'll be civil suits, I could be prosecuted. . . ." I stopped. I was thinking of the lawyer murdered on his sailboat.

"You're really afraid of these people, your so-called friends! They've totally silenced you!"

It was an insulting claim, and I raised my voice despite myself. "They can't silence me! Listen. I'm out of this Program. I promise you that. But I need more time."

Now she was getting angry. "I've given you fifteen years!" She stopped to calm herself. "For fifteen years the company always came first. Your ego came first. Ahead of your family and especially ahead of your son, who needed you to be something other than an authority figure who only noticed him long enough to tell him how he wasn't meeting your high standards."

"That's completely distorted!"

"You still know nothing about him! If you did, maybe you wouldn't be dithering about whether it's okay for Whitehall to kill a few more people while you consolidate your financial position!"

Something about her words disturbed me. "What do you mean?"

She stopped and closed her eyes and took a deep breath. She seemed to be struggling with something. "I mean . . . there's loyalty, and then there's complicity. I can't be married to a man who would knowingly put his financial interests before other people's lives. Because then I'd be part of it. If you can't choose, I'm going to have to."

I felt exasperated. I was so close to being free and she was throwing a monkey wrench into the whole thing. "Anne, I am trying to extract us from this gracefully."

"There is no graceful way out of this, Jim! You can't finesse it, the way you finessed all those little towns and city councils and Chambers of Commerce. You can't finesse death squads." She stood and gathered her things, and I stood up next to her. To my surprise, she threw her arms around me and held me with what seemed like desperation. I had the sense of something hidden, but I was too confused to do anything but intimate its uncertain shape down there among all the grief and frustration. Finally she pulled back. Her look was strange: a sad, Renaissance smile. There were tears in her eyes. "You can't have it all this time, Jim. So maybe you have to try to figure out what's most important and hold on to it as hard as you can." Her last words sounded almost like a threat: "Because that's all you're going to keep."

23

I turned thirty years old in jail, the day the Militants threw every-thing out the window with their national bombing campaign. Happy Birthday, Miss Cortright. The police had put me in a cell with a steady stream of women who'd been picked up for prostitution and shoplifting, and I spent four days listening to sad stories and learning jail slang from my "cellies." Finally all the Democracy Northwest people were released to a flurry of cameras and nasty insinuations by the Government and their Media agents.

I had a hard time getting my momentum back. I guess I'd been nurturing the hope that the violence against the Militants and the Civil organizations would further discredit the Administration, but part of that involved someone like James Sands coming out publicly, and the Media charging to the rescue, and at the moment neither of those things looked likely. The violence was growing on both sides, and the peaceful future I dreamed of seemed more unattainable than ever.

I was tired. Several gray hairs had sprouted since I'd plucked out the first one nearly a year ago, and they reminded me of all the things that doing good work didn't provide. Old friends of mine had husbands and babies, while I was living in one bedroom and working sixty hours a week for subsistence wages. The world would always need fixing. When could I sit back and fix my own life? In a hazy, completely unrealistic way, I thought that maybe when this government was overturned Lando and I could find out where things might go with us. I imagined living at his house, sleeping every night in the White Room. It was a fantasy—I didn't even know his real name—but was it any greater of a fantasy than a reformed America with its most powerful criminals in jail? I kept both visions in my head and I went to work every day like a plumber or a carpenter, hammering away at a better world.

As far as the election, Governor Cox and his Commissioner of Elections had thrown up one roadblock after another, all the while wringing their hands at their helplessness. Our attempts to get the Federal Government to facilitate a vote went nowhere. It was a case of States' Rights, they insisted. President Matthews even proclaimed that it was really about Freedom. Folks needed freedom to resolve their own issues, he said in his homiest voice, not have the Federal Government interfering all the time. I wanted slap the smirk off his face.

"It's a new world out here," Dan said. "Cox is pulling this stunt as a test for the Feds. If they can make it stick here, they'll wheel it out whenever they need it."

Our members, though, were in no mood to let this test succeed. Since the hour of the Governor's announcement, there had been a growing crescendo of phone calls to the DNN from our membership, begging us to organize a demonstration, and as they kept coming in, I started feeling the energy again.

"Where would it be?" Dan asked.

Shar had obviously been thinking about it already. "I'd say, outside the Federal Courthouse here in Seattle. This is a really a Federal issue: They refuse to ensure our right to vote. Plus, it's downtown, the streets are narrow, and if we get the kind of turnout we got for the National Business Symposium, it will shut the city down."

"No," I said. "We've already done that. We need something bigger. People hate Cox and they hate what he's doing. He's got a fifteen percent approval rating. It's time to show him who the real boss is."

The idea that developed was to shut down the entire state. Demonstrations in the major cities, along with a general strike and as much pressure on legislators as we could bring to bear. The demonstration would be open-ended, persisting until the Governor gave in. I had told Lando long ago that the people were ruled by consent, and that one day we would take away that consent. Now was the day.

We talked about the municipal Unions, which ones might go out and which wouldn't. Janitors, teachers, maintenance workers, the people who processed papers and answered phones. Truck drivers and port workers. There was still one important group we were uncertain about: the Throwaways.

Joe Simic had caused a small riot in Akron, Ohio, three months ago, demonstrating on behalf of voter reform, but he'd been coy since then. We'd heard that he'd organized as many as thirty thousand Throwaways in Washington, Oregon, and Idaho, recruiting heavily among ex-loggers and ex-airplane makers. Whether they would join us was another question.

"He likes you, Emily," Shar said. "Why don't you call him up and find out where he stands?"

Joe had been especially gracious toward me since I'd told him about the infiltrator in his own organization. After the Symposium protests he'd come over to the offices to congratulate us, and since then we'd worked with him loosely on a few campaigns. Mostly his issues: the fight to maintain a minimum wage, the battle to reinstate the eight-hour day. They were good causes so we were willing to get behind them. We weren't sure what loyalty we would get in return. That was how dealing with Joe was. On his issues, though, he made a wonderful partner: helpful, well-organized, with a staff of black-coffee-and-cigarettes field people who commanded from the top down and backed up anyone on their side of the fight. As it turned out, Joe was scheduled to be in Seattle in three days.

He came into my office in the afternoon with his usual large friend in tow, who I now knew was stereotypically named Tony. The big man was in his usual polo shirt and blue blazer, while Joe was in the same uniform he always wore: a light brown canvas jacket and blue jeans. They laughed, as they always did, at the gag picture of me with my head Photoshopped onto a weight lifter's body, and I caught a dubious look in Tony's eyes when he saw my poster of the Earth with the phrase HONOR THY MOTHER. By the time they sat down in the small space, the whole room smelled like tobacco smoke, but I'd surrendered to that long ago.

"I liked your little to-do in Akron," I began on a positive note. "I think you got the message across."

He gave an understated grin. "Yeah, I think they heard us."

"You came out for the vote!"

"Yes, we did." He cocked his head and let loose the hint of a smirk. "'Course, between you and me, it wasn't just the vote."

I leaned back in my seat, crossing my arms. "I heard a rumor that you made a stink about the vote in Akron because their state Senator opposes you on minimum wage. Breaking some windows killed two birds with one stone."

His light brown eyes creased up at the edges. "That's the way the game is played, my dear Emily." He turned to Tony. "I like this girl!"

I gave him my sweetest smile. "You are a very cynical man, Mr. Simic."

The two of them looked at each other and had a good laugh. "So I understand you're planning on stirring things up out here," he said.

"You already know what's going on with the vote, don't you?"

"Why don't you fill me in? I'd rather hear it straight from you."

I went through the tortured history of the ballot reform, how we'd gotten it through the legislature only to have the Regime's people slow it to a crawl. "When it became clear that they couldn't stall it any longer, they decided to just cancel the vote. Then, of course, the Militants started up—"

"Those Militants . . ." He shook his head. "You should be thanking your lucky stars they're around."

"Why?"

"Because we've got an extremist Regime trying to pose as the Center. That's why they gave a green light to these Right-wing attacks—."

"You really think the Government—?"

"I don't just think: I *know*. Because I know some of the people involved. Not the ones killing people—that's probably Whitehall, or the Government, but the ones attacking some of the Civil Society offices, yeah. I know them from the old Union days."

I tried to accommodate the strangeness of it. "But why would a Union person turn on the Civil Society groups. It doesn't make sense."

"These people have their own story, and it's a particular story. In their story, they can only keep their jobs if the economy picks up, and groups like yours are obstructing the Masters who know how to run the country. Which threatens their jobs. Which threatens their family. Which means you're the enemy."

"But . . . it's completely the opposite! It's the greed and incompetence of the people running the country that threatens their jobs."

"Of course. But then you get into facts, and facts don't matter a whole bunch when you're barely holding on. These folks have got their own Web sites, their own news channels. They got a whole set of facts that tell 'em that *they're* the smart ones, the hard-nosed, commonsense workers, and you're just Patagonias: rich people who went to college and want to lord it over everyone else." He softened his voice. "I know: It ain't pretty. I'm just telling you this so you'll understand. These people are scared. They've lost control of their lives, and when you're powerless, carrying a gun and blowing things up makes you feel pretty powerful again."

"Joe, if you know who some of these people are, why haven't you come out about it? Why don't you expose them?"

"In due time, but that's a side issue right now. You notice, they don't attack me or my people. They're sympathetic. Which means they could become supporters. I prefer to approach it from that angle."

It sounded as if he wanted to use them as his own shock troops someday. "Well, I find them a little hard to ignore, since our office might be the next one they blow up."

"I hear you! But I think the real issue is the ones behind these people, the Government and the private security companies, and we're not strong enough to take them on head-to-head yet. And even though you may not believe it, these attacks are helping your cause. I talk to a lot of the kind of people that you don't. People whose idea of politics is listening to talk radio down at the beauty parlor. And you know what? They don't like these attacks on the Civil Groups. They don't like Whitehall. They don't have a real sophisticated view, but they got some basic ideas about what America stands for that can't always be manipulated. When the time comes, some of them—not all of them—but *some* of them are going to stand up. That's when we go after Whitehall."

It sounded good, but at the same time a little too convenient for him. I couldn't let it bother me right now. "So what are your thoughts on joining this march, Joe? Are you ready to stand up?"

He looked thoughtful for a moment. "I completely sympathize with the predicament you're in. I think you're absolutely right in making a stand and doing whatever it takes to make them hold a vote with legitimate ballots." He stopped there, a look of righteous sympathy on his face, but no commitment whatsoever.

"So does that mean you'll march with us?"

"That's a separate question, and I can't give you an answer quite yet. How is it looking for you without us?"

Typical Joe Simic. He wanted to see how good a chance we had of winning before he joined us. I stifled an irritated sigh. "The State Employees Union and the municipal Unions of Seattle, Tacoma, Olympia, and Spokane will probably sick-out. We're trying to get cooperation from the Teamsters."

"What'd they say?"

"They were surprisingly favorable."

Joe gave a secretive little smile. "Off the record, their leader's got a few scores to settle with your Governor, too."

One thing about talking with Joe: He was cued in to a whole world that I wasn't, a world that seemed so far away from our consensus building and community that it was hard sometimes to believe that we were working for the same cause. If, of course, we *were* working for the same cause. Whatever. I couldn't turn up my nose at the chance of pulling in thirty thousand people. "If this march succeeds, Joe, we all win. Your people aren't going to get better work and benefits without getting rid of this administration. You know that. It's not just about raising the minimum wage in a particular state or making cosmetic changes in a few trade laws. It's about putting the People back in power. Without that, you'll spend the rest of your life refighting the same battles. We need your help."

We looked at each other, and maybe it was my imagination, but it seemed like his sly distance fell away for a moment as he thought about it. "We'll see."

That was all I could get out of him. He returned to his working-man's irony, and he and Tony jovially said good-bye and left.

"Well?" Dan said afterwards, appearing in the doorway of my office.

"He wants to make sure he's on the winning side."

He had his own bad news. "They won't budge on the parade permit. They refuse to let us anywhere near the Federal Courthouse."

"I thought the mayor was our friend."

"It's not his show. Homeland Security insists it's a national security issue because a big crowd outside the Federal Courthouse endangers Federal judges. The best they'll offer us is down by the Stadium."

"That's bullcrap."

He raised his hands and rolled his eyes.

The Safeco Field area was the perfect protest pit. Its huge parking lot could accommodate 200,000 people, but it was surrounded by a wall of buildings with narrow streets between them, which were easy for the security services to block off. Though it was only fifteen blocks from the courthouse, a couple thousand police could contain a hundred times their own number, and would be difficult to outmaneuver. Most important to them, a mass of people marching around in the Stadium parking lot wouldn't shut down anything at all.

We had bigger problems than the venue, though. We were running out of time. It was already mid-September, and we had to change the Governor's mind or get the legislature to overrule him in time to stage a November election. We would need coordinated demonstrations and strikes all over the state. We chose the first weekend of October as the starting date, an incredibly short space to organize a major event. I wouldn't be sleeping very much for the next two weeks.

The Matthews Administration pretended to take an Olympian view of it, with all their talk about Freedom and States' Rights and letting the good people of Washington sort things out. On the local level, though, they started their intimidation campaign right away. The state Attorney General proclaimed that anyone convicted of property damage or rioting would be prosecuted under antiterrorism laws that could land them in jail for six years, and that mere trespassing could get them three years. Sheriff Tom Grundel, the neo-Fascist leader of the King County sheriffs, went even further. All of downtown Seattle was declared a No-Protest Zone, and Grundel was clear about what would happen: "We will have zero tolerance for quasi-terrorist tactics. Anyone using physical force, intimidation, or mass crowd behavior to breach the No-Protest Zone will be engaged and, if necessary, destroyed by law enforcement units." Not a very politic statement; he backpedaled on the word *destroyed* the very next day, but it got the message out to all the middle-aged, law-abiding Citizens who were thinking about making a stand: *If you go up against us, we will knock you down.*

In spite of that, the Direct Response people were starting to organize again, putting their calls out for affinity groups. Dave was one of them, so we could do some informal liaison work over the kitchen table on the third floor of the Apex. I'd just come home from work at eight thirty in the evening and he was eating a slice of thick dark sprouted-wheat bread along with a cube of cheese. I hadn't seen him around much lately.

"You want some?" He cut me a slab and motioned toward the cheese. "Help yourself."

"How's the rock looking this time?"

He was a lot less bouncy than usual, and it occurred to me that he'd been that way for a while. "Uncertain," was his reply.

"What do you mean?"

"Folks are scared. Grundel got out there and advertised that he was going to beat the crap out of anybody who didn't follow orders. That strengthens some people and it intimidates others. Nobody knows what Grundel is really capable of, and a lot of people think he's already worked out some sort of immunity for anything he does in the service of the Regime."

Their strategy would be different this time. They would have to be more mobile, mixing a few strategic lockdowns with groups of people that could move quickly and keep the police in motion. Their first target would be vehicles. They would lock down at key intersections, in front of parking garages, on the interstates, on the busiest entrance and exit ramps going into and out of downtown. Once they had snarled traffic, they would coalesce in seven groups and start moving toward the Courthouse and the Federal Building in groups of several hundred to several thousand people: enough to power through blockades or to run around them. It was a confrontational strategy, designed to create as much havoc as possible. They knew they were going to pay a heavy price, but they were using their bodies to ask a question, and that question was: *How many people are you willing to hurt to keep your privileges?* We'd have our first answer in five days.

I went into my room and lay down on my bed, too nervous to rest. By now my preparations for the demonstration had raised me to a level of constant tension and exhaustion, and I could lie there for hours worrying about all the things left undone. This had to work. The wave of violence moving across the country was getting worse, and we needed a victory to show that the middle way could work. There was something fundamental about this demonstration. This wasn't about Privatization, it was about Democracy itself, and both sides knew it. The Administration had decided to test its strength, to see whether lies and fear were sufficient to sustain their vision of the country: part dictatorship, part oligarchy, operating within the trappings of Democracy. They would dole out a few drops of power to us citizens when it was convenient, then rein it back in when it suited them. In their vision, the illusion of power would be enough to keep Americans happy. Soon we'd find out whose vision was going to hold.

24

Whatever strange minuet we'd been dancing with the Civils is over now: The Strategic Counteroffensive is in full swing. Every crew for themselves, no need to ask permission. Blowing up ATMs doesn't cut it anymore—the targets are human. The Combine finally gets some payback, killing a Whitehall vice-president in an ambush at his Hyannis trophy home, and the Gettysburg Contract snipes a notorious Philadelphia police chief. They post the video and half the world drops in to watch it, a move so cold-blooded even I have to suck in my breath. I see the footage, watch him fall, and the nightmares about John Polling start rolling through my three hours of sleep. Not that we're slacking out West. The San Francisco office of a leading war profiteer gets fire-bombed, as does our very own Weyerhaeuser Supertree nursery, where tomorrow's Corporate-run forests are being prepped to replace all those tax-subsidized clear-cuts in Alaska. Kahasi and Lilly took that one out with a fire that ended up spreading to the local suburb—bad press for the Good Guys, but in the rush of pent-up energy nobody's looking back anymore.

By now the best Regime and Corporate targets have been set up with all the protection Whitehall can sell, and it starts to show. When the FAR attacks Regime party headquarters, it turns into a firefight that leaves two comps and a guard dead. An attempt to dump blood in the lobby of General Dynamics goes bad in a way nobody would have guessed, escalating into a sixteen-year-old getting a bullet in the temple and three Friends evaporating into the Regime's secret prison system.

This is the fuck-up era, where the amateurs go to town. Banners get half-hung. Banks get half-robbed. The Michigan Militia accidentally blows up the eight-year-old daughter of a Dow Chemical boss, and a splinter group in Denver puts six rounds in a judge who, it turns out, had just handed in his resignation to protest the Regime. The most bizarre: Four comps from an off-brand outfit in California kidnap the president of the company responsible for cutting the last big redwoods and subject him to an Earth Court. The problem is, they can't fine him or lock him up for fifty years, which leaves only one alternative, which they execute with a hunting rifle they bought at the local hardware store. Admittedly, not a great loss to humanity—this was a man who took the redwoods away from generations of people to come—but it's sloppy, a propaganda-fest for media hatchet men, who, as always, focus on the heartbroken family of the greedy old bastard, and this terrible mockery of justice. They last precisely eighteen hours on the lam, and as much as people are happy to see some Corporate scum get wiped away, nobody identifies with a loser, and the Militants' status drops to an all-time low.

It's out of control now, even if we don't admit it to each other. I keep thinking back to the Polling Operation, the first killing of the civil war from our side, and that voice keeps coming back to me, *not what I meant, not what I meant* . . . Every new operation that McFarland proposes comes off to me as senseless and counterproductive, projects I would have jumped on six months ago. I argue against bombing the Boeing factory as being too dangerous, and go along with burning down the Hilton resort in Olympic National Park only because it was Tonk's project and I couldn't go against him. Mac, Joby, and even Sarah are getting frustrated, nickname me the Pacifist.

In this atmosphere, a spooky e-mail comes in over our Web site. A run of numbers two lines long, it's old-fashioned book encryption, simple but impossible to break without the book it's drawn on. In this case, a forgotten novel from the '60s called *Wild Horse*. I know as soon as Gonzalo sends it over that it's from Earl E.: *Ready for reinsertion into Target America.*

"Don't even think about touching it," Sarah says. She's sitting on the floor of her apartment with Tonk curled up around her.

"If he's still out there we at least ought to know what he's up to."

"You can't assume he's still out there," Gonzalo answers. "For all we know, Homeland was looking over his shoulder when he sent that e-mail. Maybe they're waiting for us to set up a meeting."

Sarah's know-it-all voice is grating on me. "We can't just break the security protocols because Earl E.'s an old friend of yours. Don't be a dumbass."

I stare at her. "Sarah, I'm getting a little tired of being called a dumbass."

Tonk tries to get everything back to normal. "Gonzalo's right, Lando. It's completely possible they're tracking him right now, with or without him knowing."

I look around the circle of closed faces and throw up my hands. "Okay! We never got it!"

Earl E. doesn't intend to be ignored, though. Mac calls me up a few days later, and we meet for coffee at the Athenian Café, looking down on the big orange cranes that loom far below us in Puget Sound. The Athenian is in the heart of the Market, a throwback to the '30s, with out-of-date menu items like scrapple and corned beef hash. Mac, as usual, with the smell of tobacco pouring off him. It's a relief to have him shake my hand and clap me on the shoulder. "You look like shit, Lando."

I smile and shake my head. "Thanks, Mac." In the best days of the cease-fire, I'd gotten nearly five hours of sleep a night. Now I was back to two. "What's up?"

"Earl E. contacted us two weeks ago about an operation."

I feel a little twinge of guilt that we never answered him. "What kind of operation?"

"That's what I wanted to know."

He tells me how he set it up, putting Earl E. through a long elaborate set of movements and fake meetings over the course of three days to see if he was being tracked. Finally he'd met him in the deli of a half-abandoned strip mall in Bellevue. I know why he went to McFarland. After we set up the network, he spent a lot of time out there learning about guns and explosives. The cross-training I advocated. "So what's his operation?"

"It's not good. He wanted me to fix him up with an M-203 and some RPGs. He wants to take out some Whitehall guys at the demonstration next week."

"Is he fucking insane?"

"Oh, he's got his logic. He figures Whitehall's a legitimate target, since they were linked to those Jefferson Combine murders back East. He claims nobody likes Whitehall anyway, so an operation against them's going to go over well, especially in defense of the protesters. It's all the same logic you'd use; he just comes to different conclusions."

"Has it occurred to him that exactly the opposite's going to happen? That the Regime's going to use it as an excuse for a massive crackdown?"

"I said something like that. In his mind, the more repression there is by the government, the more people will react against it."

I remember Earl E. saying that when we had that first meeting at the Super 8 Motel, but at the time I ignored it, because I wanted to get a cease-fire. Now his words are banging on my temple with a little brass hammer. I rub the spot with my fingertips.

"What'd you tell him?"

"I played along with him, of course. I wanted to find out what the hell his plan is and then figure it out from there."

"And what is it?"

He takes off his cap and scratches his crew cut. "He's made some assumptions about where the Government's going to set up their block-ades around the Stadium, and I'd say they're pretty good assumptions. He plans to set up in an office building about three blocks behind their lines and shoot at them from the back."

"Has it occurred to him that they're going to have snipers on every roof within a quarter mile of the demonstration? That as soon as he pokes his rifle out the window he's going to get blown away?"

"He's found a window behind a neon sign that's covered from the front but still has a view toward the demonstration. He took me down and showed the room. It's a good pick."

"You mean he's already rented it?" Mac nods, and I think of the twelve thousand dollars I gave Earl E. Looks like he's found a way to spend it. "Is he alone on this or has he got a crew?"

"Whitehall wiped his crew out. The ones that aren't in jail are on the run. He's solo as far as I can tell."

"I hope you said no to the grenade launcher."

"Give me some credit, Lando." His scrapple comes and he digs into it, but stops to watch as I empty most of the creamer into my cup and start tearing open packets of sugar. "You gonna have some coffee with that?"

"It's the poor man's latte."

"Right." He takes a few more bites then goes on. "Anyway, he's downshifted to a .308, but there's other problems. For one thing, the demonstrators are right on the other side of his target, so you got a high probability of someone else being hit by a ricochet or a miss."

I exhale. This is getting worse. "How's he plan to escape?"

"He's got a Seattle PD uniform. The basement of his building has an old connection to Underground Seattle. He'll egress into Pioneer Square as a cop. It's actually a fairly well-planned operation."

"So, you tried to talk him out of it, right?"

"Of course I tried to talk him out of it. I told him in no uncertain terms it was a dumbass idea that was going to get people killed for nothing. He's not hearing it."

"I'll try."

"Not going to happen, Lando. Especially with you. He's pissed at you. He thinks you sold us out with the cease-fire. And he said he tried to contact you and you wouldn't respond."

"I wanted to. Everyone else was against it."

Mac nods, looks long and hard at the idle orange cranes far below us. "Earl E.'s fighting his own war now. I'd say it's going to be a very short one."

I talk it over separately with the others. The idea gets floated, then dismissed, of tipping off the cops. Gonzalo, the man of elegant solutions, suggests we plant evidence that the security forces are on to him to scare him away, but that won't stop him from finding another place, either now or later. For all that's happened, I still think of Earl E. as the guy I sat in a tree with for three weeks.

"I think we need to put him on ice: get him to Europe or South America where he can chill."

Sarah is as practical as a pair of scissors. "To do that we'd need docs, money, probably facial and fingerprint stuff. I don't know when you last looked at the books, but we've only got about thirty thousand in cash left. The rest is overseas, and Gonzalo's trying to figure out a new way to bring it in. What you ought to be thinking about is how we're going to raise some more money."

Even Tonk's not with me on this one. "We're not social workers, Lando. If Earl E. wants to make his mark, that's up to him."

"Who are we, Al-Qaeda? We can't let him go blasting away at a demonstration. We have a responsibility here." I take a breath. "What Earl E. needs is to know he's not alone, that we're all in this together and that he's making a mistake."

"Mac tried that already."

"I haven't tried."

I finally get clearance to contact him, but Earl E.'s already dumped the cell number McFarland gave me. Only one way left. I'm thinking about Second Avenue, in the heart of the No-Protest Zone. On October 9th it'll be crawling with cops and snipers. The last place for a guerrilla.

Three days ahead of time, whatever sick sense of irony drives this world steps in to dial things up a notch. It's my mother, telling me she's going to the demonstration in Seattle the coming week.

"Mom! What are you talking about?"

"I'm a member of Democracy Northwest now. I told you that a few weeks ago!"

"Yeah, I know." She's told me the story of joining up after Franklin Seven's murder. No doubt her suspicions about me had something to do with it, too. "But, Mom, that demonstration could get really out of hand. I mean . . . stay in the back, okay? I don't want to see you on TV beating the crap out of some cop."

"Oh, Josh!" She laughs. "I was going to demonstrations before you were born! You can't let them intimidate you."

"What's going on with you and Dad? I mean, with the issue we talked about before."

That careful, guarded tone: I can tell she's figured out that someone might be listening in. "We're making some progress, but in the end your father's going to have to choose. I wish I could say it will be me, but I might be flattering myself. I don't suppose you're coming up to Seattle?"

The parody machine is really cranking here. "No, Mom, I'd love to, but I'm buried here in Portland. I'm going to let the Seattle people take care of this one."

She's disappointed. So am I. Another time when I wish this was all over, that I was hiking the North Cascades, taking Emily home to meet the folks. Maybe next year, or the year after. More likely it could happen only in some year measurable by counting in base twenty, and I couldn't get there now.

25

We had put the call for help out to the whole country, and now the responses were coming in at an exhilarating rate. Someone important on the Right seemed to have decided that voting was worth marching for: Suddenly a whole slew of center-Right groups had called to promise their support and participation. We rented a secondary office twice the size of our original one, and tripled our staff. Every day fresh energy came from unexpected directions, including a surprising number of politicians who privately expressed their support, always being sure to take our names for future reference. Most seemed sincere; some probably just wanted to be on the record in case the tide really turned. I didn't have time to weed that out right now. The vague and conflicted group of individuals that in some mysterious way constituted the People had accepted our invitation in massive numbers, and in a few days they were coming downtown with all their anger and their aspirations. It looked like America had finally decided to show up.

The Government, meanwhile, was working hard at dampening turnout. After Grundel's "engage and destroy" comment ten days before, Homeland followed up with a full-scale Media campaign, featuring lots of video of police in full riot gear, their training with the baton, the imperviousness of their body armor, the pain-inducing capacity of their weapons. Word leaked out that as many as fifteen hundred Whitehall mercenaries were being brought in at a cost to the Government of over a thousand dollars per day, each. Much of the language used was military language, carefully coordinated by the Government's "Public Diplomacy" advisers. "We will have a wall of steel up to protect Seattle's downtown core," said the local National Guard commander. News shows featured interviews of riot police, portrayed as good guys with a job to do for all of our protection. "Freedom of speech is the American way," said one captain, his Plexiglas face plate tilted up, "but we have to protect everybody's freedom of speech, not just the loudest ones." It was the kind of patriotic double-talk the Administration had been thriving on for years, but for a change its real message was clear: Get out of line and you'll get hurt. To some degree it worked.

"I don't think we're up for a riot," said one of our affiliates, the pastor of an Episcopal church in Kent. "We've got kids and elderly in our group."

"It's not a riot," I said. "It's a peaceful demonstration."

"Well, the police are talking about smashing heads."

I wanted to reassure him that no one would get their heads smashed, but how honest would that be? Instead I said, "We'll keep you near the stage."

With the Governor and the King County Sheriff so eager to get their war on, our board decided that breaking out of the Stadium parking lot and marching to the Federal Courthouse wasn't an option. The demonstration was only one part of our strategy, and as long as we stayed there in numbers, the Security forces had to maintain their numbers, and we would be achieving our goal and keeping our people safe. What the Direct Response people did was up to them.

We were pondering this when Joe Simic called and invited Shar, Dan and me over to his office in Tukwilla, a low-rent spot in a failing strip mall near the airport. Our day was already frantic, but we took off a precious two hours to meet with him. He was warmer than I'd ever seen him, personally getting us coffee and tea, offering us bags of hot popcorn. He had good news, he said: His members had decided to participate. He started going down the list of conditions before we had time to let the smiles melt off our faces: that the Throwaways be mentioned in any Media interviews and press releases, that they maintain their own command structure, that he be given a chance to address the audience between noon and 1 P.M. on the first day. The discussion took up nearly an hour, mostly between Joe and Dan, and by the time they'd concluded, we were organizing together on training first-aid volunteers and areas of the lot that could be marked off for his groups. He already had a schematic of the parking lot, our stage, and the likely police barriers. He immediately picked out the areas closest to the barriers.

Shar, who'd been biting her tongue the whole meeting, finally spoke up. She did a poor job of covering up the fact that she really didn't like Joe Simic. "Let's get clear on one thing, Joe: Nobody leaves the Stadium parking lot." He didn't react, and Shar drilled in. "This is going to be the most heavily militarized crowd-control effort since the 1970s. Maybe more. We don't want you putting our people at risk, and if that's a deal-breaker, then I guess you're out."

Joe took a breath. "Sharlene, the time comes when you have to come face-to-face with the Masters—"

She shook her head. "No! Don't even think about it! We've got strikes and marches and slowdowns and sick-ins organized all over Washington. According to polls, we have seventy-five percent support and we have the strength to bring the state to a stop until Cox gives in. We don't need a riot to make our point."

Joe looked around the room and briefly met my eyes. Finally he shrugged. "Okay! It's your show!"

We drove back to the office in Dan's tiny hybrid. "Well, we wanted a broad base," he started.

Shar was still angry. "Why do I not believe a word he says?"

I spoke up with more confidence than I actually felt. "I'll deal with Joe tomorrow, okay? He still owes me for letting him know about that infiltrator last year."

My colleagues weren't too confident, but I didn't have time to worry about Joe Simic right now. When I got back to the office, I was amazed to find Anne Sands waiting for me. She was as elegant as ever, wearing a beautiful blue-and-yellow jacket with dragons that looked Chinese.

I hadn't eaten lunch, so I invited her out to the 5 Point Café across the street, dying to know what was happening with her husband. We slid into one of the dark booths, and the barmaid came over in her low-cut dress and took our order for tea and clam chowder.

"So," I began, "things are looking very positive for the demonstration tomorrow."

I started into a description of all our alliances and plans, and she let me wax enthusiastic until I ran out of steam, and then she said, "I admire you, Emily."

"Well . . ." I was embarrassed by the compliment, but she let me off the hook right away. "I imagine you want to hear what happened with my husband."

She went into a detailed description of everything he'd told her about the Program, and as I listened to all the ins and outs I felt a profound dread come over me. It was as if all the mercenaries and profiteers of the oil wars had gotten together with the worst of Corporate America to form their own version of the Thousand-Year Reich. By the time she finished talking my chowder had cooled to a thick white glue, and a fresh sense of anxiety had killed my appetite. "Wow. Where is your husband on all this?"

"He's horrified. He wants out. But he thinks he needs to take back control of his company first. He says that once he gets rid of his partners, he can drop the Program."

"Does that mean he'll go public with what he knows?"

She hesitated, uncertain. "If he doesn't, I will. I'm giving him an ultimatum next week. My testimony won't have the same effect as his, but maybe it will get things rolling." She looked down at the table, then back to me with an awkward smile. "Of course, that would probably be the end of our marriage."

I didn't know what to say. This was strange new ground for me. "I appreciate what you're doing. I'm grateful."

It made her uncomfortable, and she brightened up all at once. "Well, you must be very busy!"

We arranged to meet at the demonstration in the morning, and I crossed the street back to my office. I half expected a dark sedan to come screeching from the curb to run me over. The murders and disappearances were turning out to be exactly what everyone had feared, and I couldn't help letting my mind wander irresistibly along the continuum of aggression that I myself had been targeted for: threats, arrest. What came next? When I reported everything to Dan and Shar, we sat there in creepy introspection for a little while; then Shar abruptly stood up. "Good work, Emily. You've clarified our schedule."

"What do you mean?"

"Tomorrow, we stop them in Washington. Next week we go after their little Program. So right now"—she smiled at Dan and me—"we just don't have time to be afraid of them."

Still, it was hard to remember that when we finally got free for a walk-through at eleven o'clock that night. Some of our people had gone down earlier and tried to mark out quadrants to stand in with temporary paint, but the police had arrested them for vandalism, and we'd heard of other "preemptive" arrests. As we walked down Second Avenue, it was clear that businesses were bracing for violence. All along the route between the Stadium and the Courthouse, store windows were covered with plywood, and the streets had already been converted into the most intimidating display of paramilitary force I'd ever seen. Each of the five intersections that faced the Stadium had a tank sitting in the middle of it, with their turrets and machine guns facing inward toward where the crowd would be. Concrete barriers had been set up in front of the tanks, and chain-link fences further narrowed the openings. There was already a heavy presence of police and Whitehall agents and they were setting up checkpoints to delineate the edges of the No-Protest Zone that they had illegally decreed. Our pictures were taken three times. As Shar and I looked over everything, our conversation tapered down to a few brief exchanges, muffled by the sense of impending violence that hung over the streets. For the first time, I felt like we were no longer fighting against an Administration or a Governor, but against a *Re-*

gime, the kind with death squads and secret police, for whom Democracy itself was the enemy. Lando had seen them that way from the beginning. I remembered that morning in the White Room, when he'd spoiled my mood by insisting that they would go down in a rage. I'd thought he was paranoid then. I wished I could believe that now.

Dave was waiting for me at the Apex when I got back at midnight. I didn't recognize him at first—he'd cut his hair nearly to the skin and trimmed his beard to a neat triangle below his lips.

"You look like a meth dealer. All you need now is a tattoo on your skull."

"I'm not getting dragged out of there by my hair this time."

It seemed like the mellow Dave I knew had disappeared with his haircut. This new persona was a little disturbing. "How is it looking for the Direct Response Groups?"

I hadn't seen him for days. We'd both been frantic, and he'd actually slept at the Direct Response meeting place a lot of nights. "The Homelanders dropped by around eight and arrested twenty-six people. Did you know that?"

"You're kidding! What were the charges?"

"Who the fuck knows! Conspiracy to express our freedom of speech, not saying the Pledge of Allegiance—whatever they decide! They took all our banners, all our freaking giant puppets, our computers, and anything that could be classified as lockdown material. I was out making a pizza run, or I would have gotten popped, too." He motioned toward the refrigerator. "By the way, there's a twenty-inch veggie in there, if you're hungry."

"That's totally illegal!"

"Like that's going to make any difference between now and tomorrow!"

I rolled my eyes. "They get bolder every day."

"Hey, after canceling an election, the sky's the limit."

We'd agreed to keep quiet about the Program for now, so I didn't tell him how right he was. "What will that do to the Direct Response Group?"

"We've already rigged a backup switchboard at somebody's house. It'll take them a while to zero in on that one. Plus, everybody can still communicate directly between affinity groups."

"So what's the plan?"

"Same as before: Converge and swarm. We've got our spots picked out and we'll run right past the checkpoints when the time comes. With enough people we ought to be able to breach every checkpoint they've got and show up right where we belong: at the Courthouse. Then we lockdown. That's when it'll get choppy, unless you guys help us out again."

"Sorry, Dave, but nothing's changed: We're not leaving the Stadium." He seemed about to say something but held back. I got a piece of cold pizza out of the refrigerator and turned on the oven. "You'd think the Governor would just give in and let us vote. He's not making the Regime any points."

"These people want war. They want some injured cops and they want some property destruction, because they can use those images to create fear, and fear is the only thing they've got left. When the smoke clears it's going to be real visible what the new rules are, and people are going to have to make a decision. And God help us then, because what scares the shit out of me is that everyone's going to just change the channel and forget about it."

It wasn't a very heartening proposition, and it was weird coming from this shaved-head guy who was using Dave's voice. He was sounding more like Lando now, and less like the loving freak-dude I'd always known. "I don't think it has to be like that."

"What's your scenario?"

"How about this: Two hundred thousand people show up, our sympathy strikes close down the city and state Government, Seattle, Olympia, and Spokane are too messy to function. We let the Corporations know there's not going to be peace until we get our vote. We inform them about the national boycott of Washington products we're considering launching, and finally when it looks costly enough on a political and economic basis, the Governor gives in and releases all the punch-card machines so we can have an election with paper ballots. We vote the jerks out of power and go on to the next phase."

He flashed his old smile. "And this is going to take how long?"

"A week to ten days, beginning tomorrow."

"That's what I love about you, Sister Emily. You've got enough be-lief for all of us." He nodded. "I'll keep you on my speed dial."

Even with all the clouds hanging over the demonstration, I went to bed worrying about Lando. Maybe because I wished I could see him, or maybe because three other Militants had been murdered or disap-peared in the last week, and every time a family came out to the newspapers looking for their child I had to examine the photo and see if it matched the face that I knew. For some reason, the Army of the Republic was miraculously untouched and their insignia was still all over Seattle: on walls, posters, stenciled onto sidewalks. **A⊕R**. Along with that was another slogan that had become prominent in the last few days, one that I'd seen at the last demonstration but that now seemed scarily appropriate. BULLETS OR BALLOTS, it said, TAKE YOUR PICK.

People started trickling into the Stadium lot at eight in the morning. They came as individuals and in busloads, walking from distant parking spots and touring curiously around the stage and the impos-ing Security barriers. I was busy checking in with the leaders of our biggest contingencies and making sure that speakers and musicians were on their way. Shar and Dan were off doing the same thing. The sky hadn't lightened much since early in the morning. It looked like we would get a misty cool October day for the demonstration. The big empty pavement was black and slick with moisture.

I found Anne Sands drinking a paper cup of tea beneath a light post, looking a little apprehensive and out of place among the younger crowd. She didn't recognize me at first because I had my hair pinned up under a stocking cap, and she lit up when she realized that I'd come for her. I felt like I needed to protect her. "Did you bring the things I told you to?" She opened her purse: eyedrops, bandages, a first-aid kit, water, sandwiches, a paperback novel, an extra cell phone battery. "Great. Let's check things out." We walked together along the police lines on the north side of the huge lot.

Each street that led away from the demonstration area had at least a hundred uniformed men in front of it—some of them in the navy blue Seattle PD uniforms, others in black riot gear, with Plexiglas face shields and shin pads. Others wore the gray uniforms of the Whitehall private police. They chatted with each other, or watched us with empty expressions. They probably didn't want to acknowledge our personhood, since they might be attacking us in a few hours. Anne seemed a little unnerved.

"When's the last time you were at a demonstration, Anne?"

"It's been twenty-five years, at least. I remember protesting against nuclear power."

"If things get ugly, stay away from the police barrier."

She was scanning the barricade of metal and concrete the police had erected all around us. Harsh words were going back and forth between the police and some Black Bloc demonstrators with bandannas across their faces who were harrassing them with cameras to get postable footage. "It looks ugly already."

By nine o'clock, people were streaming into the big plaza where the demonstration would be held. The stage had been erected on the southern edge of the lot so that our backs would be to the police lines. This had been a stipulation that came with the permit; an attempt to lessen the possibility of a confrontation. Probably a good idea. The downtown core of Seattle had been to a large degree shut down anyway by the police's own preparations and the various sympathy strikes. Between the Direct Response people and rogue demonstrators, there would be plenty of chaos without us entering the fray. I wasn't sure Joe Simic saw it the same way.

At nine thirty his Throwaways came marching in en masse, thousands of them, many of the men wearing bulky coats under which I occasionally glanced a club or a bottle. They looked raw, plainly dressed, the women with their hair done and the men often with that fleshy, unhealthy look that reminded me of television football and cans of beer. What they did look, though, was determined. Instead of marching toward the stage, they marched straight back to where the police line was, forming up there and glaring at the Security preparations. I spotted special groups of people with red crosses on their armbands, their medical people, and others with orange armbands and hats that said PARADE MARSHAL.

"I like the little prison camp they set up," Joe said when I met him by the stage. "It shows how they really feel about us."

He was wearing his usual canvas jacket with a blue plaid shirt peeking out from underneath. He had on construction boots and an orange button pinned to his breast that said MY VOTE WILL NOT BE THROWN AWAY! Tony was with him in a long overcoat, smiling at me. I introduced them to Anne then asked her to excuse us for a minute. When I'd walked a few paces away with Joe, I asked the obvious. "Your people all went to the back, Joe. I thought we said that wasn't going to happen."

He reached up and touched his nose with a piece of tissue. "Emily, today's the day."

"What does that mean?"

"This is the day the Rotary Club gets involved."

"That's not an answer. We're trying to avoid confrontation with the police, and you've moved your people right in front of them."

He hesitated. "Emily, let's you and I just take a few minutes to see who we got here. Okay? We're both busy, but just turn your cell phone off for a minute and let's have a look. I'll do the same."

I told Anne I'd be right back, and Joe and I climbed a few of the stairs leading to the stage and surveyed the crowd. The space was beginning to get denser with people now, though the official activities wouldn't begin for another hour. Media and police helicopters were pulsing overhead.

"Look at that. Tens of thousands of people, and we're just starting. You spent years writing letters, fielding canvassers, raising money, picketing, signing petitions, printing bulletins, all to convince people to stand up to this Regime. And now here they are. They are refusing to obey. They are refusing to cooperate. This is what it comes down to. Look at them. It's not just political activists anymore. There's office workers, laborers, mothers, teenagers cutting school, college kids. There's even old folks here."

"And that's exactly why we need to avoid violence or a confrontation that's going to turn violent."

It didn't faze him. "Do you think these people don't know there's going to be a confrontation? That's what they came for. They heard all that talk about 'engage and destroy' and a 'wall of steel.' They came here precisely because they were ready to face the Regime."

"A few of them—"

"All of them! Maybe they don't want to lead it, and they don't want to get hurt in it, but they are here to be organized into something bigger and stronger, that can go toe-to-toe with this Regime and its stooges, that can speak with one voice, and if you don't see that then you are badly misreading the people you worked so hard to organize. The confrontation's already on, Emily, and you need to respond appropriately, just like you did at the Business Symposium last year."

I looked back at the wall of fences and tanks. The Throwaways were taunting the police, and many of the people who came in were gravitating toward the fence now instead of the stage. Looking along the rooflines I could see snipers and cameramen silhouetted against the flannel sky. Joe Simic was looking at me intently. "I've worked with some of these people for years, Joe. They're not violent people."

"No, they are not violent people. But they're not passive people. And where we are right now is in the gap between those two things. By the end of the day, we'll be someplace different."

A certain amount of self-selection between Joe's two poles was happening as soon as people entered the protest space. Those who wanted confrontation always made directly for the crowd at the fence, while others would pause, assess the situation, then drift toward the stage, where the sound people were throwing cords around and testing the microphones. The out-of-towners were everywhere, holding signs that said NEW YORKERS FOR VOTING RIGHTS or OKLAHOMA SUPPORTS THE VOTE! There were giant puppets of Uncle Sam with a satchel of dollar bills, or of President Matthews wearing a Nazi armband. Banners said NO VOTE, NO PEACE!, and the A⊕R insignia was around, slashed out in red paint, along with others that said 2ND REVOLUTION. Some of the young people who held them were brandishing them in front of the fences.

I wondered if Lando was somewhere in this crowd, with his Henry Rampton driver's license and his young stockbroker disguise. I knew where he would come down in my debate with Joe Simic.

It took me a while to track Dan down. He'd been talking with the Seattle Police Chief at his command headquarters.

"He's not sounding too conciliatory after last time," he said. The previous Police Chief had resigned after the last demonstration, and his successor had been wary of making any deals with the DNN.

"One weird thing did happen. He kind of took me aside and said there were other actors with different agendas and that we shouldn't give them the opportunity to play them out."

"That is weird. Who was he talking about?"

"I don't know. I got the sense that he was sympathetic, but his role is bigger than him. The message is clear, though: We need to avoid a violent confrontation."

"Did you see what's going on over by the fence?"

"I don't like it."

He called Shar on his walkie-talkie, and we met up near the media tent where she'd been giving interviews for the last hour. "So what did the SPD chief say?"

"He's okay, but he hinted around that some people wouldn't mind things getting violent."

She rolled her eyes. "Great!"

"Not just on his side," I added. "We have a problem with the Throwaways. I'm positive they're going to try to breach the police line. Maybe when Joe speaks."

"Maybe we should tell him he can't speak," Dan said.

I shook my head. "I think if you try to keep him off the stage the riot's going to start right there."

Another organizer came up to Shar's elbow to tell her something, but she ignored him. "Does he realize how bad it could be? With this many people in a small space? You could have dozens of people trampled, for starters."

"He'd probably say that's a necessary part of the process."

Now Shar shook her head. "I'd like to talk with him alone and tell—"

"He's over there," I said, pointing to the other corner of the stage. "Let's go."

He was standing there with Tony and three other men. They were looking over a map of the demonstration grounds and Joe was pointing toward one of the streets, with its tank and its barriers. His companions moved subtly outward to form a protective ring around him as we approached, and he put the paper away.

"Hey there!" he said cheerfully.

Shar launched right into him. "What is that bullshit over there?"

She motioned toward the fence. "You agreed not to put your people at the police line!"

He didn't seem in the least bothered. "Let me ask you a question in return, Shar. Is this demonstration against the management of the Seattle Seahawks football team? Or is it about our Constitutional right to vote? If it's about our right to vote, why are we having it at a football stadium, instead of at the Federal Courthouse, where it should be?"

They were eye-to-eye now. "This isn't about political rhetoric, Joe. It's about people getting hurt."

Dan started in. "There's plenty of people on the other side of that barrier who'd love to see things get out of control."

"What are you asking me for here?"

Shar didn't lighten up. "Tell your marshals to move everyone back another thirty feet. And tell them to face the stage, not the cops." She was almost out of control. "Do it!"

Tony shifted a little closer, and I realized that my heart was pounding. Joe gave Shar a long, even look. Not a hostile one, but not a particularly friendly one either. "Sure."

He walked away toward the barrier with Tony, leaving us standing there. Shar was trembling. I put my hand on her shoulder. "Thank you, Shar. When his speech comes I'll make sure all our Peace Keepers are in front of the police barrier."

"I'll stay there, too," Dan said. "I'll let the police know we're trying to control the situation."

The big parking lot was becoming noticeably crowded now. Little energy centers formed at different spots, around groups of drummers or other spectacles. One man had speakers attached all around his coat and was walking in a cloud of blazing percussive sound. In another area, a group of actors in wild makeup were doing some sort of street-theater piece, shouting their lines above the din. Over at the fence, where the Throwaways had gathered, a black woman was standing on a box with a microphone, leading the crowd in a hypnotic chant: "AIN'T NO POWER LIKE THE POWER OF THE PEOPLE 'CAUSE THE POWER OF THE PEOPLE DON'T STOP!"

"That's right!"

"AIN'T NO POWER LIKE THE POWER OF THE PEOPLE 'CAUSE THE POWER OF THE PEOPLE DON'T STOP!"

"Uh-huh!"

I looked at my watch. The opening speaker would begin in ten minutes. I looked for Anne and she was standing calmly near the stage, chatting with a woman who was carrying a baby. She spoke as I approached her. "Is something wrong?"

"I don't know." I scanned the rooflines, saw the same snipers and spotters, maybe more of them. Behind the barriers, the police had brought in eight off-duty city buses, ready to take away anyone they arrested. My cell phone was ringing constantly now, a lot of the affiliates that I'd worked with during the last demonstration were touching base, looking for encouragement, an expression of solidarity. I answered all of them, even if I talked for only ten seconds to say, *Thanks for coming. We're going to win.* Now I was adding, *Stay away from the police line.* I dialed Dave's number.

"Sister Emily!"

"Brother Dave! I wanted to make sure you're okay. Where are you?"

"We are up on Olive Way, massing for another run."

"You mean you've already started?"

"Just doing a little moving around. Converge and disperse. You know the drill. We've got awesome turnout. I'm in a pack of at least five hundred right now, and we're all fast runners. There's probably twenty more groups our size. It's wild!"

"Any problems with the police?"

"A couple of arrests, nothing we didn't expect. Guaranteed—we'll be eating lunch at the Courthouse."

I closed the phone. Dan had already climbed up onto the stage to welcome everyone. His reedy voice reminded people that we were peacefully assembled to make a nonviolent show of strength in favor of our vote. He listed the many Unions that were doing slowdowns, sick-ins, or sympathy strikes on our behalf. I wished he was more dynamic. The steady roar of chants and catcalls from the people facing the police barrier formed a raucous background to his thin voice. The plaza was full, certainly more than a hundred thousand people, but at least a quarter of them were not paying attention to the stage at all, focused instead on the barrier, some three hundred yards away, and Dan kept glancing toward the thousands of backs that were turned to him. He finally introduced a folksinger who would do some political songs, rolling his eyes at me as he descended from the stage. It was a happy day in so many ways, with such a huge and varied turnout, but it looked like it was going to be long, nervous, and chaotic.

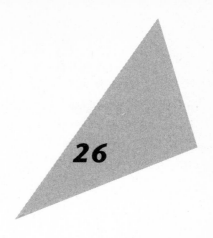

26

Ten A.M. in the No-Protest Zone, and there's a dark rainbow of security straddling every corner. Blueshirts scanning IDs, greenshirts kicking back on green trucks, brownshirts bulked out in war gear and earbuds, bristling with guns and all their favorite anti-Citizen tools: batons, chemicals, boots, and gloves. Gas masks hanging at their belts. Proud as punch behind their Whitehall tridents. *Have a nice day, motherfucker. Hope I get a chance to gas you.*

Today's theme is total compliance. Henry Rampton's ID gets scanned three times in five blocks. No talk about unlawful search and seizure here; that quaint notion went out with the Constitution. I flash all my business litter: bank statements, estimates cooked up for Web-design jobs that don't exist. Protest? Not me! I've got a meeting, Officer! I give an address, talk my way out, go through the process again in three blocks, even coming from the water side. If anything happens, Henry will be tidily in the database, pulled up in a millisecond as someone in the area when the shit went down.

I locate the Emerson Building, three blocks from where the street is stuffed up with security forces and a big chunk of Uncle Sam's war metal just for good measure. Beyond them, the ocean of the people, waving their banners at the sky. Even this early, the dim roar is making its way up the street to me, the smash of drums, unintelligible chanting, the bounding female electronic voice from the stage reading as batches of noise and words: "... *choice for the people of...*," garbled syllables, howling from the crowd, "... *constitutional right to a free and fair...*" I don't look up, but I can feel the spotters watching me with their binoculars. This is the last place I want to be right now; I'd rather be in the crowd three blocks away, but this is my own mission—me, who hooked up Early with McFarland. It's all so spookily Judges-like, the ending, where the whole network of the Twelve Tribes breaks down into atrocity and madness, sparks flying in every direction. Everyone wants to kill the Evil, and everyone always fails.

The Emerson's a small old building—four brick stories and an informal reception desk that doesn't ask me to show the throwaway ID I'd brought with me. Not a very prosperous scene here: yellowing palms, gray smudges on the walls scraped by long-ago furniture. I breeze through the lobby, note the EXIT signs over the stairwell then bounce up the ancient brown linoleum rectangles to the third floor. The smell of varnish in the dim, quiet hallway, heavy old wooden doors painted white with early twentieth-century numbers curliqued onto brass plaques. Behind one of them Earl E. is waiting with his rifle.

I find his number and tap my knuckles against the door. No answer, not a sound. "Early, it's me. Lando. I need to talk to you."

Still no answer.

"Early, open up now or I'm getting Security up here."

The thick wooden door opens a crack and his familiar face glances at me and then up and down the hallway. His hair is crew-cut now, his face shaved clean and his eyebrows bleached blond. "Get in here!" he intones, and then closes the door quickly after me. "I thought you might show up."

He's wearing black tactical gear on his torso and navy blue pants that match the Seattle PD uniform on a hanger draped over a chair. He's got the whole kit: baton, plasticuffs, a handgun in a black leather holster. From outside the window he'll look like an official sniper, giving him those crucial seconds of confusion to get his shots off. When he hits the street he'll be just another blueshirt. It feels weird to be alone in a small space with this large angry man, but I stay focused.

"Nice outfit. You look like you're all ready to go out there and bust heads."

"Cut the shit, Lando. That brand is stale."

The one-room office is set up with some computer desks and telephones that he'd probably bought used and moved in a couple of weeks ago. Stationery lying out on the desk says HELPING HAND FOUNDATION in a logo that he must have cranked out on his computer. Pens, a calendar on the wall. He knew Security might be checking out offices with a sight line to the action and he'd taken the steps.

I see a black police sniper rifle lying near the window and Earl E. picks it up when he sees me eyeing it. The window itself has a big neon sign blocking it just like the pictures Mac had showed us, but out the right-hand side there's a twelve-inch space between the sign and the building. I walk over to it and see the police barricade three blocks away. A few hundred feet beyond them I see the massive crowd of protesters, with their banners and giant puppets. The din hums in through the wavy old glass a few inches from my nose. Emily's in that crowd somewhere. So is my mother. I step away from the opening. You never know who's looking back at you.

"Nice setup," I say.

"What are you here for, Lando?"

"I'm here to talk."

"Always the politician, eh? You've even got your little politician suit on. But I already said: Nobody elected you."

"What's the plan here, Earl? You wait until things heat up, open the window, pop a few brownshirts, and duck out?"

"You got it."

"What if you miss? You realize that your bullets will go straight into the crowd."

"I won't miss."

"Everybody misses sometimes."

"McFarland didn't miss when you guys whacked John Polling. Or did you forget about that already?"

My ears get warm. "Polling was a legitimate target."

"So is Whitehall."

Can't argue with that: It's my own logic. "Look down there, Earl E.! If you start popping off rounds they're not going to automatically spot you and return fire. They're liable to panic and let it rip at anybody that looks threatening. And that's demonstrators! The people on our side! And even if they don't, even if everything comes out just the way you want and you get away clean, the demonstration suddenly goes from being about people trying to get back their right to an election, which everyone understands, to some whacko popping a couple of brownshirts, which has nothing to do with anything."

He gets louder. "I am tired of your PR crap, Lando! You think you're playing these guys, but you're not. You and your strategies don't even register with them! If the Regime's so afraid of the Civils, why did they cancel the election in the first place? That doesn't sound like somebody who's scared. It sounds like somebody who's ready to push the envelope. This is a test run for the Dictatorship, and if we don't fight back now—"

"They are fighting back! Don't you see them out there? There's got to be a hundred thousand people out there, maybe two hundred, fighting back!"

"Not yet, they're not."

"And you think you're going to get their fighting spirit up by starting a massacre?"

"It's already a massacre! Ask Franklin Seven! Ask the guy that got killed on his sailboat, or the ones who disappeared! Ask my people! Is this a style problem, Lando? Is that it? You think a nice quiet massacre is more politically correct? Corporate death squads sneaking around and killing us one by one. That's the kind of massacre they want, because then nobody ever has to make choice. Well, I say fuck that! Let's get this party started!"

I ignore it. "Where's the rest of your crew?"

"You're looking at it!" He says it fiercely but I can feel the sadness underneath.

"They all went down?"

A slow nod.

"I'm sorry about that, Early. I tried to help."

He looks down silently. "I know you did. And I know you caught shit about it."

"No regrets. What happened to your wounded comp?"

He takes a deep breath and says quietly, "Liz didn't get through. I buried her up in the North Cascades. That's what she wanted." He shakes his head, and his voice flutters. "And everybody got caught anyway! Whitehall killed two of my guys that I know of, and gulaged three others. And you don't think they're a legitimate target!"

I'm understanding where he's coming from now. Maybe a person can only handle so much loss before they snap. "Early, man, you had a bad run, but this isn't the way to make it better. Why don't you just abort this operation? Leave the gun, lock the door. You've done your part. I'll get you hooked up with some new docs and a ticket to Sweden, if you want. You'll be a hero there, dude. The Euros love us. When things chill out, you'll come back."

He's considering it, but he finally shakes his head. "I have an obligation here, Lando. There's too many dead people looking over my shoulder."

"Early . . . how many more do you want?"

His eyes slide down to the floor while he gets his head around that one, a chore I still haven't completed. "What comes next, Early? Car bombs? Blowing up the Federal Building? We can't win. Not like this. Only the people in that crowd can win."

He's intimate and distant at the same time. "I'm sorry to hear you say that, Lando. I didn't think you were a quitter." He drifts over to the window and eyes the demonstration through a pair of binoculars. "Looks like they're starting to cook down there."

He backs up and I take a look. The empty space between the police barrier and the crowd has shrunk now, but it's still there. I hear a drawer open and then his voice behind me, flat and businesslike.

"I need you to put these cuffs on until we're done here. Then we'll both go out. I'll pretend I'm arresting you." For a second he had a touch of the old confidence. "One step ahead of Whitehall. Just the way it should be."

He's holding plastic cuffs in one hand and a revolver with the other. The gun has a soda bottle taped over the muzzle in a do-it-yourself silencer. It looks a little ridiculous, like a child's toy, except I've shot them like that myself and I know that at close range there's nothing toylike about them.

"C'mon, Early! You're going to shoot me? I sat with you in that spruce tree for three weeks."

"Don't play the buddy card, Lando. That tree went down at the Siskiyou. If I have to shoot you I will. This operation's under way."

My heart starts to speed up. "Early, my mother's out there." It shocks him, sets him back the way it set me back when I found out his real name. "Listen, I'm going through that door, and I'm going to call 911 and tell the cops there's a man with a gun in the window of room 321. So you've got about sixty seconds to clear out." I slowly walk toward the door and put my hand on the knob.

"Don't, Lando! I *will* shoot you!"

My back is to him, and I can hear the nervousness in his voice, but I know he won't pull the trigger. "I have to."

I turn the doorknob, and suddenly there's a loud boom and the door comes flying into my face and slams me backwards against the wall. A sharp pain comes from my nose at the same time that a little burst of white light blossoms in my forehead. I lose my footing and slide down the wall to the floor, glimpse a dark gray uniform, and in the side of my vision, framed against the distant ceiling, I see a look of confusion on Earl E.'s face, his weapon half-raised, and then I hear clicking sounds and Early stumbles backwards and drops his gun. He crumples a few feet away from me; then I see a gray uniform move quickly into the room, pointing a pistol with a silencer down at Earl E. and briefly at me. The flash of a golden trident from the shoulder. Whitehall. He kicks Earl E.'s gun away and turns to me, and at that moment, even stunned by the door, things get even weirder, because it's Joby. His crazy blue eyes are revved up with adrenaline. "Lando! You okay?"

I roll over and manage to get to my knees next to Earl E. His black tactical garb is turning wet and reddish, and Earl E's face looks suddenly fifteen years old instead of twenty-five, a big kid who's twisted his ankle sliding into home, all surprise and pain. Looking horribly innocent and out of character in his SWAT clothes, a boy in a Halloween costume, dressed like a stormtrooper without understanding what stormtroopers really do.

Joby kneels down next to Earl E. and looks into his face. His urgent raspy voice: "I'm sorry, bro! I had to do it."

Earl E. moves his mouth like he wants to talk, but nothing comes out. Tears leak down from the sides of his eyes.

Now the blond guy who always scared people is sounding desperate. "I'm asking for your forgiveness, bro. I'm trying to do the right thing, here. You shouldn't of drawn on Lando! You shouldn't of . . . I couldn't let you shoot those people, man." He turns to me, explaining quickly. "Mac sent me. He told me to back you up."

I grab Earl E.'s arm. It feels limp in my hand, like a turkey leg. "Early! Hang on. I'll get help!"

I can see he's beyond help, though. Joby's done his job well. Earl E.'s mouth stops moving and his eyes lose their focus. He wets his pants. I close his eyes, the way I've seen it done in the movies. Jonathan Blust. Last free man of the Berkeley Anarchists. He did what was right in his own eyes.

Joby interrupts me. Joby's quietly starting to freak, and I wonder if he's not quite the cold-rage killer he comes off as. "I had to, Lando. He was set to shoot you. I heard the whole thing!" Joby's wagging his head back and forth, pushes his hands over his scalp hard, then does it again, and again, like a little kid retreating into himself, and for a second, I see Joby as that faraway kid in elementary school, the oddball one that everybody picks on or stays away from, self-stimming when he gets upset. "This is *messed up*, man! This is *messed up!*"

I look over at Earl E. He didn't even fire his weapon. How can I tell Joby that he never intended to?

"We'd better go, Joby."

Returned to the problems at hand, Joby clams up and throws the silencer down, not wanting to carry it in the streets in case we get picked up. The smell of gunsmoke has billowed out into the hall. We shut the door then clatter quickly down the stairwell to the basement and the tunnel that goes to the next street over: Earl E.'s planned escape route. The streets are clotted with little groups of uniformed cops, backed up by Whitehall mercs in Humvees and the occasional troop carrier of weekend warriors. Nobody knows what just played out in room 321 of the Emerson Building, maybe will never know, will never become history, just a sad and shabby little killing in a shabby little room that no one needs to find an explanation for, except Jonathan Blust's mom and dad, his brothers and sisters—if he has any. I don't even know. Soon to be propaganda flash for the Regime, like everything else. *Terrorist killed in settling of accounts.* Pictures, pictures, more sad and silly pictures.

The emptiness is back, the airless black futility I felt when Steve Sykes went down, except this time it's full of cops and soldiers, all around me. All I can think is, *I want out of this.* Out of the fear, out of the murders—*I want the fuck out of this!* Joby walks me to the edge of the No-Protest Zone without a word, and I head for the Pike Place Market to rendezvous with Tonk. I'm in a hurry to see him, praying he can magically find the words that make everything fit together again. The merchants look depressed and listless. The place is practically deserted. I stop a few hundred feet away, spot the café we've agreed on. I'm trying to get my head to stop banging and figure out how I'll explain what happened with Earl E. A lone customer is buying a salmon, and I stand and watch vacantly, waiting for the fish-slinging that they're famous for, some sign of everyday joy as an antidote to this whole nonsensical story. Instead the man walks it over and puts it on the counter to be weighed. It's usually a guy with a handlebar mustache and a wisecrack. Today it's a big man with thinning black hair who gives the fish a quick wrap job and seems to wave away the customer's money. Strange.

Just strange enough to make me take another look at the street. A garbage truck pulls up and blocks the central alley of the market, and two men in municipal coveralls get out and start fiddling with a Dumpster. I move behind a rack of magazines, reach out and leaf through one while I eye the street. A man steps out from the fruit stand. They're at one side of the alley. On the other avenue of escape it's two guys dressed in fleece jackets and blue jeans, one with short hair and the other with hair to his waist, but a little more bulked out than any freak I've seen lately. A woman with a baby carriage starts walking toward the café Tonk is sitting in. There's a price tag hanging from the side.

My muscles start rumbling again with whatever adrenaline hasn't been squeezed out of me fifteen minutes ago. I can't see Tonk from this angle, don't know if he's made them or not. The woman wheels her carriage into the café while I stand there paralyzed, no way to warn him, not even my HK on me to shoot him an escape route. The freak follows her in, and I spot three more men around the corner now, obvious plainclothes guys, heads rigged up with earbuds and side-arms in their hands. I back toward the other door and reach for my cell phone, but just as I'm dialing Tonk's number there's a big sound of shattering glass and Tonk comes bursting through the door of the café with the longhair hanging on to his leg. Tonk hammers him at the back of his neck with his fist and yanks his leg away, and I see him crouch for a second, blood running down his cut face, swiveling his head all directions like his old wide receiver days, looking for open field. He starts to move, and just then the woman rushes out with her gun in her hand and runs directly into him, bounces off him sideways, and before she can draw down on him he's got his hands wrapped around the barrel, twists it away from her and kicks her backwards over the other man. Now the garbagemen are moving in along with the fruit guy, drawing their guns. Tonk makes them, cuts the other way, and breaks into a run toward the fish-seller, who's out from behind the counter now, yelling *"Halt!"* with his gun drawn. Tonk stops, reverses direction, puts on a burst of speed straight toward me, and he catches sight of me, flashes a look of surprise for a split second, then picks up the other three plainclothes running at him for the tackle. He lets them close, shifts sideways, and sends one of them to the pavement, straight-arms the other right in the face and moves past him, takes the full brunt of the third slamming into him with a high tackle but manages to stagger back two steps and then start pumping his legs again, catches the man across the face with the bar-rel of his gun and casts him off. And I think, *He's made it! He's made it!* until the fucker on the ground rolls to his stomach and fires. The thunder splits the air, the street seems to shudder for a second in that eclipse of sound, and as I stand there Tonk stutters forward a few of steps, then collapses in a hideously slow belly flop directly onto his face. I hear him hit the pavement in a rustle of flesh and clothes, his face tilted toward me in a fierce grimace. Our eyes meet but I don't dare signal him. The two cops shout, *"Drop the weapon!"* and he rolls slowly to his side, he points his gun, and they open up with their pis-tols to complete his suicide. His body twitches with the impact and he slumps to the wet dirty asphalt.

Tonk is dead. There, right in front me, Tonk is dead! My mind gets stuck on that single stunning fact and for moment I can only watch as his executioners approach his body with their guns drawn, and then the fear overwhelms me like it never has before. I'm seeing myself there, lying in my own blood with everything I am and everything I hoped for wiped out by killers who'll go home and brag about it to their friends. I'm nothing but prey now, and that animal reality freezes me in place, the classic prey response. I look away from Tonk's body as if none of this ever happened. Not me! I didn't see anything! I'm not even here!

Some higher-level survival mechanism cuts through the adrenaline fog. How long have I been standing there? I shift back behind the magazine rack, glance sideways to check on the owner, who's suddenly got a gun in his hand and is advancing on Tonk. A few more seconds and they'll be sweeping the area for witnesses, pull in anyone on hand for questioning, and my answers are going to put me right next to Earl E.'s dead body at the Emerson Building. I back up slowly and move out the other side of the newsstand onto First Avenue, walk east and then north toward the Westlake metro, past the ancient Walgreens and the bookstore where we'd first flagged Emily, so long ago. Breathing in and out as deeply as I can, trying to inhale that sense of normal lives, of buildings that will be there tomorrow, of garbage cans and traffic cones and walk lights that measure out pedestrians totally apart from that last look on Tonk's face, that last painful barely focused grimace that said, *Where were you, Lando?* I want out of this!

Two blocks away from the Market, then three, through the deserted streets. The fancy department stores. I get the sudden paranoia that maybe someone made me, is looking for me now as a witness, and I turn into Saks and find myself surrounded by cosmetics. The pretty ladies with their colored cheeks, the hand mirrors, the little silk bags and glass counters. Tonk is dead, and I'm floating in a world of makeup, drifting to the escalator past mannequins in cashmere sweaters, the jaunty plaster man in a leather jacket and a woolen cap, like death is just an outing in the country. Or a day at the office. Men's Furnishings, with its white-haired salesman looking like a cashiered Corporate, like an undertaker. "Can I help you find something?"

Yes, sir, could you please help me find the reason why things get so fucked up when you're trying to make a better world? "No thanks, just looking." The strips of colored silk, the hanging suits in muffled tones

of blue, navy, gray, and black, enough to dress everyone at the funeral. I head to the casual section, wave off the saleslady, pick out a
tan Windbreaker, maroon sweatshirt, blue cotton pants, then top it
with a stocking cap and leave my old suit in a garbage can. Pay in cash
and walk out a new man, throttling my brain down to just a guy
walking on a street, feeling nothing, Tonk dead, Earl E. dead. From a
distant corner of my mind a prayer goes up: God Almighty, you cruel
lying son of a bitch, look down on this broken world and *get me the
fuck out of this*!

I'm all the way to Westlake before I find out the transit's shut down
here by the protesters. I suddenly hear shouting and a group of hundreds of people comes walking quickly around the corner, filling the
street, stopping traffic, and when some shirts come up beside them
from a cross street and start laying down tear gas to head them off,
they break into a run and go right through it, flowing around a Humvee full of brownshirts at top speed, losing a few but passing on to
whatever destination they're headed for—yes, probably the Courthouse. That's it: There's a demonstration today. That's where this
started. I walk up toward Capitol Hill, hoping to find a bus, and that
little bit of practical thought helps me ratchet it down to survival
mode. Other people are depending on me. Okay. Okay. Tonk's dead.
Earl E.'s dead. Work backwards: How'd they make Tonk? Who else
have they made?

   I should call Sarah, get the word out that we need to relocate, but
maybe her line's compromised, too. No choice. I call her and she
picks up, says quickly, "Hello hello hello." Then I can hear the strain
in her voice as she blurts out, "Hey! Is this some kind of crank call?"

   The distress code. I close the phone and throw it in a garbage can,
imagining the Homelanders or some brownshirt committee standing
over her. Fuck! Stay cool, Lando, think about the Network. Don't be
Josh Sands, the guy who fears, the guy who loses it. I duck into a coffee shop with Wi-Fi and punch out Gonzalo's line on my Internet
phone. I wait three rings without an answer, leave a message on the
voice mail: "Hey, it's Jack. That other thing turned out to be a crank
call. Sarah and Tonk had to cancel for dinner, so go ahead and make
other plans. I'll catch up with you in a few weeks."

I close it out. Maybe Gonzalo's already in a cell somewhere and Security's got units speeding to this gas station. Maybe he was just in the bathroom and left his phone next to the computer. Anything's possible. But Tonk is dead, the vultures ready to pick apart his phone records, Sarah's in deep shit. It's getting clear as Christmas: The Regime's using the demo as cover for a crackdown.

I'm twelve blocks north by now. The outbound 179 comes along and I get on, pay my fare, walk past the faces smoothed down by transit, black ones, some Mexicans speaking Spanish; then I realize I don't know where I'm going. If it's a sweep, there's a fair chance Henry Rampton's been made, too, and that stash of nineteen thousand, and my HK .32 and my computer with its memory card hidden inside the sofa are all under twenty-four-hour watch, hoping that Henry will show up for his arrest. Do I go back for the cash and the computer, or play it safe and abandon it? Think, think! About ten thousand in a safe-deposit box downtown. Little bundles of five thousand buried in the park, stashed on the roof of a tavern in Greenwood, other caches of documents and money held by Friends around the city. I get off at another hot spot and call Kahasi and then Lilly, reach them to my great relief. I give sixty-second briefings with all the bad news, leaving out Earl E. and saying as little about Tonk's death as I can. I allocate them each a cache of money, tell them to relocate and sit tight, promise to check back when I know more. They'll get the word out to the others, and Lilly will tug on the spiderweb all the way down the coast. I message a warning to McFarland.

Now I get on the 48, heading away from downtown, still not sure where I'm going. I have five hundred dollars and a pack of credit cards that might already be poisoned. I ride along in the haze, heading all the way to SeaTac while I try to think things through. Our network's been fatally compromised, and what counts now is surviving to the next round. Europe is open, just like I told Earl E, and I'm thinking how to get there. Not from Seattle—they'll be flagging walk-up tickets everywhere on the West Coast. No. Go over the mountains to Canada and fly out of Edmonton or Calgary on the fake passport that has my hair dyed black and the name of some guy from Saskatchewan on it. In an instant I see it all in front of me like a window with a beautiful sunset—the quiet café, the bridge over the canal, an old apartment with a crack in ceiling, the tolling of evening bells—just the whole peaceful green feeling of not being hunted. I could go there. I could lie low. I could live.

Crowd noise is blaring from the television and I glance up at whatever Corporate moneymaking contest is going on. But it's not sports this time. It's the demonstration down at the Stadium. The camera picks out a banner held front and center in a crowd of people facing down the cops, young people so brave and hopeful that before I can stop it, my chest clenches up and the tears come brimming out of my eyes. The banner says LONG LIVE THE ARMY OF THE REPUBLIC!

27

*I*t was almost noon, and Anne broke out one of her sandwiches and split it with me. I ate it as we wove our way through the crowd toward the chanting, taunting Throwaways. Joe's group was easy to identify because they were wearing orange buttons like Joe's that said MY VOTE WILL NOT BE THROWN AWAY! and some had hard hats or even bicycle helmets on. They'd attracted the rowdiest elements of the crowd, especially angry young males who looked ready for a fight, and the feeling got more and more intense as we approached the barrier. At the front of the crowd, the Throwaway Parade Marshals had linked their arms and were keeping the line of protesters back, leaving an undulating forty-foot space between the protesters and the front ranks of the police. Maybe Joe was going to keep his word after all. I called on my cell phone and asked some of the Peace Keepers to send more people to the front.

The Security forces had long since lost the easygoing boredom that police show in the early stages of a demonstration. Not surprising, since the Throwaways were treating them to a constant stream of insults: "Hey, lapdog! Ready to club some fellow Americans? They pay you well for that? Hey, you! Ruff ruff!" The Security forces were tense but controlled, refusing to look the demonstrators in the eyes or to react in any way. In the front row were the riot police, with their black helmets and nightsticks. The thick padding on their chest made them look bigger than normal humans, the medieval-looking head wear reminiscent of the evil commander in a science-fiction movie. They did their best to seem completely remote, but I felt sorry for them, in some ways. How much verbal abuse could a person take? "Does that make you feel good, clubbing some working people? They pay you well for that, lapdog? Hey, Brownshirt!"

Behind the Seattle PD were the King County riot police in navy blue, and mixed in with them were the Whitehall troops, distinguishable from real police only by the Whitehall trident patch on their black tactical gear. They were armed with clubs and shotguns, with the wide black barrels of their tear gas launchers sticking out of their utility belts along with canisters of CS spray, batons, stun guns. In the back were the National Guardsmen, looking queasy as they stared into the angry faces in front of them and clutched their rifles. They weren't well-trained for repression. They were the most likely to panic, as they'd done at Kent State in my parents' generation. What had they been told by their commanders? That we were all radicals? Subversive traitors? That we hated our country? I wondered if they'd brought them in from the parts of the state where Regime support was strongest, the way the Chinese had brought troops from Inner Mongolia to massacre the students of the Beijing elite at Tienanmen Square.

Now the people on our side of the fence had begun edging closer, with only twenty feet separating them from the police. The Throwaway Parade Marshals kept them from going any closer, some of them stretching out an orange rope while roving groups of Marshals tidied up the fringe of the crowds. They were like a swarm of bees ready to move at some invisible signal.

Anne touched my arm and pointed at the police. "They're putting on their gas masks."

It was true—the security forces were now strapping on their masks, checking the seals for each other with a weird touch of brotherly tenderness. One of the police commanders started hectoring our side through a megaphone, and a few cops had come out to confer with the Parade Marshals. "Move back ten feet!" they commanded. "Move back, or you will be forced to comply. Pain compliance will be used. We *will* inflict pain."

We were running out of slack now. I had to try to be bigger than I felt. I told Anne to wait for me and went up to one of the commanders, a kindly-looking man with brown hair and a walrus mustache. He was uncomfortable, glancing off to the side as if he expected an ambush. I introduced myself. "We're trying to avoid problems. Is there anything we can do to defuse the situation?"

He looked me over suspiciously. "Are you in charge here?"

"Nobody's in charge, but I have some influence."

"Yeah." My answer annoyed him—he was used to command structures. "Move them fifty feet away from this barrier and get them to face the stage."

"I'll try. Can you hold off for a few minutes?"

"I'm not making any promises."

I looked around the immediate area for Joe Simic, but the crowd was like a thick fog: The farther away a person was, the more difficult it was to spot them. At a distance of only twenty feet, most individuals disappeared. The music onstage was winding down. I looked at my watch and realized why I wouldn't find Joe here at the barrier: He was scheduled to take the stage next.

My phone rang and Dave's name flashed on the screen. Keeping in touch. I took the call, but before I could say anything Dave's voice cut me off. "Joe!" he began.

"Dave? This is Emily!"

"Shit! I dialed the wrong number. I'll call you back later, Emily."

He hung up, and I stood there gazing at my phone for a second. Why was everybody looking for Joe? It could have been a different Joe, I guessed: another Direct Response person, a woman named Joanne. I hurried on toward the stage.

The musicians were saying their last thank-yous and the leader of the Throwaways stood off to the side, next to Tony, talking on his phone. I rushed toward him. His friendly wave had an empty tone to it. It seemed to come more from habit than from any real welcome. In fact, he actually seemed slightly annoyed that I stood there as he talked on the phone.

"Have they reached Yesler?" I heard him ask. "How soon can you get to South Washington?" He listened to the answer; then he seemed to become acutely aware of me, and motioned with his eyes to Tony. After that he turned his back to me and moved away about fifteen feet, where I couldn't hear him. Tony smiled. "Great turnout, eh?"

"I need to talk with Joe, Tony. We have to get everyone away from the barrier."

Tony was unimpressed by my sense of urgency. "Joe needs his privacy right now, Emily. Can it wait until after his speech?"

"Tony, you're not hearing me. We need to get people away from the fence right now or the police are going to attack." He didn't answer, and I peered around him at Joe. One of his volunteers on the sound crew approached him and nodded and hurried away. I swallowed and looked up at the huge man in front of me. "Tony. I need to talk with him *now*! He needs to move his people back!"

It finally seemed to get through. "Wait here for a second." He started walking toward Joe and then turned to me again. "Just wait. I'll bring him over."

I stood there like an idiot. Joe covered the phone as he listened to Tony's message; then he tossed off a little wave toward me, as if he'd be right over. The musicians had finished now. The only sound was the rumbling white noise of the crowd. I didn't see Dan or Shar anywhere—they might have been back at the barrier, or in the Media Booth. The MC came on to introduce the next speaker.

I looked back toward the barrier. The police were actively brandishing their tear gas launchers and CS canisters now. The riot troops had formed into a line with their clear plastic shields held up in front of them, and I could hear the thundering as they began to pound their batons against them. The policeman with the bullhorn was still telling the crowd to move back, and so were other policemen at farther points in the line. The crowd hadn't backed up at all: judging by the movement of the signs and the raised fists that I could see from the steps leading up to the stage, it was getting more agitated.

Joe finally put his phone away, but to my surprise, he ignored me and went quickly down into the crowd, heading straight for the barrier. I felt cautiously relieved. Maybe Tony had gotten through to him after all. Joe was the one person who could move the Throwaways back quickly and peacefully. I hurried down the steps to help him, with Anne Sands behind me. I lost sight of him immediately. Then, a minute later, I saw him rise up above the crowd.

His people had improvised a platform for him in front of the police barrier, and he was holding a mic that had been patched into the sound system. I still thought he would move the crowd back, but he went right into his speech, his homespun, artless-sounding voice lashing over the audience. The entire crowd was now turned toward him, and toward the police barrier.

"Fellow Citizens! Workers. Homemakers. Students. Grandmas and grandpas, but above all, Citizens: I salute you!" He had a slow, methodical delivery that gave each word a powerful symbolism. When he said *Workers*, it was as if workers were an ancient and eternal pillar of the earth, and when he said *Citizens*, it had a mystical weight, as if we were Athenian citizens and Roman citizens and the heroic citizens of the American Revolution. "I salute you because you cared enough to come down here. I salute you because you could not be intimidated by the Regime, with their threats and their 'walls of steel.' You came to remind them of who America really is."

He was an immensely powerful speaker. Even I felt a thrill that momentarily overwhelmed the fact that the police were getting prepared for a major onslaught only forty feet away from him. Then I started getting nervous.

"The problem here is that the self-appointed rulers of this country have a different idea about who you should be. They want Americans to be obedient, to let them run the show. They only want Americans to fight when they send you or your children off to a war somewhere, and when you return they'll reward you with a pin to hold up that empty cuff where your arm or leg used to be, and tell you what a great warrior you are, give you a pat on the back. That's their idea of what a good American is. Is it yours?"

The crowd bellowed its anger back at him from all over the plaza.

Anne tugged at my sleeve, yelling in my ear. "Is this what's supposed to happen?"

The sound of the police bullhorns was barely audible now. "No!" I hollered back at her. Joe wasn't going to be defusing things just yet. I glanced back at the stage, looking for Dan or Shar, but I knew they couldn't help me now anyway. I was furious. I wanted to grab Joe Simic by the lapels and yell in his face. I began pushing through the increasingly dense mass of coats and backpacks, trying to reach the platform, but the closer I got, the more tightly packed the people were, and instead I tried to move laterally, circling toward the police barrier. I yelled his name a few times, but it was useless. I could feel the energy rising around me. I turned back to Anne. "I'm going to the police line to try to move people back. Why don't you stay at the stage and I'll find you later?"

"I'll go with you. I can help."

I thought about insisting she go back, but that would be insulting. She'd come here from Washington to make a contribution, and now was the time. "We have to hurry."

I looked at the faces as I pushed past. All ages, some of them smooth, healthy faces, others were worn-looking, tired, angry, unkempt. Noses were pink from the cold, and breath was hovering in the air. These were my fellow Citizens. I could hear chanting from a few hundred yards away along the barricade, above the sound of the police warnings: "WE ARE PEACEFULLY ASSEMBLED! PEACEFULLY ASSEMBLED! WE ARE PEACEFULLY ASSEMBLED! PEACEFULLY ASSEMBLED!"

Joe's voice went on, hypnotic, scornful.

". . . and they're still at it! Look at 'em over there: They're still trying to make you feel like a second-class member of this United States of America. With their gas masks and their shotguns. They steal your vote, and when they can't steal it, they cancel it! Then, when you want to tell 'em how you feel about that, you can't go down to the Courthouse to do it. 'Cause the way they see it, it's *their* Courthouse, for *their* laws! No, they say, you go down and protest at the football stadium, because that's *your* role in this society: to watch football and fight wars while we make the rules at *our* Courthouse."

At that moment, an orange pellet came ripping through the air and hit him in the back. It startled him, and when he turned I could see he was covered with bright orange dye.

"See this?" he said to his audience. "They're marking me for arrest. They're coming after me. Because the last thing they want is someone who reminds you that they are not the rightful rulers of this country—you are! And there is no power on earth that can ever dominate the American people by force!"

I was almost to the barrier now. I'd never felt a sense of impending chaos as I felt it then, a terrifying, crackling, explosive mood, like something out of a Greek myth. The police were in order, hulking black figures with shields and clubs, ready to move forward. Behind them the ranks of Guardsmen and Whitehall troops were prickling with black gun barrels. In the crowd, a number of protesters had slipped on their own gas masks, or had tied moistened bandannas over their faces, like outlaws. I saw sticks held down low. Our Peace Keepers were being completely ignored.

I came out into the narrow clearing and yelled at the Throwaway Parade Marshals. "We've got to get these people back!"

"Who are you?" a woman asked.

I pointed to my purple Peace Keeper armband. "I'm Emily Cortright, from Democracy Northwest. I need your help to move these people back." I turned directly to the crowd, shouting in as authoritative voice as I could manage. "Everybody, please move back!" I waved my arms over my head, as if I were signaling a jumbo jet. "PLEASE MOVE BACK! BACK! MOVE BACK!" Anne stood next to me, doing the same. A few people seemed to shuffle back a half step, but there was almost no reaction. The Throwaway marshals were watching me silently. I turned to them and yelled, "Help me!" but everyone merely glanced at me and turned back to the podium. I spotted Dan a few hundred feet away, having the same luck I was.

I felt a sharp stinging on my arm, and I looked down to see a bright stain of glistening Day-Glo color on my raincoat.

Suddenly a booming came from beyond the police line, and I noticed that many of the police had turned their heads and were staring behind them, agitated at some disturbance. Tear gas was being fired, but in the opposite direction from us, to their rear. Whatever was happening back there seemed to make up their minds. A command was given, and then I saw the Security forces lower their tear gas launchers and a row of white explosions ripped across the line.

The first few tear gas canisters went bouncing past me on the pavement, streaming pale smoke behind them and slamming into the legs of the front row of protesters. People cried out in pain, and then the powerful streams from the water cannon and fire trucks started knocking people down, hurling them backwards into the crowd and scooting them along the wet pavement. The police moved quickly forward in a ragged line, some of them dousing people in the face with CS foam, others poking demonstrators with their batons, or pushing them with their shields. An arrest team of Whitehall troops moved toward the podium where Joe was speaking. The crowd started to shrink back, and the police went after those who didn't shink fast enough. A few people had sat down in clusters, huddling together and closing their eyes against the gas. I myself could barely see; it felt like needles were being pushed into my eyes. I spun around, coughing, squinting, and trying to back into the crowd. I could open my eyes for a few seconds and then the pain would be too much, and I'd have to close them again. "Hey!" I heard, and in a woman's voice, "Please! I'm trying to move." Off to the other side, behind me, I heard cursing.

There was a general backward movement to the crowd; then suddenly, strangely, I heard people say "Let's go! This is it! Go! Go! Go!" and I felt the crowd surging forward again, like a wave, some of them striking out, some covering their heads and hurling themselves at the police like bowling balls. The police were overwhelmed in seconds. People were grabbing at shields and pushing them out of the way, stripping off gas masks, punching, grabbing batons. I found myself directly behind a riot cop, looking over his shoulder as two men came in on him. He drew back his baton and I watched it move quickly through the air until it hit me squarely in the face and then I felt the sudden hard surface of the pavement against my knees. In the background I heard little snatches of what seemed like Joe Simic's voice—then I was knocked to the ground by someone rushing past me, and my head bounced like a rubber ball. I lay there coughing, dimly felt a sudden intense force coming down on my ankle, until I thought it would snap, then it stopped, then a hand was gripping my forearm and pulling me upward. "Hey, help me out here! I can't lift her alone." I was on my feet somehow. "What's your name? Do you know your name?" My legs were paddling loosely, and there was pressure under each arm. I felt my chest heaving as I coughed. "Medical unit!" I heard someone yell, then cough a few times. "Medical unit!"

28

*A*nne had already told me she was going to the Seattle protests, and she'd made some very ominous hints about what was going to happen when she returned. Along with my secret maneuvering to regain the company, it made the days leading up to the demonstration nervous and uncomfortable, as if I were going around in a suit a size too small for me. Walter invited me to come over and watch the football game, but I was barely able to follow it, and was irritated at his questions about my wife and son.

The day of the demonstration I kept compulsively going to the news on my computer screen, homing in on the Seattle stations. The talk of some sort of showdown brewing there had been popping up all over the media, and the visuals looked a little menacing even to me. At two thirty D.C. time, I decided to close the day out early and see if it was the "smackdown" the pundits had said it would be.

The commentators were talking when I tuned in. They were in a tight shot of the police line, looking cool and determined. The anchor and his color man were delivering a chatty analysis about the ascending scale of crowd-control methods, from tear gas and water cannon to rubber bullets, chemical Mace, and finally live ammunition. They went to a wide shot of the entire street.

Holy shit! The crowd filled the huge open space in front of a football stadium. They were packed tightly with banners and a few giant puppets waving their arms above the heads. I had no way of judging crowds, but the official estimate of thirty thousand protesters seemed short by 300 or 400 percent, even in that one area. A massive amount of people: the kind of crowds they showed on TV when third world governments fell. Banners bobbed overhead with all the popular drivel of the left. I poured myself a glass of aquavit and sat down to watch.

In the foreground, the orange barricades and their mob of blue were a thin buffer zone before the relatively empty street behind them. The police were clustered around water cannon, fire trucks, and, strangely, city buses. There were quick shots of points in the area, showing mobs of radicals gathering in intersections, or jogging from one place to another. A group of radicals had gone up to the highway and locked themselves together in an immovable tangle of chains and plastic piping. These in turn were surrounded by a mob of other radicals. Behind them the cars were backed for miles. Dozens of police had waded into the knot of people on the highway, but any paddy wagon or bus was far away. It didn't seem to matter—several of the policemen wearing gas masks were dousing to all sides with canisters of pepper spray, sometimes grabbing the protesters by the hair to turn their face up into it. It seemed a little excessive.

"See, Frank, this is what they call a 'lockdown' situation. The radicals lock themselves together in ingenious ways to create the maximum disturbance possible. We've seen them chain themselves to doors by their neck. They've built high towers out of aluminum struts and then perched on top of them. Oh, they're clever. That crowd of people around them is there to prevent the police making an arrest."

"So this is a common tactic?"

"Oh, yeah. They've got lockdowns at a half-dozen different points right now. They usually choose strategic intersections, where they can cause the most confusion."

Even if they deserved it, the close-ups were hard to watch. The cops and the National Guard were wading in with their black sticks flailing in every direction, and it was obvious that they were ganging up and pounding the shit out of kids who could no longer defend themselves. The camera tended to cut away when that happened. You could only see another cop or two approaching with their batons up, and then it would move on, maybe to another fight, maybe to the aerial view again. When cops got outnumbered, it would stay fastened on the scene, accompanied with sorrowful clucking by the color man, a retired officer from the riot squad, who could describe in vivid detail the experience of the overmatched cop as he squared off against the frenzied demonstrators. Another color person, a woman who'd taken part in demonstrations some years ago, was commenting on the demonstrators' strategy. It wasn't mentioned, but I saw a lot of uniforms with the Whitehall trident on them.

I thought about Anne, hoping she wasn't mixed up in that mess, but soon those worries were swallowed up by the sheer spectacle of the images before me. The camera would return periodically to certain hot spots, and personalities began to come out: the kid with the black goatee and the red stocking cap, or the mob with the orange buttons. The middle-aged riot cop with the resolute face seemed to glare at the presumed anarchist with the black bandanna across his mouth and the BAD CORPORATE CITIZEN sweatshirt. It was a way to create characters that people could follow, like the close-ups of football players they flashed in between plays.

"That's Emily Cortright there, talking into the cell phone. She's one of the Democracy Northwest organizers—"

"Yes, Frank. Emily studied environmental sciences at the University of Washington, and then went to culinary school before enrolling in law school at the University of Oregon—"

The former riot squad cop chipped in: "Sounds like she can't make up her mind what she wants to do when she grows up!"

A little chuckle. "Her first cause was Democracy Northwest's Water Project, when they were trying to oppose the reorganization of the water utility—"

I remembered that. They'd delayed us three years in Seattle. Her name seemed vaguely familiar. Maybe I'd seen it in a newspaper, or a security report. So this was one of my old adversaries, plotting and rallying the troops.

"Randy, let's talk a little more about the protesters' strategy, here."

A diagram came on to the lower corner of the screen as the deep, reassuring voice of the former head of the Chicago Riot Squad assessed the situation. The radicals had been granted a permit to exercise their freedom of speech at the Stadium, he said, but they wanted to protest at the Federal Courthouse, which created a public safety and terrorism risk. The problem was that some of them seemed to want to break through the barricades to the Federal Courthouse anyway. On the schematic, the barricades were little yellow lines across the streets that led away from the Stadium. The radicals were red arrows pointing inward toward the Courthouse, and the police and soldiers were elongated blue and green T's opposing the demonstrators.

"So what are all those other people we see around downtown?"

"Those are groups of people trying to maneuver their way to the Courthouse. They tend to be the most extreme. I'll tell you, Frank—the police have a very wily enemy here. They're smart and they don't play fair. Look! Look at this!"

The diagram was replaced instantly by two policemen standing over a thrashing protester. They seemed to have just knocked him to the ground, but it was hard to tell. As we zoomed in, four young men in T-shirts and red bandannas came up behind and began pulling the police away. The former riot squad chief clucked. "Will ya look at that!"

A squad of blue suddenly appeared at the upper corner of the screen and swarmed over the demonstators, batons whirling. The camera cut away just as they closed in.

They went back to the Stadium with a wide shot. Something big was happening, and I couldn't make it out at first, even with the commentary. Someone was speaking from a podium only a dozen yards from the police barricade. His name was in blue letters at the lower left: Joe Simic, a self-proclaimed leader of the angry unemployed that I'd read about before. In his phony workingman costume: ". . . 'Cause the way they see it, it's *their* courthouse, for *their* laws!" Dismissing the crowd with a scornful wave of his hand, "No! they say, you go down and protest at the football stadium, because that's *your* role in this society: to watch football and fight wars while we make the rules at *our* courthouse!"

The color man had an explanation. "This is Joe Simic, of a group that calls themselves the Throwaways."

"Wait a second. Something's happening."

They changed angles just in time to show puffs of smoke coming from the police lines and then tear gas canisters the size of shaving cream cans go skittering across the pavement. Some of them were fired too high, and I saw people get hit in the chest or head and crumple. The water cannon opened up: One of them knocked Joe Simic neatly off his platform and sent him tumbling into the crowd.

The picture suddenly switched to the police barrier, and the riot cop became agitated. "Holy cow, would you look at this! Where the hell did these guys come from?"

A crowd of hundreds, maybe thousands of people was streaming into the rear of the police barrier from a cross street, running at full speed like a cattle stampede. The police began to fire off tear gas canisters at them, and then I saw a line of them raise their shotguns and open fire with what I guessed were rubber bullets. The front fringe of the runners stumbled, but there were so many of them that the others kept coming.

Even the commentator sounded worried now. "The police are surrounded."

"That can't be good."

The rear of the police ranks had completely collapsed, and the street behind them had turned into melee.

"They're starting to make some arrests here."

The police were laying right and left with their clubs and their OC spray, but in fact, they didn't seem to be trying to arrest anyone, but rather striking out randomly, in panic. The National Guard, visible as a group because of their green uniforms, seemed to have received some command to come forward and reinforce the police line toward the Stadium, because many of them broke off from the fight and kneeled beside the police with their guns pointed at the massive crowd at the Stadium.

"I don't like this," the Chicago policeman said.

The fighting had become more savage that anything I'd ever witnessed. I winced as security forces held their black shotguns up almost in people's faces and pulled the triggers, blasting their adversaries with rubber bullets. This spread the panic, and with no escape into the dense crowd behind them, the protesters were ripping guns and gas masks away from the police, firing back at them, and at the barricade. A few surged toward the chain-link fences and began to push at them. They began swarming up the fence, and it wobbled eerily before collapsing under their weight and coming down directly on the police behind it.

"My God, they're getting trampled!"

A cluster of police dropped everything and began trying to lift up the fence, but the crowd was already beginning to swarm over it, crushing the fallen men and overwhelming the police in moments. Now it was cops on the ground getting beaten, having their gas masks pulled off and their clubs taken away.

The police moved back to take cover behind the fire engines, who turned their hoses toward the fallen fence segment. There were no politics left in this crowd; they were simply enraged, rushing through the streams of water, getting knocked down and across the pavement, then getting up again and running crazily into the police lines. They quickly passed the fire trucks, which were caught flat-footed by the unexpected charge. I could see people swarming over the trucks and taking the hoses from the firemen, and then all the police who could made a sudden, rapid retreat, and the camera panned to a line of green National Guardsmen, kneeling with their rifles pointed at the crowd. Even the color men went silent.

There was a series of explosions, like a line of firecrackers, as the National Guard opened fire on the crowd. White smoke spurted out, and I could see people crumpling to the ground and writhing there. Others threw themselves flat, hid behind trucks. I couldn't believe what I'd just seen.

"Good Lord!" said the cop, despite himself. "I think that's live ammunition!"

Some of the protesters seemed to go insane, charging straight at the rows of guns. The view of the massacre had lasted only a few seconds; then the camera pulled back to an aerial shot that showed the chaos of smoke and fallen bodies, and in that moment, in an image that I immediately attributed to my own misperception, I thought I saw a flash of familiar cloth in sky blue and gold.

The view switched suddenly to a cop who was rolling slowly over on the pavement.

The commentator's tone became strangely hesitant. "The, uh, I'm told that the protesters have opened fire on the police."

There was a quick string of booming sounds, and then screaming as fleeing demonstrators began hurtling past the cameras like comets.

"What?" the commentator said, then, "The police are, um, defending themselves."

The camera swung toward a line of policemen with their pistols out firing at the crowd, and I realized that they weren't policemen—they were Whitehall. Then the camera was knocked to the ground and went gray, and quickly a new picture came on the screen. It showed a brief shot of the confused crowd, hemmed in by the wall of people behind them, then cut to a woman holding a sign dropping to her knees and collapsing face-first on the pavement. A young man suddenly clutched his face and staggered backwards into another demonstrator, who grabbed at his own shoulder with an openmouthed grimace. The picture jostled, then went into a featureless royal blue, the curtain rung down, imposed by technical difficulties, self-censorship—I wasn't sure.

I felt cold inside, like something big was rising and becoming solid in my chest. People were getting shot at close range, pieces of metal were ripping through organs, smashing bones, and somewhere in the crowd I thought I'd seen a glimpse of sky blue and gold. I dialed Anne's cell phone, but she didn't pick up.

The picture came on again, this time in a studio, with a long-faced commentator giving out the grave news. "For those of you just tuning in, violence has erupted in Seattle. It seems that gunfire from protesters there has sparked a deadly battle with police, in which . . ." Visual of two policemen lying wounded, of the water cannon and the clouds of tear gas. My cell phone rang. It was Howard Pettijohn, weighing in with his excited Appalachian accent. "Holy Christ, Jim! Are you seeing this? Turn your TV on!"

"I see it."

"Christ, it's like the opening act of the Civil War! The cops are creaming 'em out there."

I didn't know how to respond. We were supposed to meet the next Monday to go over the buyout papers. "It's pretty extreme."

He laughed. "All I can say is, it's about time! I'm sick of their crap! Which network are you watching? Are you watching Channel America? Channel's got the best coverage."

"I'm watching CNN, but they're back at the newsroom."

"I saw the first cop go down. One of the radicals must have—"

"It looked to me like the National Guard panicked and opened fire."

"The National Guard? What's wrong with you? Turn on Channel America. It's less confusing."

I switched to Channel America and it seemed like the violence had died down slightly from a half minute before. Protesters were lying wounded or simply ducking and covering in case the shooting started again, while others were being marched off with their hands behind their heads. Some demonstrators had knelt over their fallen colleagues to try to help. The cameras kept switching back to the same couple of wounded policemen while excited color men, sounding like Pettijohn, were decrying the way the radicals had opened fire. I muted the sound.

Pettijohn went on. "This'll teach those goddamned socialists. They went too far this time. They've been asking for it for years. The more they kill, the better off this country'll be."

On the screen now a small crowd of demonstrators was confronting a Whitehall trooper who was standing over one of the wounded. He pointed his pistol at them, and one of the demonstrators moved forward, then crumbled in front of a cloud of smoke.

"Holy shit!" howled Howard. "That'll shut that punk up, won't it? That's what we're payin' 'em for, Jimbo! Bring on the fucking bloodbath!"

Anne was in that crowd. Howard went on, as if he himself were standing there, rather than watching on TV. "Bring it on, boys! Bullets are cheap!"

I couldn't stand it. "Howard, will you just shut up for a second!"

A marked silence from the other side. His voice sounded hurt and angry. "Sure. I just didn't want you to miss this, that's all."

"People are getting killed out there! Or does that just not matter to you!"

The hurt had left his voice as he answered flatly in a tone I hadn't heard before, one that recalled the accusations about death squads and paramilitary groups. "People have to die, Jim. When they get this extreme, you've got to kill a few people to show them you mean business."

A long quiet. "Let's talk later, Howard." I hung up the phone.

The violence lasted only a few more minutes. After that, it was the desultory mop-up, as the crowds tried to disperse enough to let in the ambulances and EMTs, of which there was a drastic shortage. By this time, the network was starting to cut back to headquarters to show the highlights, like a football game, with the most dramatic and or violent moments carved out with accompanying commentary. They did a good job of promoting the official story, probably worked out ahead of time by McPhee/Collins, that the demonstrators had opened fire on the police, rather than what I'd seen. Or had I seen it? It didn't matter. By tomorrow I'd be saying whatever McPhee told me to.

When they flashed to the demonstration again, it became apparent that the crowds were refusing to disperse, and they seemed to have taken advantage of the confusion to go around the police barrier and move into the narrow streets leading to the Courthouse. At eleven o'clock D.C. time they were still there, lighting candles and singing songs, and I was still watching them.

Around then a call came in on my personal line. I didn't recognize the voice.

"Is this James Sands? The husband of Anne Sands?"

"Yes."

"Hello, Mr. Sands. I'm Dr. Steven Herman, at Harborview Medical Center."

I felt the way I had when they'd started shooting that afternoon, like something was happening that wouldn't soon be forgiven. Dr. Herman went on with a sympathetic blandness, horrifying news laid down in words worn smooth by the day's toll of disaster. My wife had been injured in the demonstrations that afternoon. A bullet had hit her in the spine. She was still unconscious, in stable condition. A full recovery—well, it was too early to tell.

PART IV

THE RAGE

29

I left for Seattle immediately, taking the company jet and then sending it back from the airport. I told my bodyguard to stay at home, that I needed some privacy, and Walter called to talk me out of going alone. He desisted in the face of my silence.

The hospital corridors had their usual clutter of stainless steel and Formica, the doorways filled with reclining bodies and putty-colored plastic curtains, burnished into shabbiness by the constant presence of pain and worry. My wife was sleeping when I arrived. She'd been sleeping since they brought her in, dumbed under by drugs for a five-hour operation. I wondered if she'd found out how badly she'd been damaged before she'd gone under. Tina stuck in Europe somewhere, unreachable. Joshua available only as a snide recording on a voice mail. Where was he? The doctor came out, a weary-looking Jew with black curly hair and an East Coast accent, and I had a strong desire to tell him about my Talmud-scholar grandfather, to establish some kinship in this impersonal hallway. Where was Joshua?

Dr. Herman shook my hand, briefly clasped my shoulder as he explained her X-rays, and the shattered necklace of vertebrae on them. "The bullet punctured her spleen," he went on, and I nearly fainted, coming back just in time to hear the word *spleenectomy*. I'd already contacted a specialist in D.C., and I instructed Dr. Herman to send him copies of everything. It made me feel better, like I was taking charge of the situation, but at the same time, I realized it was a situation where no one was in charge except the mysterious forces in Anne's body that would either heal her or fall short, with or without Cascadia and the Fund and all the other entities I'd regarded as the unimpeachable rulers of my life until a few hours ago. As we talked I looked past him to my wife, lying on her stomach with her head to the side and her long gray hair cut short. I sat down beside her to watch her sleep, my beautiful wife, the wrinkles at the outside corner of her eyes looking deep and irreversible below her aqua hospital cap. Without her smile, without her beautifully incised eyes and eyebrows and the fluid way that she moved, she was defenseless against her age, and she looked ten years older than the last time I'd seen her. I'd brought a family portrait taken a few years ago and propped it on her night table so she could see it when she woke up. On the wall hung cheerful pictures, drawn by grade-school children in the hapless symphony of shapes and colors of those who were not bound by reality, and I envied them.

I sat there two hours, finally reaching Tina boarding a shuttle flight to Lisbon. We had a short tearful conversation about Anne's spine; then she had to switch off until she arrived in London. My brother and my sister-in-law reached me, and it soothed me a bit to be able to be the one to dispense details, as if I were their proprietor instead of just their servant. My sister-in-law would get here tomorrow afternoon on a commercial flight. And in between all the conversations, the mutterings of the doctors in the hallway, the periodic visits of the nurse to look at gauges and make notations on charts, I was wondering where the hell Joshua was.

Somewhere around ten o'clock a young woman appeared in the doorway, then stopped short. She had long dark hair and a Mediterranean or Middle Eastern face, tall, robust, dressed in a long white cable-knit sweater and jeans. She was carrying a raincoat that had a bright orange stain on it, like the dye used to mark trees to be cut down. A strange look crossed her face, and she froze there, bobbing her head back imperceptibly, as if she'd just opened a container of spoiled food. I'd seen that expression before.

"I'm sorry. I didn't know there was anyone here."

There was something familiar about her, but I couldn't place her immediately. I stood up and put out my hand. "I'm Jim Sands. I'm Anne's husband."

She took my hand almost reluctantly. "I'm Emily Cortright." She glanced around, as if checking for retainers or bodyguards, then looked back to me.

I recognized her then. This was the woman who'd opposed me for so many years when I'd been getting established in Seattle, whom I had seen on television earlier that day. "I saw you on television," I said stupidly.

"I've seen you on the television, too." I must have blanched, because her next words were warmer. "How is Anne?"

"She's stable. The bullet damaged her spine and they took out her spleen. It's too early to tell very much." I felt my voice faltering. "The X-ray was pretty scary. A lot of, uh, spinal cord damage."

Her mouth opened halfway and she looked for a moment like she might cry, then she stepped forward and took my hand in both of hers. An acrid chemical smell came from her clothes. "I am so sorry, Mr. Sands. I am really, really sorry."

I was stranded there, looking into her dark eyes. "It's, uh . . . I guess it's one of those things that happens. Not really anybody's fault. Right?" I shrugged at my helplessness, at the sheer stupidity of what I'd just said, and suddenly my eyes started to fill up. She put her hand on my shoulder and then I felt the moisture running down my face and that spasmodic shuddering in my chest, which I tried to cover up by coughing. I turned to the side and wiped my eyes. "I'm sorry."

"You have nothing to apologize about."

Another loaded statement that I had to studiously ignore. In this situation, everything seemed to be laden with ponderous ironies, starting with the Corporate Bad Guy meeting his nemesis at the worst moment of his life. Neither of us knew what to say.

"How do you know my wife?"

"I work for the DNN, and she's been a supporter of our group. Your wife is a great woman."

"I know."

"I was with Anne at the demonstration today."

"You were?" It was strange to find out my wife had been marching alongside one of my staunchest opponents, but Anne's injury had eclipsed everything that had formerly thrown the light and shadow in my world, and it was more important at the moment to try to construct some reasonable chain of events around this disaster. That's what rational people do; we try to build a structure that contains things, and my old one wasn't working so well anymore. "What happened?"

"She wanted to be near a friend, since she doesn't know anyone in Seattle. We were trying to move the crowd back from the police lines when things got crazy. That's why she was in the line of fire."

"Did you see her—?"

"No. We were separated."

I had noticed that the area above her cheekbone was darkened. "You look like you got hurt, too."

She reached up and touched the bruise on her face. "Oh, this?" She shrugged. "It's minor. I got the backswing of someone's billy club, then I banged my head on the pavement. They were holding me for observation upstairs."

"I saw the riot on TV. It looked pretty savage."

A touch of weary belligerence came into her voice. "Twenty-six dead. A few hundred injured. So far. I'd call that savage." She glanced off to the side. "A lot of people have been pushing for a crackdown on the civil groups." Directly into my eyes: "They got it."

I felt like I'd been punched in the gut. I rifled around my foggy brain for the counterargument that society had a right to orderly streets, but this wasn't a talk show and I didn't have whatever it took to defend myself at that moment.

"I'm sorry," she said at last. "That was inappropriate."

No, I thought. *It's appropriate.* But I couldn't concede that. "I understand."

"You should know that they targeted us. One of our coordinators was hit in the ear with a rubber bullet. He's over at Swedish Hospital. The other was hit in the neck with one of those wooden things that shatter into little discs on impact. She's upstairs. They had snipers shooting, too. We have pictures of them. A lot of them were Whitehall. Your friends."

I raised my hands in front of me. "I can't have this discussion right now."

"You're right," she said. "There's been enough pain today." It became awkward. "Well, I just wanted to check on Anne." She stopped and gazed down at the bed for a few seconds, then noticed the picture I'd set up and moved closer to it. "Is this your family?"

"Yes. That's my son and daughter."

She took another step until she was leaning over Anne, staring down at the photo. Then her head rocked back, as if she were surprised at something. She spoke with a strange alarm in her voice. "This is your son?"

"Yes. That's Joshua. He lives in San Francisco. Have you met him?"

She picked up the photo and held it close to her face, with her back to me. "No," she said at last. Then, wonderingly: "He looks a lot like someone I know." She put it down, but she seemed fidgety. She glanced back down at my wife, and at the picture again, and then at me. She motioned toward the photo and said overbrightly: "And that's your daughter!" Anne must told her about Joshua, about how he despised what I did. We stood there uncomfortably for about ten seconds; then she started up on a fresh tack. "You know, Mr. Sands. We've been adversaries for a long time. My group has opposed your company on several issues."

"I know that."

"I think . . . It might be a good thing to talk. You and I. Maybe we can resolve some . . . issues. I mean between my organization and your company."

I could tell she was running some sort of game, but I had no idea what. Maybe they were ready to cut a deal, one of those corporate–NGO alliances where they came out and endorsed us. The PR on that was like gold, and it would surprise the hell out of the bastards at McPhee/Collins. I felt like I was back on familiar ground. "I don't want to be away from Anne for too long, but how about tomorrow, for lunch?"

"I'm going to be at the demonstration tomorrow."

"That's still on?"

She looked at me in amazement. "I don't think you understand, Mr. Sands. People want their vote." She reached into her backpack.

"Here's my card. I'd like to meet with you first thing tomorrow morning, if that's okay. There's a restaurant called Thirteen Coins downtown. Does seven thirty work for you?"

I felt suddenly buoyant. I'd returned to the world of doing and making, like a superhero that had temporarily lost and then regained his powers. I was in the mood to go into the lion's den. "Why don't I just come to your office?"

She gave me a funny look, then said, "Our office is bugged and we're under surveillance." She hesitated a couple of seconds. "As I'm sure you know."

I reared back at her accusation, shamed that she had made it and shamed because it was true. My brief good mood fell to pieces.

"I really don't want to be confrontational, Mr. Sands. But the things I'd like to talk to you about are intensely private and intensely serious, so it's probably best if we try to be as honest as we can with each other. Otherwise I'm afraid there's going to be a lot more sadness."

It sounded almost like a warning, but just then Anne stirred and gave a tiny humming moan. I looked down at her pale face, bent down close to her and said her name softly a few times, hoping she might come to. She settled back into her darkness and I straightened up and turned back to Emily. "Half past seven. Thirteen Coins. I'll be there."

Walter had been calling all evening, and I finally answered him. It was three in the morning in Washington.

"Jim! Thanks so much for picking up! I know you need privacy, but I've been worried sick about you and Anne. How is she?"

Anne had never liked Walter, and I suspected he knew that, but at times like this one tried to transcend old scores. "It's not good, but she's stable."

"Thank goodness. I took the liberty of putting McFee on it so the media doesn't make an awful thing even worse. They can damp it down for a few days till we get it all sorted out."

Thinking of Anne lying unmoving in her bed with her spine severed, I couldn't see how we were ever going to get this "sorted out," but I took it for what it was worth. "Thanks, Walter."

"We also talked to the hospital and Dr. Herman. I think they see the virtue of not releasing your wife's name to the media. Just use your personal cell phone and don't respond to any reporters if they track you down. In a few days they'll move on."

"Thanks, Walter."

"Has she regained consciousness yet?"

"No. Maybe tomorrow."

"Jim, I'm so sorry this happened."

For the moment, it was pleasant not to deal with the reality of the situation: that my wife had left me to march against everything Walter and I stood for, and that, in fact, I didn't dare ask him how he really felt about the day's bloodshed. For the moment, Walter and I were happy to bask in this cozy little fantasy of the ailing wife and the friend of the family.

He finished the script perfectly. "I understand you need privacy right now, but let us know when you want us to resume the security routine."

"Okay."

For the first time his voice sounded uncertain, as if he, too, was negotiating some unseen trial. "Hang in there, my friend. I'm praying for you and Anne."

The warmth and doubt in his voice melted me, and I was overwhelmed for a second by a wave of affection for the man. "I will."

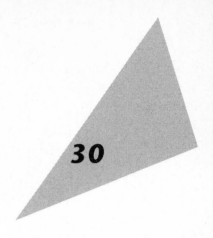

30

I tried to call Lando six times that night. I was desperate to speak with him about his mother, his family, about the proposal I was going to make to his father. I wanted to just sit back with him and say, "Wow!" just, "Wow, Lando, I can't *believe* that you are James Sands's son!" He'd always flickered in and out of my life, never quite the same person twice in a row. Lando, delinquent saint and punk hero. Lando, the poor little rich kid in the thrift store overcoat. Now he had finally become real. I could recognize his mother's features in his face, I knew about his parents' marriage problems. I wished that we could hide out for a quiet weekend and just talk and talk and talk until everything was unraveled and we found our way to what was true.

But it seemed I was in this all alone for now: For the first time he didn't pick up or call me back. I reached the Apex near midnight, and the common room on my floor was buzzing with eight other tenants. Several of them had seen the shootings from up close, and there was a weird hushed feeling, like the silence after a hammer blow. We were all wondering if this was the beginning of something bigger that we weren't really sure we were ready for. Dave had been arrested, or injured, or maybe both. One rumor was that he was in a military hospital. Another was that the Security forces had grabbed him and were holding him incommunicado. I gave my version of the day's events, leaving out everything about James Sands and his wife, then borrowed a friend's laptop to try Lando from a source less likely to be tapped. No luck.

I returned messages until three in the morning, trying to piece together what came next, checking with our media liaisons, our legal team, calling my parents to tell them I was okay. The tally on our side: Joe Simic in jail, Shar in the hospital, Dan in intensive care, half our staff put away, carefully targeted for arrest by plainclothes cops as soon as the violence started. I'd probably escaped because I'd left in an ambulance. The demonstrators had broken out of the Stadium area and gotten as far as Columbia Street, where they were camped now around candles and bonfires made of scavenged debris, waiting out the night until the next push. Despite the brutality, our people in the street had conceded nothing. Someone had gotten it together to bring food around, and I was proud that even with the supposed "ringleaders" out of the picture, the Network had stepped up and kept things going. To my amazement, all the phone lists and e-mail groups were still functioning, and already a new strategy was being stitched together around the loose idea of continuing toward the Courthouse the next morning. On top of that, organizations all over the country were organizing vigils and solidarity marches to protest what had happened in Seattle. At three, I decided I'd done enough for the night and turned off the light.

Even then I couldn't sleep. I lay there bumping down the dark streambed of the small hours, nudged by the images of the day, by thoughts of Lando and James Sands, of Anne. I kept seeing the back swing of the police baton, the image of Joe Simic after he was hit by orange marking dye. Sometimes, thinking of the police and the clubbing, my heart would start pounding, and other times I would end up wishing I could be with Lando again in his white white bedroom on that perfect snowy morning, when he'd been my boyfriend with tea and toast. At five I drifted off with that luxurious thought, and almost immediately the alarm woke me to go and meet with Joshua Sands's father.

He was already there when I arrived, dressed in a sweater and a brown shearling jacket. It's hard, in that situation, not to try him on as your future father-in-law, and to wonder if this is the way your lover will be thirty years from now. He was a tall man with big bones and thick eyebrows that matched his once-black hair. He was slightly barrel-chested, the way men often get in middle age. I could see that Lando took after his mother, with her smaller, more delicate frame and fine features, but as we talked I kept looking for that trace of Lando in him. I thought I saw it in his air of decisiveness and competence. He definitely seemed like the kind of man who could run a huge corporation. Or a guerrilla group, for that matter. He already had a cup of coffee in front of him, and he rose to smile at me and extend his hand.

"How is Anne?" I asked him.

His cheeriness flickered. "She's still out, but she's stable."

"I'm glad to hear that." At least we were starting off with some common ground, although in reality we had more common ground than he could possibly imagine. I almost thought he sensed it, though, when he asked that I call him Jim, and chivalrously flagged the waitress to order me a cup of tea.

The 13 Coins was an odd restaurant of high black leatherette booths and curtains of metal beads, with a stately sort of kitsch that reminded me of Las Vegas. The height of the booths gave them a degree of privacy, as you could see the occupants only if you were standing right next to the table. Lando's father had chosen one in the back corner.

"I appreciate your meeting with me," he started out. "I know we've been on opposite sides of the table in the past."

With all the hidden identities buzzing around in my head, it was hard to engage on the one-seventh of the iceberg that was showing. I took refuge in the menu for a half minute, but it turned out we'd both eaten before we'd come, so we folded up the big leatherette cards and put them down. He started the conversation. He was curious about how his wife had gotten involved with us, since we were so far away from their home, and I told him how she'd appeared in my office the day Franklin Seven had been assassinated.

He flinched slightly at the word *assassinated,* as opposed to, I guess, *brought to justice,* but he didn't want to contest it. Instead he glanced down at the table and then back up at me, smiling bashfully. "There are not too many groups she could have chosen that have opposed me more persistently and effectively than yours."

It was a compliment, in a way, and an admission. I decided to put it all out there. "She mentioned that she didn't like what your business had become. I know you two had your differences."

The discomfort wavered across his face and he answered with a slightly sullen tone. "It seems you know all about me and I know very little about you."

"I'm sorry. I didn't mean to put you on the defensive. I'm just trying to get to the heart of things quickly, because we have very little time. We can't do the 'I'm an Organizer and you're a CEO' thing. We just have to be two people." He considered it, nodding. I thought of Lando, and a flash of paranoia came over me. "You're not wearing any sort of listening device, are you?"

He was annoyed, then ironic. "No, I'm not wearing a listening device. You know, it's possible I'm not the monster you think I am."

"I'm sorry, but I can't take any chances, for both our sakes." I waited for any last-minute change of heart, then went on. "Should we start?"

He lifted his hand from the table to signal he was ready.

"I've read that Whitehall handles your security."

His personable air became slightly too-polished as he turned into the Corporate director again, just like that. "Whitehall is a big company. They handle a lot of people's security."

"I know, but Water Solutions is one of their clients, isn't it?"

"That's public knowledge."

"And what exactly does a company like Whitehall do for a company like yours when they provide Security?"

He sounded like he was making an appearance at a high school careers fair. "Well, they manage computer security, sometimes through an outside contractor, and they develop protocols for keeping our information safe. And of course they also protect the physical facilities, like offices and water plants. And in some cases, they protect the principals and their families."

"You mean bodyguards."

"Yes."

"Do you have a bodyguard with you in Seattle?"

He thought about it, then answered with a faint exasperation. "No! I dropped my protection when I came out here. I wanted some privacy, for obvious reasons."

We both stopped talking as a waitress seated a couple with a baby in the booth behind us. James Sands gazed at the child with that simple, joyful smile that babies so often inspire. In that moment I felt sorry for him. I saw a man who imagined he was at the top of his game, but was finding out how close and how deep the abyss really was. He put his guard up again. "You were asking about Whitehall. Why?"

I glanced at the booths around us. "Can we go for a little walk?"

He put some money on the table and we left. It wasn't a cold day for October, but it was wet and gray and I could feel the tiny tingling drops of rain hit my face as I walked. We weren't in a particularly nice area: a sort of sparse low-grade commercial zone with several empty storefronts testifying to the economic collapse. We strolled past a bankrupt clothing store that had left its skinny naked mannequins in the window. Yellowed maple leaves lay plastered against the sidewalk by the rain. James Sands waited for me to begin.

"Jim . . ." It was weird to use his name, weird that I was talking to the CEO of one of America's most hated Corporations. "We have evidence that Whitehall's hired themselves out as a private counterterrorism operation. Do you know anything about that?"

"I know they're contractors to the government—"

"I don't mean the Government. I'm talking about Corporations paying a fee for a secret program against the Militants and against the Civil Groups."

"I've seen allegations of that in the press."

"Anne told me you were involved in it."

He stopped walking, and his anger overwhelmed his professional façade. "She did! Well, that's news to me!"

"She told me that Water Solutions and other companies are funding Whitehall to kidnap or kill Militants, and to spy on groups like ours. And she said they're working with the McPhee/Collins public relations firm to discredit the opposition to the Matthews Administration."

A mixture of expressions crossed his face: a tinge of fear, the petulance of a child that's been caught. "Is this what you called me away from my wife's bedside for?"

"I'm asking you to go public about this Program. People need to know and they need to hear it from the source."

He took on a sour look that didn't quite become a smile. "Is this the deal you were offering me? I come clean about some program and in return . . . What? You pin a medal on me? You say nice things about me in the press?" He gave a tough little laugh. "No thank you, young lady! I think I'll pass." He glanced toward the restaurant, where his car was, then raised his eyebrows at me with a sudden fake gaiety. "Good try, though!" He started walking back.

I was angry at the way he'd put on his CEO mantle and blown me off, as if he was above having to answer to me or anyone else outside his group. "Where are you going?"

He said over his shoulder, "That's it. We're done."

I took a few quick steps and suddenly I was directly in front of him, furious. "Don't you walk away from me! I'm not finished, and you don't know anything! You're not some high-class executive to me: You're just a negligent father who's so self-involved that he won't even speak up to get his son off Whitehall's death list!"

He stared for a few moments, confused, then edged toward me, intense. "What are you saying?"

"Your son is a Militant! He carries a gun, he blows things up. And you can be absolutely sure that when your little Program catches up with him they'll kill him just like they killed Franklin Seven."

He stopped, his mouth hanging open from whatever he'd been about to say, his head waving slightly. It took him some ten seconds to grapple with the shock and spit out an answer.

"That's bullshit!"

"You know it's not."

"That's bullshit!" he shouted.

"Do you really think he's designing Web sites in San Francisco? Does he ever answer his phone? Does he have a work number you can reach him at? Did you ever try?"

His eyes were desperate as the pieces kept coming together and falling apart again. "Did Anne tell you this?" He changed suddenly from confused to imperious. "I need to see some proof!" he said quickly. "You can't just drop something like that on me without any proof!" He took out his phone and pressed a button, looking at me as he did. "I'm calling him right now!" He cursed and switched it off after a few seconds. "He never answers his goddamned phone!"

"Because it's a phony number! He's not *in* San Francisco."

"Where is he? Here?" I didn't answer and he shook his head back and forth, looking at the ground. "What kind of goddamned mess has he made this time?" He tried to get control of the situation again. "Okay. If this is true, can you put me in touch with him? I mean—" His voice caught. "—his mother's been hurt and he won't even pick up the phone!"

"Mr. Sands, if you want to help your son the best thing you can do is to go public about Whitehall and get their Program shut down."

When he heard that, a layer of pretense fell away. "People have already gone public. I've seen it in the media."

"Nobody on your level. If you say it, if you give a detailed account of what you know, and you name names and give details, it will help people realize what's really happening in this country."

He gazed down at the shining black asphalt, then seemed to reverse himself again. "You're . . . Even if what you said was true . . . Even if I had all sorts of information about what you say Whitehall is doing, do you think my voice would make a difference? The dirty little secret is this, Emily: Nobody in this country really cares what Whitehall does. They want to go on living in their own little world and they don't care what it takes to keep that world intact."

"A quarter million people yesterday would disagree with you."

"See, you operate on the belief that a bunch of people marching around with signs makes a bit of difference to this government. Believe me, they don't. I know that firsthand."

"Then why'd they shoot a couple of hundred demonstrators yesterday to keep them from getting to the Courthouse? Because they didn't care? Why'd they shoot your wife?"

"Don't drag Anne into this!"

"She's already in it! And so is your son! You're just like all those people you have so much contempt for: You want to believe there's no danger to Joshua, because then you don't have to make a choice. You can go on living in your own world, with your friends and your business and your status."

The anger left him all of a sudden and he seemed to take everything back within himself. He gave a long sigh. "Where is he? Is he here in Seattle?"

I went around the question. I had to make my proposal now. "If you could see your son, and he told you he was in danger and asked you to come forward about Whitehall's Program, would you do it?" He hesitated, so I went on. "To save your son's life! Would you do it?"

His eyes were on me but I knew his mind was somewhere else, tripping through a million calculations. "I'd consider it."

"You'd *consider* it." I shook my head. "That's one of the saddest things I've ever heard."

He collapsed into silence, gazing into the window of the bankrupt clothing store. At last he spoke quietly. "I'll consider it. Please, put me in touch with him."

He looked old then, like a tired, troubled shopkeeper at the end of a long day, and his day was just beginning. I reached over and touched his shearling-covered arm. His beautiful wife was badly hurt and his son was being hunted by professional killers. The *Happy* was burning right in front of him and he couldn't even rouse himself enough to pour water on it. "Keep your afternoon free, Jim. I'll do what I can."

I called an old college friend who lived in Rainier Valley, a quiet open neighborhood that afforded long view planes down the wide streets of an old postwar suburb. After that I dialed Lando's number. It rang several times; then, to my amazement, he answered.

"Eagle Maintenance. Ben speaking."

I felt like laughing and crying at the same time. "Lando!"

There was a pause. "I'm sorry, I can barely hear you, ma'am. Where are you calling from?"

I tried to read something in his voice but it was all cordial professionalism. I looked around. "I'm near Capitol Hill." I remembered our little code. "There's some liquid sunshine here. Maybe that's affecting your reception."

"Did you want to set up an appointment for an estimate?"

"Yes. Yes, I do. I have a . . . My, uh, my house on Meade Street, in Rainier Valley. The sink is leaking. Can you be here in an hour?"

There was something in the timbre of his voice I hadn't heard before. An exhaustion, or a weakness. "I'm sorry. We're swamped today. We've had some unexpected setbacks."

"It's urgent. It's really urgent!" I gave him the address. "Please!"

The silence went on so long, I was afraid he'd hung up, or that my phone had gone dead. Finally he answered in a tired voice, "We'll do our best, ma'am."

My friend and her husband had one of those 1940s houses with a giant porch out front and big picture windows that let the sunshine in on wide oriental carpets. I was struck by the comfortable normalcy of it: the big leather couch and the Guatemalan handicrafts. Somewhere people were living happy comfortable lives, with cats and plants and organic honey. I envied my friends, with their long bookshelves filled with fiction and history. They were sane, compassionate people, raising their children to be good citizens. They didn't want to be involved in politics—they had little time for meetings and they hated demonstrations—but they always showed up when they were asked to. If it became known that I was using their house to meet with a member of a "terrorist organization," they would likely lose everything.

I was too nervous to eat, but I heated up some water and sat with tea by the big front window, watching the street for Lando. Now that things were almost in motion, I was getting nervous about my plan. No one in Lando's group had been caught yet, so one little meeting would probably be an acceptable risk, but Lando had sounded different over the phone. What if his father was lying about the bodyguards, or gave away some clue to Whitehall by accident? And if Lando got caught from all this, would it be worth it? Was my agenda more important than his life? It was a scary question, and none of the answers were very comforting.

He arrived after about twenty minutes, wearing coveralls and carrying a small backpack. He was wearing a black wig and horn-rim glasses. I closed the door behind him and then pinned him against it, hugging him.

He held on to me without saying anything for a long time. I could tell by the intensity of his grip that he knew about his mother, about the massacre. Even after I wanted to let go and talk, he held on to me. My face was filled with the tickling black hairs and dusty odor of his black wig.

"Are you okay?" I asked him.

"No," he said quietly. "I'm not okay. What happened to your face?"

"It's nothing. I ran into a club at the demonstration." I hugged him tighter and murmured without thinking: "I'm so sorry about your mother."

His body stiffened suddenly and he pulled back. "What do you mean?"

I realized then that he hadn't heard, that he had no idea that I knew who his parents were. "Your mother," I stumbled. "Anne."

He pushed me suddenly away and his face became filled with suspicion. "How do you know my mother?"

His fury surprised me. "It . . . It just happened. She came into our office and made a donation. But I didn't know. Then, at the hospital, when I met your father—"

"My father?" He turned from me and put his fingertips to his forehead. "Oh my God!" He scrunched his eyes shut. "Oh my *fucking* God. It was you!"

"Lando! What is it?"

I tried to put my arms around him but he twisted away, and his anger moved him around the room in a furious little dance. "That's great, Emily! You got your wish: You finally ID'd me! Clever you!" He suddenly rushed over to the little window in the door and peered out onto the street. "Where'd that white car come from? That wasn't here three minutes ago!"

Now he was making me panic. "Lando, what is it? What happened?"

He didn't look away from the window. "What happened? Tonk is dead! Okay?" He turned on me. "But don't worry about that! That's my problem, right?" He lifted up his hands in fake jubilation. "You ID'd me!"

"Lando, I had no idea! She just came into my office. That day they killed Franklin Seven—"

"Shit shit *shit*!" He grabbed his forehead again, closing his eyes. "It's my fault! I got him killed! I never should have . . ." He looked at me with disgust. "Goddammit!"

He suddenly reached into his coveralls and took out a dull black pistol. It frightened me. His voice had the quiet urgent tone of a maniac. "Come here!" He pulled me to him. "Stay here and watch for any movement. Yell if you see anything. Do it now! Do it now, Emily! Don't fail me!"

He glanced around the hall to get his bearings then rushed up the stairway toward the back of the house. I watched outside, my heart pounding. The street was quiet. The white car had been there since I'd arrived that morning. There was silence; then I heard the ceiling creak as he moved quickly from one side of the house to the other. Nothing happened outside, but my heart was knocking as if I'd just run a marathon. "Lando!" I called out. "That white car was there when I got here! Do you hear me? It was already there!"

I heard his footsteps returning and he came down the carpeted stairs, slowly, his face neutral beneath the black wig. He put the pistol away as he approached me, then he stood there for a few seconds before he spoke. "Why did you say you were sorry about my mother?"

I was afraid to touch him, but I stretched my arm out and rested my hand on his shoulder. "Your mother was shot at the demonstration yesterday. She's in the hospital. I thought you knew."

His eyes widened and he swayed backwards a little bit, staring at me as if this might be some sort of trick. "How bad is it?"

"She's in intensive care. There's some damage to her spine." I tried to soften it. "Maybe it will be okay." He was nodding slowly, and I went on. "I thought you knew because your father left a bunch of messages."

"Believe it or not, Emily, I haven't been checking my messages in the last day or so. I've been too busy watching people get killed." He probably meant to sound acid, but his words had a weak, defeated tone to them that disturbed me. He gave a long sigh. "I'm sorry, Emily. I need to know more about how you met my parents. A lot of bad shit's been happening."

"What happened?"

"First answer my question: When did you meet my parents?"

I told him how his mother had joined our group, and about the demonstration. "I went to visit her when they discharged me, and your father was there. He'd put a picture of your family next to her bed and I recognized you."

"A picture of the family," he said. "That's so fitting." He shook his head at the floor, muttering to himself. "So this was last night. Okay. That's after, so it wasn't that meeting. And if it was you, they'd already be here."

"What do you mean, Lando? What happened?"

He sighed again. "I just need to sit down and be quiet for a few minutes. Okay?"

He looked around but couldn't seem to decide on anyplace to rest, so he leaned backwards against the wall and slid to the floor. I sat down next to him. "Lando, talk to me."

He looked straight ahead. "I saw two people get killed yesterday. First it was Earl E., the guy that asked you for help after the Siskiyou thing."

"What happened? Who killed him?"

"We did."

I didn't know what to say. After a long pause he went on in a heavy voice that made him sound all used up. "Whitehall liquidated his whole crew and Earl E. was the last one left. He was tweaked. He wanted to shoot some brownshirts at the demonstration. He felt like Whitehall was a legitimate target. I didn't, and we knew that shooting into a crowd could make them panic and open up on the demonstrators, so I went to talk him out of it." His voice rose a notch. "And that went over like shit!" He stopped to collect himself. "Then one of our guys got overeager and blew him away before I even knew what was happening." He tried to smile. "And wouldn't you know it, they massacred them anyway!" His voice became low and uneven, a croak. "Including my mother!"

I thought he was going to break down, but he managed to keep it together. After a while he gave another long sigh and started in a calmer voice. "So then I went back to where Tonk was waiting for me, at the Market, and just as I'm getting there I notice the fish guy is different, and there's garbage guys in the middle of the day. I look around and see it's all a *trap*! They were all over him." He began to quaver again, sniffing a couple of times. "And Tonk is sitting there drinking coffee out of a paper cup, and I just . . . I don't even have a way to warn him! I mean, they're moving as soon as I figure it out, and then he comes flying out through the glass door, and they're trying to tackle him and just when he's breaking away—" His voice became high and thin and his face contorted. "—some asshole just blasts him, and Tonk goes down, and he lands looking right at me, right fucking at me! He sees I'm there and I don't know what he's thinking, and I'm just . . . I can't do *anything*!"

He dropped into a deep, unseeing silence, hugging his knees, and finally saying quietly, "So I turned around . . . and walked away."

I moved close to him and put my arms around him as best I could. He managed to compose himself and go on in a thin voice. "And then I call Sarah, and she's in deep shit, and Gonzalo is gone or busted—I have no idea—and I can't even go back to my house to get a change of clothes."

He pulled away from me. "You know, I used to want to save this country, but now I hate this country. I hate its stupidity and its greed, its laziness. Its two-faced morality! These people deserve a Dictator!"

"You've lost faith, Lando, and I under—"

"I have lost the faith, goddammit! I put my faith in the People, and that was a mistake! This is a shit people! They get stolen blind by their politicians and they lick their boots. They send their kids off to die for somebody's business deal and they celebrate it like they're doing something heroic! This *great* and *glorious* People! Lazy sacks of junk food and jingo!" The tears come to his eyes again. "*Fuck* America! *Fuck* this shit country and its shit people! *Fuck* this stiff-necked nation of cowards! I'm going to enjoy watching this country go all the way down, because that's what they deserve!" He wipes his eyes dry with the back of his sleeve. "I mean, what am I doing? The goddamned brownshirts are killing my friends, they're after my ass—and I'm fighting to save . . . who? People who cheer when they shoot demonstrators? People who, if you give them a choice between cheap gasoline and saving a thousand endangered species, will choose cheap gas *over* and *over* and *over* again? What the fuck was I thinking!" The tears came again and then he barked, "I don't want to die for these people!"

I'd never heard him afraid before, and it made his death suddenly close and terrifying. I hugged him as if that could somehow protect him, and he went on in a ragged painful voice. "It's over, Emily! Democracy's run its course in this country, just like in Rome. The Republic is over."

I held on to him without saying anything. Mistaken as they were, he and his friends had hung it all out there for a magnificent principle, and they were paying a terrible price for everyone else's apathy. I finally spoke to him as calmly as I could, saying what I so often had to remind myself of when things got dark. "It's not over, Lando.

There's always greedy, abusive people who want more, and Democracy only exists because other people come forward to stop them. Temporarily." I smiled at him even though he was staring down between his feet. "So it's a little too early to give up."

I meant it, but what I really wanted was to escape the relentless demands of that better world, even for a few minutes—to hold some part of it, now. I squeezed his arm. "Hey. Come with me."

I led him up the stairs to my friends' guest bedroom. The walls were lined with books, and Lando looked them over and said with a trace of his former self, "Wow! The last of the readers! I'll bet these people can, like, name the three branches of Government and find Ohio on a map. Elite stuff."

"Just forget about all that. And could you please take off that wig?"

He turned from the books and gave a sad little smile. "Pictures are winning."

"Don't worry." I tugged at the wig until I'd uncovered his short brown hair again. "I am personally going to kick Pictures' ass. And that's a promise." He brightened up at my blustering. I was glad to get rid of the panicked faithless figure in the black hairpiece and find the man I knew, the one in the photo on his mother's night table.

I put my arms around him and he ran his hands down my body, kissing me. I started to undress him and he fell on me like he was a drowning man grabbing on to dry land. We kissed for a long time. I think we both wanted to somehow make things last. It was slow and melancholy, stretched out like the kind of light that comes in late afternoon on a summer day. We looked in each others' eyes as we made love, an intimacy that was almost embarrassing, and then everything reached its height and I rocked back and we tumbled all the way down to that warm hidden place where everything became dark and pulsing, far far down at the bottom of the ocean, where life began.

The room started filling in again, with its books and its Matisse poster and the light fixture on the ceiling with its hairline crack. I felt a faint spasm go through Lando's body, like a tiny sob, and hugged him tighter without asking him to explain anything. I wasn't sure if it was about his friends or his mother or his whole ruined family. It passed, and he became still and held me quietly from behind. He said: "Which picture was it?"

I knew what he meant. "It was your family in some sort of garden."

"Yeah, I know that one. They flew my sister and me in for my parents' twenty-fifth anniversary. My father took that picture right away, and an hour later we got into a big blowout about the Regime, which of course became a blowout about me, and I left the next morning. A really great anniversary celebration. Then, a month later, my mother sends me that photo in a nice gold frame, like we'd spent the whole weekend in a greeting card." He was quiet as he thought about it. "We've all got our pictures, I guess, even my mother. Maybe there's no escape. Maybe we spend our whole lives drawing one picture after another." He rolled over and stared at the ceiling. "I can't even go visit her." He seemed to spiral back downward into another dark silence; then he said, "I'm not going to see you again for a long time, Emily. I'm leaving Seattle. In fact, I'm leaving the country. I was on my way to Canada when you called, then Europe."

"You were?"

"Yeah. I'll come back when things settle down. That's our security protocol."

I rolled over as the last buzzing of our lovemaking disappeared. I hadn't told him my plan yet. Now was the time. "It's just . . ." I hesitated. Could I really go through with this, knowing what had happened to his friends in the last twenty-four hours? "I was going to ask you to do something. Something really important." I propped myself up on my elbow.

"What is it?"

Even as I spoke, part of me was screaming that I should drop the whole thing. The other part, the organizer part, insisted that we needed to win. "Just listen. There's a lot of hearsay that Whitehall is running a secret Program against the Militants and the Civil Groups."

"It's not hearsay, it's truth."

"I know that, but there's no proof yet. Your mother told us that your father is involved in it. That's why he's in the Media all the time denouncing the Civil Groups. It's part of his package with Whitehall." I repeated what Anne had said about the Program. "I talked to your father this morning. I asked him to go public about it."

"I'll bet he was all over that opportunity."

"He was too surprised at being confronted about it to make a decision. But I think he's starting to get it."

"Having his wife shot in the spine isn't enough to get it?"

"I think you could convince him."

He didn't answer immediately. "As Lando or as Joshua?"

"Both." I braced myself for his anger. "I already told him you're a Militant. I thought it was something he should know if he's hiring people to kill Militants."

His voice became sharp. "Did you tell him I'm in the Army of the Republic?"

"No! And I didn't tell him you're in Seattle. But he said he'd consider going public if he could meet with you."

"He'd 'consider' it." He rolled onto his back. "Gee, thanks, Dad." He didn't move for a long time. "Well," he said quietly, "we are sort of getting into the endgame here, aren't we?"

"I wouldn't put it like that."

"I would."

"Lando!"

"You're right. I don't have the luxury of being fatalistic. My friends didn't die so I could give up." He turned to me again. "The problem is, they're all over us. I don't know if we were infiltrated, or somebody rolled, or what, but if I've hit their radar as Joshua Sands, meeting with my father would be suicidal."

The doubts I'd been having before welled up again, but I put them aside. "He said he's alone in Seattle."

"Yeah, and he's assuming he's in control of this gig. I don't. Right now it would be just about impossible for me to take effective security precautions. My half of the Army is all deep blue. You really think it's worth it?"

"I do! He's one of them, Lando. If he comes out about Whitehall's Program, and names names and says it loud and long and with authority, he could have a huge impact."

"Yeah, for about five minutes."

"No. That massacre yesterday really affected people. There are sympathy demonstrations going up all over the country, and it's not just our side. When people hear that these are Corporate death squads killing Americans, and attacking Citizen Groups, it's going to shock them, and then it's going to make them angry. Whitehall will have to stop their Program and legalize all their prisoners, including your friends. And that will just be the start."

"Saving my friends would make it worth it all by itself." He looked at me with a little half smile, as if he knew everything that had been going through my head since I'd first considered asking him to do this. He ran his hand from my ribs to my hip and then back up again, stroking me as he thought things over. "It's the only honorable choice for me, isn't it?" He rested his hand at the hollow of my waist for a second. "Just like you have no other choice but to ask me to do it. It's who we are."

I wanted to disagree with him, to pull him back from the danger, but I knew he was right. He and the Army of the Republic had broken the law because they held its administrators in contempt, but the Law still stood, over and above its perversion by the Regime. I had to stand with it, whatever the cost.

"Besides," he finally added, "I'd like to talk to my father. It's time."

He put his arms around me and we stayed there, our skin touching and our faces close together, eyes closed. I just tried to shut out everything and hold on to this one last peaceful moment. He dozed off for a few minutes; then I felt him jerk awake, his eyes wide open, fearful. "It's okay," I said softly, "I'm here."

He relaxed for a little while, then he seemed to gather himself up mentally. "We have a lot to do."

"Yeah," I said, "people are going to be wondering where I am."

Lando pushed himself up with a groan and reached for his underwear. "The escalator's always moving." He sensed that I was reluctant, and he patted me on my thigh. "Don't start being sad, because once you get started, there's no end to it, and we don't have time for that."

"I'm just afraid. I mean . . . I want us to have a future."

"Hey! We'll have one." He laughed. "We'll straighten out this bullshit and then you'll see me so much you'll get sick of me!" He tugged on his coveralls. "I'll need your help setting this up with my father. What are you doing this afternoon?"

"I was planning on going back downtown. They decided to keep pushing to the Courthouse, and I'm part of that."

He scribbled something on a scrap of paper. "Hang loose until two thirty this afternoon then call this number. I'll give you instructions. It'll probably take you an hour to line it out."

"Then what?"

"Then you head back downtown, of course. Didn't you promise me you were going to kick some Picture ass? I expect you to keep kicking." He checked in the mirror as he clipped on his wig and checked it with a shake of his head. "Lookin' sharp!" He was back to being Lando again. He turned from the mirror and grinned. "Don't worry, Emily. James Sands will go *huge,* and the whole world's going to hear him."

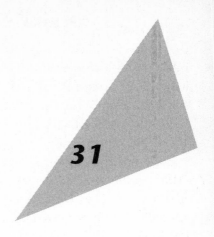

31

I'm straight now: even with the deadweight of my mother in the hospital and my comrades presently testing out Whitehall's new stress positions, I've turned down the static and my mind is clicking away. No time to disappear—there's work to do. By my count, we've lost Tonk and Sarah, probably Gonzalo, maybe his two techs, with Kahasi and Lilly now deeply deeply blue. The protocol is to get out the warning and go silent for six weeks, then begin again with the dead drops and dormant Internet accounts, slowly coax the Network back to life. Everyone has some money stashed: I pick up eight grand and a Glock stuffed into a dry bag up a tree on Whidbey Island, so I'm good for a couple months in Canada. But I've got things to do right now, and with everyone scattered, I only have one person left to call.

I pick up McFarland on a channel we've reserved for the apocalypse. Two clean cell phones, never used. I'm wondering if the High Plains guys have been swept.

"Negative. We haven't been touched."

"How did you hear about us?"

"Through San Francisco Mark, yesterday around three, by a secure line. And I got your message. We've been sweating it out here, but nothing's happened. Same with San Francisco. It looks like it's just you. How bad is it?"

"I think they got Gonzalo. Definitely Sarah. Tonk's dead. I'm sure Joby told you about Earl E."

"Yeah. I'm sorry that went down like that."

"Me, too, but I'm going to feel shitty about Earl E. later. We've got other problems right now. We owe it to Tonk and Earl E. to survive."

We've tried to keep all contacts with McFarland low tech—calls routed through phone cards, personal meetings. I'm the only gateway left to the High Plains guys, but with Gonzalo down, who knew what kind of electronic fingerprints might be smudged around the fiber-optic cocktail glass? Not to mention what Sarah might say. Rumors are that Whitehall is using some new low-amplitude wave technology that scrambles your insides but leaves your skin intact.

McFarland's not in a hurry to meet me, and I don't blame him. The fact that they hadn't grabbed me yet didn't mean I was in the clear. They might be tracking me now, hoping I'd expose another thread in the network.

"I already met with Rob." Our code name for Emily. "If they were on me, that would have been too choice a grab to pass up."

"Maybe," he said.

"I need your help with something, Mac. It's important."

He agrees to come into Seattle. It's risky, and I admire him for it. We figure out a playground in Greenwood, far north of the chaos the Civils are brewing downtown, God bless them. Riding the bus out, the massacre's the big show, and I watch it against the rolling backdrop of the calm cool suburbs and the mental image of my mother on a hospital bed. To my surprise it's not Channel America, not Hammer. Someone's turned the channel to the local station, a heretical universe where protesters aren't "Radicals" and dead people aren't perps. Maybe it's the bus driver, violating Metro rules, or somebody at headquarters. Maybe there were just too many relatives and friends with bullet wounds and club marks to turn their back on it and let the Corporates make it theirs. Somebody's pushed back, in one of the million little ways that are too widespread and decentralized for the Regime to control. In Regime gospel, it's "keeping the streets clear for lawful Citizens," but on this bus, at least, it's a massacre, with bootleg footage of women being beaten and shot, old people being sprayed in the face with CS foam, citizens on their knees being kicked senseless. A couple of Whitehall ops attack a cameramen. Another pins a teen against a car with his baton across the throat. Mixed in with all the gunplay, real-time of today's downtown. Whatever unspoken invitation went out, people are picking up on it and the Irregulars are on the move. There's crowds from sidewalk to sidewalk, banging pots and pans, thumping on drums. Black-clad tacticals and soldiers man barricades like the skirmish lines at Gettysburg.

I get off three blocks away and walk to the playground. A couple of kids are bundled up in bright winter clothes, climbing up the wrong way on a slide while their mother reads a magazine nearby. No revolution out here, and no sign of McFarland, but after five minutes he seems satisfied and comes ambling out in a Mariners cap and smoke-colored shooting glasses, leading a pit bull. He walks it over to me and I move forward to pet it. I notice the parent looking up to watch us.

"Nice dog."

"Stay on his good side. What's up?"

What's up is a big question, so I try to simplify it. "I need some Security for a meeting."

"Who with?"

"James Sands."

He smiled. "I didn't hear you right."

"James Sands. Of Water Solutions. I need to talk with him."

McFarland cocks his head, in a surprisingly good mood. "I can tell this is going to be interesting."

"Emily Cortright set this up. Evidently Sands is thinking of going public about Whitehall's Corporate repression program. He and Water Solutions are in, so he has the names and the pay stubs. If he goes on the record about the death squads and kidnappings and everything else, it's going to set off a serious shit storm. It might get our guys legalized. I think the reality of Corporate mercenaries killing and kidnapping U.S. Citizens in the United States is going to help make this country get up off its ass."

"Not if they hate us enough."

"There's always a constituency for hate. I think they proved the hell out of that one a long time before this idiot Regime was ever thought of. But listen to talk radio—that's the number one hate venue. Even there, a lot of people see us for who we are. We killed some Bad

Guys and blew up some vote-fixing machines. We attacked Corporate assets. We stood up for all the people who read the news and get sick to their stomach but don't have the time or the guts to do anything about it. They don't hate us. This Regime's coming apart, Mac. That's why there's still hundreds of thousands of people on the street in Seattle today. There's demonstrations starting up all over the country. It's happening, and this is something that can accelerate it. If the stink about Whitehall's Program is big enough, they'll have to shut it down."

It's hard to hear myself and not think I'm just giving one more in a category titled "Rousing Speeches." Do I even believe myself? The Regime may be coming unglued, but it's not going to happen in the next twenty-four hours, and Whitehall's still got enough guys to kill all of us fifty times over.

But Mac, with his Turkish-prison haircut and his long thin face, is thinking, stoops down to scratch the lethal friendly skull of his attack dog. "So what made James Sands want to talk now?"

"His wife was shot in that demonstration yesterday. I guess she was hit in the spine. Maybe paralyzed."

He looks at me strangely, probably sensing that there's an inordinate amount of emotion kicking around somewhere below my attitude. "Yeah. That'd make an impression." He stands up again. "But maybe his business is more important than his wife. It's not easy to turn on all your buddies, 'cause then you got both sides piling on. Nobody likes a snitch. I've been there."

Another allusion to some past I'd like to know about, if we ever get the chance. "I agree with you. But right now, he's the best weapon we've got if we want to put some pain on Whitehall. It's the information war, Mac. And he's got the information."

He scans the perimeter of the park, just in case. I know that Joby and probably someone else are out there, too.

"So what's all this got to do with you? Why does Emily think you could convince him?"

I take a deep breath and let it go. I'm so tired of playing people. "Because he's my father."

McFarland stares at me, turns away, and walks in a tight half circle. "You're shitting me! You're one step removed from motherfucking Satan and you never told us? Whitehall's all over him!" A wave of paranoia seems to come over him; he makes sudden piercing glances all around the playground, then back to the despicable punk in front of him. "You put me and all my men at risk!"

The mom's noticed that the water's gotten rougher over here; she's watching us and eyeing her kids. I try to defend myself. "I don't blame you for being pissed—"

"Pissed doesn't even come close! You betrayed me! You betrayed all of us!"

Something snaps at the word *betrayed*. "Oh yeah? How did I betray you? By setting up the Polling operation?"

"By never—"

"I stole my father's password!" I hiss at him. "He picked me up at the airport and I went to his house and stole his password so you and me and everybody else could blow up his water plant! And you want to lecture me about betrayal? Fucking get in line!"

I notice the mom has reached for her cell phone and I flash her a quick smile to slow her down. "Don't be alarmed, ma'am. We're just having a little political discussion." I turn back to McFarland, now in total confrontation mode. Eyes burning and hard, the receiver's off and he could go full-auto in a fraction of a second. Even his dog is growling, low malevolence from near my groin. I've never heard so much contempt in his voice: "Just a rich kid, having an adventure."

He steps toward me, but I don't back up. "Get off it, Mac! I've taken every risk you have, and done some shitty things you haven't had to. I screwed my father, my mother's lying in the hospital with a fucking bullet in her spine . . . I am *in*! I'm in deeper than you! And what I'm saying, if you can listen, is that because of the twisted fucked-up nature of my life and my family, we have a chance to strike a blow against Whitehall, a harder blow than we can ever do with bombs or bullets, and it's the best chance our friends have for getting out of this alive. And maybe waking this stupid-ass country up!"

He doesn't seem to be buying it. Neither does growling Fido: a measure of my credibility. "You know, forget it! This is my gig. I'll go alone. Maybe you're right. Maybe I'm the dumbass that's getting people killed. At this point either they're on to me or they're not, and if they are, there's no sense in all of us stepping in shit."

The woman's put her magazine away and is gathering up the kids, not liking the scene. McFarland is eyeing me, locked in his own little cloud of smoky thought. Shrugging my brand-new-jacketed shoulders at him: "So, I guess we're finished here. I'll do the meeting naked, and if it goes well I'll let you know what my next move is. Or not, whatever you choose. My half of the Army's already been cracked. There's no sense spreading the virus." I put my hand out. "Hey. Win or Die for America. It's been a real pleasure knowing you."

He puts his arm out and clasps my hand with his hard mechanic's calluses. I start to pull away but he holds on, looking into my eyes.

"I don't abandon my men," he finally says. A short pause. "And I damn sure don't abandon my friends."

I get a lump in my throat. It's so corny and boneheaded, movie crap, but at the same time, it's real. McFarland's the buried America, the America of loyalty and sacrifice that somehow got silted over by junk patriotism and the child-lust for new toys. And here it is in front of me, still alive, still burning. There's still hope. That settles once and for all the question of leaving for Canada. I won't be running. Not tomorrow. Not next week.

He calls Joby and we meet a mile away to set things up. All questions are gone now. The operation is on. Win or Die for America.

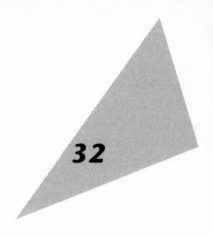

32

Emily met me outside the hospital at three. The bruise on her forehead was ripening like a plum and she looked nervous as I walked toward her. She'd come from the demonstration downtown.

"Are you ready to go through with this?" I nodded and she handed me a piece of paper. "Okay. I'm trusting you not to tell anyone we talked. Here's your instructions. Empty your pockets and leave everything in Anne's room. No cell phone or wallet. Good luck."

I read the directions as I went back to Anne's room. The doctors had given her some kind of sedative and were in no hurry to bring her around. I looked at her for a long time. She was depending on me to take care of our son, to do the one thing I'd never failed at in all our married life: to be competent. I kissed her cheek, then took a cab to a department store, where I bought all new clothes, including a navy-blue overcoat, a red scarf and a red cap, even new shoes, slightly annoyed at having to abandon my old things in the Saks Fifth Avenue garbage can because a bunch of kids wanted to play cops and robbers. I went to the corner of Third and Columbia at exactly four o'clock and waited. It was a fairly dense crowd, but seemed aimless at the moment, milling and talking to each other as if they were waiting for something to begin. There was some chanting coming from farther down the block. As Emily had said, they seemed to be getting ready for another push toward the Courthouse. I felt someone brush against me, mutter, "Excuse me," and keep moving, green buffalo plaid that disappeared quickly into the mass of people. I never saw his face. When I reached into my coat pocket I found a piece of paper with a computer-printed message on it.

All very cloak and dagger, like kids acting out something they'd seen in a movie. A bit of a pain in the ass: now I had to walk six blocks to a subterranean parking garage, go down to Orange level, look for a beige Ford LTD.

A man reading a newspaper behind the wheel put it aside and got out of the car. He had a black stocking cap pulled down to his eyes and a scarf wrapped around the lower part of his face. I'd expected a twenty-something radical like the kids Joshua hung out with in college, but from the little I could see, this man was in his late thirties, with crow's-feet around wary eyes. He looked like the kind of guy who might have blown up my water plant.

"Are those new clothes?" The voice sounded rough and uneducated, not who I expected my son to be involved with.

"Yes."

"Shoes, too?"

"Yes."

He looked me over, then patted me down. "Let's go for a ride."

He moved to the back and opened the trunk. "Get in here."

It was all a little heavier than I'd expected. It felt like a kidnapping, and I wondered if I should be cooperating or trying to make a run for it. I climbed in and watched the lid come down on me, lay there in the dark. I wasn't in control anymore, and it was getting hard to pretend that this was merely an escapade that would make a good story someday. I was lying in the trunk of a goddamn Ford LTD, for Christ's sake! Who were these people?

I felt us go up an incline and then stop at the collection booth, heard a bell ring when the gate came up, then felt the gliding and stopping of downtown traffic. The trunk smelled like oil and rubber, but I could feel a faint trickle of cold air coming in from below me, along with the smell of exhaust. Not ideal, but probably enough oxygen to keep me alive.

I tried to concentrate on my strategy. If I could talk to Josh alone, I'd try to find out how bad things were and what exactly he'd done. Probably nothing more than hanging out with the wrong people, trying to glom on to the cachet of being a militant to impress girls or something. I could see him managing their Web site, or helping them hack into government files. Some prank like that. But these days, pranks like that could get you thirty years, and hanging with the wrong crowd could get you shot. That had been Anne's crime, hadn't it?

The anger had been pretty distant, but in the dark, without anything to distract me, it took me by surprise. There, with the drive train sawing away by my head, I could imagine only too well what I hadn't wanted to: a whole lifetime with Anne in a wheelchair as her legs atrophied and her circulation got worse and nurses helped her with bedpans and bags in those long long years after her grace and beauty have abandoned her, and all because she had the audacity to stand in the street and demand people's right to vote. Why shouldn't they be at the Courthouse? Why shouldn't they have paper ballots? They weren't imagining things: I'd met the Party's sleazy "technical consultants" when I'd fought the referendums, and Howard Pettijohn had ridiculed me for not hiring them!

I thought of Matthews and the way he talked, the phony populism, the unending lies, the sickening crooked deals so huge that even I felt like a peasant when I considered them: billions funneled to companies that provided no real services, tens of billions spent on weapons systems that weren't needed or didn't work. Howard loved him, idolized his fake tough-guy act, was probably cheering on his every word as Matthews draped a flag across the casket of the single dead policeman and claimed the massacre as a blow for freedom. Matthews would never worry about Anne, as long as they'd taught those radicals a lesson down at the Stadium. *They'll vote when I damn well say they can vote!*

My fists were clenched and my breathing had become quick and shallow, but I had to put that aside for now, because Joshua had thrown a nasty curve into our already difficult situation. I had a couple of hours to snap him the hell out of it and get his head screwed on straight. Okay, so this would be my strategy: I walk in, say, *Joshua! What the fuck is wrong with you?* No. That wouldn't work. I'd need a soft approach. *Joshua, your mother is in the hospital in very bad shape. Please tell your friends that your family needs you and you have to take a sabbatical. We need you.* Okay, not exactly true. If I'd really *needed* him I'd have been in the gutter long ago, because, realistically, this was a kid who never called me on Father's Day, never even bought me an ugly tie. But maybe saying I needed him would be enough to pry him loose from his guerrilla-chic friends to where I could park him someplace safe to decompress. Maybe he could live in London or Paris for a few years. Maybe someplace without an extradition treaty, just in case.

The cold lump I'd felt at the small of my back, probably a jack, began to bother me, and I shifted around, trying to stretch my legs a little. We'd left downtown and were on some sort of curvy route without any stops. There was a series of jarring bumps and gravel hitting the bottom of the car; then things smoothed out again. We slowed, then seemed to go over some railroad tracks. More curvy road, and then we came to a stop.

The top opened and the driver stood in front of me with a piece of black cloth. We were in a small dark garage. "Lean over toward me."

I angled toward him and he slipped the hood over my head.

"Isn't this a little overdramatic?"

I felt him grab my shoulders and shake me, and suddenly his voice was inches from my face. "Shut up! I'd put a bullet through you in a heartbeat, if it was up to me!"

I heard a second voice. "Take it easy on him, Joby."

The hood came up and I was facing a tall man in a camouflage hunting coat. He was wearing a black balaclava so I couldn't see much of his face, and he had a rifle that looked like a toy suspended in one hand. He shifted his weapon so that it pointed at the ground, then spoke to me in a low, rough-sounding voice. "So, you're Lando's father."

It was strange to hear him refer to Joshua like that. "I am."

"I don't see much resemblance."

"He looks like his mother."

The tall man nodded and he spoke with an incongruous gentleness. "I'm sorry about your wife."

The expression of sympathy caught me by surprise, and I muttered an acknowledgment.

He went on in a firmer tone. "I want to tell you something about your son. He's one of the most honorable men I know. And I've known a few of them in my time. You got a lot to be proud of."

The respect in his voice disarmed me. I felt myself blushing. "Thank you."

"My guess is, there's part of you in him somewhere." There was a brief silence. "Don't lose that part."

He reached out and helped me out of the trunk. After I straightened up he said, "I'm a father, too." He stood there staring at me through the slit in his black headgear for an uncomfortable length of time, as if he had something else he wanted to get across, but all he finally added was, "Cover him up."

The short man put the hood back on and kept a grip on my forearm as he led me over some soft ground, onto pavement and up a few steps. We paused there as a storm door rattled open; then he moved me inside and lowered me onto a squeaky couch that gave off the flat smell of vinyl. "Stay there and leave the hood on," the first man commanded, then I heard his footsteps cross the rug and the door slammed shut with a cheap tinny rattle behind him.

I waited a little while with the blindfold on, then the door opened again and I heard someone approach me and stand before me. I felt the hood gently lifted from my head.

Joshua was there, smiling. "Dad!"

I stood up and hugged him. His hair was its natural brown now. He still felt light and fragile—he'd always had his mother's bones, and as I thought of that my eyes started to fill up. "Joshua!"

I hugged him again. I couldn't say anything, and neither did he. I noticed that we were in the narrow rectangle of a mobile home, circa 1970s, with cheap press-wood paneling and an orange shag carpet that was worn down to its crisscross foundation near the door. Thick curtains were drawn. It was an America I hadn't seen since I'd hitchhiked across the country all those years ago, and been picked up and invited into homes like this. A few potted plants, throwaway furniture of imitation oak or imitation leather, the television, a collection of ceramic figurines purchased from an ad in the back of some women's magazine. I'd been here before, decades ago; a rancher had offered me chicken-fried steak, a wife somewhere off in the kitchen, rabbit-ears TV antenna, his son coming in cradling a.22 rifle. For a moment I was back on that trip again, with its dust and its sleeping in culverts and cornfields. It flickered, then it was gone, and Joshua was in front of me, in trouble.

"Josh. What is this? Who are these people?"

"We'll get to that. How's Mom?"

I sighed. "Mom's in tough shape." I repeated some of what the doctor had told me, with his precise terminology of thoracic vertebrae and spleenectomy. Josh's face paled as I went on. I put my hand on his shoulder. "She's going to be okay. She's past the worst of it." An ambiguous statement I tried to sell against my own doubts. Maybe the worst of it was ahead of us. "I don't know how mobile she's going to be. It's a spinal injury, and you know how those are. But the doctor says that you can't count out human will, and you know how Mom is." I tried to buck him up with a smile, but I couldn't quite bring it off and I felt it settle into a papery little grimace. I sighed. "Josh, at this point we have to salvage what we can. Your mother needs you. I don't know who these people are or what you've been into, and that doesn't matter right now. I think you should explain that you have to take a break for a while. I'm sure they'll understand that."

Joshua didn't respond to it, just nodded his head a few times to put the idea behind us.

"Dad, let's sit down."

He pulled a cheap vinyl ottoman over to the couch and hunched down on it. He reached over and touched my knee, his face close to mine. The thin skin beneath his eyes was dark from lack of sleep and he needed a shave. "I'm sorry about Mom. I'm sorry I haven't been with you at the hospital and that I never returned your messages. I know it's been really shitty for you to be all alone in this. I'm sorry. The problem is, it's very dangerous for me to be in contact with the family right now. That's why we had to take all these precautions."

"Joshua, who is *we*?" I motioned around the room. "Whose trailer is this? Who are these people?"

"People resisting the Regime."

"That's a very foolish thing to be doing right now."

"Foolish? That isn't the adjective I'd use, but I understand what you mean. You mean it's open season on people like me. That's what

I need to talk to you about. I understand that Whitehall's running a Program to liquidate the Resistance and prop up the Regime and that you know something about it."

I tried to shy away from his broadside. I'd come here to get him out of this, not to be drawn into a discussion about Whitehall. "Whitehall is a big company. They do a lot of things."

The answer bounced off him. "This isn't *Washington Challenge*, Dad. Okay? It's just you and me, and we don't have a lot of time. I already know you're involved with their program. You told Mom and Mom told me and she told people at the DNN, too. It's out. So please don't treat me like I'm some TV straight man. I'm your son."

I felt a sharp little burr of anger at Anne's betrayal. "You're quick to remind me you're my son when it suits you. Why didn't you remind me of that when I was on my ass yesterday listening to the doctor tell me which of your mother's vertebrae were shattered? Or when the terrorists blew up my water plant and left me up to my neck in a pool of goddamned sharks?" He glanced down for a second, but he didn't argue with me. He was going to wait me out on this, and I'd need to go halfway. "All right. Whitehall. We're dealing with guys who've had their way for a long time, and that makes people take the next step. So, yeah—they're bending a few rules."

"No, Dad. No. They're not just bending a few rules. Whitehall kidnaps people and holds them in secret prisons. You already know that. They're coordinating a full-scale psyops and Intelligence campaign against Citizen Groups that oppose the Regime. You know that, too; you're part of it. Here's something you didn't know: They killed my best friend right in front of me yesterday at the Pike Place Market, and if I'd showed up thirty seconds earlier I would have been lying on the pavement in a puddle of blood right next to him."

I didn't breathe for a few seconds. "What do you mean?"

"Bang bang, you're dead! That's what I mean!" He was getting more emotional, but he didn't raise his voice. "You want the details? Okay. I'm meeting my friend at the Market: a great guy, college football hero. He's waiting for me at a café. I move in, spot some fake garbage men, fake shopkeepers. Very professional setup, but James Sands didn't raise any idiots, right? I hesitate, and that saves my stupid life, while my friend tries to run for it and gets shot three times. *Boom boom boom!*" His voice was getting louder. "And I'm standing twenty yards away behind a rack of newspapers watching it like my own fucking ghost, because if I'd walked a little bit faster, or if the crosswalk had been green instead of red, I'd be as dead as he is! Luck, Dad! A lifetime's supply of luck used up right there! Consider me out of luck!"

The horror of it was creeping up on me. Joshua was in way over his head. I tried to focus on the incident, as if grappling with that one incident could shut out all the things that were becoming clearer and clearer. "Well, who was this friend? Why were they after him?"

He took a breath and went on in a calm patient voice. "He was just like me, Dad. He resisted the Regime, so Whitehall killed him."

The fantastic nature of the whole afternoon—rides in car trunks, ski masks, guns—it all came swimming up around me. I steadied myself, suddenly seized with the need to defend my security company. "Hold on. Let's get back to what we know. Ignoring whatever your friend did to make himself a target—which I hope you haven't done. Ignoring that. You're only guessing it was Whitehall."

He looked at me like I was crazy. "Dad. Do you understand what I'm telling you? I was fifteen seconds away from getting a bullet in the chest from a bunch of guys with no uniform and no ID. Do you really want to argue about whether it was Whitehall or Homeland? Whether it would have been a thirty-eight slug or a nine millimeter?" He leaned into me, his hands on my shoulder and his face inches from mine. "Dad! These people are killers! They will kill me just like they killed my friend! You need to tell what you know about Whitehall's Program and make them stop!"

I shrank back, made claustrophobic by his proximity and his relentless return to his own death. I could sense my own panic starting to bubble up through the layers of control. "Look—" I held up my hand. "—just sit back for a second, Josh. Listen . . . Listen: I don't know what you've done, but it doesn't matter. I want to get you out of the country. I'm sending you to Europe."

"I'm not going to run away."

"Josh, this isn't a game anymore. You can't play cops and robbers—"

He cursed under his breath. "I just told you my friend was shot to death right in front of me, and you're talking about a game! It's the same crap you've been peddling since I was twelve years old—"

"This is not the time to start in with all your old gripes—"

"Yes it is! You always think your game is real, and everybody else's real is just a game! That's why it doesn't matter to you—"

"They're killing people!" I bellowed over him. "Don't you understand that? That's reality!"

He looked at me in amazement. "I just told—"

It all started rolling out. "You wanted to rebel? You wanted to piss me off? Okay, you pissed me off! You got my attention! I'm an idiot! Okay? I admit it! You win! Now, for the first time in your life, will you please try and think of someone besides yourself and let me get you out of the country? For your mother's sake? Christ, Joshua, think of your mother!"

He breathed a few times; then he answered in a quiet, determined voice. "It's not about me, Dad. It's not about Mom. It's about you. You need to find your better self. You need to be brave and tell what you know about Whitehall. They're Evil, and you have to stand up to Evil."

His self-righteous lecturing goaded me on. "And the terrorists are angels? Are we all supposed to just lie down because some tiny group of fanatics decides they want to take over? Look at those guys who killed John Polling! That Army of the Republic! That was cold-blooded murder, just like you accuse Whitehall of."

"That was justice."

"Bullshit! It's not justice because ten people decide it is! That's anarchy! Nobody voted for them!"

"When Corporations occupy our Government, it's acceptable—"

"Will you stop with that jingo!"

"That jingo created this country."

"This is now, Joshua! It's you! It's all of us! You're sitting there defending the Army of the Republic. . . . Are you out of your mind? They're murderers! I have no problem whatsoever with Whitehall killing those people. After what they did to me? Kill 'em all! I'll be happy when the last one's been exterminated!"

He went suddenly slack, then rose and walked to the far side of the tiny living room, staring at the floor. He moved back until he stood about five feet from me and he spoke slowly in a tone that was a strange mix of sympathy and pride. "There's something you need to know, Dad. I founded the Army of the Republic. Me and a few others. I initiated the Polling Operation. I helped plan and execute Cascadia."

"No!"

"You want me dead? Just stick with your friends at Whitehall. I'm sure you'll get what you paid for."

I stood up. "*No! That's bullshit,* Joshua! It's *bullshit* and you know it is!"

"It's the truth. I stole your password when I was home and downloaded all the blueprints. That's how we planned it."

I stared at his stubborn, defiant expression, and I realized then that the whole disastrous spiral that began with John Polling's murder had been brought about, nonsensically, by my own son, as if his adolescent anger and genius had been focused solely on my humiliation. My voice came out high and thin. "How could you do that?" Then it became louder. "*You're my son! How could you do that?*"

"You turned into one of them, Dad. You turned into a predator."

"I don't care what I turned into! You are my *son!* You're supposed to be loyal!"

"I'm loyal to this country!"

"Fuck this country! I'm talking about your family!"

He became quiet, looking at me with his eyes gleaming. "I'm loyal to somebody you used to be," he said. "I could care less about your silly stupid dreams of a bigger James Sands."

The contempt in his words pushed me into a rage that made me deaf and sightless. I was still taller than him, and now I rose up to my full height and screamed down into his face. "You *idiot!* In your entire life I never could have imagined you would fuck up so badly! You, with your idiot ideas and your half-baked politics! You are a failure and you know *Nothing!*" It had all become unbottled now. I inhaled to begin again; then I realized that he had recoiled from my onslaught, shrinking back with a familiar look on his face, a wounded, sorrowful small-boy expression so distinctly from his childhood and our lifetime of battles that it froze me, and suddenly my anger was gone and I completely forgot whatever I'd been about to say. In that moment Joshua became an amalgam of his boyhood and the man in front of me, and I encompassed in a fraction of a second all the arguments Anne and I had had over him. I imagined her powerless in her hospital bed, and standing silently at my side right now. She was depending on me to save our son, our brilliant, mixed-up, brave, and honorable son.

An assassin and criminal, a guerrilla chief unbowed by authority, a revolutionary who was ready to die for what was right; Joshua had become the man I might have fantasized myself as thirty years ago, if I'd had the courage and the will. It became clearer then than anything ever had been that my whole life was being weighed at this single moment, and I could choose ego and anger or I could leave those behind in whatever imperfect and clumsy way possible, and try to hold on to the one thing that was so desperately important.

"Okay." I put my arms around him, struggling to control my voice. "Okay. I love you, Josh. I don't care about the rest of it. I want to get you out of this. I can talk to Richard Boren. He'll help if we need it."

He was silent as I embraced him; then he patted me on the back and pulled away. "No, Dad. I'm sorry. I won't help you play this one. You need to go public about Whitehall."

"Joshua . . . Think of Mom. If she lost you . . ." I felt my throat tightening up. "We depend on you, Josh. Children never think of that, but parents depend on their children for happiness." He looked down without answering. He wasn't going to change his mind. I knew that. My life was being weighed. "Okay. You leave the country, and I'll go public. You leave, and I swear I'll go out the very next day and tell everything I know. I'll work with your friend Emily. I promise. Can you do that?"

The mention of Emily's name affected him, and I knew there was something there. He sat back down on the ottoman as he considered it. "Yeah," he said reluctantly. "I guess I'd do that."

I felt the first surge of relief, but now that I'd offered it, I couldn't help playing out the scenario in my mind. Howard would go berserk and spike our buyout deal. The Fund would fire me and tie up all my assets, and any help I was counting on from Richard would evaporate. I'd be weak and vulnerable. "You know, believe it or not, I've already been working on getting out of the Program."

He was cautiously pleased. "Really?"

"Yes. I'm very close to getting Barrington and Whitehall off my back. Once I do that, I'll be free: I can go as public as I want and they won't be able to touch me. But I have to do it from a position of strength."

His shoulders slumped a little and his voice lost its buoyancy. "How close is *very* close?"

"A week."

He just stared at me for a few seconds, then shook his head sadly. "I'm not sure I have a week, Dad."

He seemed exhausted, and for the first time in many years I felt like I could comfort him the way a father is supposed to. I put my hand on his shoulder. "Don't worry, Josh. This is all—"

I was interrupted by a sudden loud explosion outside the trailer, maybe a few hundred yards away, then two more quick ones just like it. Joshua whipped his head around toward the window curtain, alarmed, as a deep boom resounded, then a quick series of sharper cracks. I didn't understand what was happening, but Joshua dived to the ground and quickly turned off the lights inside the trailer. "Dad, get down on the floor!" I threw myself down and he pulled out his radio. "Mac, it's Lando. Are you there?"

The voice that came back sounded tense, but under control. "They're at the garage. You're going to have to come out the back way and head into the woods. Leave your father there. He'll be okay."

I could hear the panic in my own voice. "Josh, who is it?"

"I don't know!"

Outside, a full-scale battle had erupted, and I could hear it drawing closer. There was another roar of gunfire from only a few feet outside the trailer, and the firecracker-fast reports shook my stomach. I could see Joshua in the little cracks of light that came in past the curtains and angled across the dark floor. "Josh."

"I gotta go, Dad." He started squirming toward the other side of the room.

I could see that he was holding a pistol, and now the fear became almost overwhelming. "No! Stay here with me, Josh! You're safe with me!"

"I can't, Dad. They need me."

"Joshua! Joshua!" I was starting to panic. "*I* need you!"

He looked at me, then at the back door, then talked into his radio. "Mac. It's Lando. Go without me." He started crawling back toward where I was curled up on the floor, then raised the radio to his mouth again. "Mac! Go without me. Did you read that?" There was gunfire from behind the trailer now, and an answering exchange from near the back door. "Mac! Mac!"

Everything was silent for a second. Josh and I looked at each other; then there was a sound of shattering glass and a burst of blinding light and a concussion that went right through me. Another one came, then I heard something hit the wall in back of me and fall nearby, hissing. Immediately my eyes stung and I was coughing. "Dad, don't move! I'm coming."

The door crashed open and a nightmarish figure in helmet and goggles rushed into the room, scanning with his gun and pointing it at me. I wanted to holler, *Don't shoot!* but I was coughing too much. A second figure filled the doorway, black and demonic in his gas mask. He looked at me, then down at Joshua six feet away and pointed his rifle at him. *No!* I tried to yell, *that's my son!* but I could only gasp out pieces of words, and then his gun went off in burst of noise and flame, and I saw Joshua twist, and then the gun exploded again in one final shattering blast.

A sickening emptiness came over me, and with a weird guttural howl I struggled to my knees to attack the man who had just shot my son. As I crouched to tackle him, someone kicked my legs out from under me. "Stay down!" I could only open my eyes for a fraction of a second before they reflexively closed against the ice-pick sharpness of the smoke. I rolled onto my side, struggling to breathe, and then two more figures were suddenly above me, grabbing my arms and hauling me to my feet. I tried to look back but they were dragging me to the back door. My stocking feet brushed against something on the floor, and I felt a sensation so dark and monstrous rising up inside me that it was a relief to be swallowed up by the tear gas and the coughing, the immediate pain in my eyes and lungs that I hoped would go on and on, forever, because it was the only thing between me and the world that was waiting just beyond it.

A cool evening came around me, bumping down steps. I was still convulsed with coughing. I felt hands going through my pockets, flashlights, a voice asking if I was hit anywhere, another saying no. I kept coughing, was dragged to a car, shoveled inside between two men. Headlights on bare ground and dead leaves. Me still coughing, trying to tell them I didn't want to leave. *"My son . . . ,"* I gasped out. *". . . Ambulance!"* I kept asking about Joshua and they kept say-

ing nothing, except a man's voice from the front seat, calm and reassuring in a cold, professional way: "Don't worry, Mr. Sands. You're
safe now. Everything's going to be okay."

We seemed to be driving through a tunnel, but a tunnel filled with all
the props of the real world: shuttered gas stations, traffic lights. Everything kept going completely quiet, with objects moving around, and
walls standing, and cars gliding past, but completely silent and unreal,
like a film being shown with the sound turned down to nothing, which
made it all seem papery and badly acted, incapable of containing the
monstrous new truth that was bearing down on me. I kept wanting to
run it all backwards, to undo the last half hour and its horrible defor-
mations, but it kept jerking forward; a hotel pulled up outside the car,
a back door appeared and then receded, an elevator dropped its little
ping in the dead carpeted hallway.

"Excuse me, Mr. Sands. Walter called and he'll be here in twenty
minutes." I looked up to see a stranger, and almost immediately he
started to drift away again. *He asked me to stay here with . . . arrive . . .
can get you?*

Who is this man? Is he from Whitehall?

"Yes, sir. I'm here to assist and support you."

"I didn't want anybody in Seattle!"

"I'm with the Seattle office, sir. I live in Seattle."

"Give me my cell phone!"

"I don't have it, sir."

"I want to make a phone call." I picked up the receiver. "What the
fuck's wrong with the telephone?"

"I think it's best if you wait for Walter to get here, sir. He can explain everything."

"I want to see my wife!"

"I understand, sir. But she's still unconscious. Walter will be here
soon."

The underling started reading a newspaper and everything suddenly felt fidgety and desperate. I picked up the remote control for the
television but all I could do was stare at the mosaic of black buttons,
with their arrows and their chevrons, as incomprehensible as if I were
a monkey, because something was hanging just over my shoulder, a

big wave behind me, cresting up. Up, up, up, about to crash down, and what were all these silly buttons in front of me? I threw it onto the couch and found the power button on the set itself. A news channel came on, a commentator whose patter I couldn't follow. Crowded streets and big banners, a little flourish of exhausted propositions sputtering through my mind: *Demonstration . . . DNN . . . Emily Cortright . . .* Then I saw a banner with red slashes of paint that said **A⊕R** and the big black octopus came shuddering up out of the deep and took hold of me. A blanket! I needed a blanket! I rummaged until I found one of snowy white wool, turned off the set and draped it over the screen, pinning it at the top with a phone book and vase of flowers, suddenly overwhelmed by the image of my grandfather, forty years ago, after my grandmother had died and he was alone, blind, in a house he couldn't negotiate any longer, somehow seeing enough to stoop down and throw a cover back over the television, because in those first seven days of shivah, when the soul is traveling to the afterlife, entertainment was forbidden. The hypnotic rhythm of the prayer for the dead that I never learned but whose incomprehensible Aramaic haunted me. And I'd sat down next to the frail old man, ninety but never to reach ninety-one. He'd looked so fragile, and I knew how alone he was, alone after seventy years of marriage, and I'd wanted to reach out and hold his withered white hand, but I was afraid to. I was afraid to! And now thinking of it forty years later I felt myself start crying for him, for all that was inconsolable and beyond redemption, for the prayer for the dead that I couldn't remember, for things learned too late or never learned, for affection withheld, for the silly, easy unforgivable sin of taking things for granted, and then suddenly Walter seemed to be standing right in front of me. The prophetlike image of authority and strength. It was Walter.

I stared up at him, then slowly rose to my feet. He put his arms around me and embraced me.

"Jim, there's been a terrible mistake."

I surveyed the depths beneath his face for a long time. A tired-looking and worn face, its always-sure demeanor now carved away by some current of doubt and failure I'd never witnessed before. There'd been a terrible mistake, he said, but I could see deeper now, see that in this one unguarded moment he was admitting not to a tactical mistake, a mistake of planning, but rather to a life that was all one horrendous mistake, his own, because within the confines of that life, arranging the execution of a friend's son was a perfectly logical thing to do. It was there for an instant and then it passed, and he was back to being Whitehall's man, working me.

"Our team was afraid they might try to kidnap you . . . ," he began.

"Kidnapped! By my own son?"

"They could have been using him, Jim. Maybe he was the bait to lure you in without knowing it."

"My son is not bait and he is not being used by anyone!"

"Then what was that meeting about?"

"That's private!" I was tired of being the one to answer questions. "How did you get here so fast? You were supposed to be in Washington."

"I knew I needed to be here."

"That's not an explanation!"

He looked at me sadly. "Jim. Your son stole your password to break into the company network before the Cascadia attack. We checked your home computer—"

"Without telling me?"

"I wanted to, but you might have unintentionally tipped them off. We saw your password posted there, and we knew your son had visited, and that made us take another look at him. His apartment in San Francisco was a cutout, and then things started adding up but we couldn't get a physical location for him. My bosses decided to bring him in. They figured at a time like this, with your wife being hurt, there was a good chance . . ." He trailed off, then added, "It wasn't supposed to happen like that."

"Walter! You saw me almost every day! We drank in my office and you ate dinner at my house and you never told me Whitehall was targeting my son?"

He roused himself. "Look, you hired us to dismantle the Army of the Republic!"

I yelled into his lying face, "I didn't hire you to kill my son!"

"No," he said quietly, and his voice became cold. "It was supposed to be someone else's son, wasn't it?"

The brutal truth of it hit me like an ax and sent me reeling back without an answer. It was supposed to be someone else's son. Yes, it was. And that would have been okay, I'd been willing to sign on for that, because I had wanted the wrong things, and that seemed like the way to hold on to them. I sat down on the couch and covered my face and then my chest started bucking and my cheeks were suddenly wet and I heard my own broken voice choking on the pure shame of it. But Walter was still standing there, and I wasn't going to give in. I tightened my teeth and breathed in, and out. In, and out. Fuck it. I am James Sands, and I don't crumble.

Walter was talking, his hand was on my shoulder, but I didn't hear him. I started remembering a time I'd taken Josh to work with me, when he was six or seven. With his baby-fine light-brown hair and his slight body. He played with the Scotch tape at an empty desk next to me, sharpened pencils to stubs, pricked his finger with the stapler and cried as it bled a tiny red spot onto a piece of tissue. Afterwards I took him to the employee cafeteria and he took two Jell-Os off the counter, and for once I didn't say anything, I got one myself and we both sat there eating Jell-O, and it was something I hadn't remembered in twenty years, but now, at this moment, with all of it so brutally shattered and out of reach, it came back to me in every detail, coursing by in a fraction of a second: his pale skin, his frail, winsome features, so delicate that people used to mistake him for a girl. His little smile. Maybe that was the happiest time we'd ever had.

I felt my chest start to close up again, but I managed to sigh it open and then pushed my way through the thick atmosphere of the room over to the window. The marchers had filtered into the street below and were milling slowly to their destination. I snapped back and focused in on Walter again. He was saying something.

"Jim, listen to me. Are you listening?"

"What?"

"You need to listen to me."

"I am listening! Why don't you think I'm listening?"

He was next to me. "Jim, as painful as it is, you have to stay quiet about all this. One thing I know about President Matthews and his friends is that they're big believers in payback. If you embarrass them, they'll go after you, and I don't want to see that happen."

I laughed, but the humor of it died out before I finished the sound. "What else can they do to me, Walter?"

"Anything they want. They can say you were meeting with a known terrorist, and freeze your assets while they conduct an investigation, and that investigation can take as long as they like. Everything: bank accounts, credit cards, safe-deposit boxes. You'll be flat broke from one day to the next, right when Anne needs the best care you can get her. It's like being proscribed in the Roman Empire, Jim. They'll take everything."

My head came out of the mist for a second. "Then why do you support them?"

He hesitated, uncertain, and then he switched on his tidy little answer. "Because I'm going to outlast them. Once we get stability, get this economy moving again, these guys'll be gone and we'll go back to the way things were. Right now they're a necessary evil."

I just looked at him without answering, and his matter-of-factness dimpled a bit. "So what is this, Walter? Are you Whitehall's errand boy? Is that what you came to tell me? Keep quiet, Jim, or else? Or else you're out of the club?"

"It's not exactly like that."

"You can't silence me, Walter. I'm not saying I'm going to talk, but I just want you to know that I'm not the kind of person you can silence like that."

"I would never suggest that you were."

"But you just did!"

"Jim—" He put his hand on my shoulder and looked into my eyes. "—I am trying to protect you."

"Really?" He infuriated me with his righteous lies. "Is it really for my benefit? What should I do? Kiss your hand and ask for my son's body back?"

"Jim, you're ranting—"

"Oh, I'm sorry! Is this what you call ranting? I'm sorry I'm not more fucking composed! I'm sorry if I embarrass you! I'm sorry my family wandered in front of your bullets!" I was shouting. *"You killed my son!"*

"For God's sake, Jim! It was a mistake!" He became awkward, apologetic. "I'll tell you what, Jim: Don't worry about any of these things we talked about. I'm going to call you a doctor and he'll give you something to help you get through the next few hours and I promise I'll stay with you."

"Where's my daughter? I want to call my daughter."

"We already talked to her. She's on her way. You'll see her tomorrow."

"I want to talk to her!"

"She's in the air, she can't be reached. And right now, Jim, you'd just upset her more."

The numbness started coming on again. I got out one last protest as my head sank below the waves. "You can't silence me, Walter. I built a two-billion-dollar corporation from scratch. You can't shut me down with a threat."

"I'm not trying to silence you. I'm trying to help you make good decisions in a horrific situation." He put his hand on my shoulder. "Listen, Jim: I know about the Russians and your deal with Howard Pettijohn. I've kept it to myself even if I catch hell for it later, because I'm your friend and I knew you wanted to get clear of Barrington. I can keep that secret. No one can make this all better, but at least you can get out of it with something." He stopped and let me consider his offer for a while, then patted my arm softly and leaned close. "Do you want me to call that doctor?"

I sighed. I felt drained and restless at the same time. "Sure. Call him." I sat down, then stood up again. I started to think of Joshua at the trailer a few hours ago, but then there was the goggle-eyed figure with the gun and the next thing I realized I was hunched and panting, my vision filled with the little puddle of carpet around my feet. Far away Walter's voice. ". . . a wreck, just like anyone who's been through . . . I certainly am. I'll stick with him."

The sounds of the demonstration below were coming in through the window. Far off there were the booms of tear gas grenades being launched, police sirens. Beneath it all, rising and falling, was the roar of the crowd, oceanic and implacable. I struggled over to the glass again. From the third floor I could see the street below me was filled with people, with banners and posters floating a few feet above their heads. They were risking their lives to walk to the Federal Courthouse, where their only plan was to stand there with their candles and their colorful bits of text, because if they could stand there, it was theirs, and if they couldn't, it wasn't, and for that very same reason other men were willing to spill their blood to keep them from doing it.

These were the people my son had fought for. I felt a sudden need to go down there. It was the only thing I could do for Joshua now. I had failed him in everything else.

"I think I want to go outside and get some fresh air."

I moved toward the door but Walter was suddenly in front of me. "Don't go out there, Jim. They're going nuts down there. You don't need that right now."

I nodded my head slowly. I was a prisoner, more or less, but it didn't terribly matter because I was being crushed by something far bigger and more absolute than anything they could impose on me. This room felt immaterial, like all the other trappings of my ridiculous career. The jet. The houses. They'd always been a farce. Now Walter was offering me more of the same. I thought of Anne lying in the hospital with a shattered spine. I thought of my son.

"I going to lie down for a while, Walter. I need to get my bearings."

"Of course."

"Let me know when the doctor gets here."

I went into the bedroom and closed the door. I waited to see if Walter would follow me, then slowly and quietly opened my bedroom window, terrified that Walter would come in. My heart was pounding. The fire escape led down to an air shaft. I could feel the narrow edges of the cold black rungs and their blistered paint beneath my fingers as I descended, peering into the warmly lit interiors of bathrooms and bedrooms. More rungs, the brittle spots of corrosion, then the cement beneath my feet in this narrow air shaft. Back into the hotel. The restaurant, yes, the kitchen. An underworld of boiling cauldrons and dismembered flesh. Steam and stainless steel, calmly, to a puzzled cook: "Excuse me . . . the service entrance—?"

An alley in the cold outside air, the smell of water steeped in kitchen garbage. A side street scattered with people sloughed off the edges of the protest, digging through backpacks or scanning the crowd. On Fourth Street a dense river of people was churning slowly toward what I guessed was the Courthouse. I lurched in their direction, robotic, as if I were in someone else's body. As I neared the corner a young man and woman broke off their conversation and looked at me. "Are you all right, sir?" the man asked, but I staggered past them into the mass of people.

Inside the crowd, I felt like I saw them for the first time. There were clots of young people in ragtag clothing, but also people my own age, fat people and thin ones. A few had the pinched, worn faces of hard work outdoors; others were bursting with youth, needing a shave, the kind I thought of as know-nothing punks. Hair down to their shoulders, or heads scraped clean and blazoned with tattoos. A group of seven or eight hippie-types wandered past, banging out a slow steady beat on big drums. One of the girls was shaking a maraca. Another of them, a black woman, was leading a chant, a quick rhythmic incantation that cut into the crowd. *"Ain't no power like the power of the People 'cause the power of the People don't stop!"* The drums would answer with two beats at the end of the phrase, and she would start again. I drifted sideways into someone.

"Excuse me!"

I moved into the thick of the flow, borne along by their current. People were talking to each other, and in some areas little chants would surge up and then sputter out. I felt as if the pavement were far below. "Hey," a voice said off to the side. "I think that's James Sands!"

I staggered away deeper into the crowd. Faces seemed distant, and then suddenly close and intimate: a smile, an expression of worry, black words blotted onto cardboard placards. ". . . back alive!"

The mass was slowing and consolidating ahead, and as I moved forward the street became more and more packed with people. I saw people talking on cell phones, heard little snatches of conversation. I felt a strange sensation, that I was part of this crowd and that we were all participating in something together. Without thinking about it, I gathered the notion that the police were going to make another stand at Pike Street, four blocks shy of the Courthouse. But they didn't say *the police,* they said *the Regime.* The Regime was making a stand.

Protesters came hurrying toward us, retreating from whatever was happening ahead, but the greater tide of people kept moving forward, and I moved with it. I was safe from Walter, enclosed within the masses. The chant had grown—it seemed to come from all around me, and many other drums had picked up its beat. *Boom-boom!* *"Ain't no power like the power of the People 'cause the power of the People don't stop!"* *Boom-boom!* *"Ain't no power like the power of the People 'cause the power of the People don't stop!"* I could see the barricade clearly now, only twenty yards away. Soldiers with gas masks were poised with their rifles in front of a Humvee with a machine gun. Mixed in I could see the insignias of the Whitehall people, and riot police with shotguns and tear gas launchers, all of them masked and goggled, and suddenly I was hyperventilating again, bent over and panting with my heart pounding away so fast I thought it would explode. Someone squeezed my arm. I heard a young voice: "You okay?" I straightened up, breathed in. A stocky kid with wild hair was looking into my face. No, I wasn't okay, never would be okay. "Thank you."

There was an explosion and a canister banged painfully against my shins. I stumbled, stared dumbly at it hissing by my feet until my companion picked it up with a bandanna and hurled it through the window of a clothing store. "Fuck you!" he shouted, waving his fist across the pavement. My eyes welled up instantly, but I could still see the guns smoking and hear the thud of rubber bullets against the bodies beside me, the yelps of pain. "You can't silence me," I heard someone whisper. "You can't."

People began to fall back under the onslaught, and I heard calls behind me to link arms, to keep moving forward. They had come this far, block by block, in the face of everything. A sudden sharp smack burned against my thigh and the impact dropped me to my knees. I felt hands under my arms lifting me up, offering to bring me away, but I shrugged them off and stood facing the ranks of helmeted figures, anonymous and inhuman. "You can't silence *me!*" I snarled at them. I felt the tears running down my face and I didn't try to choke them back anymore. I said again, louder, "You can't silence me!"

I was alone now with the crowd just behind me. The security forces had formed a line and were getting ready to charge, but they were just pictures of men to me now, lies made flesh, and the rage came rising until it was singing in my ears. "I'm going to tell everything!" I yelled at them, then I picked up an orange traffic cone and hurled it across the gap. "Do you hear me? I'm telling *everything!*"

The wall of men in dark armor began advancing, step by step, hulking and machinelike, but I didn't move. "I'm not afraid of you!" A blur, the sound of shattering glass, then pools of flame exploded on the street. A savage cheering went up behind me, and the wave of black uniforms became confused and halted. They raised their bullhorns, babbling threats across the strip of burning pavement, but I didn't care anymore. I was free now. "You can't silence me, goddamn you!" I started toward them, throwing my fists over my head and screaming so hard that the hot ragged edge of my own voice was tearing at my throat. "YOU CAN'T SILENCE ME!" They began to give ground. *"YOU! CAN'T! SILENCE! ME!"*

HHEIW COHEN

COHEN, STUART,
    THE ARMY OF THE
    REPUBLIC
HEIGHTS
09/08